Ronin of the Dead

Book Two

By Keith J McIntosh

Acknowledgements

There's a lot of people I would like to thank that helped me get to this point. This, of course, is not in any particular order.

I would like to thank Pete Chaffe for introducing me to George A. Romero's movies, and pretty much the entire concept of zombies. For listening to my bullshit over the years, and for giving me a wall in which I could throw ideas against. We did it, old friend!

Of course, my wife and family for supporting me. Especially my wife, Renee, who sat with me and helped edit this monster during those long, winter nights. When it was just you, me, and Microsoft Richard. I love you.

I'm extremely grateful for my good friends, the Fergusons. Sorry, guys. It's just easier to lump you together. The pains of being married, I guess. Jason, for reading the first edit of the book, which was painful. I know. But even after reading that hot mess, he still believed in it. Bobbi, his wife, for teaching me the cold-hearted, merciless art of editing. We sacrificed much in this journey, but we will always have the orange flickering glow.

A special thanks to Robert Belland, my high school friend, who helped me put the technical side of this project together. He helped a lot with the actual formatting of the book, as well as coming up with the amazing cover art for it.

Another special thanks to Kathy Carter. My first fan. Another poor soul who suffered through the very first version of the book. Chapter by chapter she climbed this mountain with me, encouraging me to finish. Demanding that I finish. And at some points, threatening violence if I didn't finish.

This is dedicated to my Mom, Marlene McIntosh.

Love you.

Contents

Chapter 1

Elliott

"No."

"Excuse me," Ken said with genuine surprise as he leveled Elliott with a hard look. He didn't blame him. It *was* the first time Elliott disobeyed him.

Elliott couldn't help it though. He simply couldn't let Ken continue. They'd been clearing the town of the undead for three days now. They had enough supplies, and now Ken wanted to rid the town of all the undead. He had been adamant about achieving that goal. They started on the east side of town, and unlike their other trips, Ken wanted to attract as many grey people as he could handle. Each day Ken walked up ahead of the truck, and smashed and stabbed his way through the grey people who were foolish enough to follow the sound of the truck's horn. Each day, they finished in the late afternoon, when the sun was the hottest. Ken insisted on neatly collecting all the fallen bodies and putting them into piles before he set them on fire. Then they would head back to the house, with black smoky tendrils reaching into the sky behind them.

For three days they did that. Each day inching closer to Main Street just to have to start a block back the next morning from all the zombies that were attracted by the smoke during the night. Today, they had finally reached Main street and disaster followed almost as soon as Elliott honked the truck's horn for the first time. To the north, from the tiny apartment complex Momma said was mostly for divorced people, flowed a river of grey people that went back for blocks. Elliott's mind was ablaze with all the little details his stupid brain noticed. He only cared about one piece of information, though. *Seventy-one grey people!?* It was too many, but as Elliott prepared to put the truck in reverse, he saw Ken was stretching on the road ahead of him. When he was done, Ken moved into position on the train tracks. From there, Ken decimated the grey people's numbers. He simply thrust the spear forward, stab one in the face, and then he would retreat a few steps before he did it again. The grey people had no defence for the simple tactic combined with the length of the spear. Facing off with that crowd of grey people, Ken was all business. No swooping attacks, no fancy twirling movements that ended with grey people flying off in the opposite direction. Just poke, and step back.

The only downside to the method was that it took Ken hours, and more then three blocks worth of backpedaling before the grey people's numbers finally dwindled away. The whole time Elliott could feel Ken's massive swell sink more and more as time and effort wore his friend down.

Now that he was finally done, Ken wanted to organize the bodies into his silly piles again. It was more that Elliott could take.

"You can't," Elliott said firmly. "You're too tired. You need to rest. Take a break." Elliott said nervously in a clipped tone and before he knew what he was saying, he added, "I'll do it." Elliott wanted to take it back. He didn't want to clean up smelly corpses, but when he looked at his friend and the state he was in, Elliott found it was the right thing to do.

"You?" Ken looked him over once in a way Elliott didn't like. "No," he said, shaking his head. "No, that's okay. You're overreacting. I'm fine."

"Your hands are shaking." Elliott countered and, for good measure, pointed to Ken's hands. Even with those tanned leather work gloves he wore, they were noticeably shaking at his sides. Ken balled up his hands into fists, which he brought to his chest like he was trying to hide something. Maybe Ken thought his hands would magically stop shaking if he did, but they still trembled slightly against his chest.

"That will go away," Kenshiro said and looked down at him and breathed out deeply.

Elliott just looked back at him, unconvinced. He knew deep down Ken wanted to stop, but he wouldn't. He had to, though. He felt Ken's swell ease back from the shoreline and settle in the distance, and before he spoke the words, Elliott knew that he had won.

"Maybe you're right," Ken said, making it sound like a defeat, like it was something he had to accept. "I could use some downtime." Ken looked at him with a touch of guilt, but Elliott was having none of it.

"Okay, it's settled then. Let's go," Elliott said and then he reached down and grabbed Ken's spear, intent on carrying it for him so he wouldn't have to, and gave it a good yank.

Nothing happened.

The rod refused to budge. Elliott was undeterred. He just levered the rod back and forth in the dirt to create some wiggle room, and then planted his feet and lifted until his legs burned until it popped free. Elliott looked up at Ken in triumph.

"Let's go." He repeated to Ken's amused face and turned and marched off to the truck. He could feel Ken following behind him with a certain sense of satisfaction.

Back at the truck, Ken retrieved his length of rope and explained how it was to be used. Elliott understood immediately, and eagerly agreed that he didn't want to grab the grey people with his hands either. Looping the length of rope around their ankles and dragging them to the pile seemed infinitely better to him. Ken also showed him a trick to help with the rotting smell that followed the grey people around. Elliott stood still as Ken took a stick of deodorant and rubbed a generous amount across Elliott's top lip, right underneath his nose, and then wrapped a black bandana around his face. For a moment, Elliott felt like a bandit from the old westerns, the ones who held up the stage coaches on horseback. But then the scent of the deodorant filled his nose and a disturbing thought occurred to him.

"Did you use that on your armpits?" Elliott asked suspiciously and pointed to the stick of deodorant in Ken's hands. The same stick that Ken just wiped all over the top of his mouth. Ken looked at him and blinked quickly a few times.

"No," Ken simply said. Elliott frowned at him.

"You're lying." He simply stated it as a fact because it was the truth, and they both knew it, so there was really no point in arguing about it. Elliott didn't mind that Ken lied. It was a harmless lie, and he found that people told little lies like that all the time, back when they were still around. "That's gross," Elliott said in a disappointed tone. Ken only shrugged an apology as he finished tying the bandana off at the back.

That's how Elliott spent the rest of that day. Collecting dozens of dead and desiccated bodies into five smelly, disgusting piles of human remains. Ken told him not to look at the faces, Elliott soon found out that was good advice. The spear did horrible things to some of the grey people. Each body was a struggle to move, but he did it. Albeit, slowly. Ken waited for about an hour, after that Elliott couldn't keep him away any longer

"We stink." Ken broke the silence between the two

of them as they sat on the truck's tail gate. Ken parked the truck under a tree for some blessed shade from the scorching sun. They drank luke-warm water from plastic bottles and solemnly surveyed their handiwork. "I think we deserve a bath when we get back to the house."

One of the first things Ken had done during that first week, after he discovered Elliott's house had a working gas stove, was to heat water for a bath. The sound Ken made when he first slid into that small amount of hot water in the bathtub reminded Elliott of the satisfied purr of an old cat. He stayed in the tub, with his large scary pistol within reach on the tub's rim, for what seemed like over an hour. Elliott figured Ken stayed in that tub until his body sucked up most of the heat of the water.

"I don't like baths," Elliott said absent-mindedly, almost as if by instinct. However, in that moment, he almost yearned for the warm touch of the bath water. Plus, Ken was right. The two of them smelled awful. "But I'll take one." Ken chuckled slightly at that, which confused Elliott because he didn't realize he said something funny, but he smiled along with him regardless.

Ken finished what was left of his water bottle and tossed it carelessly into the back of the truck. Elliott got the sense they were moving on, so he quickly downed what he had left of his water and tossed it in the back, and hopped off the back of the truck when Ken did. Elliott's muscles protested every action he took and he couldn't help but to groan a little over it. Ken stretched his back and growled slightly as he did it.

"Let's leave the bodies as they are for today," he started to say, and Elliott knew he meant he didn't want to light the piles on fire. "I don't want to attract any for tomorrow. We're close enough to that storage lot to check it out. We'll take a bit of a break tomorrow. I think we earned it. Sound good?" Ken asked, and Elliott quickly nodded his head in agreement. They *had* worked hard, and they *did* deserve a break. "Come on, let's go." Ken said, pulling up the liftgate and closing it.

Elliott, with little thought, hopped into the driver's seat, his seat, and wondered excitedly what Ken had in store for them on their day off.

-

Elliott was disappointed to find out Ken's idea of a day off was still work, just a different variety. Ken drove them to the storage lot that Mr. Fleming and his wife owned, but their son ran. Ken cut the lock off the fence and Elliott pulled the truck ahead while Ken closed the gate behind them. Sealing them off from the grey people that were outside the fence that encircled the property. Once Ken dealt with the grey people who were stalking towards them inside the fenced lot, he hopped back into the truck and directed Elliott to the back units.

"Whoa," Elliott said as Ken drew back the covering to reveal a shiny black beast of a car that they found in the storage unit. Elliott knew it was a Mustang by the unmistakable stallion insignia on the front of its grill. The car was all black and polished to a point Elliott could see their distorted reflection in the high gloss of the hood. He had seen many Mustangs on the road, but never one that looked like this. Elliott never had much interest in cars, but someone must have made this one to look almost… mean. That was the best word Elliott could use to describe the look of the car.

It was in the first unit they opened. The one Ken planned to store extra supplies in.

"Goddamn! Will you look at that?" Ken exclaimed at the sight of it and moved deeper into the garage with his knife still in his hand to have a better look at it. Elliott followed him and moved to the corner of the windshield. Out of curiosity, Elliott glanced at the VIN plate.

"It's a two thousand and seventeen fastback Bullitt edition, with a five-point two-liter engine, and they made it in Flat Rock, Michigan." Elliott informed Ken mechanically. Ken frowned at him and stepped forward so he could have a look at the plate for himself.

"Okay," he said. "I get how you got the date and the engine size, but how did you know they made it in Flat Rock, Michigan? And where did you learn to read a VIN number?" Ken was genuinely curious at Elliott's sudden knowledge of the car. Elliott simply shrugged innocently before he answered.

"I read it once, what the numbers mean. Daddy was looking up something on the computer and it had a chart that showed what the numbers meant, and I saw it on the screen."

"And that's how you know they made it in Flat Rock, Michigan?" He asked, and Elliott nodded but then added.

"Yeah, but also, Flat Rock, Michigan, is the only place that makes Mustangs," Elliott said like it was common knowledge. Ken looked at him with a weird smile on his face.

"Ok, good to know." He sounded amused. Elliott paid it no attention as he moved to the driver's side window to have a better look at the interior.

"Can we drive it?" Elliott said, looking at the smooth surface of the tan leather seats. He looked back to Ken, who thought about it, but ultimately slowly shook his head.

Elliott could tell Ken wanted to.

"No, we probably shouldn't." Ken sounded genuinely disappointed. "I'm guessing you could hear this bad boy coming from three blocks away. All it would be is a moving beacon drawing them to us, no matter where we went." Ken never had to explain who '*they*' were. "But this unit will suit our purposes just fine. It even came complete with a hell of a getaway vehicle."

Then Ken explained the car's battery was probably dead, and if they were going to use it as a possible getaway vehicle they would have to charge that battery up, disconnect it from the car so it didn't drain down, and then have two more batteries wired up to boost the car if necessary. It sounded like a lot of work to Elliott. "Aaanndd, that's assuming the keys are in it. Why don't you move these boxes out of here and go through them to see if there's anything in them we might want, while I have a look for the keys?" Ken suggested lightly, and Elliott simply nodded and did as he instructed. He was on the clock, after all.

Elliott first emptied the storage unit out of all the boxes and stacked them on the side of the building. Ken didn't care where he put that junk. While Elliott was doing that, Ken busied himself by opening the other units in the building. It was nice being inside the fenced lot because they didn't have to worry about the noise they made. Which was good, because Ken wasn't too polite in his search for the shelves he needed for his unit.

It wasn't all work. Ken found a portable basketball hoop in the unit that was two doors down from theirs, and a somewhat deflated basketball. Ken set up the net against the opposite building and they would take breaks throughout the day to play games of h-o-r-s-e. Ken even set-up the little camp stove at lunch time and cooked some beans. They had pear slices for dessert. As an extra bonus, Elliott even found a couple three-dimension puzzles in one of the neighboring units. One featured a modern aircraft carrier, the U.S.S. Nimitz, Elliott had never heard of it before. The other one was the Empire state building, Elliott knew that was a famous building in New York. Though, he wasn't exactly sure what it was famous for.

At the end of the day, when the sun was finally high enough in the sky to deter Ken from working any further in the heat, they had the beginnings of a pretty decent storage space. Ken found enough shelves to line the opposite wall from the mean-looking car. Ken did end up finding the keys but they never started it. Much to Elliott's disappointment.

The day had ended well, at least it had until Ken started to talk about leaving La Veta again. He did this sometimes. Elliott knew why, but he didn't care.

"I like it here. I don't want to leave," Elliott said sternly, keeping his eyes locked on the space just in front of the truck. He fought the urge to say it again.

As with all the other times Ken brought up the prospect of leaving his home, Elliott felt the all too familiar bad feelings and thoughts that bloomed inside him. *Why should we leave? We have everything we need right here? I don't want to leave. If I leave, how will they find me? How would Momma and Daddy find me? If I leave the farm, I will never see my parents again.* The thought terrified Elliott into a silent turmoil he could never explain to anybody. It was a whirlwind of anxiety that threatened to burst him at the seams. He gripped the steering wheel until his knuckles turned white.

"I know, buddy, I know." Ken patted Elliott on the shoulder gently and gave his back a bit of a rub before he withdrew his hand. "Let's head back," he said, pulling them away from the subject. "I'll make us some dinner and you can start on one of your puzzles before it gets too dark."

"Okay," Elliott said, feeling the pressure inside him lessen by his friend's warm touch and soft words. It brought Elliott back from the storm. Ken hadn't always been so understanding and accepting of Elliott's moods, and he could still feel the frustration building in Ken as well, but thankfully, outwardly, he held his calm. He didn't get mad and argue with Elliott like he did when they first met. He didn't swear at him anymore either, and he took the time to say nice things to Elliott, even though he didn't have to. Ken still talked little, but he didn't have to for Elliott to notice he was trying hard to be the friend Elliott needed, so Elliott would try to do the same.

Elliott shifted the transmission into Drive and slowly took them home.

-

Elliott sat in the truck, like he was supposed to, and felt incredibly bored. Ken was inside the house, his gore-stained spear was leaning up against the house by the front door, while Ken was inside checking for grey people and looking for supplies.

This morning, Ken said they were going back into town for supplies that they could now put in the storage unit. Which Elliott said he was fine with, but in reality, he didn't want to go back to town. He wanted to stay at home to continue working on his puzzle but when Ken said he wanted to do something, the look on his face when he said it left little room for the prospect of debate. Again, Elliott was fine with that. He was happy to spend time with Ken, no matter what they were doing. Sometimes, though, he wished Ken wanted to do more fun things with him. All they seemed to do was work.

They left in the morning shortly after breakfast, as the sun was just rising above the horizon. The coolness of the previous night was still present in the air. They took their time getting into town. Now, Ken was inside his third house, and from where Elliott was sitting, he still had a lot of day ahead of him. Most of which would be spent staring out the windshield of the truck, after he had completed his other task, that is.

His role had evolved since they first started, and that was nice. It gave him something to occupy himself while he waited for Ken. Elliott now sorted the contents of the large garbage bags Ken had brought out from the house. In the back of the truck, Ken put three large plastic bins from the storage lot, and it was Elliott's job to sort the contents into those three bins.

One bin for cans, one for boxed goods like his prized macaroni and cheese, and the third bin was for various items Ken picked up from houses he thought might come in handy. The third bin was usually the slowest to fill as Ken's main priorities going into the house was food and water. After two houses, the only things in the third box were two small flashlights and a small compass that caught Elliott's fascination. He never saw a real compass before, but the moment soon passed, and into the third bin it went.

When Ken finished with the previous house, he only came back with a scrawny little bag, just a few cans really. It didn't take Elliott long at all to sort through it. He was keeping a mental tally of the food they had collected since they started. Elliott didn't want to. It wasn't information he really was all that interested in, but sometimes his brain just did its own thing. Currently, creamed corn was way ahead, and in second place were regular baked beans. There were a lot of varieties of beans. Baked beans, pork and beans, chili beans, kidney beans, black beans, green beans, and there was even a maple style variety. After all this time together, Elliott suspected Ken's favorite was the baked beans with little pieces of bacon mixed in, *Beans N' Bacon*, but it was hard to tell because Ken didn't seem to enjoy eating.

Not as much as Elliott did, anyway.

That was probably because Ken had been eating this whole time while Elliott still remembered the terrible ache in his gut from when his stomach was so empty it seemed to hollow him out completely. The bitter taste of dandelions still haunted Elliott occasionally. Elliott was glad he didn't have to eat those anymore. Those days were gone. Hopefully soon it will be a bitter memory he would have to search for in the recesses of his brain. Thanks to his new friend. Ken might just be the best friend he ever had. He hoped Ken felt the same way. Elliott couldn't tell by his wave. There was still only so much he could discern from a person's mind-beach. It frustrated him slightly, not knowing, but he was still learning.

His friend soon emerged from the house with a somewhat neutral look on his face and his usual bag of supplies. Though this bag was fairly large, Elliott guessed it was the largest bag so far, but the day was still pretty young. This was only the third house, after all.

"How'd it go?" He asked from the driver's seat as Ken approached with the bag in hand.

"Pretty good. No dead in that one, so that's nice, and there was a bunch of stuff still in the cupboard. So that's a win," Ken said and even managed the tiniest of smiles as he hoisted the heavy-looking bag into the bed of the truck. Then he went back to the house to close the front door he had just left through, as was his way, and collected his heavy metal pole which he angled into the back of the truck so a good portion of it stuck out the back of the truck. That way, it was easier for Ken to pull out of the bed at the next house. It was refinement to his method that Elliott had noticed him change in the last few days.

Elliott started the truck, shifted the transmission into gear, and let the truck roll down the road. They were slowly moving south on Poplar Street. They had finished with the houses on this block. Ken instructed him to turn left on East Francisco Street. Here were four houses, two on each side of the street with wide lots surrounding them. One of the town's nicer motels, *Inn At The Spanish Peaks,* was located on the corner. It stood out on the block a bit as it looked sort of like an old Spanish fort you'd expect to see in a western or something, but not on some random corner in a rural Colorado town. Momma said it was one of the few real tourist attractions the town had. Elliott had never been inside it and to him it was just a weird, blocky building that added a bit of character to the streets he grew up in. Ken had glared at it with a hint of suspicion as they rolled passed. The street was blessedly empty, and they both let out a sigh of relief when they saw the bare street in front of them.

Regardless of that, as was procedure, Elliott parked the truck and let out a quick blast of the horn. Then they waited. Elliott guessed they waited in silence for a good five minutes before he broke in.

"Maybe there aren't any around," he offered, and no sooner had he said it, then a shambling figure popped into view down the road, emerging from a patch of foliage that covered the corner of the property.

The awkwardly hunched grey man wore the equivalent of torn, dirty rags and struggled like he couldn't support the weight of its upper body enough to stand straight. Elliott sighed as Ken gave him a look that said it all. *There's always a zombie out there somewhere*, one of Ken's personal mantras.

The two of them opened their doors in near unison

and they both exited the vehicle and moved to the back of the truck. Elliott placed his foot on the back tire and pulled himself up into the back of the truck to sort the bag Ken brought from the previous house. Ken moved to his weapon and lifted it out of the truck before stepping casually towards the grey man down the street.

Elliott, from his vantage point standing in the truck's bed, could see two others had appeared from behind the slightly run-down looking house on the opposite side of the street. The two newcomers looked to be dressed for a party. The grey man wore a dark suit complete with a tie and the grey woman wore a light blue dress that had one strap on her shoulder broken, Elliott could see a sizable chunk of flesh had been removed from the grey woman's shoulder. It left a dark stain that seemed to cascade down the front of her dress. Ken noticed them as well. He had stopped up ahead and seemed to look around for a suitable spot to lead the grey people to before he took care of them. He soon locked his gaze on the house across the street. Elliott could see why.

The house had a wide gravel driveway that could have easily fit three cars parked beside each other. It currently sat empty.

That's where Ken will lead them.

Elliott felt he had been around Ken long enough to know these things. Ken was fond of using driveways for his piles of grey people. They were usually far enough away from anything that Ken could light the pile on fire and leave without worrying about accidentally burning down something. They were also flat and easily accessible for the grey people, so it was relatively easy for Ken to lead them there before dispatching them. Elliott smiled proudly as Ken stood in the center of the wide driveway and waited for the three figures to make their way to him. The ragged grey man was the first to arrive and the first to be put down with a simple thrust of the pole. The fancy dressed grey couple came shortly after. Ken put the man down first and then shifted his position, so when he struck, it fell neatly on top of the raggedly dressed corpse already on the ground. The grey woman fell next, and she landed awkwardly on top of the new pile.

After that, Ken walked to the center of the street where he was visible from all sides and stood with his weapon in his hands, eyes constantly searching, waiting for his enemy to arrive. Elliott kept his eyes on him, because there was a distinct possibility Ken might want him to honk the horn again. It happened occasionally when Ken felt there were more grey people around. Elliott waited until Ken turned back to look at him before he gave him their signal.

Elliott held his hand out in front of him so it was in front of his chest with his palm facing outwards and then he pressed his other hand to it, almost in a clapping motion but without the sound because Ken was adamant he was to make as little sound as possible when they were in town. It was the signal they had worked out.

When Ken did it, it was him telling Elliott to honk the horn again. When Elliott did the signal, it was a question. *Should I honk the horn?* Ken saw the signal clearly and understood it. He shook his head slowly and then held up his hand with his fingers apart for a moment before letting all but his index finger close into a fist; it looked like he was pointing to the sky, but then he moved his hand in a few wide circles with his finger pointing upwards. Finally, he dropped his hand and pointed to the house by the truck on the north side of the road. Elliott confirmed he understood with a thumbs-up gesture. At least, he was pretty sure he knew what the signals meant. When Ken was explaining it, he was going pretty fast and sometimes the weird way he said certain words made it hard to understand him. *I'm going to wait five more minutes to see if there are anymore in the area then I'm going in that house.* That's what Elliott was pretty sure he said, either that or he was going to walk around the area for five minutes to look for more grey people, then go into the house he pointed to.

As was Elliott's procedure, he waited and monitored his friend while he was out on the street. Ken never specifically told him to, but he thought another set of eyes keeping an eye out could never hurt. Besides that, Elliott wanted to be watching in case another grey person came onto the scene. Ken might do something fancy with his rough metal spear if it was only one or two. It happened rarely, but when it did, it was pretty amazing to Elliott to watch Ken's unyielding control of that spear. However, after Ken waited in the streets for a short time, it was becoming clear that no further grey people were going to show themselves. This was what Ken was hoping for. Even though, Elliott thought he looked kind of disappointed standing there alone in the middle of the road.

Ken finally signalled he was through waiting and started towards the house he had indicated earlier. Elliott watched as Ken leaned the spear, point down, against the house by the front door and pulled out his small case of tools he used to unlock doors. He was good with them. A couple of days ago, he showed Elliott how he had done it by sliding back the deadbolt on the front door of their house. It took him about a minute, and Elliott watched in amazement as the metal bolt slid back into the door. He let Elliott try, and Ken even tried to explain in great detail what had to be done, but Elliott couldn't figure out how to make it work. Ken said it required a certain feeling, and Elliott didn't know what he meant by that, so he soon abandoned his attempts. After about a minute, he figured Ken must have been successful with the lock because he was soon zipping up the little pouch and storing it back into his pocket. Elliott watched as Ken rapped rather loudly on the door, then leaned inside the house and listened intently for any grey people who might be inside. He knew Ken heard nothing out of the ordinary because Ken pulled his knife, opened the door completely, and entered the blackness of the house.

Elliott saw his friend disappear into the house, and soon after the front door slammed shut. Elliott thought that was kind of weird, but didn't think much more of it. He had his own job to do, after all. Elliott settled into his spot in the truck's bed and pulled the dark garbage bag full of goodies closer to sort it. The bag was fairly bulky and had a lot of weight to it, and Elliott forced out a sort of grunt as he pulled the mass closer to where he like to sit on the hump of the wheel well. Elliott opened the bag, and as usual, Ken had stuffed in a pile of clothes. Jeans and t-shirts mostly, but Elliott didn't have a real hard look at them. They had a separate bag for clothes that they would separate back at home. He simply transferred the clothes from one bag into another, then he made himself stop to look around himself for grey people, like Ken always reminded him to, before he dug into the second bag.

Baked kidney beans were the first can out of the bag, which was a hopeful start, because one can of beans usually meant there would be others. Elliott just hoped there wouldn't be any Lima beans. Those were his least favorite, but after two more cans of baked beans and a can of corn niblets, he stopped worrying about what he didn't want and just focused on emptying the bag. Soon though, Elliott pulled out a can of green pickled jalapeno peppers and paused in confusion. He knew what jalapenos were, what he couldn't understand was why Ken would want them. His daddy once gave him one to eat with a sly smile on his face that Elliott didn't understand until he foolishly stuffed the whole thing in his mouth and started chewing. The burning sensation in his mouth and throat were enough to send him running to his Momma with tears in his eyes. That was one pepper and now he was holding a whole can of them.

Elliott didn't hesitate when he tossed the can away.

He picked out a bit of overgrowth on the side of the road, where it hopefully wouldn't be seen by Ken, and lobbed the can overhand into that spot. Ken wouldn't miss it. He was fairly sure Ken didn't know what he was grabbing when he put it in the bag, because no one wants to eat a can of that. Elliott watched as the can tumbled into place, out of sight, right where he wanted it to. He was proud of the toss. He had gotten really good at throwing. It wasn't much of a skill, but it's what he had. He was still congratulating himself on the good toss as he stuffed his open palm into the bag, expecting for it to close in around another can.

That's when something in the bag seemed to jump up and bite his palm.

"Ow!" Elliott hissed quietly as he yanked his hand back out of the bag and instinctively shook it as if the sudden motion would shake the pain off. "That hurt," Elliott complained quietly and looked down at the offended hand just in time to see the first bead of crimson peek out from the wound.

It wasn't deep at all, just hurt a lot, and bled a bit. Elliott inspected his hand with great interest and immediately found the wound. A tiny puncture wound stood out red and angry against the gentle pink of his palm right in the meaty part by the thumb. He watched the tiny red bead of blood on his palm swell slightly before it broke off and drained to the center of his palm. That's when he heard it.

Elliott couldn't explain the sound. At first, he wasn't

even sure he was hearing it. The slight breeze around him just seemed to carry this weird buzzing noise with it. It was there for a moment, a quiet sigh that seemed to come from all around him, just enough time to register with his brain, and then it was gone. Elliott cautiously looked around him, like Ken often did, to see if he could spot the source of the noise while his brain replayed the slight sound repeatedly in his head to see if it could identify it. His brain liked puzzles, and this was as good a puzzle as any. The weird thing that struck him was the sound came from all directions at once. Maybe it was a little louder to the south, but with the short time he had to listen to it, it was hard to tell. His brain tried to place the noise but the best it came up with was a heavy, scratchy sort of sigh, the kind his great aunt would do after a coughing fit when they would visit her in the old folks home in Colorado City, but that made little sense. He listened for a moment while cradling his injured hand to see if the sound would return. It didn't, and after a bit Elliott dismissed it altogether. He had more pressing matters, like his hand.

With nothing to clean the wound properly, Elliott settled on simply licking the small amount of blood off his palm, and lacking any sort of proper medical training, he resorted to simply sucking on the tiny wound until it stopped bleeding. When he looked down, there was only a tiny speck of blood that still covered the wound. His solution satisfied him. He felt he had dealt with the problem sufficiently, so Elliott opened the bag wide to have a look to see what was inside it that had poked him.

Elliott carefully shifted some contents to the side and then he found it. It was an old style metal can opener. Momma had one just like it, though Elliott couldn't recall a time she ever used it. He admittedly didn't know exactly how this style of an opener worked. It looked more like a tiny blade that had a little hooked thumb on the top of a short blade. Elliott retrieved the pokey item from the bag and tossed it into the miscellaneous bin with the flashlights and the compass. With that taken care of, he considered the matter closed and returned to emptying the bag, more carefully this time, just in case there were any other surprises.

Elliott was digging into the bag and sorting the contents into the three bins. Well, two really, because Elliott didn't feel the third bin would fill up. Elliott was delighted to find the previous house had a score of Macaroni and cheese boxes. There were other pastas there as well, and Ken made a pretty good spaghetti and tomato sauce. It wasn't as good as Momma's, of course. She made hers from scratch. His palm still throbbed a bit. It wasn't bleeding anymore, it was just a flesh wound, but those sometimes hurt the most. Elliott pulled out a can of apple pie filling and smiled broadly because pie filling had become his new favorite treat. Cherry was his and Ken's favorite, but Elliott liked apple too. He placed it in the can bin with sudden disappointment because Ken had said these supplies would go into the storage unit. Elliott thought briefly about hiding it away for later, but then he simply placed it in the bin and made a note to ask Ken if they could keep that one can for themselves. He was pretty sure Ken would agree to that. Elliott looked into the bag. There wasn't much left inside and reached his hand in for the next can.

That's when he noticed the movement from down the road.

The moment he noticed it, his eyes snapped to the source. Of course, it was a grey person. What else would it have been? Elliott noticed the grey woman's denim pants that stopped halfway down the shin, *capris*, his Momma had called them, and on top was a simple black shirt but she had a vest on like Ken had, but this one was green and kind of raggedy. She was missing her arm, and to Elliott's displeasure, he could see ragged pieces of meat swing from the stump with each uneasy step. Elliott immediately noticed the snapping teeth and clawing arm, as well.

She can see me.

Elliott did a quick inventory of all the sounds he made in the back of the truck; he was sure he had been utterly silent. Even when he pierced his palm on that weird looking can opener, he had hardly made a sound. However, there was no mistaking what he saw. Something else struck him as odd, this one was moving more nimbly than he'd seen other grey people move. Still awkward and slow compared to normal people, sure, but the grey woman was stumbling ahead at a pace that was almost a fast walk. Which, for grey people, was practically sprinting.

The sound at the driver's door startled him. Elliott turned, expecting to see Ken's bulk standing by the door and was about to comment about the grey woman almost trotting down the street, but what he saw was dark hands reaching for him.

"Whoa!" Elliott couldn't help yelping when he felt the nails of the grey person's claw-like hands scrape across his back as Elliott jumped instinctively in the opposite direction.

He tumbled backwards awkwardly across the bed of the truck and landed hard in the back corner, his arm knocking painfully against the tailgate. He hardly felt it, though. His blood stream was spiked with adrenalin, the pain in his arm was a distant thing, and his wild eyes focused on his attacker. The dark, grimy figure that was now angling himself towards the back of the truck to get to him. Elliott scrambled to his feet and hopped out of the truck on the passenger side.

His first thought was to run away, but he had to get to the horn to alert Ken inside the house of what was happening outside. Elliott ran for the open door on the passenger side and climbed into the seat and reached over and gave the horn button three quick presses.

Honk-honk-honk

Panic had set in. Something was wrong. He knew it. The grey people shouldn't be acting like this. After all, Elliott had his superpower. It was something Ken had tested and agreed with. It was real. Ken said it made him special, so what happened? Elliott didn't know, and he had no time to think about what went wrong. Something *was* wrong, and he needed Ken to come out and fix it. Elliott locked his eyes on the front door, confident any moment Ken would appear through the doorway with his trusty knife in hand, and he would know what to do.

Ken wasn't coming, though.

Elliott's mind screamed at him. *Three quick honks.* That's what Ken said to do if he ever found himself in trouble. One press of the horn for one grey person, two honks if there were several zombies, and three quick honks if Elliott was in trouble.

Honk-honk-honk

Elliott blared the horn three more times in quick succession and would have done it again, but he had to pull his hand back when the gross-looking grey man came up to the door and began frantically scrambling into the open driver's door window to get to him. Fear coursed through him like a strange electricity he had no control over. So, when he yanked his hand away from the grey man's snapping teeth as he climbed through the window, Elliott did it with such force he fell back out the open door of the passenger side and landed hard on the gravel road.

Elliott probably would have been dazed by the rough

landing if it weren't for the adrenalin flight response he felt in his core. His back erupted in a dozen different spots of pain where the rocks of the road dug into it. In the cab, the grey man struggled to get his lower half through the open window of the driver's door. He wasn't really trying, just clawing at the material of the seats, trying to get enough purchase to pull himself forward. He was doing it, though. The grey man snarled wildly at Elliott in a way he had never seen before. Elliott could see the milky irises of its eyes contrasted by the black holes of the pupils that were laser focused on him, and him alone. Elliott could feel his heart banging away in his chest and he was sucking in air in desperate gasps as he dug his heels into the loose gravel and slapped his palm painfully into the road to push himself away from the truck.

Once far enough away, Elliott kicked out with his shoe to close the door of the truck, effectively trapping the grey man with his evil little teeth inside. He looked down the road, knowing the grey woman in the vest would be there. What Elliott didn't expect was how close she had gotten and it horrified him. She was already at the back of the truck.

"Shit," Elliott breathed as he rolled over and rose to take a quick couple of steps away to create some distance between them, as well as to give him much needed space to think. He didn't find the space he needed, though. He found two more coming in from the other end of the street and made him skid on the loose gravel to a stop.

They were a distance ahead of him yet, the two grey men. Elliott's mind logged several interesting things about them, like how the one had an oversized belt buckle that shone in the morning light, or how the other one was missing part of his ear on the right side, but he didn't have any time for that. Elliott was in trouble. It made it hard to think straight, because he felt it in his bones. He wanted to run as fast and as far as he could, but he had to push that instinct down. Ken had a plan for this, so instead Elliott looked to the south, looked between the houses for any movement, and when he saw his path was clear, he bolted across the street.

Ken had a plan for everything, it seemed. He had carefully explained to Elliot what he wanted him to do if they ever got separated. Ken spoke slow and repeated himself often, the way adults usually did with him. If they got separated outside the town, which they had never been to yet, Ken instructed him to run back to the farmhouse. He was to avoid roads and houses when possible and stay in the open, because as Ken explained it, was better to see the grey people coming than to hide from them only to turn a corner and have one jump out at you.

That made sense to Elliott.

Inside the town, however, they had a different escape plan. They agreed on a location. Here, it was a tree in the north-east corner of the field where he had accidentally broken Ken's stereo that was under the garbage can. Elliott had picked the tree because Ken wanted some place he could go where he would be safe from the grey people. Ken had suggested a house they could agree on. It was Elliott who had suggested the tree. It was a well-known climbing tree around town, with a massive trunk and plenty of thick low-hanging branches to scramble up on. All the kids in town used to play in and around that tree. Elliott said he could easily climb that tree and the greys wouldn't be able to get to him, unless grey people could climb trees, which Ken assured him they couldn't.

That's where Elliott was running to, because that's where Ken would find him. He couldn't stay here, that much was clear. So that's where he would go and as he did, he tried not to think about why Ken didn't come out of the house like he was supposed to when he honked the danger signal. Ken came up with the signal so he would know when Elliott needed him immediately, because he was in grave danger. So where was he?

Elliott felt the wind on his cheek as he pumped his legs on the ground and swung his arms to drive him forward as fast as he could go. He knew where he was going. It was two blocks away, and he knew exactly how to get there. He cut between the two houses across the road, thankful the people of La Veta didn't believe in fences. Most lots were spacious and wide open, and he easily made it to the narrow gravel alley that ran behind the houses. On his left a grey woman came into view, Elliott veered to the west to give her a wide berth only to see a grey man appear as he passed the house on his right. He veered on his path again as he made his way along the alley. Elliott looked wild-eyed around himself as he ran, desperately searching for the grey people he needed to avoid, and the more he looked, the more he seemed to find.

His stupid brain assaulted him with useless thoughts as he ran, clouding his mind when he needed it clear and focused.

Hey, did you know the grey lady is missing a shoe and there's something wet, and slimy moving around inside that wound on her neck? What do you think that is?

Elliott saw another grey man ahead of them, he was also making his way to the alley from the other side. He wondered whether he could make it passed the grey person, or should he cut in front of that bush on his right?

Hey, did you notice that the grey man was missing three teeth?

Elliott sprinted hard for the alley's end where he could turn down the road and head south, just as the grey man with the missing teeth made it to the edge of the narrow alley. Elliott's feet lost purchase on the gravel as he dug his heels in to avoid the outstretched arms. He skidded slightly as his heart dropped in his chest, but he madly pumped his legs underneath him to find solid ground. He recovered quickly and was up and running down the alley again.

Hey! They see you. They ALL see you. They're coming for you.

"Shut up!" Elliott wasted precious air to say, and he balled up his fists and gave the sides of his forehead an angry couple of bumps.

Several yards ahead of him, a grey woman stepped out from behind a shed and onto the gravel of the alley, and then immediately two more ugly shambling shapes followed it.

Blocking his path.

Hey, did you notice that there's no grey people to the south? You could probably run through those trees and cut across to the road.

Elliott turned south. There was an older looking house buried behind several large bushy trees with enormous trunks at their base that shaded almost the entire lot. Elliott weaved between the few trees between him and the road ahead, and sourly wondered why his brain couldn't be more useful like that all the time. Elliott cut onto the road as he sprinted for the intersection up ahead.

The intersection was fairly open and he could see far in all directions. As he ran, Elliott glanced wildly all around himself. His brain easily counted up all the grey people, and had no problem casually adding the fact they all seemed to be heading straight for him. Elliott's eyes watered as he tried to figure out what he had done to cause this, because obviously he must have done something wrong, and when Ken finds out, he's going to be mad at him.

At the intersection, Elliott veered to the right and started heading west towards the athletic field, and the big oak tree where he would safely wait for Ken in its top branches. He could see the top of the tree behind the house at the end of the block on the left. He also saw five more grey people do a sort of angry shuffle from between the houses on both sides of the street, and the way they did it made Elliott's brain comment that it looked like the grey people already knew Elliott was coming. They didn't wait until he came into view to get angry, like they should, because Elliott didn't think the sound of his footfalls on the loose gravel would be loud enough the stir them from this distance. When he saw them, they were already plenty angry. They were pursuing him before they even knew he would be there. *How? Why?* Some part of his brain demanded to know why the grey people weren't playing by the rules anymore. It wasn't fair. Elliott did everything he was supposed to.

This shouldn't be happening.

He pumped his legs even harder, so thankful for his new life he had now because, now he could run faster. If this happened before Ken, he wouldn't have had the energy to run this fast. Elliott couldn't help but temper that point with the other fact, that if it wasn't for Ken, he would be safe back at the farm right now. Elliott pushed these thoughts away as he focused on the grey people coming in from the sides of the road.

There were three coming towards him from the left, two coming in from between the two houses that were about halfway down the block and another one coming in from between the second and last house on the block. The right side only had the one group of two that was angrily stumbling, almost in unison, towards the center of the road. Towards him. He didn't want to leave the road. That's where Ken said he would be the safest because he could see them coming. They *were* coming. That much was for sure. He kept a mad eye on them as he ran down the street. He passed the first two of the left easy enough, but he had to dash in the opposite direction of the two on the right that lunged forward from the edge of the road. Elliott ducked his shoulder away from their grasp and could swear he felt the nails of the grey man's outstretched fingers scrape across the fabric of his shirt.

Elliott wanted to scream in horror and disgust, but he fought to keep his mind on his pumping legs and placing his feet. He couldn't afford a misstep right now. His once trademark clumsiness could be deadly at this point.

He nimbly avoided the grey woman, who was on the left-hand side of the road, and he continued down the street. He wanted to be proud of his display of speed and agility, but it kind of felt like a moot display when he looked back and saw all five of them continuing their awkward pursuit from behind him. Worst yet, he recognized the grey people turning onto the street from down the block at the intersection from when he had passed them previously; they were *all* after him.

Elliott turned his attention back in front of him because up ahead, less than a hundred yards away, was the tree. He had been fond of the tree, like all the other kids in town, but now that tree had become his lifeline. Elliott sprinted towards it with tears softly spilling from his eyes. He wasn't crying, not really, but he felt the emotions stirring inside him like an incredible pressure he harnessed to use to get his feet to move even faster. The soles of his shoes slapped the ground of the overgrown field as he crossed it and headed straight for the tree. Beyond it, his brain counted seven grey people who were currently on the field, making their way towards him with the same sort of mindless resentment. Three more came in from the west and one more suddenly popped into view from behind the field house. Elliott refused his brain's attempts to inform him about anything else, he didn't know how he did it. He just kept staring at the base of the tree as he ran towards it and tried to picture how he could scramble to a safe height the quickest. His brain remained blessedly quiet as Elliott found his route just in time as he practically collided with the tree with his arms outstretched to halt his momentum.

In the old days, the days when he was... bigger, he had a bit more trouble scaling the branches of the tree than the other kids. He still enjoyed it. How could you not? He just wasn't as naturally skilled at it as the other kids were. Jenny could climb a tree like a squirrel and was fearless with heights. Jenny would be proud of how quickly and deftly he made his way up that tree now. Elliott still didn't go as high as she had because that was madness, and there was no need for it. He found a good-sized branch about fifteen feet up from the ground that could easily support his weight and worked his way towards it. Once there, he lowered himself to sit on the branch with his legs hanging down and he steadied himself by holding onto another branch and waited to be rescued. He had made it. He did as Ken instructed him to do when the situation arose and now, he could relax.

Not that being in that tree was in any way relaxing.

He tried to calm his breathing. He was sucking in air wildly but it still didn't seem like enough, and watched with increasing unease as the grey people encircled the tree. The first one to arrive was a grey man in pants and a stained shirt, he was balding on top and had what Elliott considered being an entirely too long and unkept beard on his face, Elliott could see his cracked teeth past the matted hairs of his moustache. The grey man started clawing at the bark like he expected to pull himself up the tree by his fingertips, like he was Spiderman or something. The whole time locking his eyes onto Elliott and snarling at him.

Soon enough, the others came to encircle the tree. Elliott recognized the grey people he had ran past to get here. They had all followed him here and as Elliott looked out over the field, he could see others making their way to him as well. His brain wasted no time informing him that the number at the base of the tree would swell to twenty-six when they all reached their destination. Elliott couldn't help but to make little mewing noises as he looked down at the angry mob of snarling, snapping black teeth and dirty hands desperately clawing at him. Those at the base of the tree clawed mercilessly at the bark, scraping shallow lines into the hard skin of the tree. Those who couldn't reach the tree, just clawed the air between Elliott's shoes and themselves. Elliott didn't think grey people could jump. He'd never seen it, but regardless of that, he pulled up his feet so they weren't dangling down anymore. The noise the collection of grey people made was impressively terrifying. His brain neatly picked apart the collective growl into each individual snarl and made sure he was aware of each, and it made his skin crawl. Then the smell hit him, and just like the collective growl, the pungent odor coming off them was a strange mixture of seemingly all the foulest smells that his brain recognized. As well as a few it didn't. It was so foul Elliott tasted it on his tongue each time he sucked in another lungful of air.

"Ken will come," he whispered to himself nervously.

It was an all-out assault on his senses. There was no escaping it, there was no place he could go to, no place he could hide from it. Sure, he could close his eyes, but he couldn't close his ears or make it so he couldn't smell or taste them. His stupid brain seemed to love it, it just dissected all the information, sorted it, categorized it and stored it somewhere for later use but not before running it by Elliott first in mad flashes he had no control over, and it made it hard to think.

"Ken will come," he said again. *This will be over and we can go back to the farm, and I can go back to working on my Empire State Building puzzle, and everything will go back to normal.*

They bite people; his brain reminded him, *and if they bite you, then you'll become a grey person.*

Elliott looked down at all the hungry mouths below him with tears in his eyes. If each of those mouths were to take a bite out of him, Elliott didn't think there would be much left of him to become a grey person. They'd just gobble him up with their ugly, greedy mouths. Elliott wondered morbidly which fate would be worse, to be gobbled up completely by grey people, or becoming a grey person. For once, his brain had nothing to say on the matter, and he had to agree he didn't know which would be worse either.

Ken had said Elliott was invisible to grey people, which is up for debate now, but the little secret he kept to himself was that the grey people were kind of invisible to him as well. Grey people didn't have waves the way other things did, living things, nor did they have a mind-shore of any kind. They had nothing. In a very real sense, one Elliott wouldn't be able to explain to normal people, grey people weren't there, not like real people. From them, Elliott just felt a cold, black, sucking void. Which differed from dead people, because with the deceased, there was nothing there to feel. It was like trying to get a feeling from a chair, which was silly. What he felt from grey people was a cold sort of darkness, a void he dared not get too close to for fear of being pulled into its depths forever. Which he knew was impossible, but that didn't stop his stomach from fluttering wildly at the thought of it. He didn't know what grey people were, but he very much knew he didn't want to be one of them.

"Ken will come." He repeated, louder this time to speak over the hungry, vicious growl that was continuously erupting beneath him.

No, he will not. Elliott imagined the grey people beneath him saying. *Everybody left you. He left you too.* He imagined it to be a mocking, cruel voice. *Ken probably came out of the house and it thrilled him you weren't there. He was probably happy to be rid of you. Such a stupid, useless child. What use would you be to him? You think he's your friend, just wait, you'll see. You can't stay in that tree forever. Eventually, you'll fall, and then we will FEEEAAASSST.*

"HE WILL COME!" Elliott screamed down at the snapping mouths that taunted him as much as he was screaming at the voice in his head that said the actual words. Ken was his friend. They'd see, he'd show them just like he showed the grey people at the railroad tracks. "AND WHEN HE DOES, HE'S GOING TO BE MAAAADD!"

Chapter 2

Kenshiro

Kenshiro was in a good mood when he approached the door to the modest-looking house. It was still morning. He still felt the coolness of the air on his skin. It was refreshing. He took it as a good sign that the day would go well. He made a mental note not to keep Elliott out too late today.

The last few days they hadn't returned to the farmhouse until later in the evening. Yesterday, they didn't get back until the sun was kissing the western horizon. Elliott complained about that, because he found a couple puzzles at the storage lot the other day, and he was excited about them. Elliott couldn't wait to put them together. Last night, even as excited as he was to start on it, all Elliott did before he went to bed was empty the plastic bag of pieces all over the table, and make it so all the pieces were face-up. Elliott had to accept he was too tired to continue. It was a little heart-breaking to watch him realize and pull himself away from his prized find.

Elliott had a strange way of doing puzzles. It was just another part of the teen's weirdness. Kenshiro figured by now, he must have spent about a month with the boy, and he was still undecided as to the exact nature of his disability. Was he truly disabled, or a genius? It was hard to tell at times. Kenshiro could make a case for each. Hell, maybe the kid was both.

With puzzles, Elliott would spread all the pieces face-up on the table in front of him and just stare at all the pieces on the table for a time. Then, without any warning, he would just start constructing the puzzle piece by piece. Kenshiro watched him do a five-hundred-piece puzzle in less than an hour. He carefully studied each piece for a short time and then started to place one piece after another. Elliott simply assembled the puzzle like each piece had a number on it, and all he had to do was put them down in the right order. They would do puzzles together because Elliott said he enjoyed doing puzzles with friends, but after a while it became clear Elliott actually preferred the do the puzzle himself. The other person was just supposed to be present for it, and maybe add to the conversation. Kenshiro would have thought that doing a puzzle that way might hamper Elliott's ability to talk endlessly. Sadly, though, that wasn't the case.

That's okay, we'll make up for that tonight, Kenshiro told himself as he slid the small zippered pouch of lock picking tools from his pocket. He put the tensioner tool into place and he kept a slight, but steady pressure on it before he slid the rake into the lock and started working on the pins. It was an older house, so he was hoping it had an older deadbolt. This felt like a three-pin lock. Kenshiro kept working it for a short time.

Snick!

He placed the tools back into their respective slot in the zippered pouch and then stowed it away back into his pocket. Kenshiro forced all other thoughts from his mind as he drew the long straight blade from its sheath on his leg, and took a deep breath to center himself before he knocked loudly on the center of the door. He leaned in close to it and tried to listen for movement inside with his hand on the doorknob. It wasn't a great sign of what might wait for him on the other side of the door, zombies usually made little noise. He waited for a couple of silent breaths until he turned the knob and stepped into the house. The door opened easily, and immediately he saw a small staircase that led down into the basement and another one that led to the top floor. As soon as Kenshiro opened the door partially, he heard the telltale raspy moans of the dead from within the house. He paused, with the door still open, to discern where the sounds were coming from. It was upstairs somewhere. The staircase leading upstairs was partially obscured behind the door, so he took another step into the house to peer around it.

Shit!

The panic set in immediately as he saw the dead woman at the top of the stairs. She was right there in a badly ripped patterned blouse that hung off her frame. Kenshiro could see her bra through the torn garment. There was a old blood stain that ran down its neck from the spot on her right side where it looked like someone had torn its ear clean off.

It was an ugly wound.

The dead woman's milky eyes locked onto him as she stepped forward, mindlessly extending her leg out past the top step. Without having the benefit of there being anything there for it to step on, its body lurched forward down the stairs. The dead woman's slack body landed hard. Kenshiro was sure he heard a muted series of cracks and pops as it bounced off the stairs and tumbled downward towards him.

His mind quickly did the math, and Kenshiro darted fully into the house before the body crashed into the door, slamming it shut behind him. He turned back to the dead woman just as the dark figure was madly scrambling along the tiled floor to get to him. It wasn't even trying to stand up, it just clawed at the floor to get to him while breathlessly growling. He quickly got his bearings, stepped forward and stomped his boot down on its back. Right between the shoulder blades, and forced the dead woman back onto the floor. Kenshiro pinned it there with his weight on its back just long enough for him to drive the knife into its skull.

The raspy snarl ceased immediately when the blade struck home, and the dead woman's body kicked once and settled onto the floor. He pulled the knife free, and wiped the blade clean on the torn blouse, before he stood back up in the entranceway and listened.

There was a slight banging noise coming from the basement.

Something was bumping up against a door down there somewhere, and it seemed to be the only other sounds coming from inside the house. Kenshiro moved up the stairs to the upper floor.

He already knew there were more downstairs. He would deal with them soon enough, but after he checked the upper floor first. Zombies had a much easier time going down stairs than they did moving up them. A fact proven by the still figure in front of the door at the entranceway.

At the top of the stairs, there was a hallway to the left, that led presumably to the bedrooms and probably a bathroom. Immediately to the right was a nicely decorated living room. On the floor were a few items that were knocked from the coffee tables, probably from the dead woman who had been bumping around up here for God knows how long.

In front of him, he went through the archway that led into the kitchen. Again, like the living room, it was clear of the dead, and relatively neat. Only a few items seemed to had been swept to the floor in the house's history. Kenshiro moved quickly through it and exited another archway that led back into the living room. Through the window at the front of the house, he could see Elliott in the back of the truck sorting through the haul Ken brought from the last house.

He's a good worker, Kenshiro thought before refocusing on the hallway ahead of him, and the bedrooms they led to.

There were four doors, two on each side, spaced out equally. Two were open, the closest one on the left-hand side, and the farthest door on the right. With knife in hand, Kenshiro walked swiftly towards the open door on the left. He was confident those rooms would be clear. He had already made enough noise to wake the dead in the house, literally. The knock at the door before he entered the house might not have registered, but the epic sounds of the disturbance that soon followed should have alerted all the dead in the house. Any zombies that were able would make their way towards the sound, would do so, but he wasn't taking any chances.

He peered into the first room. It was obviously a young girl's room. They painted the walls a pastel shade of pink. There was a small bed in the corner covered in bright Hello Kitty blankets, with a nightstand next to it that was empty except for a light with some cutesy cartoon character he didn't recognize at the base. Kenshiro saw a dresser by the closet that was decorated with girlish knick-knacks but it held no interest for him. He walked into the room and approached the folding doors of the closet to search it, and as soon as he found it was empty, Kenshiro exited the room just as quickly. There was nothing in that room that would be worth finding. What would a small girl have that would ever benefit him or his friend at the end of the world?

Back in the hall, he moved to the other open door at the end. This was the master bedroom, for sure. It was a large sized bedroom with a good, comfortable-looking bed in the center of the room with matching nightstands at the sides they each had identical lamps, and alarm clocks with blank faces on them. He moved with purpose into the room, where he spotted a small walk-in closet, which he checked.

He made a note to search for clothes that might fit him, or maybe Elliott, but he doubted the man of the house would be Elliott's size. The teen was at the awkward age where he was taller than a boy but not big enough to be considered a man yet. It made finding clothes for him challenging.

Next, he moved to the ensuite bathroom that was just big enough for a sink and toilet, and maybe a little extra space for some elbow room, but not much. With the master bedroom cleared, he moved back into the hall. Across from the door to the master bedroom was the closed door on the left-hand side. Inside the room he heard nothing, so he braced himself as he reached for the doorknob and gave it a twist.

The room beyond was an office. In the middle of the room was a good-sized wooden desk with a laptop on the surface along with a few framed photographs and other things that didn't interest him. There was a filled bookcase in the corner that he would check later to see if there were any novels that might interest him. Around him, various pictures of people shaking hands and framed certificates lined the walls. He didn't recognize or care enough about them to give them a second look. The room was empty, that was all he needed to know right now, so he went back into the hall and moved to the last closed door.

Kenshiro rapped on the door, and all he heard was the corresponding echo from inside the room. *Bathroom*, he thought as he opened the door and Kenshiro quickly drew his eyes to a bloodied sink that stood out in the otherwise pristine, albeit dusty, bathroom. Something had bled a lot in this room in the past. The dark carpet of the hall hid any signs of a blood trail, but there was no hiding the dark crimson stain from the ivory white of the room. He noticed the entire basin to be covered with dull, cracked dried-out blood that looked like dried soil as it caked the sink and countertop. The room didn't have any dead in it, so Kenshiro abandoned it and left the mysterious blood stains behind to move into the hall and head downstairs.

He stepped past the dead woman's body that was on the front landing in front of the main door and proceeded down into the relative darkness of the basement.

At the bottom of the stairs a large room opened up on the left. Kenshiro could see that it room was lit by patio doors that led to the backyard towards the back of the room. It was a den of sorts. The plush leather furniture was all arranged around a large screen television that occupied the center of the front facing wall. Beside it, was a large cabinet of various electronics that he imagined were all hooked up to the television, and into the speakers he saw placed strategically around the viewing area.

Behind the leather sofa set, was a classy-looking bar that was built into the corner of the room, complete with rustic looking barstools that lined the counter area with held actual beverage taps. A real man-cave. To the right of the stairs was a partially darkened hallway lit by an open door on the side.

At the end of the hallway, ominously shadowed by the light from the open door, was a white door with a single dark blood stain that was the exact shape of a human hand right in the center. Kenshiro could tell by its size, it was a large hand that made that print. That was where he suspected the quiet thudding noise was coming from. As if on cue, something rebounded off the door at the end of the hall. He heard the sound and saw the door move slightly in time with the noise.

Something was definitely behind that door. Something large.

Before heading down the hall, Kenshiro took a quick step into the man-cave, just enough to see around the corner. He saw the patio door was slightly ajar, but other than that, there wasn't anything out-of-place inside the room. Kenshiro took a step towards the door, intent on closing and securing it. That's when a sound came from down the hallway he recognized, and it chilled Kenshiro's blood.

Aaaaaaaarrrrrrrrrrrr!

The normal wordless rasp of the undead had risen to a kind of pained scream, or maybe a kind of howl. Whatever it was, it sounded like the zombie behind the door was in pain. Kenshiro knew better, and the truth made his flesh break out in goose pimples, because the memory of it wasn't something a person forgets, and the implications of it were dire. *The Blood rage!* But that was impossible. That would mean somebody was...

BOOM!

The door at the end of the hall bulged dangerously outward as something struck the other side with substantial force. Kenshiro held fast momentarily as his mind struggled to imagine what could be behind that door that could generate that kind of force, and as if to answer an unspoken question, it struck again.

BOOM!

He saw the entire surface of the door flex under the strain, and a moment later there came a sickening crack from the door. A thin dark line appeared down the center of the door. The crack was visible in the center of the handprint. Kenshiro became transfixed on it for a moment until whatever it was behind that door crashed into it again.

BOOM!

That door isn't going to hold, Kenshiro thought to himself, like it was beyond dispute. It was an eventuality he was going to have to deal with. As he thought this, the crack widened menacingly as a significant force pressed against the other side of the door. Kenshiro gripped the knife in his hand even tighter.

And then he remembered the patio door was still open. He snapped his head to the door, and just in time. Through the glass, a zombie girl in a pink sundress was moving across the lawn towards him. Kenshiro quickly moved towards the open door to secure it.

Beyond the door was a fairly large patio area that was sunken into the ground. People who wanted to enter the patio had to move down four concrete steps from the lawn. The concrete walls were maybe waist high, and as he approached the door, Kenshiro had his eyes fixed on the female zombie in front of him. At the door, he saw another tall zombie on the side of the patio simply walk off the edge of the lawn to fall face first into a set of patio chairs with a loud crash.

They were coming for him. At least, Kenshiro hoped it was him.

He quickly closed the glass patio door, and because it didn't have a standard doorknob but some fancy brass door lever. Which were perfect for the undead's limited abilities. Kenshiro locked the deadbolt on the door. *I'll deal with them later*.

With the patio door secured, he turned back and moved to the opening of the hallway. Down at the other end, the door was being pushed apart from the inside. The crack had widened to a gap large enough to see some natural light peek through. Kenshiro saw the outline of some massive figure behind the door. Then a large, dark hand pushed through the gap, but it wasn't the claw-like bony digits of typical undead fingers. No. This was an impossibly massive fist with five meaty digits that looked like black sausages from this distance. From inside the room, Kenshiro heard frantic breathless snarling, and then a second large hand pushed through the gap. The sharp cracking noises of the door being torn apart exploded down the hallway as the massive hands pushed through the gap to reveal giant forearms. They forced the two sides of the failing door apart with horrifying ease.

There came a low, deep growl from inside the room at the end of the hall and Kenshiro saw those meaty fingers on both hands ball up into fists before they flexed outward. With a snarl and a loud crack, the door exploded outward into two distinct pieces. One piece, the side with the doorknob, flew out into the hall and then ricocheted off the wall before it fell to the floor with a crash. The other piece, the one still connected to the hinges, flew back on those hinges to bounce off the wall of the hallway. It slowly rebounded back inwards where it bumped uselessly against the hulking figure standing in the doorframe.

Fuck me, he thought with a sort of terrified awe, *look at the size of that fucking thing*! The monstrous zombie took up most of the doorframe. It was a goddamn giant, towering easily over six feet tall. Kenshiro didn't know how much taller this thing was than him, but there wasn't a lot of space between the top of its head and the top of the door frame. Nor was there a lot of space between its shoulders and the sides of the door. From the outline it looked like Frankenstein's monster on steroids. *Shoot it*. The thought came hard and fast, but before Kenshiro could act on it, the towering beast at the end of the hall howled through its ruined vocal cords and charged at him.

Zombies lose muscle mass as they age. Kenshiro didn't know exactly how much over time, but it was easy to tell which zombies had been around for a while. So normal people, over time, turn into relatively weak zombies after about a year. However, if the infected person was, for instance, a bodybuilder of some type. They would have more muscle to lose than regular people and would be stronger than you'd expect. This towering menace storming towards him was probably the biggest goddamn zombie he had ever seen, and Kenshiro couldn't imagine what kind of life would produce a living person of this size.

Too late.

The same voice that advised him to shoot a half second ago now declared that time had passed, as the snarling undead figure at the end of the hall propelled itself forward on its tree-trunk like legs with surprising speed. Kenshiro could feel its thunderous foot falls on the concrete floor through the soles of his boots. It felt like mini-tremors as the undead giant barreled down the hallway towards him. In an instant, he did the math and he wouldn't be able to pull the gun and aim effectively before this beast would be on top of him. Kenshiro cursed his inaction as he breathed in sharply and stepped forward to meet this mass of undead fury.

He needed momentum of his own to stop this charging mass of dead muscle, for that Kenshiro needed space, and he was quickly losing it to this monster. Kenshiro couldn't wait any longer, so he let his instincts step in, and he did what felt natural. He stepped forward with no actual plan for how to deal with this freight train of a zombie.

Kenshiro moved in, and breathed out as he swung his hips around and shot his foot out in a hard side-kick. The same one he had used to break a man's rib in the ring, and also the same kick that sent normal zombies flying in the other direction. Kenshiro had been using this kick for what felt like a good chunk of his life. It was maybe the second technique he had learned. He was younger than Elliott when he first used it. Kenshiro spent the next ten years turning that kick into a weapon by learning how to squeeze as much power and speed out of it as his frame could muster. In the dead years, he had to break old habits. Now he didn't have to worry about his opponent's health anymore, and started hitting with genuine force. He hit that fucking monster with the hardest kick he had ever thrown in his life. It felt like he just kicked a concrete wall, and the shock of it rattled painfully up his leg and into his lower back.

In his mind, the kick would send the beast back a few steps and he would move in low with the knife to the inside of its arms while they flailed backwards to regain its posture. A quick thrust under the chin and then it would be over. Quick and simple.

He threw the kick, and it landed solidly in its center of gravity, right where he was aiming, but all that happened was the force of the kick just got absorbed into the thing's massive momentum. Kenshiro felt something painfully pop in his leg. He had stopped the charging mass in its tracks, but when he pulled back his now injured leg, it just snarled defiantly and descended on him like a damned avalanche. Kenshiro just saw those huge hands reaching out for him, and for a moment he couldn't help but feel dread. It was only natural, but he resisted it and grit his teeth as he planted his injured leg behind him and pressed forward to hold back the tidal wave of death.

He felt something cold and heavy slap down onto his shoulder. Kenshiro realized it was the impossibly large hand of the zombie brute when he felt it squeeze. It felt like he caught his shoulder in a vise. Its fingertips dug painfully into the muscle of his shoulder to pull its meal in closer to his jaws. With the knife still clutched in his hand, he pressed his fist into its barrel-shaped chest to hold those snapping teeth at bay. His other hand caught the zombie's bicep as it reached forward. Its arm was as big as Kenshiro's thigh, maybe bigger.

Under his hand, he felt the loose skin around its

somewhat deflated bicep as it pressed forward. It made it hard to find a good grip on the arm, like he was trying to hold on to a greasy log that was baring down on him. Kenshiro growled angrily as he pushed back against the snapping force descending on him, but it was no use, it was too strong. It took everything he had just to keep it from pulling him in to those damned teeth. He had nothing left to deal with the sheer weight of it as it leaned in towards him. He couldn't let his shoulders pass his hips, he had to stay upright, which was hard because this zombie towered over him. So, instead of pushing Kenshiro straight back, it was pushing him backward into the ground. His back could only arch so much before he would fall backward with this fucking thing crushing down upon him half a second later. It would be all over after that point. He felt there wasn't a person left on this earth that could lift that kind of dead weight off their chest, it might not happen right away, but it would certainly be the end of him.

Kenshiro retreated a step to get his legs behind him and hissed through his teeth. He planted his legs and then pushed against the zombie with all his might to get enough leverage and space, so he could free up his knife hand. All his muscles, from his legs to the tip of his fingers, strained to the point it felt like the muscle would just tear free from the tendons holding it to the bones, but he persisted. Kenshiro somehow gained an inch on the dark towering figure but before he could celebrate the accomplishment, it angrily reared back its head and snarled loudly. Before Kenshiro could brace himself for whatever was coming, his entire body flew to the side and he was slammed into the wall of the hallway. Somewhere deep inside the wall, he heard a crack as the whole wall shook with the force of the impact.

Kenshiro was shaken, his right-hand still struggling against its chest to hold those snapping teeth at bay, but his left hand lost its grip on the thing's bicep as he collided with the wall. A moment later he bit down in pain as its hand clutched his side through the material of the vest. If it wasn't for the hardened fabric of the vest there's a good chance the beast simply would have ripped a piece of meat right off Kenshiro's body. As it was, it still felt like something was pinching his whole left side.

Out of pure instinct, he tried to move away from the pain, but there was nowhere to go. This thing held him firmly in place against the wall. It was a miracle he had kept his hand in place on its chest. He moved his left hand up to help push back its bearded, withered face that madly snapped at him. Its teeth mere inches from Kenshiro's face, he could smell the foulness that was brought up from its rotting depths with each snarled bite. Its blackened gums had receded horribly away from the otherwise perfect teeth to leave sizeable gaps between them. Kenshiro was close enough to those dried out and cracked teeth to see tiny pieces of old meat from previous victims that had gotten wedged in those gaps. It wasn't a reassuring sight.

Out of what Kenshiro could only assume was frustration, the mountainous zombie violently pulled him away from the wall, only to reverse his direction in an instant, sending him crashing back into the wall. The undead monster used Kenshiro like a battering ram, truly testing how solidly built the hallway wall was. Kenshiro's head whipped back and bounced off it so hard he saw stars around him, and the edges of his vision darkened slightly.

Then the bastard did it again, harder this time.

Kenshiro was ready for it, though. When the bearded undead monster viciously yanked him back, Kenshiro seized the opportunity to lift his knee up to its mid-section and wedged it between him and this thing's hulking frame.

With that in place, he braced himself for the impact with the wall. He growled in pain as its grip on his shoulder and side grew even tighter and it lifted him off his last remaining foot as it threw him back into the wall. This time the wall didn't just shake. The drywall itself folded inwards as the undead giant rammed his body against the wall with unrelenting force. Kenshiro's body sunk deeper into the wall as it just held him there, pushing against his knee as it tried to lean in closer to sink its teeth into Kenshiro's flesh. He clenched his teeth as he pushed back using his knee, which freed up his knife hand.

"Anata o fakku!" *Fuck you*! Kenshiro growled as he brought the knife down in a hard-overhand strike. In his mind, the plan was that the knife would sink into the top of its skull up to the guard, he brought all the force he could muster into his attacking arm.

It surged forward suddenly and inexplicably, driving him slightly deeper into the collapsed drywall, and the sudden motion ruined his one chance. The knife glanced off its large skull, tore down through its left ear, and sunk uselessly into the base of its neck.

"Maji?!" *Seriously*?! Kenshiro complained loudly as the zombie mountain opened its mouth and roared at him. With its ruined vocal cords, the sound that came lost the effect and sounded more like it was loudly clearing its throat. His eyes couldn't avoid looking down into the depths of its rotten throat as the sound gurgled up from it. He stared at the dried-up looking paddle of a tongue and the dark flesh of its throat beyond, it was only a moment though.

Then he was flying.

Just before he was about to pull his knife free from its tree stump of a neck, the large chilly hand painfully holding him in place pulled him free from the wall and it pivoted and tossed him through the air like he was a rag doll. Kenshiro felt an unnerving weightlessness for a moment as his limbs scrambled to find purchase on anything to slow his momentum, but he felt nothing but the open air as he sailed away from the dead bearded giant.

Until something struck his legs.

It had thrown him back into the living room, so far and so hard, the back of Kenshiro's legs collided with the edge of the plush leather sofa in the center of the room. Suddenly, the world spun crazily as he flipped backwards awkwardly over the arm of the sofa to land dazed and disorientated on the floor. He landed hard, but mercifully, he landed on all fours.

Get up! Get up! Get up! An old familiar voice screamed inside his head as he struggled for a moment to get his bearings.

Honk-honk-honk

The sound of the truck's horn filled the room, and the implications of it filled his mind like an explosion of awareness. *Elliott's in trouble.* No, not just trouble. He direly needs help. The three-horn signal was only to be used in emergencies. Elliott knew that, and Kenshiro didn't think the teen would be too quick to use it unless he was truly afraid.

In the depths of his gut an all too familiar feeling of grievous failure lit a fire inside Kenshiro. In a cruel instant, it reminded him of the first time he felt this feeling of absolute defeat and loss. Back when he still had something to lose. Here and now, he had something to lose again. And it was in that exact moment he realized how much of a loss it would be if he lost Elliott forever. No more chatty truck rides, no more playing catch in the afternoon, and no more silly little moments. That, and so much more, Kenshiro would lose forever. Because of his failure, because he thought he could keep Elliott safe. How foolish he was to think he could save someone in this world. He couldn't save anyon-

I have to get outside. NOW!

Kenshiro jumped to his feet just as those giant hands were already reaching for him again. It was a gift to be free, and he wasn't too keen to feel those fleshy vices clamp down on his skin again. Kenshiro was sure his whole left side was purple underneath the vest. He quickly darted to the right, removing himself from the towering zombie's line of attack, and easily caught its right arm by the wrist. He swept to its side and roared as he drove his shin into the back of its knee in a powerful leg kick. He was feeding off the burning he felt in his gut, harnessing the fear he had inside himself to something he could use. The kick buckled the leg and its immense weight suddenly became a problem as it fell onto its knee. Still holding its beefy forearm, Kenshiro brought his other leg forward and smashed it into its face, more out of habit than necessity, because the massive zombie didn't seem to even notice, and he followed the kick up by twisting its arm until it locked its shoulder, which propelled it forward.

Kenshiro saw his opportunity and reached forward to wrap his hand around the handle of his favorite knife that was buried uselessly into this thing's thick neck. He didn't waste any effort on half measures as he gripped the handle so tight his knuckles ached and used every muscle he had to yank the blade free. He fully intended to strike back down with the knife and pierce this motherfucker right behind the ear, but before he could bring the knife down, the thing suddenly lurched forward towards him.

Kenshiro lost his grip on its wrist before he could move out of the way. The bearded monster's arm swung back towards him and caught him in the ribs with its large forearm. It didn't exactly hurt, his brain didn't register any actual pain, though it knocked the wind out of him and sent him sailing backward into the big screen tv. It was like getting hit with a three-hundred-pound pillow. Again, he was thankful for the combat vest for taking the brunt of that blow.

He heard a crack come from the tv and felt it give slightly as it fell back against the wall behind it. Somehow, it still managed to hold his weight and Kenshiro rebounded back onto his feet, but in the process, he lost his grip on the knife and it went flying somewhere off to the side. The angry undead beast of a thing didn't even bother to rise onto its feet again. It just turned towards him and launched itself forward on those massive legs. The bearded undead monster flew towards him with its arms wide like he was going for a flying bearhug, and in the center of those arms was its massive bearded face with its open mouth and its lips curled back to reveal gross-looking, elongated, dried out teeth, with rotten bits of flesh in between them. It felt like trying to avoid a tidal wave, but thankfully, he didn't have to think about what he did. Reflexes and instincts took over at that point. Kenshiro dropped and pushed off his legs as hard as he could and dived out of the way. He didn't have time to worry about the landing, he just launched himself to the side and braced himself for the impact. Something brushed against his side as the two of them sailed carelessly in their respective directions.

The undead monster crashed into the lower half of the tv and the tiny stand it was resting on. The television held up well under Kenshiro's weight, but there was no contest with this monstrous fucking zombie's mass. The tv stand folded immediately. Kenshiro fared a little better. He crashed painfully onto the floor in front of the couch, rolled and then tumbled into the coffee table at the end.

Both he and the zombie struggled to get to their feet. Kenshiro hopped up with relatively lightening speed and as he did, he listened frantically for the truck's horn from the front of the house.

For Elliott's signal.

All he heard, however, was a banging noise coming from the back patio door. Kenshiro risked a fevered glance in the door's direction only to be rewarded with seeing the tall slim zombie he saw fall into the patio earlier. It smashed its forehead into the large window in the center of the door. His heart dropped when he saw the large crack shoot across the glass of the door. *Well, that's fucking awesome*. It was time to end this. Kenshiro reached up for the pistol and turned up to the large undead form, just in time to see a large black shape flying at him.

The tv.

Kenshiro couldn't believe something that large could move that quickly. When he first saw the dark shape, it was just a large black twisted mass that was flying threw the air at him. He forgot all about the pistol and dropped down to duck under the object. He didn't know how, but Kenshiro swore he could feel it as it sailed by him, another inch and he probably wouldn't have a head right now. The ruined tv tumbled out of sight somewhere behind the bar before he heard the angry snarl from the undead beast and Kenshiro just knew the towering zombie was on its feet and coming for him.

Kenshiro grabbed the edges of the coffee table he had crashed into and tore it away from the couch as he rose to turn back to the zombie hulk snarling behind him. He held the coffee table in front of him with both hands as he met the thing head on.

They both only got in one step before they collided and Kenshiro jammed the coffee table between them. The legs of the table caught the zombie in the chest, and Kenshiro's muscles strained painfully as he struggled to hold the zombie at bay. It clawed wildly at his face but thankfully the table held him far enough away the fucker wouldn't be able to reach him. It could grab his hands and easily forced him to let go of the coffee table, but thankfully zombies didn't think like that. It pushed forward against the table, just as he knew it would. Kenshiro retreated a step so he could pivot and use the table and the undead beast's own momentum to swing it towards the couch. Once it was lined up, Kenshiro dug his heels into the carpet and growled loudly as he pushed with every ounce of his being.

Every joint ached as he pushed. The towering zombie had lots of undead muscle and immense power, but Kenshiro had living muscle and body coordination. He locked his arms in front of him, dipped his shoulders and lowered his center of gravity, and used every bit of leverage he could muster to push this thing back into the couch. It hissed madly at him as Kenshiro forced it back one step, then with the next step, Kenshiro brought the hulk up against the couch. There was nowhere else for it to go. Kenshiro sucked in a lungful of air and pushed it out as a growl and he kept the pressure on, forcing its massive upper body further back.

That's when he heard the distinct sound of glass breaking.

Kenshiro risked a look to the patio door and saw the two figures, the tall zombie and the one with the pink sundress, stumble headfirst through the door. They crashed onto the floor, with the tiny zombie woman in the pink dress falling onto the tall, gangly looking male zombie. They squirmed drunkenly amongst the broken glass of the door for a moment, before getting their bearings enough to get to their feet and their weird looking milky eyes locked firmly on him.

And don't forget about Elliott.

A voice inside his head cruelly reminded him that every second he wasted in here was another second he lost that could be spent getting to his friend. The intense fear of the unknown fueled him, and he pushed the undead beast back even further until it was almost at the tipping point. Then he let his grip on the coffee table slacken for before he leapt forward and slammed his shoulder into the flat surface of the table. The zombie hulk couldn't adjust to the sudden increase in force, and he clumsily fell back into the couch into a sitting position. Kenshiro saw his chance. He thought about just stepping back and shooting the fucking thing and being done with it, but then he remembered the large screen tv this thing hurled across the room. Instead, he leaned heavily on the table, pinning the undead monster in place for the time being. The giant zombie thrashed wildly and uselessly against the table.

Kenshiro saw his opportunity and fear told him this might be the only one he got, so he made the best of it. Kenshiro used it to pull the small .22 caliber pistol free from its holster on the front of his vest. He stuck the barrel of the pistol into the snarling bearded face of the zombie giant he had pinned on the couch. He didn't aim, at this range there was no chance he would miss.

POP.

Kenshiro simply pulled the trigger once and instantly a tiny hole appeared in the center of the hulk's forehead. Immediately, its angry breathless howling ended as its huge thrashing form settled into the couch like someone had taken its batteries out. But Kenshiro wasn't done. There were others in the room that needed a bullet.

Kenshiro sprung back from the table and used his free hand to toss the table aside. It would not rest idly on top of the monstrous form on the couch, and he didn't want it tumbling forward and risk affecting his next shots. Plus, they pissed him off, and it just felt good to fling something to the side. It crashed against the wall as he stepped into a classic shooter's stance while raising the pistol up to a two-handed grip. Sight, pause, fire and repeat.

POP-POP

He fired two shots in quick succession, first shooting the tiny zombie girl neatly in the forehead, and then placing a bullet in the face of the tall one behind her. This time it was the tall one's turn to be on top of the zombie heap as the two of them fell to the ground.

Elliott.

The singular thought drove him forward towards the stairs in a mad sprint. His entire body seemed to protest the sudden motion. As Kenshiro limped madly for the stairs, he pushed the pain aside. He took the stairs three at a time as he bounded up the steps and reached for the doorknob to the entrance to the house. Feeling the seconds ticking away, like Elliott's life was now an hourglass draining its sand into oblivion. He pulled on the door, only to have it open slightly before it violently struck the corpse on the floor by the door.

It was the zombie woman in the torn blouse from what felt like a lifetime ago. He looked down at its compact frame as it blocked the door. Kenshiro cursed loudly as he reached down with his free hand and grabbed the corpse. He howled in frustration and pain as he tossed it down the stairs. Kenshiro didn't wait to see how it would land at the bottom. Once the body was out of the way, he forgot all about it. He reached for the doorknob and yanked the door open. His eyes painfully adjusted to the day's light, and he discovered he had a rather nasty headache as the light struck his eyes. Kenshiro ran across the lawn towards the truck, frantically looking for signs of his friend. He stopped in his tracks when he saw a strange movement from inside the truck.

Is that...?

He instantly recognized the zombie by how it moved, and for a fevered moment, he thought the figure inside the truck was all that remained of his friend. An undead husk of the once lively, talkative teen he knew. No. It wasn't Elliott. Thankfully after a moment, he saw this undead husk was from someone else. *How the fuck did it get in the truck?* He thought briefly before he decided that, right now, it wasn't important. Kenshiro took a breath and tried to collect himself as he scanned his surroundings for any signs of his friend, or where he might have gone. All he saw was an empty street and a few zombies down the road, making their way to the south.

Which was weird.

Kenshiro had fired his pistol three times in quick succession only a few moments ago. His ears were still ringing from the sound of it. By all rights, any undead in the street should be making their way to him with all the noise he was making. Kenshiro then looked back into the truck and noticed the figure inside was clawing at the passenger window, which was also facing south. His heart sank cruelly as another piece of the puzzle fell into place. *Elliott's bleeding.* He didn't know how it happened, which was the worst part of this equation. The not knowing part. He was certain Elliott had bled. That would explain the sudden rage of the behemoth back there. It explains why all the exterior undead seemed to be uninterested in all the noise he had made, and why he was now seeing them making their way inexplicably to the south.

The tree.

The meeting place the two of them had agreed upon was also to the south. Kenshiro knew exactly where it was, one block south and about a block and a half to the west. That's where Elliott would be, and that's where he was going. He didn't think about what he would find when he got there. He would deal with that later. First, he had to get there.

Kenshiro forced his fears to the side and focused on his new aim. *Get to the tree.* He hurried up to the truck. The dark undead figure inside desperately clung to the passenger door. It didn't seem to notice Kenshiro until he opened the door, and by then it was too late for it to do anything. With pistol in hand, Kenshiro opened the door to the driver's side of the truck. As expected, the thing inside turned back and snarled menacingly. Kenshiro paid it no mind as he simply grabbed the zombie by the ankle and pulled it roughly out of the truck through the driver's door, and promptly shot it in the face when it settled on the ground.

Before he hopped into the truck, Kenshiro pulled the magazine free from the small pistol and replaced it with a fresh one that he stored in one of the front pockets of the vest. He stowed the magazine that only had six rounds remaining in his pants pocket for later use.

He climbed into the truck, closed the door and fired up the engine in one motion. Kenshiro yanked the transmission into drive and slammed his foot down on the gas pedal, and spun the steering wheel to the right. The truck responded by digging into the gravel of the road and jumping to the right. The back end of the vehicle swung out behind him as the rear tires sprayed gravel behind the truck. Kenshiro turned the wheel back when the truck faced west and let off the accelerator until the wheels found purchase, and the truck shot down the road.

He was doing thirty-five miles an hour when he approached the first intersection at the end of the block. Up ahead, he saw a dark figure stumble forward through the intersection ahead, and as far as Kenshiro was concerned any dead on the road were fair game at this point. The only thing that mattered was getting to Elliott. *Fuck the zombies, fuck the noise, and fuck this goddamn truck.*

He lined the truck with the zombie, stepped down on the gas, and madly cranked the wheel to the left. The back tires spun, and the truck drifted dangerously into the turn, but Kenshiro had done the maneuver before. Usually for fun. The back end of the truck slammed mercilessly into the zombie making its way south through the intersection. A loud metallic bang came from the back passenger side that reverberated throughout the truck. He didn't look, if he had, he imagined he would have seen a broken undead body go flying off in the opposite direction. Kenshiro eased off the gas to stop the back end from drifting on the loose gravel as he sped down the road, when he steered into another zombie. The undead woman in the checkered shirt and jeans didn't even glance backwards. Kenshiro hit the zombie with the front driver's corner of the truck. He watched dispassionately as it violently rebounded off the hood of the truck and then disappeared underneath it. The vehicle bucked underneath him as he drove over its body, and left the zombie rolling in the gravel behind him.

Ahead of him he saw three others, two on the road and the other one was meandering through the parking lot of a decent sized Mexican themed inn. He only concerned himself with the two on the road. Kenshiro took the one, a portly looking dead man in greasy-looking coveralls, on the driver's side again as he moved down the road at what felt like a dangerous speed. The dead man hit hard and left a dark stain on the hood of the truck when its skull collided with the steel. There was a loud crunch of the plastic of the headlight assembly crumpling under the force of the impact with the body.

Again, the truck bucked as it crushed the body under the wheels as he drove on. The second one he took on the turn, this one was a smaller figure, a child, and there was a time when that fact would cause him to pause. However, that time was long behind Kenshiro. It was an ugly thing to do, but it had to be done, and Kenshiro wasn't in the mood for half measures. He took that one at the turn to the right. The undead child had reached the intersection and was only a few steps into it when Kenshiro spun the wheel and hit it with the passenger corner of the truck as he turned the corner with a loud bang. The body disappeared under the wheels and the truck's back end kicked up slightly as he continued down the road. He risked a look in the rear-view mirror, but the massive dust cloud behind the truck obscured any view of the child's body.

Ahead of him, less than a block away on the left-hand side, was the extensive field where he first met Elliott. Kenshiro fought the urge to step harder on the gas pedal. The truck was already fishtailing dangerously on the road, and he wildly whipped the steering wheel back and forth as he kept the truck moving in a somewhat straight line down the road.

There was a dead man on the right-hand side of the road as he turned the corner and, out of spite, he steered towards the lone hobbling figure. The back end of the truck swerved as it bore down on the zombie ahead of him. It was taller than Kenshiro originally thought. It struck the passenger side of the bumper and flew off to the side instead of being sucked underneath the vehicle like the rest. Kenshiro just swerved the truck back into the center of the road as the body flew off out of sight.

Ahead of him, he saw the top of the massive tree above the rooftop of the last house on the right-hand side of the block. Fear and self-loathing stung his eyes as the truck approached. Kenshiro didn't know what he would find and he feared the worst, but made a solemn promise that every zombie he encountered, no matter who, was going to be put down once and for all. If he couldn't save Elliott, he was going to make every last one of those motherfuckers pay.

As he pulled up, he saw the edge of the undead mob, stained zombies pressing mindlessly forward towards something he couldn't see. In his mind, he pictured the center of that undead mass feeding on what remains of his only friend in this world. His mind's eye cruelly showed him pictures of bloodied arms and clawed hands digging at the body, tearing it apart. Just like…

The trunk of the tree came into view and he let out a single sob as he saw, a short distance amongst the thick branches at the bottom of the tree, was Elliott waving excitedly from his perch.

He's alive!

Every other thought in his mind vanished like smoke and a crippling sort of pressure with suddenly released from somewhere in his gut. He's alive! *Now* Kenshiro could save him.

The truck charged onto the field and came to a shuddering stop twenty feet from the mob at the base of the tree. Kenshiro barely gave himself enough time to put the vehicle into park before he opened the door and practically leapt from the cab. He pulled the small pistol from its holster on his vest. Kenshiro approached the large cluster of undead bodies encircling the large tree with a singular purpose. He risked a look to Elliott and used his free hand to motion for him to stay put, and then went to work.

Pop-pop-pop-pop-pop-

He didn't count them, or even really look at them in any meaningful way. He just looked down the sights of the pistol, lined up his shot, and fired into the crowd. Kenshiro fired off the entire magazine. Ten bodies fell gracelessly onto the ground before any of the mob even noticed his presence. They continued to focus on the tree and its trembling occupant. With practiced grace, Kenshiro replaced the magazine in the pistol with a fresh one. He stowed the empty magazine, and released the lock on the pistol's slide before the first zombie in the crowd recognized a second living presence and turned to face him.

Pop-pop-pop-pop-pop-

Kenshiro put a bullet into that zombie's face before it took a step and lined up his next shot, fired the pistol a second time, before its body even hit the ground. He worked his way left, and the bodies fell in a tight sequence before he got to the edge of the crowd, and then he worked his way back to the right. More zombies turned away from the tree to face him. He was apparently making enough noise to justify taking their interest away from the tasty morsel in the tree. Kenshiro shot those immediately. Gunshots rang out and more bodies dropped almost mechanically. His ears were ringing despite the relatively small noise the pistol made. He was glad he wasn't using the Beretta on his hips or he'd probably be deaf by now.

By the time he reloaded his weapon for the third time, the undead numbers around them had dwindled down to just another half dozen. He stepped closer to the tree while looking down the sights and promptly put another two down. Four left. He looked around himself quickly for the others. He knew there would be more. There were three approaching from the road behind the truck. There was a singular slim figure moving in from the west, and from the south he spied six in a loose group stepping onto the field at the opposite end.

"Stay there!" He yelled up to Elliott in the tree.

Kenshiro walked up to the three by the truck and quickly shot them in the face, checked his surroundings again, only to find in the distance to the south there were more coming, maybe ten. Kenshiro didn't stick around to count them, just confirmed they were still in danger. He had little time. He turned back to the tree to shout back to Elliott it was safe for him to come down. Before he could utter a single word though, he saw Elliott was already easing himself down from the tree and was placing a foot on the ground.

"Ken!" Elliott screamed desperately as he stumbled over the fallen bodies of the undead that were once encircling the tree. Ken holstered the pistol and ran to his sobbing friend. Elliott ran towards an embrace, but Kenshiro had other things on his mind.

"Did they bite you?" He couldn't control his tone when he got to the teen, and instead of receiving the boy's hug, he harshly caught him by the shoulders. Kenshiro knew he was shouting at the poor kid, but he couldn't help it. He held Elliott firm in his hands as he madly scanned over the boy, looking for it, the mark. The darkened wound that signified doom in the new world.

"What?" Elliott asked, confused by the rough treatment.

"WHERE DID THEY BITE YOU?!" He spun Elliott around so fast he yelped a little, he roughly ran his hands over every inch of exposed skin. Kenshiro even lifted his shirt to check for blackened wounds.

Kenshiro didn't realize at the time but his heart was

racing far more now than it had madly driving the truck through the streets, faster now than when he exited the truck with the pistol in hands. He didn't even notice the machinegun pace of his heart pounding away in his chest. He was at the finish line. Elliott was alive and seemingly unharmed. Kenshiro wouldn't believe it though. He had lost too much getting to this point to believe in a happy-ending so easily. Kenshiro spun Elliott around to face him again and looked at him with what felt like a wild expression on his face.

"Where are you bleeding?" He shook his friend's shoulders roughly. Elliott's red face pleaded with him as he held up his hand shyly, before he saw it Kenshiro felt his stomach drop and prepared himself for the end. On his hand, was a tiny red dot in the palm close to the thumb.

"I poked my hand with the thing." Elliott was crying harder now, like it was a secret he was confessing. Like, he had done something wrong. "I didn't mean to. I'm sorry. I'm sorr-," he was about to say again, but Kenshiro didn't let him finish as he pulled the teen in and wrapped his arms around him and clenched his friend in his arms.

"No," he said once sternly into the boy's ear. He wanted to say more, but he was afraid his voice would fail him. So, he quietly shushed him instead, while Elliott sobbed into his shoulder. Ken gripped his friend. He was whole and safe, and although they were still far from *completely* safe, he allowed himself this moment. In the back of his mind, he was keeping tabs on the encroaching zombies. They weren't safe, but they could have this.

"I don't know what I did," Elliott whimpered softly. "All the grey people could see me, Ken. They could see me, and they were really angry. I didn't mean to do it." Ken shushed him softly as he gently pulled the teen away from him to look him in the eyes.

"It's the blood," Kenshiro explained and nodded towards his semi-injured hand. "It drives them crazy. Even a little blood will do it."

"Well, I didn't know that," Elliott whined loudly through the tears. Kenshiro tried to think if he had mentioned it to the teen. Elliott had a habit of forgetting some things, but he was having trouble thinking and quickly abandoned it. It didn't matter.

"Here," Ken quickly peeled off his leather gloves and handed them to Elliott to wear. "Put these on, cover up the wound." It was laughable to even categorize it as a wound, but he didn't make the rules. If someone exposed fresh blood to the air, the undead would come. That much he knew. Elliott quickly put on the gloves and when he looked backed up to Kenshiro with his red, puffy face, he looked strangely serious.

"Are you crying?" Elliott asked, and it sparked his tone with genuine interest.

"No," Kenshiro said defensively, just as a stray tear betrayed him, escaped his eye and ran down his cheek. "Yes, whatever, I was worried about you." Kenshiro suddenly felt embarrassed by the emotion, but Elliott just tilted his head oddly and smiled his best smile.

"That's ok," he said with a strange wink. "I was worried about you too, buddy." He said with a quirky tone, like he was trying the line out to see if it fit, and then patted Kenshiro's shoulder deliberately with his newly gloved hand two times. He seemed to think about it for a second before throwing in an additional pat for good measure. Then Elliott smiled to himself as if to say: *Yeah, that should do it*. Kenshiro looked at him with a confused look, while Elliott just let him before finally adding, "I'm ready to go home now." Kenshiro chuckled at that and mussed his hair.

"You're a weird kid, but I love it," Kenshiro said, and he meant it. The teen had been a blubbering mess right until the point he saw that tear, and then he switched gears to be… supportive? Caring? He didn't know what Elliott was going for, and he would bet the teen didn't have a clear picture of what he was going for there either. Once whatever he was trying for was achieved in his mind, then Elliott switched gears again, and now he looked rather bored.

"Let's go," Kenshiro said, and they parted and Elliott headed off towards the truck while he spared a look at the remaining threats in the field.

In the west, the lone female zombie was closer now, not a threat yet, but she was close enough he could make the features of her face. Oddly enough, there was something about that one that was familiar, but Kenshiro couldn't put his finger on it. Maybe she was famous, like an actress. He didn't know exactly, but he was sure he had seen its living face somewhere. The south, however, was a different story. That was the direction he felt the real threat would come from. There might be one or two that might wander in from the other directions, but the real numbers were still to the south.

True to form, the south had the only numbers that could be threatening. By now, the loose mob grew to a size of fifteen haggard and shambling figures stalking across the field with their collective gaze squarely fixed on them. The front runners of that group were more than halfway across the field.

Behind him, he suddenly heard Elliott whisper something. It was clear by his tone Elliott wasn't talking to him. *He's probably talking to himself*, and Kenshiro didn't hear exactly what he had said but something about what he heard sent alarm bells ringing in his head.

"Wha-," he started to say, but then Elliott said the word again, and this time there was no mistaking it.

"MOMMA!" Elliott screamed excitedly and instantly Kenshiro remembered where he saw the undead woman.

Every morning when he awoke from her couch and left her house, Kenshiro would pass three pictures on the wall that she was in. After this much time, he had all but memorized them, and now his heart dropped from his chest as Kenshiro stared into the undead face of Emily Newman.

Oh, sweet Jesus, no. Not her. Not now. Not like this. He pleaded with the universe to do the impossible.

In his time with Elliott, he had come to know many things about the teen. Right now, however, only two things burned in his mind. One, his absolute best friend in the world, was a girl named Jenny Hagerty. She was younger than he was by almost two years and had the cutest face and long, silken blonde hair. Elliott talked about her constantly and, of course, he had to show Kenshiro a picture of her. He instantly recognized her from the zombie child he stabbed in the face on the front lawn of her family's property when he followed Elliott down the road to the Newman residence. So, he had ended Elliott's best friend. Kenshiro never told Elliott that fact. He didn't know how the kid would react to it. At the time, he felt it was just better if Elliott continued to think she was safe somewhere out there. Now, Kenshiro just didn't want Elliott to know.

The other thing he knew that burned him, and left him feeling hollow inside, was that there was nobody on this earth Elliott loved more than his mother. And now, she was hobbling awkwardly towards them. It crushed him because Elliott didn't seem to understand what he was seeing.

"Elliott, get in the truck," Kenshiro said firmly as Elliott jumped up and down, waving madly at the figure.

The teen didn't pay him any attention, worse yet he bolted forward towards it. Like he would if he was running towards his real mother; but that undead woman wasn't Emily anymore. Kenshiro sprinted forward to intercept the boy. He caught his friend roughly around the middle and held him back as he protested loudly.

"What are you doing? Stop it! Let me go." He growled as he fought wildly against Kenshiro's grasp.

"That's not her, Elliott, look at her!" He struggled against the boy.

"You don't know!" He yelled. "She said she would come. She did. She promised she would come back, SHE PROMISED! LET ME GO!" Elliott howled as he twisted and squirmed like a wild animal in his hands as he struggled to pull him back to the truck.

The whole time Kenshiro pleaded with Elliott that the cruel, disgusting thing walking towards them was not his mother, but he was having none of it. He lifted the boy up, intent on simply carrying him back to the truck and stuffing him into the cab if he had to. Elliott responded by kicking out wildly with his legs. Every now and again he would painfully strike Kenshiro's shins with his heels. Elliott suddenly reared back and elbowed him gracelessly in the cheek with enough force that Kenshiro saw stars and briefly lost his grip on the teen.

That's all Elliott needed. He sprinted forward for a step and Kenshiro feared the worse, but then he stopped. He stopped so suddenly that his shoes skidded on the ground a bit and, the boy's body threatened to just pitch forward with the excess momentum.

"Momma?" He said quietly and just stood there in the field, still as a statue. Elliott stared at the figure in front of him, it was close enough to be affected by Elliott's weird ability if it was in effect right now, but with all the noise the two of them had been making, Elliott was just as visible to the undead as they were to him. Kenshiro froze in place for a moment because, deep in his bones, he felt something had changed in the boy and he suspected whatever it was, it wasn't good.

"Elliott?" He called out cautiously as he looked to the south and made a mental calculation of how much time he still had before he had to start shooting again.

It wasn't long, and Kenshiro was making a plan, thinking of what he could say to the teen to get him into the truck. He didn't want to shoot Emily, undead or not, in front of her son. He hated the world with a fiery rage for bringing them to this point. What cruel heavenly force would be so venomous as to put this in front of them? However, when his friend turned back, he forgot all about it.

"She's not there." Elliott's eyes were wild like dinner plates when he looked at him. No, not *at* him. Elliott had a ghostly sort of confused expression that made him think the teen wasn't looking at him as much as through him. "Why is she not there? I don't feel anything. Why don't I feel her? This isn't fair. I should be able to feel her. I waited all this time... Like I was supposed to. She should be there." He went on with the strange quiet conversation he was apparently having with his shadow.

Kenshiro didn't understand any of it. He understood the emotion behind the words, but the words themselves made no sense to him. Elliott's pupils pivoted about in their sockets as they searched for... something, whether it was internal or external, Kenshiro couldn't tell.

"She said she would come back, and she did, but she's not there? So? Where is she? NO!" The boy trembled in his own body's sudden fury and he reached up and slapped the side of his forehead with enough force to immediately leave a red mark after he removed his hand. "No, no, no, NO!"

Kenshiro had seen enough. He didn't know what he would do, what he should do, but it was clear he had to do something. He stepped in a grabbed the boy's hands before he could strike himself again. That seemed like a good place to start.

"Stop that."

"NOOOOOOOOOOOOOO!" Elliott shrank down to his knees as he screamed his pain uselessly into the world, the ferocity of it was shocking, but that wasn't what struck Kenshiro.

What struck him was how much the teen sounded like a certain boy from Japan. Who one day, on a not-so-lonely Tokyo highway, looked into his own mother's dead eyes and felt the world crash around him. Kenshiro would never forget that night no matter how he tried, and his friend's cries just reminded him of the complete and utter devastation. The ugly rawness of it came rushing back in that instant, because some wounds didn't heal, no matter how much time has passed. It crushed him to see this tiny, sweet teen falling apart on the inside, but what could he do?

What would Emily do?

"Come on," Kenshiro said, stepped forward and lifted the teen up. He was like Jello in his hands as Elliott weakly rose to his feet. All the fight had left his body. "Let's go," Kenshiro said softly, tried to sound fatherly, in the way he wished his own father had but never did. He didn't know what he could do to soothe the teen's soul, maybe nothing, but right now he knew he had to get him out of here and back to the farm. They could figure out the rest later. It didn't feel like near enough, but it was all he had.

"No," Elliott protested weakly, "I can't leave her, Ken." He whimpered as he looked at him pleadingly through his tears. "We can't. We have to help her, Ken. We have to." Elliott looked to him for answers, but he didn't have any. None the teen wanted to hear, anyway.

"I only know one way to help her, buddy." His voice broke as he said the words he didn't want to say. He wanted to walk away from this whole situation, but his friend needed him to be stronger than that. "You know that." He added and Elliott broke into fresh sobs and beat his hands softly against Kenshiro's chest a few times before he looked up at him with a red face and a trembling lip. He nodded before sinking his head down and leaning into Kenshiro's broad chest for support.

"I know." Kenshiro felt the crushing weight of the words as Elliott spoke them. He understood what had to be done. "But we can't leave her…" He looked around their surroundings with abject disgust before adding, "Here."

"Oh, there's no fucking way we're leaving her here, she's coming with us." He said firmly, like it was a universally understood fact, because that's how he saw it.

He shared the teen's disgust at the idea of *this* being Emily's last resting place, out in the open amongst the dirty corpses of the other zombies, to be forgotten forever as the sun and elements rotted her away to dust. Not. A. Fucking. Chance. "I'll take care of it. Just head back to the truck and wait for me inside." Elliott nodded solemnly in his vest and then gave his mother one last pained looked before he tore himself away and trudged back to the truck. Defeated.

Kenshiro waited until Elliott was safely inside the cab, and the door was closed. He pulled the small pistol free once again and used his free hand to motion for his friend to duck below the dash of the truck. Elliott didn't need to see this, and if Kenshiro was being honest, he didn't want Elliott to see him do it either. Kenshiro had already put down Elliott's best friend. Elliott didn't know it, and if Kenshiro had a say in the matter, he never would. But this? There was no walking away from this stain. He would always be the person who shot Elliott's mother. Sure, she was undead and maybe an argument could be made that it was necessary. Merciful, even. He would always be the one who ultimately pulled the trigger though, even if he didn't see it, Elliott would always know it was him.

Goddamn this world!

Kenshiro's brow furrowed as he raised the pistol to Emily's undead face. Her once pretty face twisted into a snarl as her slim hands clawed at him from ten feet away. He put his index finger on the trigger. *Love him if you can*, he suddenly remembered the line from the letter that was in his left hip pocket: *her* letter.

"I will keep him safe," Kenshiro whispered to the air between him and Emily. "I promise."

He prayed that somehow, deep inside that shell of rotting flesh and evil intent, the real Emily Newman could hear his words. Then he pulled the trigger and ended her forever. He would like to think it was hard to pull the trigger, but it wasn't. There was no difference between that trigger pull and any of the others that came before it. Though, when Emily's body fell listlessly to the ground, it felt like someone had punched him in the gut.

It was suddenly hard to breathe.

It was done, and for at least the time being, he had to put it behind him. He had a job to do yet. With the pistol still in his hand, he approached Emily's body and scooped her up in his arms. The body weight little; he kept his eyes on the awkwardly moving crowd from the south as he carried her to the back of the truck. Kenshiro looked at them with a renewed disdain as he lowered the tailgate and eased Emily's body into the back of the truck before closing the gate behind her. The nearest member of the undead crowd from the south was maybe fifteen feet away. He had plenty of time to move around to the driver's side and hop into the cab. Fifteen minutes from now he and Elliott could pull into the farm, safe and sound.

Fuck it.

He was already safe, and now that Elliott was tucked away in the truck's cab with his ridiculously minor wound covered up, he was safe, too. Kenshiro wanted some vengeance. He wanted someone or something to pay for what they made him do. He had done it, and now it was time for the zombies to pay the fucking piper.

Kenshiro strode towards the nearest zombie with the pistol raised up level with its skull. He shot him quickly in the forehead and then picked his next target, walked up to it, and he fired again. He fired until the slide locked back on the pistol, then he replaced the spent magazine with a fresh one and continued walking up to the zombies and shooting them promptly in the head. It was petty and useless. Zombies didn't feel pain, or anger, or remorse, there was no way to hurt them. Still, it felt good to shoot them, in a way. Each shot made the heat inside him burn hotter. Kenshiro could never describe in words how much he hated them. He cursed each body as it went down. By the time he was done, the field immediately in front of him was clear, and he was breathing hard.

Farther south, he saw more. *No! That's enough.* Kenshiro wanted more. He had so much more anger inside of him he could purge, but right now, that wasn't what was important. He still had Emily's boy to look after. He had strayed maybe twenty feet from the truck on his spree. He looked back at the truck without a clue how he was going to approach the sobbing figure inside, but it was time to leave.

The ride back was quiet except for the noise of the tires crunching down on the gravel road and the slight sounds of Elliott's sobbing. The boy had his head on Kenshiro's lap. He didn't ask nor did Kenshiro offer, but Elliott just sort of moved in and snuggled up to him on the bench seat of the truck. Kenshiro didn't resist it; he let the boy move in close and put his hand on the teen's scrawny shoulder. Now and then, Kenshiro rubbed his back slowly and hoped the sobbing teen found it comforting. For all intents and purposes, they had won the day. The undead had marked them, though. They were leaving the danger behind them as they drove back to the farm where he was confident Elliott's special ability would keep them safe for the night. They even walked away with a small number of supplies from the houses they did search. It didn't feel like a win, though. The air in the truck was one of defeat and loss. They both felt it, like they just lost an unseen member of their group.

Which they did.

Definitely for Elliott, the poor teen never stopped believing he would see his parents again. It might have been the hope of seeing his mother again that kept him going this whole time before Kenshiro showed up. When he got to the teen, Elliott was definitely on his last legs. Hell, the first time he saw Elliott, he swore the kid was just another zombie walking down the street. Since then, he had learned of the undying affection the teen had for his parents, especially his mother. Emily had a special bond with her son. That much was obvious from the things Elliott said about her, like she was the great shining light in his life. The way he talked about her reminded Kenshiro of his own mother. As faint and faded as they were, he remembered one thing. At the time of her death, she was his everything. When her light was snuffed out, he remembered how cold the world felt after that. He didn't want Elliott to lose that hope. As naïve as he thought it might be, it kept the kid going when most people would have given up. Sure, there was a part of him that knew this moment would come, there would come a time when Elliott would eventually realize that his parents were gone forever.

Nowadays, it was only natural, everyone loses that hope eventually. But there was no part of Kenshiro that wanted it to go down like it had today. To have that hope ripped away in such a visceral manner. In the back of his mind, he still heard Elliott's screams echo around his head. He fired a lot of rounds today, but he only remembered one. The one bullet that turned Elliott's hopes to ash.

Kenshiro never believed it for a second, though, that Elliott's parents were alive. Especially Emily. Kenshiro didn't believe the author of the letter in his pocket would ever leave Elliott alone like that. She would have to be dead for that to happen. *The most precious thing in this world to me*, he remembered. By now, Kenshiro had memorized the letter. It was the only connection he had to the actual woman. It wasn't much, but it felt palpable. Maybe it was all in his head, but he felt some weird connection to her. From everything Elliott had said about her, all his little 'Mama said' moments, and the words she had left for him , Kenshiro felt in some small way he knew her. He knew a piece of her, and it was a good piece, one that Kenshiro latched onto. Even though, he might not be willing to admit it to himself yet. *I have nothing to offer you.* She had also written that, but she was wrong. She couldn't have been more wrong. She gave him Elliott, after all. He felt he owed her something for that.

Kenshiro felt he should say something to sooth the teen but for the life of him, he couldn't think of anything. Nothing that felt genuine, at least. So, he felt it was better to say nothing at all than to just jump in with something fake and insincere. Plus, he was fighting his own demons at the moment. Kenshiro was in a dark mood and didn't feel his input would benefit either of them right now. Best to let the moment be what it is, which was horrible and disastrous with just a hint of hopelessness, and maybe just a smidge of utter failure for added flavour.

He drove the truck slowly into the yard and stopped in front of the house in the usual spot. Kenshiro went over to the passenger side and lifted the small teen out of the truck and carried him into the house. Elliott didn't resist at all, just threw his arm around him and buried his head into the fabric of the combat vest. He was sobbing weakly and whimpering something he couldn't make out into the vest. Never in his life had Kenshiro been at such a loss of what to do, never had he felt so impotent. He carried the teen up to his room. He felt it was as good a place as any, and Elliott didn't seem to object as they made the trip up the stairs and into his room. As gently as Kenshiro could, he set his friend's relatively small body onto the bed and told him to rest.

"I wanna see… Momma." He said, though he did not try to leave the confines of the bed. Kenshiro shushed him gently.

"Trust me," he wanted to give his friend a serious look so he would believe he was telling him the truth, but Elliott sank into the bed and buried his head into his pillow and didn't look up. "You don't. Let me get things ready for you, then we'll give her a proper-," He wanted to say funeral, but it didn't seem like the right word, "-Send off." It still didn't feel right. He couldn't think of a word that fit the mood. "We'll do it together. For now, just rest up a bit. I'll come get you when everything is ready." Kenshiro added at the end, in hopes it might make a difference to his friend, and maybe it did, because Elliott nodded his head into the pillow. Satisfied for the time being, he gave Elliott one last quick rub on the back before he headed back out into the yard.

"Ken?" He turned back at the door to Elliott's weak sounding voice and the teen was looking at him with his head resting on the pillow. They locked eyes. "You're still my best friend." For a moment, they looked at each other. Something inside Kenshiro broke, and his eyes watered slightly. *HOW?* The silent question was immediately followed by, *WHY?!*

"Thanks, buddy." It was all Kenshiro said before he turned and walked back out the door before the teen could see the fresh tears running down his cheek.

He closed the door to Elliott's room. Thankfully, the air inside the house was still cool from the night before, and the afternoon heat hadn't quite filled the house yet, but it would. Kenshiro sank against the wall and wiped the stray tears from his cheek. *Fuck me, what a day.* It was all a blur. If he tried to look back on the events of the last hour, he found nothing but shadows. Like, too much had happened in such a short time frame for his brain to process. The fight he had with the undead behemoth seemed like a lifetime ago. Like it was a distant memory. Unfortunately, his injuries weren't distant enough for his liking. When his body gently fell against the wall, his brain received raging hot complaints from half a dozen places on his body. He winced and breathed through his teeth until the pain subsided. It had been a hard day in every sense of the word, and now that

Elliott was safe and relatively sound; he saw the finish line ahead of him. Just a little more and then he could rest and try to put this all behind him. If that was even possible.

Just a little more.

The adrenalin of the day was working its way out of his system, revealing fresh injuries he didn't even know he had, and turning his muscles to lead. As he pushed himself off the wall, he grunted. He felt battered, bruised, and tired. Kenshiro felt like he had been run over a couple times with a car. There was nothing more he wanted than to just lay down and close his eyes and let sleep take him away from all of this. He would literally shoot a stranger in the face right now for a Coca-Cola with three cubes of ice in the glass, just the way he liked it. As he eased his sore body down the stairs, he forced all thoughts of the past pleasures aside and focused on what he had to do yet. There was more struggle ahead. *Do it for Elliott*, he told himself as he made his way down the stairs and into the living room. *Do it so he doesn't have to. You owe him that much.*

In the living room he approached the large plush couch, his bed. He had a kind of taken the room over since his time here. Elliott didn't seem to mind as long as he kept the space tidy. In front of the couch, he dragged the vest's zipper down and painfully peeled the combat vest off, letting it drop to the floor. A part of him was happy to be free of its weight of the thing. He felt like he could breathe a little easier now. He reached down and plucked the tiny automatic pistol from the vest, checked the magazine and made sure the safety was on before stowing the weapon in his back pocket. Kenshiro steadied himself for the next part, because he didn't expect taking off his sweat-soaked shirt would feel too pleasant either. He was pretty sure he had broken a rib on his right side. At the very least, he cracked it. He reached up and growled painfully as his body protested the action from several places, and struggled to pull the sticky shirt off his body. Kenshiro threw the shirt without a thought onto the chair in the corner. The chair he sat in when he first spoke to Elliott. He looked himself over as best he could without the aid of a mirror.

There was an ugly, and massive deep purple area that seemed to encompass his entire love handle on his left side. It sort of looked like the shape of a large hand the behemoth used to grab him. It suddenly reminded him of the animalistic panic he felt when that large, chilly hand clamped down through the rough fabric of the vest. On the right side, from where the stabbing pain came from with every medium size breath he took, he saw a linear contusion about halfway up his rib cage. It also was an ugly deep purple color; he couldn't remember exactly how he had come across the injury, but he remembered being tossed around like a rag doll by that fucking undead giant. On his right shoulder, he saw four tiny baby bruises from where those large icy fingers dug into the flesh of his shoulder, and a half dozen other that dotted the exposed flesh of his arms. He didn't have to remove his pants to know there was probably a bruise on his thigh, too.

And I won that fight.

He chuckled painfully. It wasn't the first time his body paid a hefty price to come out of a fight on top, and probably not the last. He reached for a fresh shirt from the pile of folded clothes he kept at the end of the couch, neatly stacked and orderly, of course. He eased a simple grey t-shirt on and went into the kitchen and retrieved the bottle of Tylenol they kept in a cupboard. The label said each tablet had five hundred milligrams of Acetaminophen. Kenshiro shook four tablets into his hands and opened the fridge door to retrieve a lukewarm bottle of water. The fridge didn't work after all. They just used it for storage. He took the pills with a swallow of water and looked out the window to the south of the house. From here, he could see the entrance into the property and the big metal gate. He made a mental note to close that gate as soon as he got outside. He didn't expect any undead intruders with Elliott's ability sheltering them from their notice, as long as they kept the noise down and the lights off at night. Besides that, they wouldn't be going anywhere soon, at least not until their respective injuries healed. Both physical, and emotional, they would need time before they could face the world outside that gate again. He already had a list of things they could work on to avoid this kind of clusterfuck in the future.

First things first.

Kenshiro left the house with two white bedsheets he had found in the hall closet in his left hand, and the tiny automatic pistol in his right hand. He highly doubted any zombies would roam around outside the house, but he wasn't in the mood to fuck around anymore today. He approached the back of the truck and eased the gate down; he was right underneath the teen's window and he didn't want to risk bothering the boy. Right now, he wanted Elliott to rest and try to put this out of his mind for a time. If that was even possible.

He reached into the truck bed and as gently as he could; he pulled out Emily's body and carried her to the opposite side of the house. He laid her body carefully onto the grass. The whole time trying not to look into the twisted, dried up face of her corpse. That wasn't Emily. Emily was the woman in all the pictures with a long mane of brunette hair, a full face that had a smile that brightened up a room. He didn't know her. Kenshiro sometimes had to remind himself of that fact. After the time he had spent in the house she made for her family, and seeing the pictures every day of the memories she shared with her loved ones, he felt he had grown to know her. Not to mention, all that Elliott had said about her. Kenshiro sort of filled in the blanks of the woman he didn't know and created an ideal picture of her in his mind.

It hurt him how similar the picture was to his own mother, the other woman in his life he didn't really know, and who he had also created an ideal picture of. He knew it wasn't who they were. The reality of people is that they seldom live up to your expectations, and it was a cold comfort to know dead people never let you down. He would never meet the real Emily Newman now, not that he ever believed he would, and the chances of running into someone that knew her well enough to dispel his preconceived notions of the woman were dismal. Like with his own mother, Emily would always be what he thought she was. That was the person he was burying today.

He spread out one bedsheet beside the body and then placed Emily in the center. Using lengths of twine he had cut, he first tucked the legs together and tied them with a single length of twine fastened around her calves. He then did the same with the arms wrapping two longer lengths of twine around the wrist and again around the elbows. This made it easier to wrap the body in the bedsheet. It had been a long time since he had done this for anybody. He only had done this twice before.

After that, the concept of burying people became silly, though he had a short list of people who he was sure were wandering the California landscape he would still do this for. He lifted one edge of the bedsheet up and over the body and tucked the edges in where he could. He then took the opposite edge and did the same, securing it again with more lengths of twine at the neck, elbows, and knees. With that done, he spread out the other bedsheet beside the freshly wrapped and secured body, moved it onto the edge of the sheet so he could tuck the edge into the twine. Then, with great care, he rolled the body into the sheet and when it was done, he secured the same spots with more twine. With that, Emily Newman's burial shroud was complete. He wished he could do more for her, but no amount of scrubbing and make-up could bring back Emily's true face. Now, at least, Elliott could look upon her body and not be tormented by how the undead blight twists the human body up. He didn't want that for his friend. He had been through enough already today.

Kenshiro left the shrouded body in the house's shade while he ventured over to the rustic-looking barn that Elliott's father had set up as a small workshop. It was easy enough to find a shovel. The real problem he had was finding a suitable spot to make the grave. It didn't seem like it should be his choice to make. Such a monumental decision as someone's last resting place should be made by someone who loved them, but he didn't want to bother Elliott with it. It didn't seem fair to make the teen decide, either. Why should he be burdened with it? So, he wandered the property looking for a suitable spot to bury Elliott's mother without the benefit of really knowing what he was looking for. He knew he didn't want the grave to be in view of the boy's bedroom window. He didn't know how much longer they would be here, and Kenshiro didn't want Elliott to see his mother's grave every time he looked out his window in the morning. That just seemed cruel to him. Unfortunately, that still left a lot of property.

Luckily, he found a spot that he thought would work nicely. On the west side of the house, there was a large deciduous tree. He didn't know what kind exactly; it had a sturdy-looking trunk and the crown of the tree was spread out and filled with healthy-looking large leaves that provided a large area of shade around it. On the north side of that shaded area was a slight break in the shrubbery that lined the west side of the property. Through the break you could see that vast Colorado vista spread out for miles beyond it, seemingly all the way to the horizon. There you'd be able to watch the sunset right until the point it dipped out of existence under the horizon.

That's where he would bury her.

It was a pleasant spot, maybe the best spot he might find in this miniscule piece of Colorado. It's where Kenshiro would want to be buried if he had to be buried here, and if he had a choice in the matter. He walked up to the edge of the shaded portion of grass that was in line with the break in the bushes and kicked the shovel into the ground. In a movie, this would be easy, simply a matter of doing it. A minor inconvenience to be endured before they could get down to the business of real grieving. In reality, digging a grave was incredibly hard in the best of circumstances. Kenshiro had left the best circumstances behind the moment he saw the undead behemoth this morning, and the day had improved little since. His body protested, seemingly with every motion he took. He considered going back in for more painkillers, but in the end; Kenshiro felt he might just have to accept the pain for what it was and keep going. He hoped cutting away the top layer of sod would have been the hardest part. He soon found the soil underneath didn't last long before the hole he made descended to hard-packed clay with rocks embedded in it. They were bigger than his fists and he had to pry them out with the edge of the shovel. His back ached terribly and soon sweat ran down his face freely, and his clean new shirt became saturated with sweat and clung to his body as he worked. His body screamed at him to stop but Kenshiro grit his teeth, sucked in deep breaths despite the pain in his ribs and kept going.

He was half-way done the grave when he heard the front door of the house open and saw Elliott's slim figure exit the house. Kenshiro waved once but Elliott didn't come over, instead he moved in beside the shrouded body of his mother. The boy dropped himself onto the ground beside the body in the shade. Elliott looked to be crying again. Kenshiro couldn't blame him. Kenshiro turned back to his work and left the teen to his mourning.

"Elliott?" He walked up to the teen some time later, who was sitting cross-legged on the ground with his head bend down. His one hand was resting on the covered forehead of his mother's body, and quietly tried to get his attention. Elliott looked at him. His face showed the swirl of emotions he must be dealing with. "It's time."

He had finished the grave a half hour ago, but he didn't want to rush the teen. So, he drank a bottle of water, cleaned up a little and went back into the house to grab another fresh shirt. This one was a light blue button-down shirt with short sleeves. He had done everything he could think of to put off this last part as long as he could, and if Elliott wanted it, he would be more than happy to give him more time, but it was time. They both felt it.

"Ok," Elliott said with a breath, like he was preparing himself for it. He wasn't crying right now. The tears on his cheeks had dried up some time ago, his face was still red and puffy, and more tears definitely were threatening to burst forth at any moment, but for now, the teen seemed resolute in what they had to do next.

"Ok," Kenshiro said more to himself than to Elliott. He stepped forward as the teen rose and backed away from the body. Kenshiro bent down and scooped the shrouded figure into his arms with his friend in tow behind him, and walked Emily over to her final resting place. He placed her body down beside the ugly looking grave. Kenshiro suddenly became ashamed of the grave he had made for her.

He could have done a better job, cleaned up the edges a bit for her and maybe removed some of the exposed roots. It would have to do.

He backed away from the body and stood next to Elliott, who had his head down, quietly looking at the body beside the hole in the ground. It was heartbreaking to see him look down on that body wordlessly. *Is that what I looked like when my father told me my mother was gone forever?* He couldn't help but wonder as he looked down at his wounded friend.

"Did you want to say a few words?" He asked Elliott cautiously.

The boy never looked up. For a moment Kenshiro didn't think the teen had heard him, but soon after Elliott took a few deep shuddering breaths, like there was something he wanted to say, but he was fighting for the words. He took one more deep breath, seemingly to steel himself for what he was about to say. Kenshiro waited and let his friend take as much time as he needed.

"Bye momma," Elliott said finally with broken words. After he got the words out, he broke into soft sobs once again.

Kenshiro reached over and put his arm around his friend and pulled him close into his side. He didn't have any other way to comfort the teen except just to let him know he wasn't alone in this. It didn't feel like enough though.

"Ok," Elliott said, suddenly wiping his nose on the sleeve of his shirt, leaving a noticeable snot trail on the fabric of the sleeve. "Your turn."

He looked down at Elliott, taken off guard by the request, mostly because of how naturally it came out. He looked at the boy's expectant eyes as Elliott returned his gaze.

"Uh," Kenshiro was at a loss for words. He could say something, and he even felt that some part of him suddenly wanted to speak, but he pushed that impulse back down into the darkness of his soul. Whatever it was, it felt too raw to be exposed to the light of day. He feared the few words he could say might bring forth some part, some emotion, of himself he wanted, no, needed, to stay buried. "Goodbye, Emily," he said, even if it was awkward sounding.

A quiet moment passed between them, like neither one of them really knew what they should say or do next before he spoke again.

"You can go inside," Kenshiro gently offered. "I can finish this up." Referring to the ugly end process of the ceremony where he would lower the body into the hole and then bury it. Elliott didn't need to be here for that and part of Kenshiro feared how he might react.

"No," Elliott said with a quiet firmness that suggested there would be no further discussion on the subject. He looked up at him with tears in his eyes, but behind those tears, there was a sort of humble determination. "Momma would want me to help." His bottom lip shuddered when he said the words, but it didn't change Elliott's resolve.

Kenshiro had to respect that.

"Ok," he said simply

The two of them awkwardly lowered the body into the ugly grave as gently as they could. The body fit easily because when he dug the grave; Kenshiro used his own dimensions as a guide. So, in an actual sense, Kenshiro had dug his own grave. He would have gladly traded places with Emily though, and he would smile contently as the weight of the dirt pressed down on him, knowing Elliott was with his mother again. He could die knowing he had done some real good before he left this world. The world didn't work that way, though. You worked with what you had, and all Elliott had now was him, and Kenshiro would make that work. With the body in place, Kenshiro left to grab another shovel. When he returned, the teen was looking mournfully into the grave with his shovel in his hands. Kenshiro approached, he touched the boy slightly on the shoulder for comfort, and then the two of them finished the job of laying Emily Newman to rest.

They both shed more tears as they worked. It was a struggle not to feel the immense sadness that was hanging in the air. He couldn't explain it, but as he worked, Kenshiro had the acute feeling he was burying his own mother. Like it was Atsuko Watanabe in that grave instead of Emily, it felt real and raw. It made every shovelful harder. He could only imagine what Elliott must be going through, but as he looked over, he saw the boy's red face was fixated on his work as his tears slipped from his face and fell into the dirt of the grave.

He's tougher than he looks, Kenshiro thought as they worked.

Emily would be proud.

Chapter 3

Elle

Elle had to admit she liked the feeling of the soil between her fingers. She didn't think she would. When Emilio first suggested helping him with his little garden, something inside her resisted the idea. It was Maggie. She knew that much. Elle didn't want to be near the helicopter because she didn't trust herself around it. She couldn't be sure of her feelings, so she felt it was best to avoid it altogether.

The first time Emilio asked her, she was in the serving line at lunch and admittedly she was in a bit of a funk that day. Elle didn't remember exactly what she had said, but she remembered not being proud of how she said it. After that, Emilio waited a whole week before he asked again for her help, and something about the word *help* struck her. It resonated within her like the soft ringing of a bell, and for a moment she forgot about the pain in her left hand and the emptiness she felt inside. *I can help*, something inside her replied. She breathed deep.

"Ok," she relented softly, knowing full well Maggie was up there on the roof. Waiting for her. She took her food and joined her sister, Bill, and now Martin at their usual table in a bit of a daze.

It had been ten days since the horror show at La Guardia, maybe more. Elle didn't keep track of the days too well anymore. These days, the only measure of time she focused on was by the pain in her arm.

The first couple of days had been sheer agony. At rest,

her arm felt like it was slowly being cooked in an oven. Heat seemed to radiate painfully from the ruined flesh of her hand and wrist. However, the real pain happened when she moved her arm in the wrong way, like if she were to twist her hand at the wrist. Then, her brain screamed at her like her skin was being torn apart by whatever she was doing, and strongly advised her to stop doing whatever it was immediately. God help her if she bumped the wound against something. When that happened, the world turned red and she would have to sink to her knees until the pain subsided. Elle took Tylenol by the handfuls, but she still found it impossible to sleep comfortably through the night. One wrong turn in the night and she would bolt straight up in her bed/couch, clutching her arm and hissing through her teeth like a crazy person to keep from crying out and waking her sister. Like with all things, the pain dulled over time.

After that first week, she could feel the pain lessen more each day, like someone had their hand on the pain output dial, and each day turned it down a notch. If she started this journey at a ten on that dial, she felt today she was at a steady five. It still hurt, but now the pain only existed on the outer reaches of her mind.

Turns out, Emilio didn't really need her help. Honestly, it wasn't much of a garden. He had three wooden shelves that he placed on their backs so the shelves were pointing towards the sky, then he placed them end to end and filled the spaces between the wooden shelves with dirt and made small little planters out of them.

"That one's yours," he said simply pointing to the left most planter, which currently had its available space split with neat rows of carrots on the one side, and strawberries on the other.

It was simple, really. He gave her a planter and made

her responsible for it. He didn't have to, though. Emilio could easily manage the few plants he had by himself. Before this, he had never once asked for help from anyone in all this time. Elle instantly suspected Martin, or maybe Bill, had a hand in Emilio suddenly needing her help with his few plants, maybe both, like this was some form of therapy for her. She knew they were watching her this last week. She felt their eyes on her.

It was enough for her to want to walk up to Emilio and tell him to take his pity job and shove it up his ass. It was at those points, she reminded herself to breathe, really breathe, because the truth of it was that people cared about her. They just didn't know how to show it, and if she was being honest with herself, she didn't know how they should show it either.

She couldn't explain it, but she was not the same person who left for La Guardia. It was a weird feeling to have. She knew who she was, but she also knew she was different somehow. As if now, she was just going through the motions, trying to mimic the old Elle everyone knew as best she could, and it was exhausting. All day long she second-guessed herself by asking: "What would the old Elle do?", or, "What would the old Elle say in this situation?"

It was hard to live not trusting your first instinct. Like the person she had become was unsuited to live her old life, and nothing seemed to fit right, and nobody was truly familiar. That first week, she found she was snapping at some people for nothing. She damn near got into a screaming match with Derek over what happened to Jackie and had to be separated by Nathan. She didn't remember what they said in that brief interaction, but she cried for the entire afternoon. She cried a lot that first week, over the stupidest things it seemed. It felt like she was a balloon trying to navigate a maze of needles. She was either whole but feeling an incredible internal pressure, or completely broken and deflated. There was no middle ground.

-

Elle flinched slightly when she heard the rooftop door close. Whoever it was, just let the hydraulics of the door slam it shut. Elle was glad her body didn't respond to the sudden noise like it had. Baby steps.

"Cómo estás, Elle?" She heard Emilio's annoying, upbeat voice call out before he came strolling around the corner holding his watering can. Which meant lunch is over, and the kitchen was cleaned and prepped for dinner already. Elle skipped lunch today. She just didn't want to bother with it, and she hoped her absence wouldn't provoke too much controversy.

"Bueno," she said gingerly. During the time they spent in the Prescott, she felt Emilio was secretly trying to teach all of them Spanish.

She responded with '*good*' because she didn't know the words for, '*I haven't cried my eyes out yet*', and partly because she didn't want to ruin Emilio's good mood. If that was even possible. Emilio then continued the conversation in Spanish but this time she only caught a few words of what he said, something about the weather, but she could only look at him with a slightly apologetic look.

"We're not there yet, and it's too early in the day for Spanish lessons. How bout we just keep it in English? So, I don't have to worry about getting a headache trying to figure out what you're saying." Emilio chuckled slightly.

"Okay, okay," he said, putting his hands up and patted the air in front of him with a wide friendly grin on his face.

How does he do it? She has asked herself that frequently. The man was stuck in an office building that was surrounded by a million undead that wanted nothing more than to peel the flesh off his bones. All his friends are gone, his family too, along with everyone else in the world, and he still sounded cheery. *Fucker*, she thought with playful bitterness. The truth of it was she enjoyed the light he brought to her surroundings. Elle was pretty sure everyone did.

It was hard to hate someone who made you feel good. His company would be a welcome distraction.

"I was just saying how nice the weather was today. The sun is out. The day is warm, and my babies are growing." He gestured to the planters. Emilio had a certain affection for his pet project, which in all reality was still in its infancy.

The strawberries were doing well, and were producing little marble sized berries that were still too small to eat. The ripe ones, Emilio gave those little berries to people he thought deserved them. The last week, since the infection set in, he had been exclusively sending them to Jackie in her morning oatmeal. It wasn't much, a tiny gesture, but it was something he knew would lift her spirits, so he did it without question or hesitation. She respected that.

"Yeah," she agreed, and she looked up and over the tiny green patch of life. "But the rain barrel is getting empty," she cautioned and nodded toward the large plastic garbage can Emilio had set up to the side so it was close to the garden, but still far enough away from the outcropping of the helipad that it could collect rainwater. "If it doesn't rain soon, we'll have to bring water up."

"Oh man," Emilio said with another chuckle. "Mason would not like that."

Mason had already established that clean water was for people, not plants, and nobody wanted to test Mason's resolve on that issue.

"Don't worry about it," he said with a dismissive wave of his hand. "It's got to rain sooner or later, right? Maybe I can convince Kate to go around and collect all the toilet water from the bowls. What do you say, eh?" Elle smiled at the idea.

It used to bother her that Kate had become the resident go-to for items. She didn't like the idea of everyone using her sister to get them things, but her sister didn't mind at all. In fact, Kate drew pride from it. After seeing her in action, Elle had to relent the point. Her sister had a sense of purpose. She filled a role within the building and it gave her a sense of belonging. Elle couldn't take that away from her. It's not like Kate would let her, anyway. At this age, Elle couldn't seriously forbid anything, because Kate would do it anyway, and just not tell her about it. She would rather be informed than to have Kate be all secretive about it. Like Elle was when she was at that age.

"If you think you can convince her to collect stale toilet water, go ahead. I can't even convince her to clean her side of the room." Emilio laughed out loud at that. He was usually quick to laugh.

"Ah, she's a good egg. Reminds me of my own *hermanita*," Emilio said and, for a moment, he was distant and quiet, "She was a pain in my ass too, growing up," he added, not really talking to anyone in particular. Emilio's facade slipped and exposed the raw center. It broke her heart.

"Hey," she said, to steer the conversation in another direction. "Where did you get the dirt for these?" Elle waved her hand over the planters like a game show host introducing a prize to a contestant.

"Kate," Emilio said simply, as if Elle should have already known that.

"Yes, obviously, but where did she get it?"

"Umm, I think she got it from a bunch of houseplants. Like dozens of them. I guess people keep plants in their office around here. I wouldn't know, never worked in an office. Why? What're you thinking?" He said with sudden interest.

"And the seeds?"

"Kate brought me the seeds too, and before you ask, no, I don't know where she got them from. I asked her for it, and three days later she showed up at my doorstep with a bunch of seed packets in her hands. Why?" He asked again, even more curious now. "What are you thinking?"

"We should make more," Elle said, nodding to the planters. "Do you have more seeds?"

"A few, but not much." Emilio rubbed the tiny dark hairs at his chin. "You know, I thought about that too, a while back. Might be too late now though, too late into the season. We'll have to wait until next year to do more planters up here." He said, pondering the idea out loud.

"We won't do them up here," Elle said definitively and with a sly grin.

The idea had bloomed in her head, and now it was taking a proper shape inside her mind. They could do this. It could work. "We'll plant them inside. In fact, we should move these downstairs too," she blurted out and then looked up to see Emilio's confused and concerned face. The concern annoyed her, but she pushed it aside and took a deep breath. "We'll find a large office that has a lot of windows and faces the south side," Elle pondered aloud. "One that's close to the top, we'll empty it out and turn it into a greenhouse. We could grow food all year round. Besides that, it would probably be better for them to grow inside, like what if we get a really severe storm?" It was a weak point. The weather this year has been pretty amicable, but

New York suffered through got some monster storms from time to time. She looked over and saw Emilio mulling over her idea carefully.

"You have a good point there. Plus, we wouldn't have to worry about all the wind from the chopper either." Elle didn't even think about the havoc the rotor wash must play on the plants every time Martin took off. "That could be a problem when some of these plants get bigger." It was endearing to her that suddenly the tiny garden had become *their* project.

Then, they both heard the unmistakable sound of the roof door closing. In unison they looked towards the corner of the building and waited for whomever it was to round it. There was no one else up here so whoever was coming up to the roof was looking for one of them. Deep down she felt a familiar tension, a pressure, an anxiety. Whatever it was, she became very concerned about the things she didn't know. Like who was going to be coming around that corner? Was it her sister, or one of the other residents? Or maybe it would be the stumbling, groaning figure that haunted her dreams on some nights? She squeezed her fists tightly and released them to keep the feelings at bay until Martin came into view.

"Hola Martin, qué está pasando?" Emilio called out and waved. Elle found out recently, to her annoyance, that Martin was practically fluent in Spanish. She gave him a smile and a wave as he approached. He answered Emilio back and the two of them had a brief conversation in Spanish. Elle understood none of it. Emilio gestured to the planters, and Martin looked like he was concerned about something before he nodded in agreement. She realized they were discussing her idea of moving the planters inside and setting up a greenhouse without her, and that was the last straw.

"You two lovebirds need a moment, or can we switch back to a language we *all* speak?" Elle said, trying to sound funny, and failing in her opinion. She still had an edge to her words. She had to work on that.

"Lo siento," Emilio said, smiling innocently before realizing he was still speaking Spanish. "Sorry. I was just telling Martin about your idea."

"Yeah, I like it. It's a good idea." Martin sounded almost proud.

"Thanks. It's going to take some work, though," she said, putting the plan together in her head.

"Sure is." Emilio smiled.

"Well, it's a good thing we have plenty of time on our hands." They all shared a single depressing chuckle at the poor joke. The realization of just how right Martin is was still something the people of The Prescott tried not to think about. "Say, Elle, can I borrow you for a second? There's something I need to talk to you about?"

"Of course." It wasn't something he needed to ask. She glanced at him with a look of concern. Elle tried to surmise what Martin needed to say to her that he felt he couldn't say in front of Emilio. They said their goodbyes, and Elle promised Emilio they would talk more about the greenhouse later before she followed Martin.

Elle knew where he was taking her before they even got to the metal staircase that led up to the helipad. She didn't know why though. Regardless, she was proud of herself when she stepped onto the staircase and climbed it without hesitation. She felt she *should* hesitate, like the smart thing to do would be to stay away. Every instinct she once trusted was telling her to turn around. Elle followed wordlessly as they stepped onto the concrete of the helipad and made their way toward the helicopter, towards Maggie, and towards the bloody scene of where Jackie lost her hand. It was burned forever into her memory. Elle still remembered the nightmare she had where Jackie's severed hand came to life and started walking around on its fingertips. Elle still felt the icy grip of those fingers wrapped around her throat.

She looked at Martin as he approached the rear passenger compartment door and reached out for the handle. Elle felt the knot in her stomach suddenly tighten, and she was about to call out to him to stop for reasons she didn't have, or care about. She just knew she didn't want to see inside the compartment. Before she could, though, Martin flung open the door without a second thought. In that moment, as the door was opening, she hated him more than anything else in this world. *Doesn't he know what happened in there? How could he be so goddamn insensitive?* Her brain cursed as the door open and revealed… absolutely nothing.

"The Three Amigos did a pretty good job." She didn't hear what he said right away. Her brain was still preparing to reel away from something that was no longer there. The inside of the compartment was spotless. It was a completely different shock from what she was expecting.

It's gone, all of it. The inside of the helicopter looked like it was fresh off the factory floor. Maybe she shouldn't have been so surprised. After all, it had been some time since she last saw it. This is how it *should* look, but Elle was stunned by how normal and nonthreatening it was.

"What? Who?" She remembered Martin had said something about amigos, and for a moment she thought he was talking about an old Steve Martin movie she saw once when she was a kid.

"Kate, Blaine, and that tall guy. Jacob. They cleaned it," Martin said, stepping back to admire the cleanliness of the compartment.

"They did?" She felt genuinely surprised, and even risked a step closer to inspect the inside cautiously, fearful that she would instantly spot something they missed, a tiny dark brown speck, anything, and it would taint the moment. She scanned over every surface, even risked another step closer, but there was nothing there that wasn't supposed to be.

"Yeah," Martin said, with a hint of admiration in his voice. "Kate and Jacob practically insisted on it. It took them a couple of days. They washed it out-," He continued on with the whole process of how they managed the wipe away the stains inside of Maggie, but Elle wasn't really listening. Well, she was, but inside she focused on the fact her friends had done this amazing thing, and never spoke a single word about it to her. *Why didn't they tell me? Were they afraid I'd freak out?* She suddenly decided none of that mattered when she felt the knot inside of her loosen, and maybe it was her imagination, but something about her felt inexplicably… lighter. "You got some good friends there," Martin said in a fatherly tone at the end of his spiel.

Elle turned towards him, took a step and threw her arms around Martin in a fierce hug.

"Wha-? Uh?" She had caught him off guard. She had tears in her eyes, so she could forgive him for thinking something was wrong. To his credit, he simply returned the gesture and remained quiet. There was nothing wrong, quite the opposite. She felt it inside like a strange warmth.

Elle couldn't explain what she felt, well, she could, but she couldn't explain the why's and how's of it. Seeing the inside of Maggie, and all traces of what she was sure would blemish the vehicle for the rest of its life removed so utterly and completely, gave her hope. It was silly, mostly because Maggie was not a person. The helicopter was an object. It didn't have feelings that could be wounded. In that way, it wasn't frail like people were, but still, Elle felt a weird connection to Maggie. Especially after La Guardia, because in a way they both shared in that experience and they were both stained by it. She realized that's why she hadn't been up here, and why, just now, she felt a terrible anxiety at seeing the helicopter. Elle didn't want to be reminded of her own stains that she carried around with her. The knot inside her tightened when the door opened because, on some level, it felt like Martin was exposing her own ruined core for the world to see. But instead of seeing the embodiment of her own demons in dried blood stains, she saw the promise of being made whole again. It was a gift, maybe the greatest gift she had ever received. The gift of hope. She knew she wasn't there yet; she knew there would be more nightmares, more times when the knot in her stomach tightened uncomfortably. But now, for the first time, she realized that it didn't have to be like that.

"I *do* have good friends," she said and her voice broke into a half sob, half laugh.

"Yup," Martin said uncomfortably. *Poor guy*, she thought sympathetically. Martin did not know what this moment meant for her. Worse yet, she knew she couldn't explain it to him, not right now anyway. "You got a good bunch there." She couldn't help but chuckle at his awkwardness as she drew back away from him and quickly swiped a few errant tears from her face. "Are you okay?"

There it was, awkwardness aside, Martin's inner father couldn't help but shine through. He didn't release her completely, instead he held on to her by her shoulders, his warm hands barely applying any pressure at all. Just enough to know he was there, but not enough to stop her from leaving if she wanted.

"I'm fine." Elle looked into his unconvinced face. "I swear to you, I'm fine," she said again.

"Well, okay then. Good." Martin pulled his hands back like he was releasing a baby bird from his grasp.

"What did you want to talk to me about?" She asked quickly, changing the subject, mostly to spare Martin the awkwardness of talking about feelings, which she knew he hated. Martin seemed glad for it as well. He nodded solemnly, getting his mind back on the business that brought him to the roof.

"Mason wants to go on a run," he stated cautiously and just let it hang in the air for a moment to sink in.

Before he even breathed his next breath, she knew exactly why he was here. It wasn't for permission. The run was going to take place whether or not she was on board. No, what Martin wanted to know was whether she was going to come. She was confident enough in their relationship to know that there was no pressure or expectation on Martin's part, but he needed to know if she would be in that passenger seat or not when the time comes.

"Food supply is getting low. Emilio has been complaining about it for days, and I'm sure you've noticed the smaller servings of oatmeal. It's time. It's probably past time really, but nobody is in a hurry to get back out there since, well, you know." She did. Elle knew all too well. "Plus, I guess Jackie's infection is getting worse. Bill gave Derek a list of antibiotics to try to find. It's getting bad," he said and let his voice trail off at the end. He didn't need to tell her. She, like everyone else at The Prescott, was painfully aware of her condition. It was all people talked about, and usually the first piece of information people asked about if they didn't already know the latest news. In a community like this, bad news travelled fast, especially when it involved a member of Mason's crew. The sworn protectors of the Prescott.

She felt bad. It was only natural, because the whole time Martin was talking, she wasn't thinking of the food shortage, or Jackie's desperate need for medication. Elle had only one thought that flashed in her mind like a bright red neon sign on a dark night.

Seeds.

"When do they want to leave?" She asked, looking into Martin's eyes for the first time since he showed up. A fact that wasn't lost on Martin. The question took him back. She had skipped right over the part where he would have gingerly asked her if she was up for the task, while gently reassuring her that nobody was forcing her to go if she didn't want to. *Seeds*. This was an opportunity, a chance to create a more stable food supply, which they desperately needed. She knew what she had to do, and strangely enough, the thought didn't horrify her.

Though a smart person it probably would.

"A couple days," Martin said like he was delivering bad news. "Three at the most."

"OK, two days," she said while mentally creating a list of things she would like to get done before then. "I'll be ready," Elle said, to Martin's mild surprise. "Now, I don't mean to be rude, but there are some people I need to talk to, and suddenly it feels like I have a million things to do and only a little time to do it in. We'll talk again soon." She suddenly turned away from Martin and headed for the stairwell.

"Elle, wait." Martin called to her and stopped her in her tracks.

"Yeah."

"Well," he said, suddenly at a loss for words. "I guess I just thought that this would go differently than it did."

"Yeah, me too," she said with a warm smile. "But I'm strangely okay with it. I promise we'll talk more later, but right-."

"Fine, go," Martin said, waving her off with good humor. "Don't let me keep you from whatever you got going on. We can talk later." She was already on the stairs when he finished.

"Find us a place for the greenhouse, and I'll take care of the rest." She said with gusto as she approached Emilio after coming down from the helipad.

"Yeah? Are we doing it?" Emilio asked with equal parts of anxiety and excitement on his face as he looked back at her. He looked to be tidying up and getting ready to head back down but she secretly suspected he was trying to eavesdrop on the conversation that was happening on the upper deck. She couldn't blame him. If the roles were reversed, She might be inclined to try to listen as well.

"We are," she confirmed, "but we're not doing it alone. We're going to need some help."

"You got someone in mind." Emilio stated with a grin.

"A few people, actually."

-

"No," Jacob said without even looking up from the chessboard. She found her little group easy enough in the common room on the fortieth floor, nestled into plush leather chairs that they arranged around a tiny table that had a chessboard on it, with Bill and Jacob gazing at the board. Well, Jacob was gazing. Bill actually looked kind of bored, if Elle was being honest. Blaine looked up from the book he was reading and waved, and she looked around the room but Kate was nowhere to be found, which wasn't really a surprise. She was hard to contain for any length of time.

"No? What do you mean, no?" She asked with humor, trying to sound indignant and maybe overshot it a bit.

"Do I look like someone who is equipped for heavy labor?" He joked and keenly eyed Bill. "Besides, I got this geezer on the ropes here. I got him this time. I can feel it." Jacob looked back to the board. Elle gave Bill an inquiring look and when he met her eyes, Bill smiled humbly and shook his head ever so slightly.

"Oh yeah," Elle winked at Bill. "What's your winning strategy?"

"So far, I think he's planning to wait until I die from boredom," Bill said. He and Blaine chuckled lightly at the joke.

"Shush, you." Jacob glared at his friend.

"What?" Blaine dropped his book and asked defensively. "It was funny."

"And accurate." Bill chimed in and they both had another laugh at Jacob's expense.

"God, these two," Jacob complained silently before moving a pawn forward on the board. "So, what do you need help with?"

"Emilio and I are planning to make a greenhouse in one of the offices on the upper levels. I need your help to move some stuff around." Elle tried to say it as sweetly as possible. Blaine wasn't a problem, all she had to do was ask him and he would be in, same for Kate. Jacob, however, required a little pageantry sometimes.

"I'm not much good at moving shit around anymore, I'm afraid," Bill said gently. "But that sounds like a good idea to me." Bill promptly moved his knight forward and took the pawn Jacob had just placed. Jacob looked hurt by the move. "I'll help where I can." Bill smiled at Jacob before neatly placing the pawn among the others he had collected along the side of the board. You didn't have to be a chess master to see that Bill backed Jacob into a corner on the board, and it was only a matter of time before Bill ended it.

"You know, you shouldn't take the obvious move all the time." Jacob declared smugly as he moved his bishop forward to take Bill's knight. He held the piece up in celebration and looked at each of them as if to say: *See, I'm getting better at this.* Elle had to admit she felt sorry for him.

"You don't say," Bill said simply and moved his rook forward from behind his line of pawns to take Jacob's bishop. It was Jacob's last bishop. Jacob could only look on in stunned silence as Bill moved yet another piece of his to the side.

"Bill," he said. "You know I love you, and I hope you don't take this personally, but fuuucck you." Jacob said in mock frustration and threw his head back before letting himself fall back into the chair he was in. "I hate this fucking game," he said finally, in utter defeat.

"You know Kate beat him, right?" Blaine chimed in from behind his book, just to add insult to injury, and left it to hang in the air.

"What?!" Jacob yelped and then look first at Elle, and then snapped his attention to Bill.

"That's right, she did," Elle added, suddenly caught up in the moment's playfulness.

"You're lying."

"She did," Bill said innocently with a shrug of his shoulders. "Once." He was quick to add at the end. "She must have caught me on a bad day." He weakly offered the excuse no one had asked for and waved off the past defeat.

"Uh-huh," Elle muttered, unconvinced.

"Why don't you guys make it interesting?" Blaine said and let his book drop when he felt he had everyone's attention. "Why don't you play a game of chess for it? If Elle wins, you help her with whatever she needs done, and if Jacob somehow miraculously wins, you can do something for him." Blaine, the chubby, adorable devil, had an evil smile on his face the whole time he suggested the bet. Elle looked over Bill's shoulder and locked eyes with Jacob, both their eyes narrowed with a certain sinister intent.

"I like that idea," Jacob said with a sudden intensity in his voice while keeping his eyes locked on hers. It took everything she had to not break at the sight of the tall, thin, gay man with a wild mane of curls try to look menacing while sitting in a chair that was too small for his frame.

"I like that idea, too," Elle said, matching his false bravado almost perfectly.

"Ok," Bill said, lifting himself from his chair. "I know better than to get in the middle of a cat fight."

"Hey!" Jacob said, acting hurt. "What about the rest of our game?"

"Son," Bill said with a smile as he eased himself into the empty chair beside Blaine, who had put his book down and looked like he was getting ready to enjoy the festivities. "You can only keep a fish on the line for so long. At some point, you have to decide whether to reel him in or let him go."

"Oh, burn." Blaine added with a good-natured laugh.

"You're kind of ruining my vibe here, Bill. Just saying." Jacob chuckled and then turned back to Elle as she was settling into the chair. "If I win, you bring my meals to me, wherever I am in the building." She could feel Jacob's excitement at the prospect.

"What if I don't know where you are?" Elle asked innocently as she set up the board.

"Then you fucking have to come find me, I guess, I don't know, but for a-," Jacob considered what would be an appropriate amount of time for this mild form of slavery. "-A month. Yes, an entire month you have to bring my meals to me," he said proudly as he sat back and thought about the luxury of having his meals brought to him like a fucking emperor or something.

"Should I call you 'M'Lord, too?" Elle asked mockingly while keeping her gaze down on the board as she set up the pieces.

"Sure, if it makes you feel better about it, why not?" Jacob said with genuine mirth in his voice. Elle finished setting up the pieces and moved her pawn forward with a wide grin on her face. The trap had been sprung. No point hiding it now.

"Wait," Jacob said, seeing the sly amusement on her face. It took everything she had not to laugh out loud when the bravado he had a moment ago drained from Jacob's face. *He's catching on.* "What am I missing here?" he asked.

Jacob suddenly looked at his comrades on the leather couches. Bill's face held an uncompromising grin. While Blaine had his hand up to his face to hide the smile on it, but it wasn't working. It was Bill who broke down first.

"You ever wonder why Kate only beat me that one time?" He asked through a gentle chuckle.

"No," Jacob responded with an irritated tone that silently added; *of course not. Why would I?*

"It's because, that was the time I helped her," Elle said with a sinister smile. Jacob looked at her with a confused look as he put the pieces of the scheme together inside of his head. She knew he understood when Jacob narrowed his eyes at her in a mean look, before turning his attention to Blaine and Bill.

"You guys are assholes," he said bitterly and then resigned himself to his fate and moved his own pawn forward, beginning the game.

-

The game took about ten minutes from beginning to end. Elle didn't want to waste a lot of time playing with him. They had work to do, after all. Jacob came out of the gate strong, probably still feeling sore about being hustled into a game he wasn't ready for. Boys were like that, even the gay ones. He brought his queen out early, which for her was a real rookie mistake, or a sign she needed to watch out for a strategy. Unfortunately for Jacob, it turned out to be the former one. Three moves later, she plucked his queen off the board and tucked it in alongside the board on her side, some place where Jacob could easily see it. Because that was part of the game too. After that, all she had to do was sit back and let Jacob hang himself with his own mistakes. Mistakes that she didn't forgive.

"So how long were you in the chess club?" Jacob asked hours later, without a hint of bitterness in his voice. He was too tired.

Emilio found what she thought would be a perfect spot for their needs on the forty-fourth floor, close to the top of the building, in what used to be some high-end financial firm she never heard of.

On the south side, he found a conference room that had at least thirty feet of full-length windows that made up the entire wall of the room. The first job was to empty the vast space of all its contents. They rolled all the leather office chairs that were around the massive conference table into the adjacent offices until they stuffed both smaller rooms with chairs. Blaine even started lifting the chairs up and throwing them into the back of the room.

They would not dispose of the massive conference table in the center of the room so easily, though. The table took up the bulk of the center space of the expansive room. They made it of a shiny black material that Elle didn't recognize. Maybe marble? Whatever it was, there was no way the four of them could lift it on their own. She could have gone and grabbed some extra hands. God knows there are enough bored people around.

The real problem was that even if they could move it, there was no way they could fit the conference table out of the double doors that led out of the room. It was just too wide and too long to maneuver out the door. Jacob surmised the table must come apart, even though it wasn't overly apparent how, and left to retrieve some tools from God knows where. It took the rest of the day for the four of them to disassemble the massive table, and move its parts out of the room to where they left them in the hallway. Leaning against the wall, for the time being. Emilio had to bow out with his usual smile and a wave to go start preparations for dinner, and surprise surprise, it was rice with a serving of beans and fruit. That left the three of them to complete the job.

"All the way through junior high, and part way through grade ten," Elle said casually as they descended the darkened stairwell towards the common area on the Fortieth floor.

She felt the boys were looking forward to a break. The greenroom lived up to its name in that it was very warm within the confines of the room. When they finally left for dinner, she and Jacob had a thin film of sweat on their brows, while poor Blaine was practically dripping, but he didn't complain. None of them did.

"Huh," Jacob said absently ahead of her as they approached the forty-second floor's landing. "Why'd you quit?" He asked casually, as if it was the next logical question, and it would almost be impolite not to ask.

"I hit puberty," she began, "and after that, boys were more interested in my *chest* pieces." She smiled with great satisfaction as her friends groaned, almost in unison.

"That's not right." Blaine complained breathlessly.

"You're not gay," Jacob responded to him. "What's your problem with it? Well, other than it was a horrible, horrible joke."

"I have a niece Elle's age. I don't need to hear that stuff," Blaine said in mirth, but after he finished, his error hung in the air awkwardly. Elle corrected him inside her head, *you* had *a niece*. They walked in silence for a while after that. "So, where are you going to find all the dirt and stuff for all these other planters?" Blaine asked, breaking the unnerving silence of the stairwell.

It was a good question given the amount of work they had done already, and how much was still ahead of them. Too bad she didn't have a more reassuring answer to it.

"I was hoping Kate could help with the soil, and I was hoping someone on Mason's crew could pick up some seeds on the next run." She lied without the benefit of knowing why. Immediately after she had finished, Jacob snorted bitterly.

"Good luck with that. Those guys are assholes, and last time I checked, you weren't really high on their friend's list." When she heard him say it, a part of her cringed internally.

He was right.

After the La Guardia mission, she had been on the outs with Mason's crew. She suspected some of them, namely Derek, still held bitter feelings over what happened to Jackie. Elle couldn't do anything about that. She lost a few nights sleep driving herself crazy trying to think of what she could have done differently during the mission to prevent what happened, but in the end, she had to accept what happened and her part in it. Elle knew she wasn't responsible, but she also knew she wasn't blameless. None of them were, not even Jackie. They all played a part in the tragedy that befell Jackie, and they all had to come to terms with that at some point.

"Sure, but they have to realize what it is for. We *all* have to eat. If we put enough effort into this, we might make enough food for everyone, and maybe then we wouldn't need to go on so many runs. In the long term, it would be better for all of us." Blaine looked to Jacob.

"Sure, but that would require someone in Mason's group to think ahead, which they're not really great at," Jacob said and then turned to Blaine. "Heads up, we have incoming," he whispered. That's when Elle first heard footfalls ascending the stairs from below them, and then saw a light on the wall of the forty-first floor. Her friends ahead of her fell silent as they approached the next landing.

Jacob was the first to reach the landing, followed a couple steps behind by Blaine and then herself. A sense of foreboding filled her as Elle came to realize whoever it was coming up the stairs was probably a member of Mason's crew. She silently prayed it was Nathan.

"Out of the way, queer." Derek's gruff voice boomed

throughout the small space and below, she saw his shape forcibly shove Jacob aside as he stepped up onto the landing. Blaine stepped down onto the level at the same time and made room for Derek to pass.

"Why do you have to be such an asshole?" Blaine protested weakly as Derek was about to pass, an all-too New York way of dealing with confrontation. Derek could just have easily given him the finger and moved on. Instead, he answered the question, in his own way.

"What the fuck did you just call me, fuck wit?" Derek growled angrily as he suddenly turned towards Blaine and stepped towards him. All Blaine could do was back himself up against the far wall or risk colliding head on with Derek's sudden rage. "Huh? Speak up, Nancy, I didn't quite hear you." He bellowed.

"Hey," Jacob said gently, trying to sooth the situation over. "He meant nothing by it. You know how he speaks before he thinks some-," It was when Jacob gently placed his hand on Derek's shoulder, just a friendly gesture to help punctuate his words, that's when pandemonium broke out.

Derek pivoted violently and rammed his clenched fist up into Jacob's abdomen. Jacob easily stood a foot taller than Derek, making punching him in the face possibly problematic. She didn't know, she wasn't a fighter. Neither was poor Jacob. The fist sunk deeply into his center, removing all the air from Jacob's lungs. Her tall friend hunched over, dropped the flashlight in his hands as his arms wrapped around his stomach, and he sunk to the floor, trying desperately to breathe.

"You think because you're fucking tall you can step up on me like that, you fucking faggot, huh?" Derek howled down at Jacob. At that moment, Derek looked like a rabid dog barking at something he already killed, taunting it. It was more than Blaine could take.

"What the fuck-," Blaine raised his voice in a way that echoed in the stairwell. He meant business, but it wasn't enough.

Derek just refocused his rage on Blaine. He turned and grabbed Blaine by the shoulders and pushed him across the space of the landing and slammed his body into the concrete wall. Elle watched in horror as Blaine's head whipped back and struck the wall audibly. Blaine probably could have recovered from that, but then Derek kneed him in the groin. Blaine folded immediately and dropped to the ground. Derek couldn't have stopped that from happening if he wanted to. All of Blaine's weight just fell to the floor.

"You motherfuckers better learn some goddamn respect," he yelled down at them. Elle felt her blood turn to ice and the surrounding air seemed to thicken with the intensity of the moment. Derek's rage radiated off him and filled the darkened landing with a genuine sense of danger. *He's going to kill them*, she thought inexplicably. "All the shit we go through so you fuckers can eat; you want to talk to me that way? Maybe do more than just take up space and shit out the food I provide you."

Stop it!" Elle stepped forward against her best judgement and used both her hands to slap Derek's back, completely forgetting the flashlight that was clenched in her hand. She watched helplessly as the metal of the flashlight's housing collided with his shoulder. "Just stop it."

What am I doing? she thought to herself as she watched her body move on its own. She had to do *something*. She knew she couldn't just sit by and watch him beat the shit out of her friends like that, but *this* felt like a mistake.

"And *YOU*!" Derek spun around to face her with his face twisted up in anger. Elle instinctively took a small step back. He angrily shook his finger in front of her as he spoke. "You are the absolute *last* person on this goddamn planet I'm going to take shit from. Be warned, you little bitch, you're on thin ice with me. You better just stay the fuck away from me for the foreseeable future. FUCK YOU!" He leaned in and screamed the last bit.

She could feel the heat of his breath on her face and, for a moment, it felt like her heart was going to burst out of her chest. It felt like the end. She didn't know why, but something inside her informed her this was it. Elle prepared herself for the blow that never came. Derek, instead, stormed up the stairs and cursed again as he rounded the corner at the top of the stairs. His curses filled the dark space like a dog's bark, and caused her to jump.

Derek left her there, shaking in the stairwell, with her friends wounded on the ground. Unharmed yet somehow still injured. All she could do was stand there uselessly, listening to the quickened drumbeat of her heart pounding away in her chest with such ferocity she could feel it behind her eyes. Everything had happened so fast. She didn't have time to adjust to the change. *He just attacked*, she thought madly inside her head. It was Blaine's loud, pained groan that woke her out of her trance.

"Jesus! Are you guys alright?" She cried and turned to drop beside Blaine.

"No," he said weakly while he continued to cup his groin and his face twisted up in pain.

"We just got our asses kicked. We are most certainly not alright," Jacob said as he struggled to get himself to a seated position on the other side of the landing.

"I can feel the pain from my balls in my teeth. Ugh." Blaine groaned loudly. Elle rubbed his back, unable to really do much else. She was ready to help him up, but considering what had just happened to him, she didn't want to rush it. He waved her off, rolled over onto his side, and lifted himself up to sit against the landing's wall as well. "I wish he would have hit me in the face instead," Blaine said as he readjusted himself on the floor to find a comfortable position.

"Not me, I have to *look* at your face." Jacob casually let the joke hang in the air, and Elle genuinely found it funny, but she didn't allow herself to smile until Blaine cracked and let out a pained, mournful kind of laugh.

"Fuck you, don't make me laugh. I'm not entirely sure my nuts are still attached." Blaine struggled to shoot back at Jacob while half chuckling and half groaning.

"No, fuck you. I can't believe you called him an asshole. That was stupid." Jacob was still holding his sides when he said it, and to Elle`s surprise, it wasn't exactly in jest.

"Yeah, I know. I should have kept my mouth shut and kept walking," Blaine said regretfully and, in a way, it sounded like it was a bit of an apology. To Elle, it was adding insult to injury.

"It wasn't his fault," Elle said, because she felt she had to. "He didn't say anything that deserved *this*." She spread her arms wide to show the whole fucked up situation that had just occurred and her friends were still recovering from. "Like, what the actual fuck was that all about?"

"What can I tell you? Haters are gonna hate." Jacob leaned heavily against the wall as he lifted himself off the ground to a standing position, though he quickly found the pain in his gut prevented him from standing fully upright. Elle watched his face wince in pain before he settled into a hunched position he found was comfortable. "Jesus, I need to do some sit-ups or something. I don't think one punch is supposed to hurt that much."

"Yeah, that guy is an asshole. Help me up." Blaine held out his arm to Elle. She grabbed on to him, planted her feet, and help hoist him up to a standing position as well. By the look on his face, it might have been a mistake to get up so early. "Like, who goes straight for the nuts? That's just a dick move," Blaine said, immediately after which she and Jacob looked at him with a weird look on their respective faces. The pun hung in the air unnoticed by Blaine until he looked up at the rest of him with a wide grin, and then all three of them burst out into uncomfortable giggles.

The levity of their comments seemed to wash away the taint that was left by Derek's sudden and insanely violent outburst, but it couldn't wash away the physical effects. Jacob remained hunched over like he was carrying an enormous burden on his shoulders, and poor Blaine looked like just standing was painful.

It saddened her to see her friends so accepting of what had just happened to them. It's one thing to see your friends grievously assaulted for no real reason, but it was entirely another heartache to watch them struggle to rise to their feet while they placed the blame for the assault solely on themselves. *What are we becoming?* She thought nervously as she stood there watching her two friends struggle to stand and making jokes. She briefly thought about mentioning this to someone but quickly found she didn't have a real clear idea of who she would tell.

Especially after La Guardia. The more she thought about it in those few seconds, the more frustrated she became because there was no one she could think of who could, or would do anything in response to this… crime? *Do laws even exist anymore?*

"We should have Bill check you guys out," she said

because she felt it was the only real thing she could suggest at this point. There was a tight knot in her gut. Elle hadn't felt it like this in a while, but unlike the other times, she knew why. Once again, she found herself amid incredible violence, and once again, she was virtually untouched by it. She would have much rather Derek punched her full-force in the face than watch him take apart her friends like that while she just stood by. *Was this because of me?* The knot tightened even more when she considered Derek's reaction was because of his feelings towards her, because he blamed her for what happened to Jackie. Even now, there was a small voice inside of her that agreed with him. But this?

"I. Am. Not showing Bill my balls." Blaine declared and then took a cautionary step, winced painfully, and then added. "We'll see what it feels like when I pee. If I pee blood, I'm definitely going to see him, but I think I'll be fine."

"You sure?" Elle asked, fully aware how much like her mother she sounded like at that moment. Blaine forced a smiled and nodded, then she looked at Jacob, who just shrugged.

"Don't look at me. I just got punched in the stomach. The thing that hurts the most is the fact I can't take a punch." Jacob put on a fake smile and tried to soothe over how much he hurt. "Seriously, I'll be fine, but I don't think I feel like eating anymore."

"I could lie down for a while," Blaine said, testing the waters. "I have that bottle of tequila that would go down good right about now," he said, looking down the stairs. Maybe he was mentally preparing himself for the descent ahead of him and possibly calculating the pain that might be involved.

"Fuck that, we're finishing that joint when we get back,

we earned it." Jacob shot back.

"I think I love you," Blaine said, sounding completely genuine. She had to admit she was envious of their relationship.

She had watched their friendship grow from the very beginning when they had all first showed up in the building. It was endearing to watch two men who probably would not have associated too closely normally, find such a deep friendship in this place. Sure, she had Kate. Some nights when she couldn't sleep, she would still look over to her sister and thank whatever God was running this show that she still had her. But it wasn't the same as what Jacob and Blaine had. They accepted each other for who they were. Who they really were, no facades, whereas Elle felt she had to be *something* for Kate. She felt she had to hide her darkest thoughts and feelings from her sister, like Elle should shelter Kate from some great evil she wasn't ready for, but it wasn't always like that. She remembered a time she didn't feel the need to distance some aspects of herself from her sister.

"Is there anything I can do?" She asked, watching the boys begin their slow, cautious descent down the stairs. It left her stunned by how the two of them could pick themselves so quickly and just move on from what happened. However, the boys stopped in their tracks. Jacob looked back at Blaine with a look of genuine curiosity and interest that worried her.

"Should we?"

"You just said you weren't hungry," Blaine complained and Elle could see his shoulder visibly slump from behind.

"Oh, buddy, that was before. This is now," Jacob said with a renewed, if somewhat strained, excitement. Elle had a good idea what was coming, judging by the weird look of childish excitement on Jacob's face. She probably could have offered, but it had slipped her mind and now it seemed like if she offered to do it now, it would just take a certain amount of wind out of Jacob's sails.

"Whatever, dude. I'm going to get fucked up and watch a movie on the laptop and try not to think about the pain in my crotch. You do you." Blaine casually shrugged and continued down the stairs.

Elle's heart sank when, even from the back, you could tell each step was causing him a measure of pain, and there was a long way to go before his and Jacob's level. *This is all my fault.* It was a familiar thought. One she had many times over the last couple of weeks. Elle seemed to use it as her unofficial motto. She had asked for their help. If they weren't in this stupid stairwell helping her, none of this would have happened. She got a jolt of frustration when she realized she was doing exactly what Blaine had done. Blaming herself for something when the full blame should rest squarely on Derek's shoulders.

"Could you bring us our food?" Jacob asked somewhat meekly, like she might refuse.

"Of course," she said, and then smiled at him sweetly before adding, "M'Lord."

"Ew, I could get used to that," Jacob said in jest while still slightly hunched over.

"Yeah, I bet you could," Blaine chimed in behind him and down the stairs a few steps.

"Can I call you my serving wench, too?" Jacob asked sweetly, turning back to Elle.

"Only if you want to get punched in the stomach again," she replied, and she got a few laughs with that one as they continued down the stairs.

-

They parted ways one floor down where Elle said her goodbyes and promised to see them soon, before she opened the door to the common area. She entered the makeshift cafeteria in a foul mood and found the dinner rush in full swing, which made her mood even worse. Elle quietly waved to a few people who noticed her entrance like everything was normal. Like she didn't just witness her friends just get assaulted by one of the people who was supposed to be tasked with keeping them safe.

She immediately saw her sister at their usual table with Bill and Martin. Kate's head popped up from her bowl and she waved at Elle to get her attention. Elle waved briefly before walking towards the table. She looked over to Emilio, who was behind the counter with one hand holding the book he was reading and the other holding an empty spoon that was hovering over the bowl of heavily sugared oatmeal. They shared a wave as Elle walked through the eating area.

"Hey Elle, where are the guys? They're not coming?" Martin asked casually.

The knot weighed her down from somewhere deep inside. She took a breath. Elle wished Martin hadn't asked at all because now she felt she was at a crossroads about what to say, and she didn't know immediately which course she should take. The indecision was infuriating.

"Elle?" Martin looked at her with sudden concern. She didn't know what he had seen on her face, but whatever it was concerned him enough to speak up about it. "What's wrong?"

With that, the interest of the entire table perked up, and suddenly, all eyes were on her. In a way, she was thankful because now there was no point in trying to hide the truth. She breathed in deeply, and just spoke and let it all come out naturally, no filter.

"Derek, just beat the shit out of Jacob and Blaine in the stairwell." She leaned in with a hushed voice. It was one thing to be honest, it was another to declare it to the entire room.

"You're kidding!" Kate said.

"What the fuck? Why?" Martin asked at almost the same time, but in more whispered tones of outrage.

Bill just shook his head in a sort of muted disappointment, a gesture that sadly fit his character almost to a tee. Elle didn't know if it was old age or experience with him, but Bill didn't get overly excited about anything. Maybe it was both. Whatever it was, it was a quality she hoped she'd learn for herself.

"Because he felt like it, I dunno," Elle said defensively, and then reconsidered. "Well, Blaine called him an asshole in passing and then things went south, Jacob tried to step in and it all went to shit after that."

"Are they hurt?" Bill inquired, staring into her eyes. She knew what he really meant; d*o they need me?*

"Jacob got hit in the stomach, and Derek kneed Blaine in the balls, so yes, they are a little beat up, but they are content to walk it off. They're probably downstairs now, tying one on and smoking a joint. I'm supposed to bring them their dinner."

"Yeah, sounds like they'll be fine," Bill said, content the matter was resolved. "Is this about the greenhouse?" He asked suddenly.

"I don't know. Why would it be?" The question caught her off-guard. Elle didn't see the connection between the two things. She could only think of one reason for Derek's behavior, and that wasn't something she needed to vocalize. They knew.

"That guy is just an asshole. I can only imagine what kind of cop he was," Martin said with a certain disdain.

"I've known cops like that my whole life," Bill said distantly, while sipping his coffee. "Not all of them, mind you." He was quick to correct, before continuing. "But there always seems to be at least one bad egg that spoils it for the rest of us. Maybe I should mention it to Mason?" Bill put it out there for the table to consider. "He seems reasonable. Maybe he might speak to Derek about it, could be worth a try."

"Pttf." Martin and Kate snorted in unison. Martin paused and looked over at her sister with a look of curiosity. Obviously surprised she shared Martin's dislike for the man. Elle wondered if it would surprise him that most the people in the building shared the same opinion on some level.

She had never known a police officer like Derek Peters, and she had to admit when he first burst through the front doors of the Prescott building wearing the easily identifiable POLICE vest over a white shirt and tie, it comforted her to have a figure of authority present. It was natural. Who wouldn't be happy to have a cop around while the world was collapsing? Or a few members of the military? When the time came for the hard questions of their survival to be answered, the rest of the group, including herself, were all too happy to hand over the reins to the people they thought were better equipped to deal with the situation.

"I don't think you'll get too much traction out of the Major," Martin said.

"I think that's a bit pessimistic, it's worth a try at least. I'm not expecting him to lose his shit over it, but at the very least he should be made aware of what's going on with one of his guys." Bill gently defended his position. "You got to give a man a chance to do the right thing, or else he never will."

"That's nice. Who said that?" Kate said, turning to Bill.

"My wife used to say that all the time. It was her thing. She believed in second chances, and third chances," Bill said, sounding a little distant when he said it. They all understood why.

"Maybe." Martin let the issue drop and continued eating his oatmeal.

She couldn't blame Bill. She believed, to some degree, they all felt the validity of what he was saying. Elle didn't know when it happened, exactly. Things like this happened in degrees that are almost imperceivable individually, but only noticeable when you look back on it. At some point, everyone stopped feeling like they were survivors, and started accepting that they were more akin to prisoners within the concrete and steel of the Prescott building. It's how she felt, and from what she had observed from the others, the quiet way they talked, the muted way they went about their day, they felt it too. Elle recognized the look in their eyes that was lacking… something. Hope, maybe. She didn't know, couldn't articulate what exactly wasn't there, but just knew some dark shroud had descended upon them.

"Did you have any luck finding some dirt?" Elle asked her sister, desperate to change the subject at the table, but also for her own wellbeing, needing to focus on something positive.

"Some." Kate began with a shrug of her shoulder. "It's surprising how many people liked having plants in their office," she said, addressing the entire table before tucking a few stray strands of hair behind her ear and turning towards Elle. "I found six pots so far. I started looking at our floor and I plan to work my way down. How much dirt are you going to need, anyway?"

"As much as you can get." There was no humor in Elle's voice. She tried to think of how many tiny plant pots they would need to fill one of their bookcase planters. She didn't know exactly, but she knew it would be a lot more than six pots.

"I'll keep looking then."

"Thanks, I really appreciate your help on this," Elle said, taking a moment to add a little something more than just thanks. It was true. It was a straightforward thing to do, and completely forgivable, but sometimes she was guilty of forgetting how supportive her little sister truly was. Elle smiled warmly when her sister summed it up beautifully.

"I got your back, sis." Kate said it like a passing comment, like something that didn't even need to be said aloud, but Elle never tired of hearing it.

"You looking for dirt?" Bill chimed in. "I know where you can get a lot of it."

"What? Where?" Elle perked up at Bill's comment.

"The lobby," Bill said and Elle's heart sank a bit. "There are two enormous pots in the lobby, both filled almost to the top with dirt. They used to have trees in them, like years ago, *actual* goddamn trees. Thought they would enrich the Feng Shui of the lobby or some shit like that." Bill was slightly animated as he spoke, like he was amused by the idea. Elle had to admit, she had completely forgotten that Bill used to work with the maintenance firm that was contracted to maintain the building. "Of course, the trees died, and they later replaced them with plastic ones, but the dirt is still there. Two big pots, each probably has enough dirt in it to fill a bathtub."

"Really?" Elle considered the possibility of it, and the

potential complications.

"Yep."

"Tell me more." So, he did.

Elle vaguely remembered the pots. She hadn't been down to the lobby since the first time they started moving up the building to get away from the amassing horde of undead bodies collecting around the entrance. None of them have. There was no reason to go down there for anything. They had emptied out the tiny clean-looking bodega that was on the far side of the lobby. The only thing down there was the vast cavernous white marble space, and an angry hissing mob pressed up against the large, front-facing windows.

Back when they still had power, and it became obvious by the line of undead in front of the entrance that no further people would arrive, they closed the security gate. A wide, steel gate descended from the ceiling. She still remembered the loud whine of the electric motors emphasized the finality of the moment. The loud metallic clank as the gate settled into place punctuated the unsettling fact, they were locking themselves in as much as they were locking the undead out.

Elle remembered the pots after Bill explained where they were in the lobby. She remembered the two large pillars in the lobby that rose all the way to the ceiling. One was on one side of the lobby, close to the entrance to the hallway that led to the elevators and the stairwell door. The other was directly across from it, maybe twenty or twenty-five feet, closer to the bodega.

She had the image of the massive pots in her head, and she was thinking if they indeed filled those pots with dirt, that would be a superb start to their project. How much soil did plants really need to grow? Six inches? She and Emilio could do a lot with that dirt. They could stretch that out a long way, but how to get it?

"Hmmm. Thanks," Elle said, still half buried in her thoughts. "That could be very useful."

"We're not supposed to go down to the lobby." Kate broke in, sounding very much like a nosy child. Elle couldn't tell if it was on purpose or not. That was part of Kate's charm.

"I know." Elle responded defensively. "Still good to know."

"I'm just saying that because you're always telling me not to go anywhere near the lobby. So, if you were to do that, it might be a smidge hypocritical," Kate said with a fair amount of amusement as she held out her index finger and thumb and looked at Elle through the tiny space she had created between the digits.

"Yes!" Elle snapped back firmly. "Thank you." With that, she gave her sister a look that warned the message was received, and Kate now proceeded at her own peril. Kate only smiled back, content with her victory of getting under Elle's skin in almost record time. Little sisters could be like that.

"Well," Bill announced while placing his spoon in his empty bowl. "I should go check on Jackie and see how she's doing." He rose slowly from his seat.

"How is she doing?" Elle asked, feeling bad she hadn't asked sooner.

"Not bad," Bill said cautiously. "She has a pretty severe infection in her arm. Her fever's a bit high for my liking, but given how much she can still swear, I think she's going to pull through."

"That's good." Martin sounded genuinely pleased. "You got her on antibiotics?"

"We have those?" Kate asked, sounding both shocked

and somewhat impressed.

"I have some. Honestly, she should probably be on an I.V., but we don't have those. We'll have to make do with what we have. It's not much, but it should be enough." Bill shrugged, which wasn't very reassuring, but then again, he probably wasn't trying to sound reassuring. Some things you couldn't sugar coat. "I should get going. I'll catch up with you guys later."

"You want some company?" Kate chirped, as Bill was turning to leave. Elle could see the answer to Kate's question in the dark features of his face before he ever said a word.

"Sorry, kiddo," Bill said with genuine disappointment. "I don't think it would be a good idea. Jackie's not too thrilled with the idea of visitors at the moment. We got to respect that."

"Oh-kay." Kate wasn't even trying to hide her feelings. With that, Bill waved to them and left. Elle watched him as he dropped his dishes off with Emilio, and said a quick word to the man before Bill walked out of the lunchroom.

"Why did you want to go?" Elle asked her sister once Bill had departed the room. Kate just shrugged.

"I dunno. It's something to do. I'm bored." She confessed.

"If boredom is the biggest challenge you faced today, then I'd say you had a pretty easy day, and that's a good thing," Martin said. It was such a dad-thing to say, he probably meant it to sound humorous or worldly, but Elle suspected it came off a little condescending. Kate didn't seem phased by it though, she just stuck out her tongue at an amused Martin.

"Do you want to hang out with the boys tonight? We

could probably get a Monopoly game going." Elle suggested, feeling guilty because she had been neglecting her sister lately and hoping this would be a way to make up for that. She knew Blaine and Jacob wouldn't object, Blaine adored Kate like she was his own niece, and Jacob... Well, Jacob deep down would do anything for Kate, Elle knew that. There was definitely an affection there, even though they had shown that affection by constantly sassing each other like a pair of squabbling siblings.

"Really? That might be fun." Kate perked up at the suggestion and Elle smiled outwardly while nodding, but inwardly, the gears of her mind were turning. She was thinking about the greenhouse, the things she had to accomplish, and a future where her friends might not be eating sugary mush twice a day but might actually enjoy proper food.

"Yeah, I think everyone could do with a little fun right about now," Elle said, thinking of the events on the staircase and wondering how the boys were recovering from their wounds. "Why don't you head down to our level and grab a few snacks for tonight." A few snacks, it sounded like they had a huge pantry to choose from, they had two small packets of M&M's, and a snack machine sized bag of Doritos. That encompassed the bulk of their personal food stores, all thanks to Kate's diligent searching throughout the building. They have been saving them for over six months now. "Something for us to share. I'll meet you down there after I have a bite to eat, Okay?"

"You want to come, Martin? Monopoly is better with more people." Kate turned to Martin in an endearing fashion. He was still new to their little group, and it was nice to see her sister include him in their game. Martin looked like he didn't expect to be invited and it surprised him, but quickly warmed up to the idea. That was the moment Elle caught his eye and tried to subtly convey that they needed to talk.

"Um. Sure, why not? Just let me go drop my book off," he motioned to the bookmarked paperback on the table. "And I'll be right down."

"Great." Kate jumped up from her chair, taking her cue perfectly, even if she didn't know it, and said her goodbyes and headed off out of the eating area. Elle was looking forward to it too. Sure she was still anxious, but she knew it would be good for her to relax with her friends for a night. She had been secluding herself for too long already.

"What's going on?" Martin said with a keen interest when Kate was clearly out of earshot. As was his nature, Martin kept his tone quiet, so whatever was said went no further than the confines of the table. Not that anyone was listening, but Elle has found that Martin didn't think too highly of people.

"Who decides where we go for the supply runs?" Elle asked, trying to sound casual and nonchalant.

"Why?" He asked almost musically. Elle suspected he knew damn well what this was about.

"Because I think we should go to Queens, specifically the Jackson Heights Shopping Center. There's a huge grocery store called Food Universe." Elle said innocently, knowing full well it was pointless. Martin was too smart for such games.

"And? What else is there?"

"There's also a small garden shop my mother used to go to, *The Ye Olde Garden Shop*. It's in the same strip mall. It's a tiny shop, mostly for apartment dwellers, but it's full of seeds." Martin smiled with a certain amount of satisfaction as she explained.

"Huh-uh. Figures. I knew something was going

on when I saw the three amigos hauling Emilio's prized plants downstairs. Then a couple hours later, I see Kate rushing up the stairs with a couple dead office plants in her hands." Martin had a smile on his face as he went on like he solved some grand mystery. Knowing how people liked to talk, it would surprise her if anybody in the Prescott *didn't* know about the greenhouse yet. "I wish you would have told me. I could have helped," he said sounding slightly hurt that she might keep something from him.

"You do help," Elle said reassuringly, before adding quietly, "and you will help."

"I have a feeling I'm not going to love the job you're going to give me."

"Relax. It's easy. All you have to do is convince the others that we need to go to Jackson Heights."

"Ok, well, that doesn't sound so bad. It shouldn't be too hard. We haven't been to Queens in awhile. I should only have to suggest it, really." It sounded like Martin was more thinking out loud than actually talking. He looked at the table, but then he looked up. "How are you planning to convince Nathan to break from the group to get these seeds? I assume it's going to be Nathan you're going to ask, because I can't imagine the others will be too thrilled to do you a favor at the moment," Martin said, thinking through the problem as he saw it.

"I'm not going to ask Nathan, or anybody else," Elle said, and then paused for a heartbeat to brace herself for the next part. "I'm going to get the seeds myself."

"The fuck you are!" Martin blurted out; the sound of his objection echoed throughout the room. In the next moment, there were eyes on them. Martin shrank slightly under the gaze from the others and Elle looked around, suddenly nervous someone had discovered her plans.

"Jesus! Keep your voice down." She hissed.

"You're not doing that." Martin pointed a stiff finger at her with a sudden air of authority. Which lasted only as long as it took for the words to leave his mouth, before he retreated and let his finger drop to the table. "Are you insane?" He persisted more gently. "You can't possibly be serious."

"I am serious. It needs to be done, and you keep saying all the time how we can't trust the others. And I don't know what you think I'm going to be doing, but what I'm planning on doing is running into the store as fast as I can, grabbing a few packets of seeds that might help us feed these people more than just brown mush, and then running out of that store just as fast." Elle looked him dead in the eye so he could see her resolve for himself. "I'll be in and out and back in the helicopter before the others even know I went anywhere. All you have to do is get us there."

She made it sound so easy, so simple. How could he refuse? Truth of it was, she hadn't actually put a lot of thought into what she would do once she stepped out of the helicopter. That part of the plan still seemed too far away to warrant much consideration. At least, that's what she was telling herself.

"I don't know," Martin said as he rubbed his scalp. Elle could see the gears working away behind his eyes. "Maybe I should try to talk to Nathan and see if I can get him to keep an eye out for some seeds. Grocery stores have seeds too. He might run into this gardening store for us." He sounded like he was trying to convince himself it would work as much as he was trying to convince her.

"Great," she said with mock enthusiasm. "Do that, but I'm still going," Elle said sternly.

"I could stop you from getting into that

helicopter." Martin threatened her, weakly.

"But you won't," she said, testing the waters and judging Martin's reaction before she continued. "Because you know we need it, and you realize it needs to be done. I'm not stopping you from talking to Nathan." Secretly, she had her fingers crossed it wouldn't have to be up to her to do it. Her life, up to this point, did not equip her for this kind of work. She knew that. It was a fact she felt was tested and proven to be true. If someone else agreed to do it instead, even better. All she cared about was getting the seeds. Elle didn't care how it came into her possession. "But if it comes down to it, I'm going." She locked eyes with Martin. He looked back at her with sad eyes. The eyes of a man who had lost.

"You could've died," he added mournfully. The raw emotion in the quiet statement caused her to pause. "Now you want to go do it all over again." He shook his head as he broke eye contact with her. She felt there was a lot he left unsaid, and she loved him for both what he might have said, and for why he didn't say it in that moment. She wanted to reach out to him but she also felt that would cross some invisible line between the two of them.

"I'll be okay." It was all she could think to say and felt wholly inadequate, but she still said it with conviction for Martin's sake.

"Huh-uh. Sounds about right," Martin said, sounding utterly unconvinced. Martin then looked into her eyes as if he was searching for something, Elle suddenly became nervous he would find her lacking somehow. She didn't know if she could handle it if she recognized that on his face. "You're going to give me a heart attack, you know that? Martin said finally. "But you're right. It is worth doing," he said with a quiet firmness. "It doesn't have to be you though-," She was about to object, but Martin cut her off by holding up his hand. "Trust me, I know what you're going to say, but at least let me talk to Nathan before you go making any actual plans."

"You're the one who said we shouldn't count on them."

"I'm aware, but it's better than the alternative. Much better," he said, mildly annoyed at having his own words thrown back in his face. "Just let me talk to him. We'll talk about it more tomorrow and we'll go from there. I'm with you." He said, suddenly switching tones. "I am. We'll get this done, even if we have to do it ourselves, but we still have to do it right. No mistakes." He cautioned.

"No mistakes." Elle confirmed. She satisfied him with what he saw in her face because he leaned back in his chair and nodded, seemingly to himself, as he breathed out a long sigh.

"Now, I want to go freshen up before the game, so if you'll excuse me," Martin said with a grin before he rose from his seat.

"Freshen up?" She asked, genuinely curious.

"Yeah." Martin slightly lowered his head and sniffed his button-up shirt. "I'm starting to smell like a three-day-old fart. Figured I'd go clean up and put on a fresh shirt. Maybe I'll surprise you all and put on some deodorant," he said with a smile. She didn't remember seeing him smile a lot before, but recently Elle had noticed it more and more. In the short time she had gotten to know Martin, she understood one thing above all; she should have reached out to him sooner.

"Careful, Jacob gets a bit frisky after a few drinks. He might not be able to help himself," she said, keeping her voice dead serious. For a moment, Martin's middle age face shifted to one of genuine worry, which caused Elle to giggle wildly at the man's sudden concern Jacob might hit on him. Martin smiled when he discovered the joke and gently fingered her before he headed off.

"Oh," Martin turned back, as if he just remembered something. "Are the boys more of a bourbon or a scotch crowd?"

"Yes," she said simply and a second later added a wink. Martin chuckled.

"My kind of people." Martin smiled and then turned to walk away, leaving her alone at the table. Which suddenly became a very lonely place when it was just the anxieties in her head doing all the talking.

Elle didn't have to wait long before she felt invisible eyes on her. She looked around the space, but everyone else was engrossed in their own day. She left the table and went over to the serving counter and, after another brief recounting of the events in the stairwell to Emilio's muted shock, she collected her lunch. Elle sat quietly at the empty table and breathed deeply as she ate her food. After she was ready to make the trek in the dark stairwell, she went back and picked up the boys' lunch.

"You got that?" Emilio asked, gesturing towards the tray in her arms. Elle didn't hesitate. She just nodded and reminded Emilio she used to be a waitress as she steadied the tray in her hand before saying goodbye and heading off towards the stairs.

She awkwardly switched the tray to her other hand as she reached up and grabbed a flashlight off the hooks on the wall by the stairwell door. Elle held the flashlight in her dominant hand and rested the weight of the tray onto her forearm as she reached for the handle of the door and moved into the darkness of the stairwell. Elle braced herself for the loud echo of the door closing, but she still felt a tremor course through her body as the sound rang out in the small space like a gunshot. As the sound died away, Elle was left alone in the darkness with only a small beam of light to show her the way down the stairs. *Yeah, I was a pretty good waitress*; She thought to herself as she followed the beam of light from the flashlight. *But I didn't have to walk down three fucking flights of stairs in the dark*! Another thought crept into her head after she took her first step towards the stairs. She suddenly had a striking fear that somewhere in that darkness below her, Derek was waiting for her like a spider waiting for a fly to land on its web. She paused, took a deep breath to steady her nerves, and pushed herself forward down the stairs. If Derek was down there, which was unlikely, she wouldn't give him the satisfaction of her fear. He didn't deserve it.

With the tray of food held in her arms and the beam of light fixed on the stairs leading down, she cautiously stepped down the stairs. She was determined not to drop the food, not to fail in this small thing. She had promised, and she would deliver, as promised, even if doing so was only important to her. She needed this. Elle needed a win. It seemed small. Who was she kidding? It *was* small. But she felt if she could do this, maybe she could see the rest of the greenhouse project through. Like, it might be some cosmic sign. If they could make a viable greenhouse that produced, maybe she could convince Mason to see the worth of expanding it even more. All they needed would be more dirt and more seeds.

So, you can what? Spend the rest of your lives living on a high-rise? Of course not, she thought. They didn't have to live here forever. She didn't like to admit it, but she agreed with Mason on one thing. She also believed the undead would eventually rot away to extinction. It was only a matter of time.

Two more years.

That is what Mason had said before in the past, but the vision of the undead she had encountered at the airport haunted her. Those zombies seemed to have plenty of meat on their bones, and they still moved with surprising speed. At least she thought so.

So maybe two years was optimistic, but she couldn't see the undead lasting longer than five years, but could *they* last that long? Did they have access to five years' worth of fuel for the helicopter? She didn't think so, and she imagined if she pressed Martin hard enough, he would eventually confirm it as well. They needed the ability to produce their own food, and she felt it was up to her and her merry little band to show the people in charge it could be done.

She descended the stairs and thought about her group of friends, a motley bunch of people who had defied all conventional norms just by hanging out with each other. Elle didn't know when it happened exactly. They all just seemed to gravitate to each other, like all they needed was the right circumstances and time. She couldn't speak for the others, but she had grown to love them all dearly. They had become her new family. All other friendships pale compared to the people in her group now. The once cherished friendships she remembered having with other people she grew up with in the same neighborhood shrunk away to utter meaninglessness when compared to what she had found in the seclusion of the Prescott.

She felt the weight of those relationships, she felt she had to protect them from the future. She didn't know if she would succeed. It seemed these days every decision, every thought, every damned feeling had with it the possibility that she could be mistaken. There was only one thing she was sure of. She had to try. That much felt true. Maybe in doing so, she could improve their living conditions, and possibly their overall health. They had to start now, though. All the rewards from this project wouldn't come for months, and winter was coming. The winter's cold was another problem entirely, but they would cross that bridge when they got to it. It was a problem for later.

Elle opened the door to the boys' floor. Blaine and Jacob turned one of the large conference rooms on this floor into a pretty impressive man-cave when it became apparent that they would not be moving any further up the building. She turned the corner of the hallway and the powerful scent of marijuana that still lingered in the air struck her. On her approach, Elle could see Jacob, Blaine, and Martin talking excitedly at a weird diagram that was drawn onto one of the full-length windows facing the hallway. Beyond them, she could see her sister setting up the Monopoly game on the large table behind them, seemingly oblivious to the excited conversation going on in front of her.

There were many opened ornate bottles of what she just assumed was some fancy high-end alcohol on the large conference table beside the game board. Elle also saw the two crystal glasses on the table she knew Blaine and Jacob like to drink from. Beside the posh glasses, was a plain white coffee cup that could only be Martin's. Elle suddenly felt a slight pang of guilt. Her mother would have blown a gasket if she knew Elle had brought her little sister into a situation where people were drinking *and* smoking dope.

"Elle!" Jacob caught sight of her and called out before he rushed out into the hall to meet her. "We did it!" He exclaimed excitedly as he approached her. His glassy eyes looked at her excitedly and she definitely smelled alcohol on his breath, but the stain of the attack in the stairwell had utterly vanished. "We did it, and it's fucking brilliant. You're going to love it." He looked at her expectedly with a big smile on his face for a moment before he looked down at the burden in her arms. "Oh, let me help you with that. I totally forgot you were bringing our food down. That's awesome." His hands shot out, and he grabbed a bowl in each of his long, thin hands. He brought it up to his nose and smelled the contents of the bowl with an appreciation of someone being handed his mother's home cooking. "Mmmm. Mushy!" Jacob said with false excitement.

"What's going on?" Elle asked nervously, nodding to the diagram on the window.

"Hey!" Jacob yelled back to the others, completely ignoring her. "Elle brought food!" Blaine perked up and waved through the strange diagram. Martin met her eyes through the window, and then looked away suddenly with a look that Elle thought might be shame. She smiled inwardly at what she thought was the cause.

"Come on." Jacob nodded for her to follow him back to the game room. "You're going to fucking love this." Elle gave him a quizzical look that she was thankful he didn't see, as she followed him back into their game room.

"Hey, Elle." Blaine greeted her as she entered the room. He took his bowl of food from Jacob's hand and looked down into it with a sort of appreciation. It was food after all. "Yum," he said blandly. "I guess it's better than nothing, and it's still warm. Thanks." She nodded to him as he scooped up a spoonful and put it into his mouth. "You going to tell her?" Blaine's glossy eyes focused on Martin.

"Me?" Martin looked up in shock. Elle could see a tinge of panic in his glossy eyes. It was clear Martin was not handling the marijuana well.

"It was your idea," Blaine said with a partial mouthful of food.

Martin explained his idea slowly and with great detail. The image hastily sketched onto the hallway-facing window of the room was the layout of the lobby. Elle recognized it from the beginning of their tenure in the building. The plan was to construct a moveable partition that was big enough to conceal the people behind it from the undead eye's out front. They would move into the lobby, and using a hand-truck from the delivery van in the parking garage, they would move the large pots back into the stairwell. Jacob knew what materials they needed to construct the partition. He even had a rough mock-up sketched onto the window beside the layout of the lobby. It seemed like a good plan.

Then Blaine dropped the bomb.

"We're going to do this while your on the run."

"Why?" Elle shot back.

"So, Mason won't find out we did it. Seemed like the easiest answer," Jacob quipped

"We're not telling Mason?" Elle was shocked.

"Did you tell him about your little seed heist?" Jacob shot back. Elle shot a stern look at Martin, but it was Jacob who confirmed her suspicions. "Yeah, he told us. He told us all about it. We told you we had your back, now we're going to prove it. Let us take care of this for you."

"Do you like getting your asses kicked?" She leveled Jacob and Blaine with a hard stare.

"Not personally."

"It'll be worth it," Blaine said with a confidence that surprised everyone.

What could she do? Elle could see by the looks on their faces they wouldn't budge on the issue. Those sweet, lovable assholes. She didn't know if she wanted to hug them or slap their faces. It was Kate who broke the stalemate from behind the Monopoly board.

"Are we gonna play or what?"

Chapter 4

Kenshiro

They couldn't afford to rest too long. His mentor's words nagged at him. *If you're not moving forward, you're falling behind.* He used an analogy of rowing a boat upstream to get his point across. Trevor Dixon was a hard man, but he wasn't wrong.

How long had he been here? A month? It felt like more. How much longer could they stay here? Kenshiro couldn't say. One thing he knew for sure. He had totally fucked up his usual timeline. By now, Kenshiro should have emptied the town out completely. He should have already established a storeroom and secured it, and if he was being realistic, Kenshiro should have been down the road.

He knew in the beginning having the teen would change things. How could it not? He had a whole other person to take into consideration now. He tried to be flexible; God knows Kenshiro made concessions for the boy he would have never made normally, and mostly it had worked out. Inside him, though, habits made from the struggles of the new world and forged into finely honed instincts did not die easily. They scratched at the insides of his head and whispered inside his mind that it was time to go, and if he stayed here too long, doom would soon find him and his companion.

"Are we going into town today?" Elliott asked as he set his plate aside and reached for his bowl of canned oranges. Kenshiro could sense the apprehension in his voice.

"No," he replied firmly and let it hang in the air. It slightly disappointed him when Elliott visibly relaxed upon hearing the news. "I thought we'd take a break today." He added, despite all the objections coming from the lizard part of his brain. "Yesterday was a hard day."

He wanted to say more, something to let his friend know he understood what he was going through. Something to raise his spirits and give the boy hope for a future that wouldn't include the people Elliott loved the most, but he couldn't find the words. Probably because they didn't exist. In the end, he left it at that.

"Yeah," Elliott confirmed distantly. "Yesterday *was* hard."

Kenshiro gave Elliott a day to recover from the tragedy of burying his mother and to come to terms with the finality of the fact he was an orphan. It seemed generous to Kenshiro. It was more than he had. He also felt the best thing he could do for Elliott was just give him the space he needed to work through it. He didn't know what Elliott was going through, and he honestly didn't want to get caught up in the teen's emotions either. Kenshiro had his own demons, he didn't think he could handle Elliott's as well.

The next day, Kenshiro came to see that decision as a mistake.

-

Kenshiro let the undead man fall while he held the knife firmly in his hand, the blade slipped free from its eye socket as the body fell back. It was the last one to settle on a floor that was already heavily populated with corpses. Kenshiro was in another ranch-style house, so the entire house was on a single level, which made clearing the house relatively easy because there were fewer places for the dead to hide. Following his tested and true method, he first knocked loudly after he opened the door and waited for a spell for his target to come to him. Given the layout, though, he soon opted to move into the house where he felt he would have more room to work. Turns out, that was the right decision to make.

When the last body came to rest, he waited, breathing in the foul stench of the house while carefully listening for sounds of movement from the rest of the empty home. It was at that point he noticed the back door was open, which would explain the larger-than-normal number of undead inside the small house, that had been a concern earlier. He closed the door leading to the back patio before he returned to the spacious living room. Kenshiro pulled his length of rope from a belt loop at his side. Kenshiro quickly wrapped it around a zombie woman's legs.

Then he stopped.

A sound seeped through the air that his brain registered, at first, as a dog's bark. That was what it sounded like, but that was impossible. No dog would be within a hundred yards of the undead and if they did, they certainly wouldn't be barking. Even dogs are smarter than that. He moved to the front door for a look and his eyes instantly locked on the empty truck parked out front. His brain came alive with a painful jolt when he saw Elliott was nowhere to be seen.

Not again, a voice screamed inside his head and Kenshiro burst through the door with wild eyes, frantically searching the area for his friend. It didn't take long to find Elliott, though. He just had to follow the sound.

"What the f-," Kenshiro looked down the road from where they had started their day. Elliott was there in the middle of the road. In took Kenshiro's brain a moment to slow down enough from the adrenalin jolt to process what he was seeing.

He recognized Elliott immediately, and he also recognized the bat in his hands. Kenshiro witnessed Elliott savagely raise it over his head. *Where'd he get a bat?* Kenshiro thought as Elliott brought the bat crashing down onto... something. A bag maybe?

At this distance and with his adrenalin-addled mindset Kenshiro had, it was the best it could do, but that's not what he was focused on.

Elliott angrily cried out as the bat crashed down and made a dull thumping sound that Kenshiro could hear even at this distance. There was a rawness to the action, a primal sort of brutality. That's what struck him the most. Kenshiro had seen people in the depths of rage before, many times in the course of his life, both before and after the zombie incursion. The sight of it did not bother him. What struck him was how foreign it looked on the boy's small frame. Kenshiro couldn't quite explain it but seeing Elliott's face twisted up with rage like that as he brought the bat down felt like a failure to him.

Then Kenshiro noticed the black shape on the ground move slightly.

Kenshiro didn't run. He dropped the bag on the sidewalk as he walked towards his friend. When he saw a dangerous situation, he didn't run. He didn't want to spook the boy, and he wanted to keep his options open. Kenshiro speed-walked up to Elliott like a father about to scold his child. Secretly, he hoped that's all that would happen. He felt the lizard brain scratching to get out.

"ELLIOTT!" He barked sharply at the boy. "Stop it!"

If Elliott heard him, he made no sign of it. Elliott raised the bat up and growled angrily, and then his entire body pulled the bat down on top of the zombie's body. As he neared, Kenshiro risked a look down at the pulverized undead body on the ground. Elliott had been busy for the short time Kenshiro was in the house looking for supplies.

With the bat in hand, Elliott must have smashed every bone in its body. The zombie on the ground wore dark pants with a checkered button-down shirt. It was hard to discern the colors of the garments because it entire body looked dark and wet. Bodily fluids were being forced out of the spots where bones protruded through the skin. Its limbs twitched slightly. Kenshiro could see where Elliott fractured its extremities repeatedly. He saw the weird angles of the zombie's arms and the way they moved weakly on the pavement. Elliott shattered the undead man's legs so badly its pants looked like someone had filled them with a lumpy paste instead of actual legs.

"Right now!" Kenshiro bellowed.

Elliott just roared again as he brought the bat down on the zombie's sunken chest. It made a squishy noise upon impact, like he was smacking a wet sponge. The zombie's expression was unchanged by the blow. With no structure left to support it, all it could do really was turn its head a little and snap its jaws. Elliott made sure of that. Kenshiro rushed forward immediately following the blow. He timed it so he could reach the boy before he raised the bat up again.

"Elliott!" Kenshiro growled his name as he grabbed the boy's arm, maybe a bit too forcefully, but he didn't feel he had the benefit of half measures. He wasn't the one holding the bat, after all. Elliott responded immediately and violently to his touch.

"GET OFF ME!" He screamed with every ounce of his being as he wrestled away from Kenshiro's grip. Elliott sounded like a wounded animal as the sound of his cries pierced Kenshiro's ears. Elliott spun away from him and when he turned back to face Kenshiro, Elliott had the bat raised over his shoulder, ready to strike. "GET BACK!" He wailed loudly.

Elliott's cries probably would have gotten the attention of every dead ear within three blocks, maybe more. Kenshiro was thankful for the work they had done up to this point. It gave him time. He had more options now.

Kenshiro took a half step back. Not a retreat from the boy, though. He simply stepped back into a fighting stance. He raised his hands up. Externally, it might have looked like he was surrendering. He was trying to look nonthreatening, but in no way, shape, or form was Kenshiro surrendering. His hands were up to protect himself, if need be.

Inside its cage, inside Kenshiro's mind, the lizard brain was already working out how to handle Elliott.

If he attacks, I'll move forward, closing the distance between the bat and myself. The blow will come on the left side, downward angle. I'll shoot my left arm out and catch it early and at a weak deflection angle. I'll quickly strike the throat with my right arm, and while maintaining control of the bat, I'll pull back my arm and hit him in the solar plexus, paralyzing his diaphragm and making it impossible to breathe. Naturally, the body will double over slightly, and I'll reach up with my right arm and wrap it behind his neck, and pull his face down into a sharp knee. All the while this is going on my left arm will snake around the boy's right arm and lock into an armbar, immobilizing the shoulder joint and disarming him at the same time. A quick twist and lever of the arm and the shoulder joint should po-

JESUS CHRIST! WHAT'S WRONG WITH YOU? Kenshiro screamed inside his head at the lizard brain, and it rattled the door to its cage inside his mind. It sensed danger and was frantic to get out. Kenshiro just breathed and looked at the boy with his hands up. He would defend himself, of course, but no more.

Kenshiro looked into Elliott's frantic eyes. He looked like a wild animal that had been caught in a trap. Hurt, angry, and terrified. He was looking for a way out. A way forward out of the corner he had backed himself into. Kenshiro had mixed feelings as he looked at his pained expression. He wanted to comfort the boy, to shield him from the inner turmoil. Elliott was tensed, and he had the bat ready to strike over his right shoulder, which wasn't ideal.

"Put the bat down," Kenshiro said firmly while keeping a watchful eye on the business end of the weapon.

"No!" Elliott cried out. "You can't tell me what to do! An..and you can't be mad either!" He shouted with a certain amount of indignation. Kenshiro checked their surroundings quickly, hoping the boy's outbursts weren't drawing any unwanted attention. So far, they were alone. "I've seen you," Elliott said, like he knew a dirty secret. "You do the same all the time. Worse. You've killed *sooo* many of them." Kenshiro didn't like the way Elliott said '*killed*'.

"Not like this, I haven't," Kenshiro said calmly and nodded to the shattered figure on the ground snapping uselessly at the sky.

Is that what he thinks of me? He thought sourly. *I thought he understood.* It felt like a mild betrayal. Like this whole time, they had an agreement that Kenshiro would deal with the zombies, if Elliott didn't think he was a monster after he saw how he did it, which admittedly could be unsettling.

"Never like this. You want to kill a zombie? Great, by all means kill it. But this," he motioned to the body on the ground again. "This isn't what I do. You're not killing it, you're punishing it, and that's not right." He couldn't help the bitterness in his voice. He just hoped it didn't make things worse. Elliott seemed to take his words like a physical blow. He even took a step back.

"What does it matter? You said they can't even feel it."

"Yeah!" Kenshiro couldn't help but to raise his voice at the boy's stubbornness. "Exactly! So why are you doing it?" Kenshiro stared at him with cold eyes for a time, to let the boiling anger inside himself cool to a steady simmer. "These used to be people, Elliott. You shouldn't treat them like that."

Kenshiro wanted to say more. He wanted to drive the point home like a knife tip to the brainpan, to ask the boy how he would like it someone destroyed his mother's zombie like he had done here to this poor undead fuck on the ground. How would he feel about that if he saw it? But he didn't. It felt like too much, and judging by Elliott's facial expression, he understood, or he was trying to, but something inside him fought it.

"It's not right." Kenshiro added at the end solemnly.

"You don't know what it's like!" Elliott had tears freely flowing from his eyes now. He looked like he was on the edge of a full-blown sob, and yet Kenshiro saw the rage persist. Elliott used the end of the bat to point at him.

Kenshiro saw his chance, and he didn't waste it.

His arm flashed out and Kenshiro felt the hardness of the bat in his palm as he snatched it free from Elliott's grasp. One moment Elliott had the bat in his hands, and the next it was in Kenshiro's. Elliott looked at him with a stunned expression, like he had just seen a magic trick performed right in front of his eyes.

"You're right," Kenshiro said calmly, trying not to make any sudden movements with the bat that would startle the boy. "I don't have a fucking clue what it's like. I have no idea what's going on inside that head of yours. In fact," he said, lowering his grip on the baseball bat. "There's really only two things I know with absolute certainty." He stepped forward, and watched with indifference as Elliott stepped back away from him. Kenshiro stepped over the ruined zombie on the pavement. "One, I know how to kill zombies." Kenshiro grinned before he pulled the bat over his shoulder like it was a golf club. He grunted slightly as he swung the bat low and connected with the side of the helpless zombie's skull. Gore splashed across the asphalt, followed closely by teeth that rattled across the surface of the road like dice. He looked at Elliott for a moment in hopes it would give his next words weight. "And two, I know you can beat the fuck out of these things all day, and you still won't feel better." He tossed aside the metal bat without a care for where it landed and stared at Elliott to see if he understood what he had said. The boy seemed better, calmer maybe, but Kenshiro could still see there was a measure of turmoil and confusion going on behind those blue eyes. "Let's go." There was nothing else that he could think to add, so he turned back to the truck and motioned Elliott to follow. Kenshiro secretly hoped he would.

"I hate them." He heard Elliott say quietly from behind him.

"What?" Kenshiro turned back to him and met his pleading eyes.

"I hate them," Elliott said again with venom in his voice. The boy hadn't moved from his spot. Instead, he stood over the decimated form of the zombie in the middle of the road. He looked down at it and then back to Kenshiro with those sad, confused eyes. "I hate them *so* much," he said looking down again at the corpse as the first sob racked his thin frame. Elliott clenched his fists at his sides and

Kenshiro could see him shake with unbridled fury.

Kenshiro's heart went out to the teen. There was no doubt in his mind that Elliott did indeed hate them. The depths of which Kenshiro might not know, but looking at the teen, he believed it was with every fiber of Elliott's being. Which Kenshiro saw as part of the problem. In Elliott's case, that part was fairly large, because in the short time he had known the wiry-framed teenager, Kenshiro accepted one inalienable truth about him. Elliott had little in the way of a middle ground when it came to his emotions. It was all or nothing with him. He had seen it too many times not to be wary of it.

This was different, though. He saw it in the boy's madly searching eyes. Elliott looked like someone who had never hated anything in his life. Now, for the first time, he felt it truly and honestly for the undead, and Elliott didn't know what to do with the emotion. Given Elliott's warm, loving personality, Kenshiro could easily believe Elliott never truly felt the white-hot heat of hatred in his soul. He did now, though, and the foreign emotion tormented him.

"Hey," Kenshiro said in the most pacifying voice he could muster as he stepped back to his friend to get his attention.

He didn't know what he was going to say, but when Elliott looked back at him red-faced, Kenshiro knew he had to say something to calm the storm going on within him. But what? He couldn't tell Elliott not to hate them. That would be unnatural, like telling a fish not to swim. He should hate them. In Kenshiro's humble opinion, it was an important factor to one's survival. Besides which, Elliott's expression didn't say: *Should I hate them?* That wasn't the question on the boy's face. It was more like, *what do I do with this thing inside me?* In that, Kenshiro was lost, as always.

For the first time in recent memory, Kenshiro wished his father was here. He would know what to do. He was always good with people. Takeda Watanabe could always connect with them on a genuine level that they respected. Except for him, of course. Kenshiro and his father always struggled to find middle ground, but it was his father that always made sure they got there, eventually. Kenshiro remembered a night shortly after the accident. The bandages he wore were still fresh, and he awoke in the night screaming. He still remembered the dream, and on some level, it still bothered him. It was the first time he really felt happy when his father rushed into the room. He took his next cues from what his father had said to him on that dark and lonely night.

"It's okay," Kenshiro said, trying to mimic the warmth his father had that night. "Really." He added when Elliott looked unconvinced. Kenshiro stopped in front of him, thought about hugging the boy, and then decided against it. Instead, he reached out with his hand and simply placed it on the boy's bony shoulder. "It's okay. Just breathe," he said slowly and then took some deep, deliberate breaths to show Elliott what he was looking for. "Just breathe." Again, he looked into the boy's eyes as he took slow breaths in the hope Elliott would change his shallow, erratic breathing to match his.

"I don't…," Elliott said and then stopped. "I mean..." He searched the ground between them for his words. Kenshiro leaned over him and shushed him softly.

"It's OH-kay," he said again. This time with emphasis. He watched as Elliott let out a final sob before he sucked in a deep breath of air, and letting it go in time with Kenshiro's breath. They took two deep breaths in synch with each other. Kenshiro secretly hoped the worst was behind them. By the look on Elliott's face, though, they weren't out of the woods yet. He still looked like he was struggling with something.

"I want to go home," Elliott said quietly, and for added measure he looked up at Kenshiro with those big, sad blue eyes that were almost begging him to agree.

"No," Kenshiro said softly, but firmly, as he removed his hand from the boy's shoulder. "We have a job to do here."

Elliott needed to understand that they couldn't stop what they're doing because he was in a bad mood. They had to keep moving forward, especially on the days they didn't want to, because that's what surviving is.

"There are no other zombies around." Part of him hoped Elliott would snicker, as he normally did, at his pronunciation of '*zombie*'. It mildly disappointed Kenshiro when it didn't come. "There's no danger to us right now. No reason to leave. We're staying, and we're going to finish what we came here to do, and then we can go home."

"But I want to go now." Elliott whined softly.

"Listen," he said and then paused for a quick breath to calm himself. "I know you're still upset. I get it. You don't have to do anything. If you want, you can sit in the truck and keep a lookout. That's fine, no problem, but we're not leaving yet and that's final." He put a bit of an edge to his tone when he said '*final*,' in hopes Elliott would take the hint that maybe he shouldn't push too much more on this subject.

"Ok," Elliott said weakly, and then a moment later he added, "I'm sorry... about him." He looked down at the broken figure with a look of shame. A part of Kenshiro felt that was appropriate.

"That's fine. I'm just glad you're ok. I was really worried when I came out of that house and you weren't in the truck." Kenshiro replied.

CHAPTER 4

Worried was a gentle way of putting it. He wanted to scold Elliott for the white-hot panic he felt when he realized the teen was missing again, but in the end, he decided Elliott had been through enough today, and scolding him would only push Elliott away. So, he tried guilt instead.

"I'm sorry," Elliott said again. "I didn't mean to make you worry." Kenshiro smiled and waved it off. "You hate them too, don't you, Ken?" Elliott looked up to him.

"I do," he admitted almost immediately.

Kenshiro didn't feel any shame in it. Maybe a better man would have paused at the question, but he didn't need to. The answer was obvious. A better question might have been: How could he not hate them?

"I really do, but the trick is not to let that hate change you. You can't let it take over and start deciding, because that's when mistakes happen. People die when that happens." He let his words hang in the air for a moment before he turned back to the truck. He was going to call back for Elliott to follow, but a small voice inside his head reminded him of something important. "I hate them," he first reiterated before continuing. "But at the same time, I kind of feel sorry for them." He paused. Searching for an easy way to explain a complex concept and being further bogged down by why it was even important to make the distinction. It didn't take long for him to abandon it completely. "I don't know, it's weird." He looked down at Elliott's perplexed face. *At least he's not crying.* "Come on," he waved to Elliott to follow him back to the truck. "Let's get you cleaned up," Kenshiro said, and he motioned to the front of Elliott's blue button-down shirt that had the dark stains of a splatter pattern on the front. He knew Elliott was particular about how he looked, he liked to look tidy, and he would not be happy when he realized how messy pulverizing a zombie to paste can

150

be. That alone might be enough to keep him from repeating the events of today.

"Ew, gross." Kenshiro heard, to his slight amusement, as Elliott complained loudly from behind him.

-

"Can you teach me to fight zombies?" Elliott looked over to him earnestly when Kenshiro hopped back into the driver's seat at the end of the day. Kenshiro looked at him for a moment before starting the truck. "You know, like you do."

"I don't fight zombies, Elliott. I kill them. Besides that, I don't think it's a good idea," Kenshiro said, it was a knee-jerk reaction to the question. He thought back to Elliott bringing that bat down savagely on the crumpled zombie on the pavement. Remembering the twisted expression of rage on Elliott's face as he did it. He seriously questioned Elliott's ability to keep his head straight when he was in the thick of it... and yet. "Maybe," he said as he thought it over more. "Maybe it wouldn't be a bad idea to teach you the *right way* to deal with them. You know, in case the time comes..." He didn't want to finish the thought because it might upset Elliott to consider a time when Kenshiro wouldn't be there. Elliott didn't seem to notice the dire possibility that hung in the air between them. He perked up when it became apparent that Kenshiro might actually consider his idea, which in a way he was. "Yeah, ok."

"Yes!" Elliott said excitedly and actually pumped his fist by his side to punctuate it.

"But." Kenshiro raised his finger to Elliott to caution him. "It's just training. When we're out and about like this, nothing changes. You still keep a lookout in the truck, and I clear the houses. No dealing with zombies on your own, no leaving the truck without telling me, and no stupid shit like what happened today." He finished with a bit of an edge on his voice that brought Elliott's excitement level down a notch. "Okay?"

"Yeah, okay. I can do that. No problem."

"Now," Kenshiro said. He then reached out and put the transmission into drive. "We have to find you the right weapon."

-

Kenshiro had an idea for what the '*right weapon*' might be. During his downtime in the evenings, he had plenty of time to think about it. He secretly wondered if this time would come. Kenshiro believed in his heart it was inevitable. He could tell himself he could keep Elliott safe all he wanted, but the truth was the boy had to take care of himself. He wouldn't always be there. Hell, it's already happened. Twice! Kenshiro felt like a mother bird looking down at her chick in the nest, knowing full well it was time to push it out of the nest and pray. He might have waited, but Elliott asked, and part of him knew it was for the best. Elliott's unique gift wouldn't save him from them once the enemy was aware of him. Kenshiro cruised the empty north side of La Veta, looking for a suitable piece of rebar.

After an hour, and twelve zombies later, he found a truck parked off the side of Moore Avenue, close to the train tracks. Someone had abandoned it with several other trucks with a similar logo on the doors that Kenshiro didn't really pay much attention to. The trucks had the look of work vehicles and he figured it must have been a construction crew of some sort.

The utility truck that caught his eye from the road had a prefabricated truck bed that had steel cabinets built into the sides of it, and on top of the passenger side were two metal forks, one at the front and one at the back. In between the forks, Kenshiro saw a bundle of ten-foot-long rebar lengths that were strapped in securely. He found a hacksaw after he picked the locks on the cabinet doors, and cut off a three-foot length for Elliott.

"That?" Elliott looked at the length of steel, unimpressed. "It's not as long as yours is," Elliott commented, and sounded mildly disappointed. Kenshiro resisted the urge to tell a joke Elliott probably wouldn't understand and carried on.

"It's also not as heavy. Trust me, once we get this all sharpened up, it'll do the job. It's really a lot handier than it looks." He gave Elliott a bit of a fatherly grin while presenting Elliott with the unsharpened, rusty length of steel. "You know, I had one like this when I first started out."

"Really?" Elliott said with a strange mixture of awe and surprise as he took the rebar in his hands. He shifted it in his hands, this way and that, to get a good look at it. Then he looked at the rust stains on his hands. "It's kind of dirty, though." He mumbled, as if he didn't want to hurt Kenshiro's feelings.

"We'll get it cleaned up for you." Kenshiro chuckled as he hopped into the driver's side of the truck.

"Can I drive?" He heard Elliott ask behind him. Kenshiro looked back and Elliott had a hopeful expression on his face. He was holding the rebar in his arms like it was a trophy he had just won.

"Sure." Kenshiro relented and eased out of the seat. "Put that in the back, though." He pointed to the rebar as he passed Elliott. As stupid as it sounded, even to him, he didn't want Elliott to get rust stains on the seats. "Do you want to make dinner tonight as well?" Kenshiro joked lightly as he climbed into the passenger seat and Elliott was settling into the driver's seat.

"No," Elliott said with absolutely no humor. "I just wanted to drive."

When they returned to the Newman property, Elliott had gone and checked the chickens after they had returned. Kenshiro stood by the side of the truck, watching the boy intently as he entered the ramshackle building, just to be safe. Elliott exited the chicken coop with an egg held high in his hand. He looked triumphant, and Kenshiro took some solace that he also looked genuinely happy as he walked up to the house.

"You know," he said, looking down at the egg in his hand as they walked back to the house together. "I was feeling pretty bad this morning, but I'm feeling better." *Beating that zombie to a pulp might have helped*, Kenshiro thought sourly to himself, and then corrected himself, because it didn't matter. Elliott was acting a little more like his old self. That's what mattered.

"That's good," he said simply.

"Kenshiro?" Elliott stopped right before the steps that led up into the house. Kenshiro stopped and turned back to him. Elliott looked… worried. "Do people who get killed by the grey people… go to heaven?" Kenshiro could tell it was a hard question for the boy to get out. "I saw that grey man today, you know the one," he said like there was a possibility Kenshiro might have thought he was talking about some other zombie, other than the one Elliott inexplicably took a bat to. "And I wondered about it … And I got really upset because I thought maybe…" he looked shamefully down at the egg, like the words he was looking for might be written on the shell. "Maybe they didn't." Kenshiro was glad his friend was looking down at that egg, so he couldn't see the stunned look on his face.

How the hell am I supposed to answer THAT?

"I don't know Elliott. All I know is that they're gone, and we're still here. That's what's important," Kenshiro said, not even trying to hide the defeated tone in his voice. "Come on, I'm hungry. Let's go eat." He waited for Elliott to bring his eyes back up before he just gave the boy a slight shrug. *It's the best I got*, the gesture said.

"Okay," Elliott said as if he was conceding a point and followed him into the house.

After they finished dinner and the dishes were washed, dried, and put away in their appropriate cupboard, Kenshiro saw there was still plenty of light left in the day. *No time like the present*, he thought to himself before he called Elliott to join him outside.

He put Elliott to work on his new weapon. The first task Kenshiro gave Elliott was to clean the bit of rust on the shaft using a steel brush Kenshiro had found in the workshop and some WD40. After that, he had Elliott coat the shaft in motor oil, to protect it from rusting more in the future, before wiping off the excess oil with a rag. Then, he handed Elliott the file he used to sharpen his own spear and set the boy on the long, arduous task of filing the blunt end to a fine point. Elliott was happy to be given the job and seemed content to just sit on the back of the truck's tailgate and work the end of the rebar with the file.

While Elliott worked on that, Kenshiro went about putting together a suitable target for them to work with. Luckily, he didn't have to look far. Elliott, a while ago, had mentioned Emily bought hay bales for her pet project with the chickens. He also mentioned, in the next breath, that she had bought way more hay than she actually needed and kept the extra bales stacked under a tarp behind the chicken coop.

Just as promised, behind the little building were three small bales of hay neatly stacked on top of each other. The tightly wrapped cubes of hay looked like large chests, but they weighed a surprising amount. He wrestled the top one off of the stack and struggled to carry it over to where Elliott had his target set up for his pitching. Elliott stood one hay bale up length-wise for his baseball target. It stood about three and a half feet off the ground, so Kenshiro stacked his on top of it in the same manner.

When completed, the two bales stacked on top of each other were taller than he was, which was perfect. He just hoped they didn't topple over when Elliott struck the target. They looked sturdy enough. After that was done, he went back to Elliott's father's shop and retrieved a can of spray paint, and returned to the hay bales to make his target.

He sprayed bright red lines on the upper hay bale until he had a pretty good approximation of an average zombie shape, about the same height as Kenshiro with a round circle for the face because it needed to have a chin for it to be effective. For effect, he gave the round face a pair of angry-looking eyes and a set of jagged lines for the mouth. It was almost a comical rendition of their enemy that was both entirely too scary looking, and didn't do justice to the genuine horror of the zombie plague at all.

It would have to do.

-

"No, no, no," Kenshiro gently corrected after Elliott lunged forward toward the undead bale of hay. His form was improving. He moved in quickly and with good intent, but his angle of attack was still off. "You're coming in too straight again." Elliott moved away from the target and looked back at him. Kenshiro could see the boy had a thin film of sweat on his face as he looked to him for instruction. "Here." Kenshiro took the two fingers of his right hand and jabbed them up underneath his chin. "Like this, at an upward angle. And when you pull it free, pull down to your hip, not to your belly." Again, he mimicked the motion he wanted Elliott to follow when Kenshiro pulled the shaft free from the target in the air in front of him, as if he was holding an invisible weapon of his own.

"Oh, okay," Elliott said like a lightbulb had suddenly come on in his head. Kenshiro didn't get too excited about it, though. He had said the exact phrase, the exact same way, about a dozen times now. It didn't signify his understanding, it's just how Elliott said it. It was getting late; the sun had secretly dipped under the western horizon without either of them noticing. Now they were losing the light, but Elliott was unphased by it, and Kenshiro felt he should take however much time the boy would give him to train.

"Again," he said and motioned to the target. Wordlessly, Elliott lined himself up in front of it with the somewhat sharpened end pointed menacingly towards the bale-zombie's face. Kenshiro heard the teen suck in a lungful of air before Elliott sprung forward. The shaft's point came up and sunk into the hay bale right under the red-painted chin of the zombie's face.

"Good!" Kenshiro cheered the boy on from behind when he saw the tip rose into the hay. "Now yank it back!" He shouted excitedly, caught up in the boy's moment of success, maybe a little too much. Elliott did as instructed, mostly. He yanked the shaft free from the hay bale with substantial force. Unfortunately, he pulled the shaft straight back to his center instead of to the side by his hip. Elliott drove the blunt end of the shaft straight into the meat of his thigh.

"Ow!" Elliott cried out in pain and dropped the shaft to the ground. Both hands fell to the spot on his leg where the weapon hit and he limped painfully around the scene. "Ow, ow, ow. That really hurt," Elliott said with a surprisingly calm voice as he continued to walk off the charley horse in his leg. Kenshiro bit his upper lip to keep from snickering. He warned Elliott about that.

"That's why we don't sharpen both ends," Kenshiro said, unable to hide a bit of a smile. "Are you okay?" He asked after Elliott continued to limp around him.

"Yeah, I think so. It just really hurts." Elliott stopped in front of him and tried to massage the affected muscles. He looked up and Kenshiro could see his eyes had locked onto something in the distance. He was looking towards the front gate, and he knew before Elliott even spoke. "Look." Elliott said as he lifted himself up and pointed towards the road.

Kenshiro turned and looked towards the front gate leading into the property. It didn't surprise him to see a figure awkwardly making its way down the road. The zombie wore what looked like work clothes and had a kind of hefty frame. Before he did anything else, Kenshiro did a quick check of his surroundings to make sure there weren't any others he should know about. He had a certain tinge of pride when he noticed Elliott doing the same. They were alone, and even now the figure walking down the road was carrying on like it did not know they were there, all thanks to Elliott.

"This is actually good," Kenshiro said, looking first to Elliott and then to the undead man on the road. "HEY, ASSHOLE!" He yelled, and the zombie changed immediately, answering his call. Suddenly it was stalking towards them with its arms up and its fingers stretched forward. Kenshiro looked back to Elliott, who looked a touch confused.

"Do you want me to deal with him?" Elliott thumbed towards the approaching zombie with a newly humbled look on his face. "He looks kind of big."

"No. I'll do this," Kenshiro said as he pulled his work gloves free from his back pocket, and bent down to pick up the length of rebar. "It will give me a chance to show you size doesn't matter, when it's done properly." Kenshiro thought back sourly to the undead hulk.

"Oh, okay," Elliott said the same way he'd been doing all night, at the same time, looking a little relieved.

"Okay, you see how it's coming towards us with its hands out straight in front of it like that?" Kenshiro asked as he bent down to Elliott's eye level to look at the zombie coming towards them. "Those hands will clamp down on anything it can get a hold of, and then it pulls itself in for the bite. Then it's all over. What we're learning to do is shoot in between those arms and strike before it even has time to grab you. That's why we have to be fast, and then we need to yank the shaft free before the body falls. If we don't, there's a chance the body will pull the shaft down with it when it falls, and then we have no weapon. Get it?" He looked into the sweaty teen's eyes.

"Oh, okay," Elliott said without missing a beat. Kenshiro frowned at him, wondering if maybe he was doing it on purpose, as some kind of joke, but the boy just stared back at him somewhat blankly. Kenshiro let it pass, it didn't matter anyway, instead he just stood up straight and waited for the undead man to get closer.

"Ok," he said once he felt his target had stumbled close enough. "Watch closely," Kenshiro said and stepped forward.

The undead man looked remarkably untouched. Kenshiro couldn't discern just by looking at it how the man had died. There were no obvious bite marks, no stains on its faded blue button-down work shirt or its jeans. As far as Kenshiro could tell the former man in front of him might have died of natural causes. *Wouldn't that be something*? Kenshiro thought briefly as it approached. *To survive the undead all this time, just to die of a heart attack or something.* He mused before ridding the thought from his mind to focus on the next few moments.

When it was within ten feet, Kenshiro readied himself. He used his back foot to launch himself forward. Kenshiro could feel the sole of his boot dig into the ground to propel himself. He felt the wind shift abruptly against his face as his momentum carried him forward. The undead man in front of him stood maybe half a foot taller than Kenshiro, and he could tell the zombie had a longer reach as well, but none of that mattered.

The zombie didn't have a chance. Kenshiro thrust the sharpened end of the shaft up into the fleshy part under its chin and drove the point up into the undead man's brainpan. The tip was kind of dull. It took some effort, but Kenshiro knew it hit home when the body of the zombie spasmed once, and that was his cue. Kenshiro pulled the shaft towards his hip, like he wanted Elliott to do, and the hefty zombie fell into a heap at Kenshiro's feet.

"See?" Kenshiro said looking back to Elliott. "Nothing to it."

-

The next day Elliott came down the stairs and declared he didn't want to go into town, he wanted to stay home and train. Kenshiro couldn't deny a request like that.

After breakfast, they started by going into the yard. The sun was still low in the eastern sky and the air still had a bit of coolness to it, which was good. They would be sweating soon. He took Elliott through his usual morning exercise routine. They talked idly at first while they stretched their bodies. Kenshiro winced slightly when they stretched to the side. His ribs were still sore from the skirmish with the brute of the zombie from a few days ago. Though he couldn't blame them, it's not like he'd been babying the injury at all. Pretending the pain didn't exist unfortunately didn't stop it from hurting. The pain was definitely better than it was. Kenshiro had a hard time sleeping that first night. Since then, he had been popping five hundred milligrams worth of Tylenol pills each day like they were candy to keep the pain at bay. He was looking forward to a time when he could take a full breath and not have to worry about a jolt coursing up his spine.

The next part wouldn't be fun. His ribs would not enjoy this one bit. He and Elliott set upon doing the core exercises. Doing each in twenty-five rep increments, they did sit-ups, push-ups, leg-lifts, and squats. In that order, until they ultimately did one hundred of each. Four circuits. On a good day, it might take Kenshiro fifteen minutes to work his way through it. This was not a good day. It took the two of them, he guessed, well over a half hour.

Elliott had recovered from his starvation. Kenshiro thought so, anyway. His cheeks had filled out, his skin looked better both in texture and palette, and to Kenshiro's knowledge he wasn't having any more dizzy spells. Elliott was weak, though.

They started with push-ups, and before he even got finished the first twenty-five increments, Elliott was struggling. Sit-ups weren't much better. He couldn't focus on Elliott too much because Kenshiro was struggling as well to complete them. His ribs violently protested each sit-up, but he grit his teeth, swallowed the pain, and pushed through because he felt he had to set a good example for the boy. The leg-lifts and the squats were easier, but they too revealed their own minor aches and pains. His back twinged a bit during the leg lifts, and during the squats, he felt a slight popping sensation in his right knee at a certain point in the bend. *I'm fucking falling apart*, Kenshiro thought to himself on more than one occasion.

Elliott struggled throughout, so much so, Kenshiro often stopped what he was doing to cheer Elliott into the next exercise. That, and he didn't want to get too far ahead of the struggling teen. On shaky arms, Elliott pushed himself up off the ground, each push-up threatened to be his last but never was. The sit-ups he audibly grunted on the back half of the twenty-five. Kenshiro, occasionally, had to remind the boy not to hold his breath when he struggled.

"Keep the air moving." He would say when the boy was red-faced with exertion. "Breathe."

When they first started, if someone was taking bets, Kenshiro would have cynically bet a considerable sum of money that Elliott would have given up on the whole thing. He would have walked away from it., either because of boredom or inability. During the routine, Kenshiro saw a lot of emotions take shape in the boy's face. Pain, frustration, sure, maybe even a little anger directed at Kenshiro. That was only natural. But also, when the body wanted to quit, he saw the thousand-mile stare of an indomitable will. The icy stare of someone who did not see quitting as an option. He'd be lying if he said he knew it was there all along, and seeing it now wasn't a guarantee of future performance, but it was a good start.

When it was done, they both rose from the final squat, and looked at each other with sweaty faces. Kenshiro smiled and nodded to Elliott that they had completed their task, which Elliott responded to by comedically flopping to the ground as if all the bones had suddenly been removed from his body.

"That was so hard." Elliott whined mockingly from the ground. "We do that every day?!"

"Yep," he lied. It was important, sure, but Kenshiro didn't do it primarily for the exercise anymore. The undead provided plenty of that.

Back when he was alone, it was a good way to pass the time, to work out the demons growing inside, and maybe it helped keep him sane. Gave him something to focus on. Lately, he found he didn't need it as much. He had Elliott now to keep him centered.

After a bit of a break, and a bottle of water each, they went back to the hay bale zombie for more practice. Elliott produced a pair of cloth work gloves with the telltale Mechanix logo on it. He never said where he got the gloves, and Kenshiro never asked, though he suspected they were his father's. They fit well enough, though obviously too large for the teen's hands. They would do for now. He had Elliott stand still in front of the target as he had yesterday. Kenshiro he stepped up and made minor adjustments to his stance. Elliott had a bad habit of leading with his shoulder.

"We want to bring the weapons forward, and keep the targets back." Kenshiro instructed as he gently repositioned the teen's stance so that Elliott squared his hips and shoulders to the target. "That's better. That looks good."

Elliott had remembered the over-under grip he had showed him last night. Elliott's back hand gripped the shaft with his palm up and the front hand, the one that guided the point to its target, gripped the shaft with the palm down. In Kenshiro's humble opinion, this was the best way to hold the weapon against a zombie. It had the best defensive options in case things went south on the way in. Elliott could easily raise the shaft up and put it between him and the zombie's snapping jaws. If it came to that, he would have a better chance of sweeping those arms to the side with this grip and then counter-attacking to the side of the jaw. He didn't tell Elliott any of that, though. That wasn't for right now. First, he had to perfect the thrust.

Elliott dug his back foot into the ground before he launched himself forward towards the target with a sort of gusto that would have made Emily proud. It was clear he wanted to do well.

He was doing… okay.

Kenshiro had taught enough martial arts classes in his time not to expect too much. He found many people were too new to the concepts of most martial arts and just basic fighting. Evolution built people to fight. The modern world had made them soft. Kenshiro believed that. He thought that before the undead came, and the undead incursion only confirmed it. Even he was unprepared for them when the time came. He had the skills, possibly, but he lacked the will to do what needed to be done. A lifetime of holding back, avoiding injuries, and following the rules had crippled him when it came time to act. Elliott wouldn't make those mistakes. After all, he wasn't teaching Elliott martial arts. Kenshiro was teaching him how to kill zombies.

"Not bad. You're still too far away, though, and you need to brace your front arm." Kenshiro calmly corrected and held his arms up in front of him as if he was holding an invisible weapon of his own. He darted forward and attacked the air in front of him to demonstrate. "You can't let that front arm collapse the second it meets resistance. We need to use your weight to push that point home." Kenshiro pointed to the newly sharpened tip of Elliott's weapon.

With the way he showed him to grip the shaft in his hands, Elliott had a good eight inches of steel poking out past his front fist, more than enough to enter the brainpan… at the right distance. That's what Elliott was learning right now more than anything else, his range. Kenshiro found in his experience that a person's range is something that is learned more often than taught. Each person is different. Different heights, different arm and leg lengths, all important variables in figuring out one's range. That sweet spot where proper form and structure can propel your weight into your strike with a slight rotation of the hips and shoulder. Like connecting a circuit to allow the electricity through.

"Again."

Elliott had two problems with his range, and it was the same two problems most beginners have. He was too far away, or too close to his target when he struck. When he was too far away, the point of the weapon might not pierce the brain, which wouldn't kill a zombie. If he was too close, he was basically colliding with the target. Elliott sacrificed all space between him and the zombie for one poorly aimed attack. If the point didn't strike home, he would be in trouble. Elliott would have no room to defend, and no time to do it before those teeth descended upon him. Unfortunately, the only real fix for that was time and repetition.

"Good. Again." Kenshiro smiled at Elliott when the teen finished his strike and looked back for his approval.

He was getting better.

"I think you're ready for the real thing," Kenshiro said reluctantly. Elliott *was* ready. His form had improved throughout the morning. There was still a lot for him to learn, but there was no better teacher than experience, unfortunately.

"What?" Elliott chirped, turning away from the target while lowering the weapon in his hands. Kenshiro knew by the look on his face that Elliott knew exactly what he had said, and it did not thrill him either. "Like a real, *live* grey person?" He asked tepidly. Kenshiro resisted the urge to correct him and continued.

"Why not? Your stance is better. You're hitting on target *and* solidly," he said, and it was the truth. A few times Elliott had hit the hay bale so hard he knocked the top bale completely off. "You're ready," Kenshiro said, trying to sound reassuring, but by the apprehensive look on Elliott's face, he was failing. "Trust me, we'll be safe. You'll be fine." Elliott still looked unconvinced. "I got a plan," Kenshiro said and then carefully explained it to Elliott to try to alleviate his concerns.

"That could work," Elliott said once he understood the plan, and he perked up a bit. He still looked nervous. Kenshiro couldn't blame him for that. He would be too.

Kenshiro left Elliott to sharpen his weapon on the tailgate of the truck while he searched for a zombie for the teenager to kill. Turns out it was a little harder than he expected. He walked the entire perimeter of the property. Kenshiro was about to give up on it entirely when he walked up to the dense shrubbery that made up the natural barrier on the west side. He walked along the line of bushes and looked out, where he could, over the western expanse. They were alone. *Never a zombie around when you need one*, he mused to himself when he decided to approach this from a different angle.

He and Elliott went into the house to make lunch, but not before he left his stereo-bucket trap by the hay bale zombie. Kenshiro placed it in full view of the kitchen window, and let Kenny Rogers play while they retreated into the house. Kenshiro made macaroni and cheese with a side plate of little strips of beef jerky and dehydrated apple slices. He also treated Elliott with a pitcher of lukewarm grape juice, which was slightly better than lukewarm water. They ate in a comfortable silence, both content to simply chew while lost in their own respective thoughts, like two old friends would.

After lunch, they cleaned up and washed the dishes. Kenshiro kept a watchful eye on the windows for any movement outside. After that, they retired to their own quiet place in the house to read. Elliott took the kitchen table, as was his habit, and spread out several comic books that he wanted to read. Usually, it was a mix of new comics he had found in town, and a few choice comics that were his favorites. He sat at the table with the pitcher of weak-tasting grape juice and a glass and quietly read through them while sipping on his juice.

Kenshiro had moved the big recliner over to the window that faced the front gate some time ago, this was his spot to read. It had a good amount of light for reading and a nice breeze that came from the open window that kept his perspiration to a minimum. More importantly, it gave him a good vantage point of the entrance onto the property, which was important to him as well.

Kenshiro finished a few chapters of his book before he heard Elliott quietly call out from the kitchen.

"We got one." He didn't yell. Elliott knew better than that, even though the sound of the stereo outside probably would mask any sound he could make inside the house. Regardless, Kenshiro was quietly pleased. It showed progress. He marked his book and set it aside for later. Then he looked out the window to the front gate as he fished the stereo's tiny remote out of his pocket and held it in his hand. He didn't see any further movement at the front. It mildly disappointed him he missed the zombie coming through the gate. Admittedly, Kenshiro had gotten into the book he was reading. He didn't linger on the regret, though.

Like someone had flipped a switch in his head, Kenshiro had a job to do now. He wiped all other thoughts from his mind.

"Just one?" Kenshiro quietly called back as he moved through the arch separating the living room from the kitchen and dining room. He saw Elliott leaning close to the window facing the stereo, presumably watching the zombie outside. He moved in beside the boy and followed the teen's gaze out into the yard.

"Yeah, I think so," Elliott said as they both watched the undead man clumsily circle the plastic trash can in front of the hay bale target to find the source of the sound.

This zombie was not one of the 'clean' ones by any stretch of the imagination. *This one had seen some hard times,* Kenshiro thought to himself as he gave the undead man a quick look over. This one had died at the hands of many zombies, that was clear, but apparently, it turned before they could finish the job. He was an absolute mess. What clothes it still had on showcased several bad tears that revealed more flesh than they covered. Blood-stained shreds of its shirt hung from its shoulders to reveal a large flap of flesh that had been torn free from its abdominal region. Little dark strands of whatever remained of its insides hung freely from the wound to its waist and swayed sickeningly with each awkward step it took. The lower half wasn't much better. Tears in the material revealed deep chunks of meat that had been ripped away from its thigh. Its head was untouched, except for the usual ravages the undead virus infected upon it, and the right ear. Which, by the looks of the wound, was missing.

"Go make sure," Kenshiro said to Elliott as he pressed the pause button on the tiny remote in his hands and immediately the leathery voice of Kenny Rogers coming from outside disappeared out of existence. "Quietly." He added as the boy moved off.

"I know," Elliott replied with a touch of annoyance in his voice as he disappeared into the hallway.

Kenshiro stayed at the window for a time to watch the ravaged zombie circle the trash can and scanned the surroundings for signs of any others that might be approaching. He didn't see any. Kenshiro moved to the front door of the house and checked the two lengths of rope he had prepared for this moment. One was about a twenty-foot-long version of the looped section of rope he used to move zombies around. In all reality, it was a lasso. The second piece, his piece, was just a long section of rope of indiscriminate length. He needed nothing fancy for his part.

"I don't see any others out there," Elliott said as he came softly bounding down the steps

"Okay, good." Kenshiro handed Elliott his rope. "You're clear on the plan?" Kenshiro asked the teen and regarded him until he replied.

"Yes," Elliott said confidently enough for Kenshiro to believe him. It wasn't a complicated plan, and versus a single zombie it should be fairly straightforward. Regardless, nameless worries nagged at Kenshiro and reminded him nothing involving the undead was straight forward.

"Alright," Kenshiro said while pulling his combat vest down from one of the large hooks mounted onto the wall. He zipped it up in one smooth motion and looked back to the boy, who had on a façade of cold seriousness, but his eyes betrayed him and showed his apprehension to the world. "We'll do it like we discussed. Stay out of sight, and stay quiet until the time comes, and if you see another zombie out there, run back to me immediately." He looked down into the boy's eyes. They looked like the eyes of an animal nervously on the lookout for a predator, which, given the circumstances, was appropriate.

"Okay," Elliott said simply while nodding solemnly once.

"Okay, let's do this." Kenshiro hoped to inspire confidence in the upbeat and relaxed way he said it.

Truth was, he was nervous too, Elliott would be dangerously close to one of the undead. If everything went according to the plan, he would be perfectly safe, but still. He was letting Elliott get in front of the danger, which was counter-intuitive to Kenshiro, like it was unnatural and cruel to be doing what he was doing in this manner. He made it his job to protect the boy, to keep him safe for Emily, but here he was preparing to throw the boy into the fire. *You ARE protecting him*, a stern voice reminded him as he reached for the door. *He's already in the fire, you're just teaching him how not to get burned by it.*

Kenshiro hoped that was true.

He opened the sturdy wood door, and then paused for a quick look outside before he slowly but steadily opened the screen door. He had oiled the noisy hinges some time ago, so now the flimsy metal door opened smoothly and silently. The pair cautiously stepped out into the world, keeping their eyes open for the enemies they might not have seen inside the house. Kenshiro could hear the wet sounding moans of the dead man around the corner by the hay bale and after a moment he became convinced that was the only one he heard. He looked back and nodded to Elliott, who nodded back before promptly moving off the front step and disappearing around the other corner of the house. Kenshiro waited until his friend was out of sight before moving forward along the opposite side of the house. His hand dropped the sheath on his leg and he silently pulled the long straight blade free and held it in his right hand while his left hand clutched his length of rope. Kenshiro moved up to the corner of the house and hugged the wall as he peered around the corner.

The ripped-up zombie was there, idly stumbling around the trash can stereo in loose, lazy circles to locate the source of the sound it heard just moments ago. Kenshiro took in a deep breath as he looked around his surroundings. He had a good vantage point from where he was and could see most of the property; he was also very aware of the spots he couldn't see. The only undead Kenshiro saw was still the one by the stereo, and surely by now Elliott would be in position, or close to it. It was time to move.

"HEY! DICKFACE!" He called out to the zombie, who was turned away from him. Once the sound of his voice covered the distance between them, the undead man instantly reacted.

It didn't turn and look in Kenshiro's direction, no, it simply pivoted its entire body towards him as if it was being violently pulled by strings. Like it already knew exactly where the sound was coming from before it even saw him. It was almost like an undead version of echolocation, Kenshiro had seen it many times, and it still impressed him. Its eyes didn't even lock onto him before his arms came up with those clawed hands in front, the dried lips pulled back as the jaws snapped reflexively. It was in full attack mode.

Kenshiro slipped his knife back into its sheath as he moved away from the house and towards the approaching dead man. He moved swiftly to get ahead of the stumbling zombie in order to get him turned away from the house.

"Okay Elliott, he's not looking. Move!" Kenshiro called out to the boy as he kept his eyes on the horror show in front of him, it was frantically clawing at him from a safe distance as Kenshiro slowly retreated into pace with it.

Beyond the zombie, he could see Elliott move out from behind the far corner of the house with his looped rope in hand. He kept himself low as he gingerly moved in behind the dead man. Kenshiro looked the zombie in the eyes and braced himself for the next part.

"Keep looking at me, ugly," Kenshiro said to the zombie as he stared him down and slowed his retreat, letting the zombie get even closer to him. Dangling the meat a little more in front of its mouth to keep its focus forward. "NOW!" He called out when Elliott was in range.

Kenshiro violently slapped the zombie's dried, cracked hands straight down. Elliott didn't waste any time and followed Kenshiro's instructions to the letter. The moment he cried out, Elliott was in motion, and when the zombie's hands were forced down, Elliott was already putting the looped section of his rope over the zombie's head. Gravity took care of the rest. Elliott pulled his end of the rope when it sunk below the undead man's elbows. The slack loop tightened and constricted, immediately pinning the zombie's arms to its side.

"Pull it tight and tie it off!" Kenshiro shouted back to Elliott, and he immediately saw the rope constrict even more around it. The rope dug deeply into the dead flesh of its arm. Kenshiro saw tiny cracks rip open around the rope from the tension. It looked painful, but the undead man didn't even seem to notice. Its milky eyes remained locked onto Kenshiro as it weakly fought against its restraints and continued the bite the air between them.

"Okay, got it." He heard Elliott say and then saw the boy step out from behind the zombie they had just tied up.

"Ready?" Kenshiro eyed the boy carefully as he moved into position and gave him a nod. "Switch!" he said, and they moved in unison. Kenshiro darted suddenly off to the right, and Elliott moved into the zombie's view from the left.

"Hey! Hey! Look at me!" Elliott chirped loudly to draw the zombie's attention back from Kenshiro's retreat. It worked perfectly. The dead man turned to Elliott and snapped in his direction, while Kenshiro swiftly moved in behind it.

He took his length of rope in his hands, gave himself plenty of slack, and whipped out the portioned section and hooked it around the zombie's neck with ease. He gave himself more slack, almost five feet of it on both sides, and then with a flick of his right wrist, the rope shot out and snaked around its neck again. The dead man took a pained step forward towards Elliott, who moved in step with the zombie. However, one step is all Kenshiro allowed it. With the slack removed from the makeshift bridle, he owned the zombie. He clenched the rope and kept the zombie locked in place by its own stubbornness. The undead man didn't even register the rope around its neck, it just pushed forward against it to get to its meal. It didn't have a spare thought left to consider what was holding it back.

"Okay, I got it. We're good," Kenshiro said as he held onto the zombie's reins, holding it in place with its arms tied down by its sides. Elliott would never get a better chance.

"You got it?" Elliott asked from a safe distance in front of the zombie. He looked nervously at the bound zombie, like it could break free at any moment.

"Yes," Kenshiro said confidently from behind their undead prisoner.

"Are you sure?"

"Yes!" He said again with a bit of annoyance in his voice. "Now hurry and grab your lance." He barked while holding the reins at arm's length. He held all the cards on the zombie. It didn't have the strength, the leverage, nor the intellect to mount any sort of real resistance.

Elliott turned sharply and bolted toward the open tailgate of the truck, where his weapon was waiting for him. It forced Kenshiro to pivot as the bound zombie shifted slightly to follow Elliott. He moved with it because he didn't want to risk the undead man tripping on his own feet and then falling to the ground. Kenshiro watched Elliott put on his gloves before he retrieved his weapon from the back of the truck and walk back to stand in front of the zombie with the weapon readied in both hands. He took a few moments to double-check his stance and his body position relative to the zombie. Kenshiro groaned slightly as the boy took his time to make sure everything was prim and proper. Only then would he be ready to strike.

"Elliott?" Kenshiro finally said, and the boy fidgeted with his hand position on his weapon. Kenshiro didn't hide the annoyance in his voice. Instead, he used it to urge the boy on gently.

"I know." Elliott shot back with his own mild annoyance. "Hold on, I'm getting ready," he said as he was giving himself a quick once-over to make sure everything was to his liking. It tempted Kenshiro to let the zombie lurch forward a step to provoke the attack, but thought against it. It probably would have the opposite effect to what he was looking for. He would just lose the boy's trust and he'd probably scurry away from the undead man like a nervous mouse. Kenshiro held onto the reins, took a deep breath, and simply waited.

"Okay," Elliott said after a moment. "Here I come." He warned no one in particular as he lowered himself into his stance in preparation.

Given his vantage point from behind the mangled

zombie, Kenshiro couldn't see much of the boy's attack when it happened, but the effects were immediately apparent. Elliott shot forward toward the bound zombie with a certain blank expression on his face. Kenshiro couldn't see the impact, but he knew it happened by the sickening, wet cracking sound as the tip punched through the zombie's palette to get to the brainpan. The zombie seized up tight for a moment before all its remaining life drained from the body and it fell to the ground. Elliott yanked his weapon free the moment before the body fell and stepped away from it while it settled. Kenshiro let the reins drop with the body and he looked at the teen with pride and enthusiasm.

"Perfect." He proclaimed. Elliott grinned.

"Really?"

"Well, it's dead and you're still alive. That's about as good as it gets. Yeah. Well done," Kenshiro said and stepped forward with his fist. Elliott needed little encouragement and eagerly bumped it.

"Yes!" He said after and pumped his free hand. The excitement wore off pretty quick however, when Elliott peered down at the sharp end of his weapon and the black fluid that coated it. "Ew. Look." He presented the stained end to him with obvious disdain.

"Yeah, that'll happen, but you can just wipe it off with a rag. It's not a big deal," Kenshiro said and waved it off. "Help me with these ropes." Kenshiro bent down at the corpse's neck to retrieve his rope while Elliott untied the one at the back before he pulled it free from under the body. "Alright, let's clean this up, and we'll do it again"

-

Kenshiro was sleeping, or at least, he thought he had been. There was a dream that he almost remembered. He lost it in the darkness. All that remained was the lingering feeling of it. Like wisps of a perfume that still lingered in a room long vacated, it only left an impression, a vague fragment of... something. Something bad. Which wasn't unusual. So why wake up? Not that he was awake, not fully, anyway. He was getting there. Like an air bubble rising from the depths of the ocean, his consciousness was coming alive, and with it came awareness.

There was a sound from the outside world. It was quiet and sudden. Like air moving. His mind hardly even registered it as being something that happened. What are the chances it was something he should be concerned about? But then he heard another noise.

A noise his sleepy brain recognized.

It was a soft sounding groan, like the quiet death wail of a seagull. It was the sound of wood flexing. There was a spot on the floor about a foot from the entrance into the master bedroom, his bedroom, that was a little left of the center of the hallway. If you stepped on it just so, it would produce that exact sound. Kenshiro had been in this house long enough to categorize all the little sounds it made, and where. One final realization crashed through his sleepy mind like a lightning bolt, lighting everything up in a flash of adrenalin. He wasn't alone.

He awoke like someone had suddenly thrown him through a glass window and into consciousness. Kenshiro was more of a passenger, stuck holding on white knuckled, as the vehicle he was in suddenly quickened to break neck speeds. He was aware of everything that happened. Even if he had no active control over it, the lizard brain had bust in and taken over. It snarled into the driver's seat and said: *just sit back. Let me take care of this part.* Kenshiro bolted upright and had, in one quick motion, swung his leg over the edge of the mattress and planted it firmly on the ground, while his right hand dropped to the holster on his leg and his left hand shot out in front of him as if he expected to brace against something that might fall into him. His eyes shot open and in the darkened room he saw the impossible.

There, standing in the doorway, was a frame that was familiar to him. His heart instinctively ached for it. She stood about as high as he remembered, with the same long dark hair that hung down and tickled her shoulders, with the same round face and soft features. She wore the Capri length blue jeans she liked, the ones with the slight tear in the thigh, and the dark blue blouse that he bought her for her birthday. It was her. He knew it; he knew because of what he felt inside. The longing, the remorse, the guilt flooded inside him in an instant. *That's impossible*, he shouted inside his head, and yet, some part of him pleaded with the universe it was true.

The lizard brain had already pulled the pistol on his leg free; he felt the cold steel of the trigger press into his index finger ever so slightly. The lizard brain was about to raise the pistol to the target in front of him when something inside him screamed for it to stop. *No*! Another jolt ran through his body, freezing his motion, and shaking the illusion in front of him until it evaporated into the truth in the space of a blink.

"Ken?" Elliott's voice cut through the darkness. It shook him to his core. One second it had been *her* standing there like a vision, he would swear it, and the next it was the boy standing there in all his awkward teenage glory.

"Elliott?!" He called in the darkness as he shook the cobwebs from his mind. Kenshiro lowered the pistol to the mattress and removed his finger from the trigger. "How many times have I told you not to sneak up on me like that?" He asked, hoping the boy didn't have the exact figure in his mind.

"I was going to knock," he said sheepishly. Only then did Kenshiro notice his one fist raised and poised to knock on the door. He was telling the truth. Small comfort now to his frazzled nerves. "I had a bad dream," Elliott stated simply.

"Oh yeah," Kenshiro said while holstering the pistol before raising his arms in a big morning stretch. "What about?" The moment had passed.

There was no danger, so he switched gears. He casually looked to the window and saw the dim light of the beginning of morning, well before the sun had actually risen. The eastern sky beyond the window was a pale blue color still. *Fuck, it's early yet*, Kenshiro thought as he rubbed his face. He was awake now, though. He had a strong feeling there would be no going back to sleep for him.

"Elliott, what is it? What was the dream about?" He asked again blandly as he watched the boy's darkened silhouette in the doorway.

"I don't want to live here anymore, and I'm kinda hungry," Elliott said in his own bland tone. *Wait?*! Kenshiro thought, suddenly confused. *What did he say*? He knew what Elliott said. Kenshiro wasn't *that* tired. He asked anyway.

"What? What did you say?" He pricked up his ears for the response this time. It fully piqued his interest.

Since he first met the boy, he has been trying to convince him to leave this place. He had developed a subtle process in which to approach the problem. It should have been easy. A type of decision that required little discussion because it was so obvious. No matter how safe they made it, the food would still run out. The simple fact is they had to leave eventually. Cause and effect. Simple. Not so much, however, when you have deep emotional attachments to the place you lived like Elliott did. '*This is my home*', he would say, as if that alone was an answer. He had been adamant and unmovable. Kenshiro then came at the problem a different way, and since then has been dropping brief hints of places they could see, embellishing almost to the point of lying about how grand a spectacle they were. According to the things Kenshiro had said, the Grand Canyon is the biggest crack in the earth's surface, which Elliott knew wasn't true, so Kenshiro covered the lie by simply saying it feels like it when you're standing in front of it. He might have also mentioned the Mississippi river is so wide you couldn't see across it and that, somewhere in Kansas, was a ball of yarn the size of a house. Elliott really liked that one.

"I said I don't want to live here anymore, and I'm hungry. That's what I wanted to tell you," Elliott said with a casualness that concerned Kenshiro somewhat. He could have been talking about the weather with the blasé tone he had when he informed Kenshiro he was finally willing to leave the only home Elliott had ever known. It made him question the boy's actual intention.

Why now? He wondered as he stared at the boy's darkened figure in the doorway. Could this sudden change of heart really be just because of a dream? Does it matter? This is what Kenshiro wanted, after all. Why should he question it?

"Can you make breakfast?"

"If we leave, we're not coming back, not for a long time." He warned Elliott gently as he rubbed his hands down his face once before he reached for his shirt from its spot on the floor.

He wanted the words to sink in for a moment. While trying to seem nonchalant as he put on his shirt, Elliott had to be sure. He did not lose the irony of the situation. Now, he was pushing back against the very thing he wanted. Their roles had completely reversed. Kenshiro didn't mind, though. He could handle a little irony, if it meant Elliott understood what he was agreeing to. This wasn't a vacation, or a brief trip to the neighboring state. This was an agreement to leave the comfort and relative safety of this place behind. Possibly forever.

"I know," Elliott said with a yawn that left Kenshiro utterly unconvinced that Elliott understood the gravitas of what he was saying. Kenshiro gave Elliott a moment in case there was anything he wanted to add to what he had said, which of course he didn't, before Kenshiro spoke.

"Okay," he said simply as he rose from the bed, stretched once more, before he turned back to Elliott. "Go brush your teeth, and I'll make breakfast." He knew they would talk about the other issue soon enough, he would make sure of it, and they would probably have many more conversations about their departure before the day was over.

First things first.

Chapter 5

Elle

Martin deserved an Oscar for the casual way he mentioned the market in her old neighborhood. He waited until after Derek had suggested a grocery store located in the Bronx. Just raised his hand up and called out the address. The whole time Mason was searching the large map at the front of the conference room for the spot, Elle's heart was racing. She let out a small sigh as Mason circled the location on the map and the conversation moved on. The last stop would be a market in the Lower East Side of Manhattan.

After that, the meeting was over. Everyone had an hour to prepare before they would depart. Elle and Martin spent that time going over the plan once again while they did the pre-flight inspection.

The flight to the Bronx took no time at all. Martin expertly followed the natural landmarks to the market in Soundview. The first location was to the north of a wide greenspace, which Elle could see the remnants of various recreational fields. Beyond that, circling the market on the south, was a collection of massive apartment buildings and expansive parking lots.

The undead spotted the landscape below everywhere she looked.

Martin dropped Maggie out of the sky like it was a rock. Elle gripped her thigh as her stomach leapt into her throat. While in the back, she heard Dennis yelp excitedly over the intercom. Martin madly slowed the descent a moment before the landing skids slapped down onto the pavement. The next instant someone in the back opened the compartment door and the soldiers all quickly filed out. The sounds of gunshots filled the air shortly after. Elle stepped out and saw the firing line around the craft drop their targets. The expansive parking lot ahead of her was filled with corpses of all kinds and shapes, new and old. *They've been here before,* Elle thought as she looked out over the littered parking lot. As soon as the shooting started, it died away, and the soldiers quickly moved into the grocery store as they reloaded their weapons. The immediate area had been cleared. In the distance, and all sides, the dead lazily approached them with out-stretched arms.

The clock was ticking.

Martin moved into position with his rifle and picked off the targets he felt were getting too close. They didn't want Elle to have a rifle. She had a pistol, and instructions only to use it if necessary. She had a different job. Elle moved around to the other side, the side of Maggie that faced the entrance to the grocery store. Once there, she went to the storage compartment door and threw it open. Shortly after, Derek exploded out of the store pushing a mostly full grocery cart at a dangerous speed.

"Make it quick," He barked as he shoved the cart towards her.

Elle dug into the cart with both hands and started tossing cans of all kinds into the compartment without even looking at what she was grabbing. She had to move. She didn't have time to peruse the contents of the cart. As soon as she was done, Nathan came with his cart and swapped it out with the freshly emptied one. Again, Elle frantically dug into the cart and madly shovelled its contents into the helicopter.

Elle focused on the cart. She stood in the swirling

downdraft of the main rotor, heard the sounds of gunfire all around, and felt her own anxieties claw away at her insides. *Keep it together!* She thought madly to herself as she worked and tried not to notice the smell of cordite and rot that filled her nostrils.

Dennis's cart was filled with large bags of oats and rice that he thankfully lifted out of the cart himself and placed into the storage compartment. Dennis winked at her as he pushed his cart back into the store. Mason exited the store with his soldiers flanking him with their rifles raised. Mason angrily shoved the cart towards her as he followed his men back around the craft. Soon after, the shooting started in earnest again. Elle did her job and pushed the empty cart well away from Maggie before she closed the compartment door just as Martin was coming around the nose of the helicopter. Nothing needed to be said.

It was time to go.

Elle hustled towards her door, and saw the approaching wave of undead and couldn't help but be reminded of La Guardia. She threw open her door and climbed in a moment before Martin and the soldiers retreated back to Maggie. Like a choreographed dance the men filed into the craft and moments later Elle let out the breath she was holding as Maggie shot into the sky. Below them, Elle could see the hundreds of gnarled faces raise their collective gaze into the sky, tracking their meal as it escaped their grasp. The higher the craft climbed the more undead she saw until Elle was certain the entire population of Soundview was descending upon the little shopping center.

One down.

Five minutes later her eyes caught a motion to her left. She looked over to see Martin using the last two fingers of the hand on the cyclic control to tap it twice. *Channel two.* Elle quickly, and as subtly as she could muster, reached down and switched her intercom channel to two.

"You ready for this?" Martin's voice came over the intercom as soon as she switched it over.

"Yup," she lied. She didn't know if she was ready, so she settled on what he wanted to hear. It would have to do.

"Just get in and get out. Don't be afraid to walk away if things don't work out. We can try again later," He paused slightly before adding calmly, "No mistakes."

"No mistakes." Elle repeated back to him before they took turns switching their intercom channels back to the main channel. It felt good to say it, like just saying it enough times would make it come true. Just to be safe, Elle said it a few more times in her head as the helicopter cruised over the rooftops of Jackson heights. *No mistakes, no mistakes, no mistakes.* Elle looked to her left, and she saw the immense green of St. Michael's Cemetery stand out against the greys of the city. They were close to their target. As if on cue, she felt the sickening feeling in her gut as the craft started its descent towards the street level.

Martin slowed the craft, banked wide and turned Maggie in a lazy half-circle while quickly lowering them towards the landing zone Martin had picked out on in the parking lot. Thankfully, the parking lot was utterly devoid of cars, except for a trio of compact sedans that were parked in the far corners. The downside being, there weren't as many obstacles between the encroaching undead and the helicopter. There were zombies wondering on the parking lot. They must have heard them coming from miles away, Elle could see them down on the asphalt with their heads craned upwards and arms stretched out to the sky as if they were praising God. Martin landed the craft as close as he could in front of the large Walgreens store with the nose pointing towards the north-west corner of the parking lot.

"Fucking-A! Nobody said there was a Walgreens here too." Dennis' excited voice burst out over the channel.

"We'll go after. The food's first." Mason's gruff voice cut in suddenly. "Two carts. Then if we're still good, we'll hit the pharmacy." It wasn't a question, it wasn't a suggestion, it was a command.

"Oorah!" Nathan said in response. Elle heard the sound before, mostly in the movies, but she didn't really know what it signified. To her, it was just another way a soldier agrees with something, but she didn't know for sure.

The skids of the helicopter touched down hard onto the asphalt of the parking lot, shaking the occupants and blowing dust and debris all around the landing area outside. As a minor dust storm kicked up around them, the landing area was partially obscured. As before, as soon as the helicopter settled onto the ground, the soldiers in the back opened the doors wide and exited with their rifles ready. Elle breathed in as she removed her headset while the sounds of rapid gunshots rose up all around her.

She exited the cockpit into the fierce downdraft of the main rotor, and Elle kept her head low as she moved around to the other side of the craft. The men had already formed a loose perimeter around the helicopter. She reached down and grabbed the cold steel of the pistol as she pulled it free from the holster, and felt the grim weight in her hands as she moved in between Martin and Nathan in the line.

Ahead of them, across the long and wide parking lot, was maybe two dozen dirty and twisted figures lumbering slowly towards them. Every few seconds, she would see one jerk suddenly away from them and slump to the ground like a puppet who had its strings cut.

Just shoot the gun. A voice inside her spoke up as she looked over the rapidly diminishing crowd in front of her. She picked out one zombie, a long-haired man in dark pants that had a tear down one leg, and a Led Zeppelin t-shirt that was horribly stained. The oily strands of its hair partially obscured the front of its dark and twisted face. She raised the pistol up and carefully looked down at the sights at her target. Elle's hands were shaking, which made aiming the small pistol down range seem nearly impossible. *Just shoot.* She breathed out and gently squeezed her index finger on the trigger.

Bam!

The pistol kicked wildly in her hands, and although she knew it would happen and expected it, Elle still flinched away from the shot. Momentarily taking her eyes off her target, maybe for less than a second, it still felt like a failure. She had to do better. She looked at her target, the shambling mess in the worn-out rock-and-roll t-shirt, upright and moving towards her group.

Towards her.

Elle breathed out forcefully and tightened her grip on the pistol to steady the sights on her target. She breathed out and fired again.

Bam!

She watched with a bit of satisfaction as her target suddenly fell backward as if some invisible force had struck it. It didn't last, though. As soon as it landed on its back, she could see it struggle to rise up. Out of the corner of her eye, Elle saw the barrel of Nathan's rifle shift slightly towards her. He fired, and Led Zeppelin zombie struggling to rise suddenly had a significant piece of its skull obliterated. The zombie felt back to the asphalt and Elle witnessed as what was left of its head bounced off the pavement.

"Nice shot!" She heard Nathan shout at her after he had killed her target. Even though he was only a few feet away and yelling, she could barely hear him. "Save your bullets, though. Wait until they're closer." He continued in a clipped tone as he tried to speak over the sounds of the helicopter and the gunfire. That was the signal she had been waiting for. Someone had seen her shoot her weapon. Elle accomplished that part of the plan. Now she just had to wait for the soldiers to clear the parking lot and move into the store.

Elle lowered her weapon. There was no longer a point in firing it, she wouldn't hit anything at this range, anyway. She took what felt like a fleeting moment to survey her surroundings. It was strange to see how familiar everything was, and yet, so absolutely foreign to her eyes. Elle had been to this shopping center with her mother more times than she could remember. Her parents' building was only a few blocks away on eightieth street.

On Sunday afternoons, rain or shine, her mother would walk to the Food Universe grocery store and buy groceries for the week, and she would stop in at the Garden Shop to talk to her friend who worked there, Barb. Frequently Elle would accompany her on these trips. More often than not, Elle would complain about it, especially in the summer, when her friends would sunbathe in the back of Becky's house and talk about the boys at school. That was what was important back then, not walking down thirty-first avenue with an armful of bags weighing her down listening to her mother talk about things that didn't interest her, all while dodging questions about herself. Elle was just another stupid teenager. Maybe all teenagers were stupid, because now her breath caught in her throat when she thought about what she would sacrifice to have those lazy Sunday walks back again.

The Jackson Heights Shopping Center had definitely

seen better days. All this time, its dozen neglected storefronts had been collecting trash and dust for almost two years now. During that time, nature and all its elements had been doing its work. All the store windows looked grimy, so much so it was hard to see inside through the film on the windows. A multitude of the windows featured nasty cracks and there were even a few that were shattered completely.

One window in the Weller Killam Realty office looked liked it had simply fallen to the asphalt. Like whatever was holding the pane in had finally let go, and the whole sheet just slipped from the frame and crashed onto the sidewalk. Elle could see the window's debris, even at this distance, and it kind of looked like tiny gems on the pavement. There was garbage and debris everywhere, blown in from all around Jackson Heights. She could see several places in the distance where leaves, paper, and other such light materials had collected into neat little piles. The wind from the main rotors lifted all the debris around them and forced everything violently out to the side. Even now, she could look out over the vastness of the empty parking lot and see plastic bags and random pieces of trash settle into their new resting places on the asphalt. She wondered how much of this dust she would wash off herself later on. Right now, Elle felt as if every inch of her body had a thin film of filth on it. She tried not to think what might be mixed in with that dust and focus on what was ahead of her.

She risked a glance at the Garden Shop, but quickly looked away. She was fearful just looking at the store might jeopardize the plan in someway, like a simple glance was enough to raise Major Mason's suspicions. It was silly to think just looking it would give everything away, but none-the-less she didn't let her gaze linger too long. The store's front was less than twenty feet away, practically a stone's throw. She wondered if Martin had purposefully landed

Maggie closer to the store for her benefit. Two things stood out immediately.

First, the 'Y' in the raised letter logo of the store had fallen down and Elle could see it lying on the sidewalk in front of the store. The second thing she noticed, to her disappointment, was that the security gate was down and secured. She didn't know for a fact if they secured it, but why wouldn't it be? What would be the point of lowering the gate just to leave it unlocked? It was a setback, for sure, but Martin had a pretty simple solution to the problem.

"Just shoot the lock."

He explained the best place was directly in front of the keyhole, which was maybe one or two inches off the ground. She had to get close enough she couldn't miss, crouch down, and fire while using her free hand to shield her face and eyes. Elle would probably have to shoot it more than once in order to free it up. The way Martin explained it seemed easy, nothing to it but to do it, but to Elle it didn't seem like such a simple process. It seemed dangerous and fraught with complications that she wasn't so sure she could overcome.

You're in it now. There's no turning back.

Elle's heart pounded away in her chest, trying desperately to keep up with the anxieties in her mind. She reminded herself to breathe and ran through the layout of the store as she remembered it. Downrange, she saw that the immediate threat of the undead were falling away. Any second now, she expected the soldiers to turn and make their way around the nose of the helicopter to the grocery store. That would be her cue to step into action. Across the parking lot, she could see the undead seep onto the scene from up seventy-seventh street, and from around the corner of the shopping plaza where it backed onto thirty-first avenue. Everywhere she looked out past the parking lot, it had undead slowly working their way towards them. Those sad-looking hunched over figures represented the ticking clock they were fighting against to succeed.

Elle saw motion to her left. A moment later, she heard Martin's voice through the noise of the engine.

"Magazine!" He shouted. Elle had turned just in time to see Nathan shift back while letting his rifle fall to his side, his hand still firmly gripping it with his finger off the trigger. Nathan reached into one pouch on his vest and pulled out a magazine. For a second it looked like he was about to hand it to her, but then from behind her Martin stepped forward and grabbed the offered magazine from Nathan. Once it was out of his hands, Nathan turned back and raised up his rifle to his shoulder to take a few shots at an approaching zombie in a blue dress. His target's head violently jerked to the side before it slumped to the ground. When Nathan finished, he trotted out of sight and followed the others around the body of the helicopter. The clock was ticking.

Five minutes.

Elle turned back to Martin just to see that he, too, was watching Nathan leave with great interest. When it was clear they were alone, Martin brought the rifle to bear on the Garden Shop entrance with the barrel aimed low. He fired three quick, well-aimed shots.

Tat-tat-tat.

She watched Martin fire the first shot, mostly because it caught her off guard, but after that she turned and looked towards what he was aiming at. Elle looked at the tiny copper-looking circle in the center of the thick bar at the bottom of the gate. It was the obvious target, and from this distance, it was hard to see any actual damage being done. Even through the noise of the helicopter engine and the gunshot, she still heard the wisps of a metallic rattle as the bullet hit home. Elle watched as the impact shook the whole gate. She saw the second shot rip a large hole in the center of the lock's face but it was the third shot that made her heart jump. On the third shot, the entire gate bounced up from the impact. For a moment, she saw the gate rise a couple inches before its weight brought it back down again. The lock was free.

He did it!

"Nice work, old man!" She yelled in his ear as she patted him on the back. Elle then sprinted towards the store before he could respond.

The plan after they had taken care of the gate was for Elle to smash out the glass at the entrance by using the pistol on her leg like a hammer. With the safety on, of course. Martin made sure of that point. As she hurried towards the shop, however, she suddenly got a better idea that might save her some time. After all, it seemed silly to use a gun like a hammer, when you could just use a gun like a gun. Elle slowed her paced to a careful walk a mere ten feet from the door, reached down and pulled the large pistol free from its holster. She fired three semi-aimed shots at the door. At this range, she couldn't possibly miss a target as large as an actual door.

Bam-bam-bam!

The first shot punctured the glass, and in an instant the glass went from a solid pane to a collection of a thousand dime-sized fragments, that made the door look more like a shiny mosaic wall. The next two shots just punched out finger-sized sections of the mosaic and passed into the interior of the store. Satisfied it had done its job, Elle quickly put the pistol back into its holster. She hoped she wouldn't need it again. Elle reached down and grabbed the gate by the handle on the bar along the bottom, braced herself because she couldn't afford half-measures, and yanked the gate up with all her might.

It rose freely.

Though not easily. The gate was heavy, well, heavy for her anyway. Thankfully, it was spring-loaded. So, the higher she lifted the gate, the lighter it became. Initially it was a heavy weight to lift, until the gate was at waist height, and after that it rose freely of its own accord. The last obstacle, the front entrance door with its shattered glass that inexplicably stayed in place, was the only thing between her and the seeds. *Fuck it*. Elle's adrenalin-fueled mind thought the moment before she grunted as she kicked the door savagely at the metal plate customers used to pull the door open. It rattled in its frame, held in the place by the large metal deadbolt, but she wasn't trying to kick the door open. The broken glass of the pane fell inwards into the store like a cascade of diamonds and spread out across the entranceway. Elle quickly ducked under the push-pull bar and entered the shop, being careful not to lose her footing on the loose glass, and ran into the store.

An imaginary clock was ticking down inside her head as she bolted down the long center aisle of the tiny store. She ran past the display of pre-made flower and vegetable baskets that had long since died and rotted away to nothing. All that remained was a pencil-thin stump sticking out of the soil and the sticky-sweet scent of decay. She ran past the racks of various long handled garden tools that hung from the wall and past the shelves that held their smaller hand-held cousins. Rakes, shovels, and little hoes. She ran past a display of neatly stacked bags of soil. At least half a dozen little piles littered a tiny section of the store on the left-hand side. Everything they would need to make a fully functioning greenhouse that might be capable of producing enough food for everyone was right here.

A part of Elle cursed her situation as she moved past all those things they gravely needed. She cursed Mason and his stubbornness. She cursed all of them. Elle blamed all of them for making her and her friends go to such extremes to prove their idea was a viable one. *First things first*, she told herself as she moved past the bags of soil. They would show them it could be done. Make them see the value of the project and the promise it could hold for all of them. Maybe this could be how she sees them safely past the undead epidemic. Maybe.

All other thoughts evaporated as Elle came to the back of the store. She stood in front of the six-foot-high wooden display cases that lined the three walls at the back. The expansive display had a dozen tiny shelves on each wall and housed every seed you could imagine, all neatly arranged in alphabetical order. It looked like a massive bookcase, in a way. Elle knew they dedicated the left wall to various flowers and different houseplants, so she paid no attention to it. The other shelves held what she was looking for: the food.

"Holy shit!" Elle exclaimed breathlessly as she stood in front of the wall of seeds.

Emilio made her memorize a list of seeds he wanted her to get. She didn't know exactly what he based his selections on, but he made her repeat the list back to him until he was confident she had it. Beans, broccoli, cauliflower, carrots, spinach, kale, onions, bell peppers, and tomatoes. She had said the list in her head many times over the last twenty-four hours.

In one smooth motion, she unzipped her jacket and pulled out the stylish leather handbag she had strapped across her shoulder underneath. She started at the top of the list in her head, scanned the shelves of seed packets until Elle came across the ones she was looking for. The fact it was all in alphabetical order made finding the seeds she wanted very easy. Elle wasn't picky when she came across the different varieties of beans that the shop had for sale. Elle just simply ran her hand along the entire shelf the beans were on and scooped up as many packets as she could into her hand. Dozens maybe.

Some packets fell to the floor as she frantically stuffed the them into the purse. Elle paid no attention to them as she moved on to the broccoli packets, and scooped them up in the same fashion. The clock in her head was loudly ticking away. Elle madly crammed seed packets into the leather purse as fast as she could before moving on to the next item on the list. She forced herself to try to move faster as she hopped to different sections of the shelves, quickly scanning for the items she needed before swiping her hand across the shelves to collect the packets in her hand. Elle would then stuff them away into her purse as she moved on to the next section.

Elle kept her eyes on the shelves as she moved to the right-hand wall, *Tomatoes*, a nervous voice barked out in her head as her eyes scanned the section she thought she would find them. Once found, she darted forward, grabbed a handful of the seed pouches and stuffed them into the leather handbag. When Elle had completed the list in her head, she moved the handbag back to her side so she could zip up her jacket again.

The handbag was out of sight, but she could feel its bulk slightly sticking out on her side. She hoped no one would notice. It wasn't her biggest concern. Right now, her focus was getting back to the helicopter as quickly as possible, before her absence was noticed. With the leather handbag stowed away again, Elle turned and bolted for the door like the building she was in was on fire.

She approached the door too fast. Her nerves got the best of her as she ran through the dimly lit store towards the light of the open door. As Elle skidded to a stop in front of the door, her feet flew out from under her on the broken glass. She felt herself go down even as her momentum still carried her towards the door. She reached out and her right arm grabbed a hold of the counter, but it wasn't enough. Elle landed hard on her butt. The shock of the impact rattled her slightly, but not enough to phase her. She reached down to push herself off the ground again and felt tiny pinpricks on her palm.

The glass! Her brain reminded her a moment too late. The damage was done, Elle lifted her hand to inspect the palm.

It wasn't too bad. There were just two tiny cuts in her hand. One right in the center of the palm, and another between the first and second knuckle of her middle finger. They looked like paper cuts and only oozed enough blood to highlight the injuries. Elle carefully wiped her palm on the dark material of her pant leg as she reached up with her other hand to pull herself off the glass covered floor. The wind blowing through the door cooled the sweat on her brow as she bent under the push-pull bar of the door and stepped into the light of the outside world.

Her eyes quickly adjusted to the full daylight, and the first thing she saw was that none of the soldiers had returned to the helicopter from the grocery store yet. *I made it*! *I still have time*! Elle scampered out from the doorway and towards the thumping helicopter. Martin stood by Maggie's side with his large menacing rifle up at his shoulder, every couple seconds it barked out a shot. Martin kept his eyes looking through the small scope mounted at the top as he shifted the barrel to carefully aim at another target before he fired again. He snapped his attention her way and Elle gave him the thumbs-up. Mission completed. As she hurried to the nose of the craft, Martin grinned and nodded once before he went back to his rifle's scope and continued firing downrange.

Elle risked a look back when she reached the smooth, rounded nose of the helicopter. Just a quick glance before she continued around to her post in the cargo compartment. She saw there was maybe a dozen zombies close enough to the helicopter to be a concern, and fifty feet behind them she saw more coming up the streets around the corner of the last store in the plaza. Elle didn't bother trying to count them, it was just a quick glance before she moved into her position and unlatched the cargo compartment door. When Elle swung the door open wide, a feeling of unease struck her.

She stood by the open cargo door nervously tapping her foot on the asphalt, waiting for the first soldier to appear through the store's entrance, feeling the unease in what she saw persist. It wasn't the number of the undead, though. It was definitely a concern, but she felt Martin could easily handle a loose mob of a dozen given he had enough bullets in his rifle. That wasn't it. She dissected the brief memory as best she could with the panicked, lightening charged mind she was currently working with. Elle was about to forget about the whole thing, just push the feeling down so she could focus on her task, then it hit her.

Were they moving faster? She asked herself, even though she already knew she didn't know the answer.

It was a hard thing to confirm because she only had the information from a brief glance to work with. It didn't seem like enough to be sure. Maybe she had been mistaken. Still, the uneasy feeling continued, like something had changed, something important.

Dennis's bulk coming through the doorway of the store

was the first thing she saw. Something that big was hard to miss. Her eyes locked onto the cart he was pushing a moment later. He dashed across the distance between the store and the helicopter in what seemed like a few long strides. Dennis nodded to her as he gave the cart a gentle shove towards her before he released the handle and reached down for his gun, clearly readying himself to head back into the store.

"Hey!" They both heard Martin's voice bark out from the front of the craft, despite the all-consuming noise of Maggie's engines. They both turned towards the noise and watch Martin hurry over. "Get Mason and the others. We're going to have to leave. Right. Fucking. Now."

"What?! Why?" Dennis frowned deeply, showing his confusion at the change in their situation.

"There's too many of them. They're coming too fast. We need to leave." Martin looked back over his shoulder nervously. It was clear he was anxious about being away from his post for too long. "Give me a magazine." Martin commanded, and held out his hand expectantly. Dennis nodded as he pulled one free from his vest and handed it over. "Go tell the others and then come back and help me." Martin stuffed the magazine Dennis gave him into the back pocket of his jeans before promptly turning back and running to the other side. Almost immediately after he was out of sight, gunshots started up again.

"Guess we better haul ass," Dennis shouted almost whimsically before he turned and ran back into the building, leaving her there somewhat dumbfounded.

We're in trouble! A voice inside her said, but instead of standing there pondering the implications of it, Elle dug into the cart with both hands with a renewed fervor. Elle snatched up the cans and tossed them sightlessly into the open cargo door. She forgot all about the garden shop and the seeds. The prospect of a viable greenhouse vanished from her mind like smoke in a stiff breeze. There were only the cans in front of her and the insurmountable feeling of doom that was growing in her gut.

Faster! That feeling said to her like it had an actual voice and, somehow, even in all the noise and chaos that was going on around her, it was whispering it clearly into her ear. *You have to move faster!*

It taunted her like a schoolyard bully, anxiously awaiting the failure of another. She breathed sharply through her clenched teeth and tried to ignore it. Elle wanted more than anything to just turn and run away from all of this, but there was nowhere to go. It was a familiar feeling to her, the feeling of being trapped and all the anxiety that the feeling brought with it, but she didn't give in. Elle tried to use it, like a secret reserve of energy, to help push her hands to move faster.

Moments later, she saw movement flashed out of the corner of her eye. Her heart jumped until she turned her head to see Nathan and Dennis burst through the grocery store doors with their rifles held low in both hands. The two soldiers moved with purpose as they rushed around the nose of the craft and disappeared on the other side. A heartbeat later, the sounds of their rifles added to the steady drumbeat rhythm of Martin's. She threw two more cans into the cargo compartment before Derek and Mason exited the store in the same manner, however they spun to the left and headed down the sidewalk of the plaza. *Where the fuck are they going?* She cursed inside her head at them for a breath and then returned to the cart to scoop up more cans in her hands.

Elle clawed furiously around the bottom of the cart basket for the last few cans. She tossed them into the open compartment door and then pushed the cart away from Maggie like she was angry at it. Which maybe she was, she didn't know. Her emotions were just a swirling mixture of anxieties, fears, and other bad feelings at this point. Elle was still in control; she knew that, but just barely. Elle turned back and closed the compartment door; she knew it was a mess in there. She had started packing the compartment with ambitions of being neat and somehow tidy, but that had devolved to simply throwing handfuls of cans and just praying that they didn't fall out somehow. With the door closed and the cart stowed away, Elle looked for what had to be done next. Where was she needed?

Her heart suddenly dropped at what she saw.

She parked the cart by the building roughly in line with Maggie's tail, so when she turned back, she could see out past the tail of the craft. She saw Martin, crouched in a firing stance, with the rifle tucked into his shoulder. He looked like he knew what he was doing. He looked through the scope of the rifle, utterly focused on what he was shooting at, which was the problem. Martin didn't notice the undead Mets fan trotting, *fucking* trotting alongside the sidewalk in front of the storefront towards him.

No!

It was the only thought her mind could coherently fashion as her body leapt into action. She didn't think about it; Elle didn't have to. She just acted. As her body sped up towards the subject of all her recent nightmares, it felt right. She knew the price of inaction was far greater than the risks presented in acting. Elle didn't fight it, quite the opposite. She couldn't move fast enough. Inside her head, she screamed for Martin to just pivot his gaze slightly to the right. Then he would see it and deal with the gracelessly jogging zombie in the Mets jersey, but he didn't. It would be up to her.

Seconds stretched out into separate lifetimes. Elle didn't wait for some voice inside her to tell her what she had to do. She couldn't wait for one of the others to notice the approaching zombie. She knew what had to be done. Elle had the means to act. She felt its weight in her hands. The cool smoothness of the trigger beneath her fingertip. She was a little unsure about her body's will to act, though. She knew what she wanted to do, but was unsure her body would do as she commanded.

Since La Guardia, she felt like she wasn't in total control of herself anymore, like outside forces she didn't understand were messing with her ability to control her own body, and sometimes her own thoughts. There was a lingering part of her that wondered if her body would actually respond, or would it just freeze up like an overworked computer that needed to be rebooted. Her doubts vanished though when her leg move forward, and then she raised the pistol up to eye level and cocked her head slightly to the side to take aim down the sights like Nathan taught her.

"Hey!" A desperate sort of scream leapt from her throat as the feeling of impending doom reached a boiling point inside of her.

Bam!

The bullet tore mercilessly through the cheek of the undead man. Elle witnessed the entire bone structure of the zombie's face shift and distort as the projectile did its cruel work before it burst out the back of its head in a spray of bone and gore. Elle felt something cold spray her left cheek. She flinched away from it instinctively, but still had a mind to watch the undead Mets fan fall to the pavement of the sidewalk.

I'M THE RIDER! This is MY fucking horse! Elle

yelled triumphantly inside her head, and a cool wave washed over her being as the fresh corpse settled. It felt good. It felt like a repudiation of all her fears while redeeming herself in her own eyes. She wanted to scream it until her throat hurt like a battle-hardened Valkyrie, but she had other matters to attend to.

Martin's eyes snapped to the loud gunshot as his body moved away from it in a sort of automatic reflex. She met the surprised look in his eyes with one of her own. The relief spread over his face when he recognized her. Elle noticed he was hit by the spray from the gunshot as well. His right side had a collection of blood droplets that were so dark, they looked more black than red. He looked like he wanted to say something, but movement to the side caught his attention. Martin turned his rifle towards it before he aimed and fired. After that, Martin's focus return solely to the undead running towards them. She saw an approaching undead teenage girl in short-shorts lose half her forehead to Martin's bullet before its body slumped to the ground. Elle tried not to pay attention to the fact the undead girl looked a little older than Kate, as the body settled on the ground as she, too, shifted her focus back to the space in front of her.

Martin and the others were doing an exceptional job keeping all the newly frantic undead mob at bay. As soon as one stepped into their kill range, they put it down as quickly as possible. Most times, it only took one bullet. Problem was, as soon as one zombie fell another trotted up behind it, and then another one, and another. By the looks on the soldier's faces, this was an unexpected problem they hadn't encountered before, and they looked worried.

"Magazine!" She heard Martin shout beside her before she heard him fire two more spaced out shots.

"I've only got one more." Nathan answered and even

though the noise of the helicopter's engines made his voice sound distant, Elle could still hear his desperation. Which quickly turned to frustration a moment later. "Where the fuck is Mason? We need to go." More gunfire punctuated the statement. There was a response. She heard it, but Elle lost the words in the chaos happening all around her. Besides that, she had her own problems, and it was jogging stiff-legged towards her.

Elle breathed in and gripped the pistol in her hands as she locked in on its approach. The undead man wore dark pants and a dark-colored t-shirt that bore the same stains from the elements as all the others, but was free of any tears or obvious stains. It was impossible to tell how old the body was when it had turned, because the disease twisted and dried out the face to such a degree it was hard to discern anything about it before it became an undead menace. Judging by his size and haircut, though, she would have guessed middle-aged. The zombie definitely had a dad look about him. A portion of his right cheek had been torn away at some point. Elle could clearly see its gross-looking back teeth through the wound. It was the zombie's only real distinguishing feature. It firmly locked its pale milky eyes on her and its mouth snapped at the air between them while its rotten hands formed into claws as it reached out uselessly for her. There was no place to go.

Bam! The pistol barked loudly in her hands, and the unremarkable zombie dad fell to the ground.

Two paces behind the zombie dad, was a woman in a faded and torn blue sundress, and behind her were two more quickly approaching Elle, not the group. Three sets of milky white dots were all locked on her. Elle took a bold step forward with the pistol raised. She put the sights squarely in the middle of the undead woman's snarling ugly face and pulled the trigger.

Bam!

The bullet struck home and the woman's complete face seem to collapse inwards in a sickening fashion before a black jet of gore exploded out the back of its head. Elle retreated a step while keeping a keen eye on the other two stumbling over the newly fallen body.

As Elle let them approach, she breathed deeply, watching them get closer. She looked down the sights of the gun as they stalked closer. She took a moment to ponder how many shots she had taken with the gun so far, but quickly abandoned the idea when she found it would take some effort to recall anything beyond a few seconds ago. The slide will lock in the back position when the pistol runs out of bullets, and it won't fire anymore. She worried about the idea of that happening at an inopportune moment. Like, right before a set of snapping jaws descended upon her. She pushed the thought from her mind, instead focused on the spare magazine in her left pocket and reminded herself where the slide release button was on the grip. Elle took a moment to visualize the reloading process in her head. She ran through the motions of it, tried to see herself doing it, and then she shot another zombie in the head.

Bam!

She imagined at one point the zombie, who had the top of his skull blow off like it was a baseball cap in the wind when the bullet struck his forehead, might have been a younger teenager at some point. Judging by the board shorts and tank top he wore, and his small proportions. Elle cringed away from the dark matter that was visible to the world after the bullet did its gruesome work. She was happy when the body fell from her view.

Behind it, the other one took a clumsy step forward, got its foot tangled in the bodies on the ground and tumbled gracelessly forward. Elle watched its forehead bounce off the pavement from the fall. She saw her chance and stepped forward with the gun in her hand and shot it in the back of its head.

Bam!

Elle heard shouting and saw a commotion in her peripheral vision; Elle feared the worse when she turned her head, but instead of seeing the firing line being overtaken by the undead. She saw the whole line slowly retreating towards the helicopter. Nathan shouted something at Martin and he immediately turned to her with a look of excitement.

"We're leaving. Go!" It was all he said. It was all Martin *had* to say. Her entire being was waiting for those words. Elle kept the pistol in her hands as she turned and ran as fast as she could to the co-pilot's door.

When she came around Maggie's nose, Elle saw Mason. He was on the sidewalk in front of the Food Universe firing upon a group approaching the tail rotor from seventy-seventh street. He too was slowly stepping towards the passenger compartment doors in between his shots. Elle reached for her door when she noticed the black sports bag Mason had strapped across his back and hung down by his hip. Medical Supplies.

Good.

Elle thought of Jackie as she holstered the crimson-stained pistol, and hopped into her seat and closed the door. She looked down at her red-stained palm. Her cuts had bled more than she suspected and she had smeared the blood over her entire palm. Elle thought nothing of it as she wiped her palm on the dark material of her pants and then touched the bulge under her jacket to reassure herself she had the seeds. That was still a success.

Assuming they survived the next few minutes.

Martin was the first to jump into his seat. Elle noticed he didn't have his rifle with him anymore, but before she could wonder where it had gone, the soldiers fell into the back of the helicopter in short order. Derek practically lunged into the passenger compartment at the same time as Mason entered on the other side. Mason closed and secured the door on his side while Derek fell awkwardly into the back seats before quickly correcting himself as the others entered behind him.

The sounds inside the cabin erupted in frantic shouts for Martin to take-off, punctuated by the odd gunshot as Nathan and Dennis fired out the compartment door from inside the helicopter. Martin shouted something inaudible back to the soldiers as Elle looked past him at the rapidly approaching herd. Her mind flashed to what had happened to Jackie and inside her head she screamed for someone in the back to just close the fucking door so they could leave this place. Martin didn't wait for the soldiers. Thankfully. Elle watched him ease back on the cyclic control. The engine revved up a tick and the craft rose gently into the air.

The shouts and gunfire inside the cabin died away as quickly as they had started. Someone in the back, she didn't know who, closed the passenger compartment door, and a warning buzzer that Elle wasn't even aware of died away inside the cabin. The excitement ebbed as Martin hovered Maggie over the rapidly expanding crowd of undead beneath them, and it became clear they were safe. Everyone in the cabin took a moment to breathe as they found their seats, and stowed their weapons before strapping themselves in and putting on their headsets. Herself included.

"What the fuck was that about?" Dennis's voice was the first to be heard over the intercom.

"Is everyone okay back there?" Martin asked a second later, and they all responded with a chorus of voices.

"Since when can those fucks run like that?" Derek complained. "Like, you saw what I saw, right? They were running. I haven't seen them do that since...," Derek's voice trailed off.

"The beginning." Nathan finished Derek's sentence for him. "I know. It was weird. What do you make of it?" She didn't know who Nathan was talking to. Elle kept her eyes forward as Martin banked Maggie to the west, but it was Mason who responded.

"I don't know," he said somewhat disinterested.

"Do you think it was just a pocket of fresh ones, or something?" Nathan spoke up quickly.

"I don't know"

"There are no more '*fresh ones*' out there, not in the city, anyway." Derek cut in abrasively.

"We're in the city." Dennis challenged him back with some amusement in his voice.

"Fuck off, you know what I mean. If there was anyone else in this city, we would know it by now. That was no goddamn 'pocket' of fresh deadheads." Derek shot back with a truth they had accepted a long time ago. They were alone in the city. "Those fucking things came at us like they were on crack or something." It was hard to get the image out of her mind. There was a definite change in their behavior, that much was clear to Elle, but she was no expert about the nature of the undead. Until now she had enjoyed the relative safety of The Prescott, but here she was taking her cues from the others. The soldiers were the ones with the actual experience, the ones who entered the fray and gunned down the menace. If anyone could comment on their behavior, it was them. Unfortunately, it seemed this was a fresh development for them as well, and they seemed spooked by it. "And I'll tell you another thing," Derek continued. "They weren't like that when we first landed."

"I noticed that too." Dennis chimed in. This time the humor was gone from his voice.

"Uh, Boss?" Nathan said, cutting into the conversation. He sounded nervous. "I'm kind of low on ammo. I'm on my last mag."

"Me too. Damn near blew my entire wad on that one," Dennis joked. It was at that point, trying to ignore Dennis's use of the word 'wad', when Elle casually looked at the displays in front of her. Her eyes locked on the one she recognized. It was the compass, clearly showing them travelling west.

They had three stops planned on the run. The next stop was in Brooklyn, which is to the south. So why was Martin heading due west? There was only one thing she could think of that was straight west of here. Before she could ponder the point further, Derek's next comment confirmed her suspicions.

"I think we should head home, boss. I don't think we can risk another stop with the rounds we have. We have enough food for the time being. What do you think?" Dead silence filled the cabin for a moment, and the only sounds that were heard were the engines overhead. She imagined all eyes in the back were on Mason while he contemplated their next course of action. Elle knew what she was hoping for.

"Agreed. We have everything we came for. Let's head home. Martin?" Mason called forward.

"Yep." Martin acknowledged the command. "Heading

home now," Martin said, but Elle noticed his hand on the controls were steady and the craft didn't waver from the course it already was on, it didn't need to.

They were already heading home. Elle believed Martin had probably done the battlefield math in his head while he was in the thick of it and simply decided on their next best course of action. *What if Mason still wanted to do the third run?* She wondered nervously for a moment, thinking of the potential fallout if Mason suspected Martin had decided the next course of action without him. But the soldiers in the back continued on with their conversation, completely unconcerned with what was happening in the cockpit.

"Thank God," Nathan said breathlessly.

"Yeah, after that one I could use a stiff drink. Like, what the fuck?" Dennis complained almost jovially, obviously pleased they were heading back to the Prescott.

"I'd still like to know why the sudden change in the deadheads' behavior. It might be important to know. Maybe we caused it somehow, I don't know, but we should keep an eye on it, just in case," Derek said, sharing his thoughts with the rest of the group.

"Yeah." Nathan readily agreed. "We don't want to run into that again, but if it happens, it could be a sign of things to come, and if that's the case, we could be in trouble. That could change everything." He finished on a dire note and Elle's mind snapped to the angry, stumbling run that the undead had managed. Something all of them didn't even think zombies were capable of anymore.

Since taking up residence in The Prescott, there has been one underlying hope everyone had latched onto. That they could somehow outlast the undead. No one person came up with the supporting idea, it happened over the course of the first few months of their confinement within The Prescott.

They watched the encroaching army of corpses that filled the streets below them and as people watched; they made observations. The residents talked to each other at great length about what they saw. They shared ideas and theories, and they formed a consensus that the zombies below them were still rotting even as they walked freely through the streets.

What happened with the stiff-legged running mob had challenged the accepted idea that zombies were rotting away to nothing. Elle could tell that news shook the soldiers. How much? She would never know. She doubted they would share that information openly.

"What changed?" Derek asked quietly over the intercom, almost like he was talking to himself.

"They shouldn't be able to do that, right?" Dennis said an instant later, paying no attention to Derek's question. "Like, how long has it been? Two years? They shouldn't be able to move like that anymore because the muscles and shit are too weak, right? "

"That's what I thought," Nathan replied.

"Will you bunch of pussies shut-the-fuck-up?" Mason growled over the intercom sternly. "This is the first time we've run across something like that. It might be an isolated incident, it might not, but there's fuck all we can do about it now. Next time we plan, just in case, we'll bring more ammo if need be but-,"

"We're getting low on those back home as well." Nathan cut in unexpectantly.

"Then we'll get more." Mason shot back abrasively. "Point is, we don't need to lose our shit over this. The only way we are going to win this race is one mile at a time. Lets worry about the mile we're on now before we panic over the next one." Elle didn't see it but she imagined the soldiers in the back were nodding their agreement. "We'll get back to the base, unload what we've got, and start planning for the next one. One run at a time, that's how we'll get through this. We're soldiers, after all. We don't panic, we plan." Mason finished with an amount of scorn in his voice, like he expected better of his crew. Like they had failed him in some small way.

After that, the intercom fell silent as everyone in the back took Mason's words to heart and settled into their seats for the rest of the ride. Elle looked out over the cityscape as they approached the east shore of Manhattan. Through the dull greys of the buildings in front of her, she could see the shiny green hues of Central Park and she knew it wouldn't be long before she could officially put this all behind her. She absently looked down at the reddish-brown stain of blood on the palm of her right hand, but as she scanned the area of the stain on her hand, something Derek said replayed inside her head. *What changed?* A thought popped into her head that changed how she looked at that innocent stain on her hand.

What if she caused the sudden change in the undead in the area? What if they sensed the fresh blood on her hand and it caused them to go crazy? It wasn't the craziest theory she had ever heard before. The timing was right. When she had gone into the store, whole and unbloodied, the zombies behaved in an expected, almost manageable way. However, it was shortly after she had exited the store with her hand freshly injured and bleeding that the zombies started acting up with a renewed sense of vigor.

It's not a lot of blood, she thought as she traced the outline of the stain on her palm with her other hand before immediately countering the point. *Maybe it doesn't have to be.* She heard somewhere, back when the world was whole, that sharks could smell blood in the water from miles away. *Miles*?! She reminded herself that zombies couldn't smell; they didn't even really breathe, but then a more horrifying thought came to her. *Maybe they didn't have to smell it*, maybe zombies could just sense it, like some supernatural ability.

Given the nature of their enemy, it didn't seem far-fetched to her at all that they could have some strange ability to sense blood like an apex predator. Quite the opposite, it seemed likely. She shrunk a bit in her seat as she considered the possibility and the ramifications of the tiny amount of blood smeared on the inside of her palm, causing the undead rampage. Her right hand rested on her thigh as she balled it up in a fist. Elle tried to look casual and unassuming, but something inside her promised her she would be discovered.

SHIT! Elle cursed inside her head as she frantically thought back to the shopping plaza and ran through the events after the injury occurred in the Garden Shop. Elle needed to remember if anybody had actually seen the blood. She was confident Martin hadn't seen it because he would have mentioned it immediately. His damned fatherly sensibility wouldn't allow him to ignore it, but what about the others? Only Nathan and Dennis had been close enough to her to see it, and they were too preoccupied with what they were doing to notice. At least, that's what she hoped.

She couldn't be sure. Elle wasn't even sure if the injury was, in fact, the cause of the zombie's sudden change in behavior. In the end, she didn't think it really mattered if it was or wasn't, because the truth of it was they had no way to know for sure. The problem then became, what would the men in the back believe? It wouldn't take much convincing, and if it came to it, if she was discovered, then the blame would be solely placed on her shoulders. She was pretty sure she knew who would lead the charge against her. Derek. She had sure made a volatile enemy in that asshole. Elle couldn't say exactly why he felt she was solely the reason the La Guardia mission ended with Jackie losing her arm, but he did, and it didn't look like he was going to let go of that feeling. She wouldn't give him more ammunition to use against her, not now, not when she was so close to the finish line.

Elle innocently brought her bloodied hand up to her mouth and did her best impression of a cough while spitting into the center of her hand. She felt the warm spittle splatter against her palm, and Elle lowered her hand with the same outward appearance of casualness and routine. With her hand resting once again on her thigh, Elle worked the spittle in her hand with her fingers until she with certain she had greased the entire area of the stain with the wetness. Then Elle pressed her palm hard into the material of her pants and wiped it down the length of her thigh. For good measure, she mirrored the motion with her other hand, so, by chance, if someone was looking in her direction, it would look like she was nervously massaging her thighs. Like she was trying to relieve some tension, which shouldn't be hard to believe, and given the situation, they would probably expect her to be a little tense. It wouldn't be a hard sell. She *was* tense.

Elle ground her palms into her pants once, twice, and then peered down as she slowly flipped it over so she could inspect her work. She struggled to breathe out her relief as she looked down at her mostly clean palm. Elle could see the angry red marks on her hand from the tiny cuts she incurred when she slipped on the glass, and there was still a scattered line of dried blood that ran across the top of her palm, but other than that it was clean. The little that remained looked more like dirt or rust than blood. She looked at the cuts for a moment while silently saying a prayer. After an intense moment of staring at her hand, she became convinced the bleeding was behind her. Elle settled back into the chair just as Maggie banked to the right. Below them she recognized The Prescott's rooftop.

"Home sweet home.," Dennis said fondly over the intercom.

"Yeah, good to be back." Nathan added as Martin brought them in on approach.

Elle's eyes immediately noticed the figures on the walkway below the helipad huddled close together, watching them approach. When her gaze locked on them, she instantly recognized their forms and suppressed the giddy sort of happiness at seeing her friends together. *They made it.* A calming voice reassured her. This was a good sign. At the very least, it meant they were safe and unharmed. Whether they moved the giant planters out of the lobby, that was a different question entirely, but their success wasn't more important than their safety. Seeing them there and feeling the weight of the full handbag against her side was all the success she needed to end the day on a high note.

We're almost home free.

They were so close to pulling off this silly little covert operation under Mason's radar, it just created another anxiety inside of her. Elle had watched enough Jets games with her stepdad to know that the promise of victory can sometimes open up the possibility for failure, and usually does if you started celebrating too soon. '*Something can always go wrong*,' her stepdad loved to say occasionally. In her mind, all she needed was for her sister and her friends to keep their mouths shut long enough for the soldiers to move into the building. Surely, they could manage that. Surely.

Maggie's skids touch down with what felt like buttery smoothness from inside the cabin of the helicopter. A sharp contrast to the abrupt landings she experienced throughout the day, but a welcome one. As soon as the craft settled onto the tarmac, Martin powered down the engine and the incredible noise above them died away. The soldiers in the back opened up the side doors and filed out of the cabin. Elle was eager to leave the helicopter. She looked over to the stairwell and saw Kate and the others sheepishly walk onto the helipad, and wait for her on the outskirts of the tarmac. Elle looked over to Martin, who was idly watching the digital displays in front of him as he calmly unbuckled himself and removed his headset to store behind the seat. She realized he was in no hurry to leave the cockpit.

"Did you get it?" He said immediately after the rear passenger doors were closed, leaving the two of them alone in their seats.

"Yeah," she said loud enough for him to hear over the decreasing sounds of the engine. Elle was going to continue but Martin cut in before she finished.

"Thank God," he said, visibly releasing some of the tension inside him. "I don't want to go through that again, whatever that was." He didn't need to say more. She knew what he was talking about and waited until he finished before she broke in.

"About that," she started apprehensively, "I think I caused that, the change, I mean."

"What? How could you-," Martin started to say, but Elle silenced him when she held up her injured hand. She could see he was confused by what she had said. Then his eyes locked onto the tiny pink cuts in her palm and the rust-looking stains of the remaining blood. At first, he was true to his character and showed concern, but shortly after that, she could see him put the pieces together inside his mind. "When did this happen?" He asked. He was all business, because he understood the implications of it.

"I fell on some glass inside the shop," she said as he

nodded thoughtfully, still inspecting her upheld palm.

"They're not huge. They look like paper cuts. Did it bleed much?"

"A bit. Not much, but maybe it doesn't have to be a lot. I don't know," she said, feeling defensive about it. She wanted Martin to dismiss the whole idea, to scoff at the possibility this was her fault, but by the look on his face, she knew he thought otherwise before he even spoke.

"Maybe," he said, pulling back from her palm. "Makes sense, I suppose. You were right to keep this under wraps. They don't need to know about this," Martin said, thumbing back to show Mason and the other soldiers. "God only knows how they'd react to it," he added bitterly.

"They *should* know about this, though. If it's true, if blood causes the undead to go bat shit crazy, they should know about it," Elle said, spelling out the difficult position she found herself in.

The part she left out, and the part she was pretty sure Martin understood, was that she didn't want them to know it was her that caused the emergency. She already had the failings of La Guardia pinned on her. Derek certainly wasn't shy about expressing his feelings. The others, she was sure, felt the same way, if to some lesser extent. They might not blame her for Jackie's bite, but they agreed she was indirectly responsible for it, which was bad enough in her eyes. She didn't want to think about what might happen if they found out about the blood because she'd rather spend her energy making sure they never found out about it.

However, they *had* to find out.

Information like this is important. She knew that, even if it was only a suspicion. Lives were on the line. She couldn't risk their lives and the lives of everyone in the

Prescott because she was afraid of the repercussions. Which she was, but not just for her own sake. If she learned anything from the incident in the stairwell, it was that Derek could make others pay for her mistakes. Maybe it was some long-forgotten scrap of chivalry in Derek's soul that wouldn't allow him to abuse a woman, not physically anyway, but Elle found terrorizing her friends even worse. She couldn't allow it to happen again. She struggled to think of a way to stop it if it did, so at the very least she could try to take away a reason for it.

"No argument here," Martin said. "It doesn't have to be you, though." She looked at him, confused. "Give it a couple days, and then I'll mention it to Dennis or Nathan over lunch or something. I'll make it seem like something I've been thinking about. Let them stew over it for a while. By the time it gets back to the others, they won't remember if they had a cut or not at the time. Hell, I'll even suggest maybe one of them cut themselves shaving that morning to sow some doubt. Don't worry about it. I'll make sure they know," he said and then looked through the windows at the back. "Let's go before they think we're up to something." Martin smiled broadly, probably because they were up to something, and they were so close to being done.

Elle opened her door, exited the cockpit and then she stepped down onto the strangely reassuring solidness of the helipad. Her heart fluttered for a moment as it overwhelmed her with a giddy feeling knowing she was back safely at The Prescott. So much so, she took in a sharp breath of air when she felt her foot touch down. It was good to be home, even if it was a strange home. A vertical concrete and glass island in an undead sea of icy hands and snapping teeth. Kate broke away from Blaine and Jacob the moment Elle fully stepped down from the helicopter and ran over to throw her tiny arms around Elle's waist.

"I was worried," Kate spoke in her jacket, and Elle struggled to hear her over the dying sounds of the helicopter's engine. "I know you told me not to, but I couldn't help it after what happened last time."

Even with the surrounding noise, Elle could hear the stress in Kate's voice. She hated putting her through it, but Elle understood the need. It was a sacrifice that she had made for the two of them, and given what Kate had been through and all she had lost, it seemed wholly unfair. Especially now.

Elle swallowed her guilt down and held onto her sister as her eyes locked on the movement of the soldiers. Mason had one hand holding his rifle by the pistol grip while the weight of it hung by the sling, his other hand secured the sports bag strapped across his shoulders close to his side, he kept his head down as he made a beeline for the stairway. Blaine and Jacob quickly sidestepped out of the large man's path and watched him go down the stairs. Dennis had another black sports bag and was unfurling it while Derek was opening the cargo compartment door. Nathan stood close by and tried to hide his shame by looking professional, and mostly it worked, but when his eyes met hers, there was a shared understanding of what was happening, she could see a hint of shame in his eyes.

"Come on," Elle bent down and spoke into her sister's ear. Elle led Kate back to where their friends were standing. She could see by the classic New York what-the-fuck expression on both Blaine's and Jacob's faces, that the soldiers had started to unload their share of the food they brought back. As she neared, they looked at her and their expressions brightened.

"Hey, how'd you guys make out?" She asked, confident Maggie's dying engines would mask her voice enough to avoid possible eavesdropping from the soldiers.

"Hey," Blaine said while watching the soldiers closely. "Good. We're golden. We got both pots loaded into the stairwell. "What? ah?" Blaine stammered slightly, not sure how he wanted to word his question. Jacob was less subtle.

"What the fuck is this all about? I highly doubt they're loading up that bag to take down to Emilio." Jacob, to his credit, kept his voice conversational, which kept his words from the soldiers, but he pointed abruptly toward the other men.

Elle casually looked over to see Dennis holding the sports bag while Derek reached into the cargo compartment with both hands and brought out a can of food in each hand. Which he casually tossed into the bag before reaching back in to the compartment to repeat the process. She saw the bag had some heft to it already, and she also saw Nathan watching her and her friends watching them. His face was neutral, but she still had a growing feeling of unease over the situation. Elle put on her best smile and gave Nathan a seemingly friendly wave.

"Yeah, maybe don't point like that," she said sharply as she turned back to Jacob and Blaine to get them to focus their attention on her. It worked, maybe a little too well. Blaine suddenly looked concerned while Jacob looked hurt that she would talk to him in that tone. She took a calming breath, and secretly hoped they were as well. "They're taking their cut." Elle tried to make it sound like it was the most natural thing in the world. Like she was explaining a sad fact to a child for the first time.

"Wha-?" Blaine began and was cut off by Jacob immediately.

"I fucking told you, didn't I?"

"That's not what's important right now, though," Elle

said calmly and yet sternly, to divert their outrage. "Look at me," she said sweetly to Jacob. "They've been doing it the whole time. It sucks, sure, but there's nothing we can do about it unless you're willing to head out there with them. I hear there's an opening," she said with a touch of sarcasm in her voice, which in her experience, New Yorkers responded to sometimes better than cold logic. She paused for a moment to watch Blaine and Jacob look at each other.

"Point taken," Blaine said reluctantly, and Jacob just looked sour.

"I got the seeds, you got the soil, we did it! We're done. Let's stick to that and not worry about things that have been going on that we didn't know about, *and* we have no control over. We've had enough excitement for one day." She softened her tone as she went and, by the end, she sounded like she was gently pleading with them.

To some extent, she was. She felt tired suddenly.

Elle wanted nothing more than to just get something to eat and sit in a quiet room for a bit. Elle understood their outrage. She felt it too when Martin first explained it to her, but there was nothing they could do about it and maybe on some level, she could even condone it. Elle had been on two missions so far and she felt like she had aged ten years. She didn't sleep well some nights, and that after *two* missions. Those guys have been doing it soon after Martin and Maggie first showed up, and that was a long time ago. She quickly found she could forgive the skimming; it was human nature after all.

"Yeah, you're right. It just pisses me off. They're no better than the rest of us," Jacob said with a frustrated expression on his face.

"Actually, I think her point is, that they are." Blaine looked at his friend, who shot him an incredulous look. "Not in the biblical sense, but they provide a crucial service that none of the rest of us can do. Hey, I'm just saying." Blaine finished with a shrug.

"You business-types are all the same," Jacob said it like it was an inside joke between the two of them. "But I get your point. Besides, it's not like I'm going to stop them, especially Dennis."

"Aw," Blaine whined suddenly and Elle turned to see what he was looking at. "They're taking a canned ham." She didn't see it. Elle saw Dennis zip up the sports bag and lift it over his shoulder while he and Derek joked about something she couldn't hear. It annoyed her to see them so goddamn jovial while they took their cut. Elle let out a puff of air and turned back to her friends.

"Ugh, you like canned ham?" Jacob asked, not even masking his disgust.

"At this point, I do," Blaine answered, turning back to the rest of them with a sad face.

"Don't worry," Elle said as the soldiers moved towards the stairwell. She didn't exactly see them move out, but just felt their presence as they neared. "Emilio will make something special for tonight. He always does on the first dinner after a run, and we can sit down and tell each other about the crazy shit that happened today."

"I like that plan," Blaine said.

"Me too." Kate chirped in cheerfully.

"After we unload the food and do the post-flight inspection, right?" Martin asked, unexpectedly close from behind her. Elle yelped and jumped away from the sudden noise.

"Jesus!" she shrieked and then turned and promptly slapped his chest, to which Martin just twisted away from the playful blow while slightly smiling. "What the fuck are you doing sneaking up on me like that?"

It was a genuine shock, but to her surprise as soon as it came, it went and after the moment had passed, the feelings of fear and anxiety went with it. She was clearheaded, focused, but not single-minded. At least, she thought she was. Elle was tired, that much she knew for sure, but she felt a strange, but welcome, sense of calm now that she was home. She hoped that meant progress.

"Did Derek or anyone ask for the pistol back?" Martin asked with sudden interest when he noticed the weapon was still holstered to her leg. She was a little surprised herself when she looked down and saw it there. Elle had forgotten all about it.

"Umm. No. Nobody said anything about. They just packed up their shit and left."

"I guess that means you get to keep it," Martin said with a smile, but she could tell he wasn't joking. "Stow it under your seat for now, and let's get this post-flight done," he said to her, and she just nodded. "And you guys? Are you helping with the unloading or what?" Elle smiled inwardly as Martin's sudden commanding nature took the boys by surprise. In all other things, Martin was a cool-headed team player, but with Maggie, he was in charge.

"Umm, yes?" Jacob answered cautiously.

"Aaanndd, you brought something to carry the food down with, or were you just going to haul it by the handful?" Martin stared at him without a trace of humor on his face. Elle had to admit she enjoyed watching Martin put Jacob on the spot like this. Jacob and Blaine seemed to squirm slightly, like they were suddenly uncomfortable in their own skin.

"He's just fucking with you," Elle said finally, letting them off the hook. They visibly relaxed while she and Martin smiled broadly at each other. "Emilio should be by soon with some boxes. You can unload the compartment onto the ground. I'll help until he does."

"Can I sit in the pilot's seat?" Kate asked, looking up at Martin with those big eyes.

"Sure. I'll even show you what all the buttons do."

"Hey!" Elle cried out in mock jealousy. "You never showed me what the buttons do."

"Yeah, but she doesn't cause me as much grief as you do. So-," with that said, Martin twisted back to Maggie, with Kate in tow behind him, and walked back to the cockpit.

God, it was good to be back.

Chapter 6

Elliott

When Elliott awoke the morning after burying his mother under the large tree they used to have picnics underneath, he found the world around him had suddenly changed, and without his permission. At least, that's what it felt like. He was still in the exact same house, still ate at the same table he always had. Everything in his little world was still in exactly the right spot, and yet... everything was different.

Now everything around him was haunted by these little ghosts, not actual ghosts, of course. Those weren't real. Elliott knew he was being haunted by his own memories. His cruel brain gave everything a faint little life all its own. If he looked at something, anything, for too long, his mind would dredge up a memory associated with it.

He was brushing his teeth that morning, as he liked to, when the first *ghost* struck. Elliott had looked down at the brush after he had rinsed it off, and was suddenly reminded of the memory of how he came into possession of that toothbrush.

It was when his mother took him to the dentist in Walsenburg, Doctor Melnor, for a routine cleaning and checkup. Elliott didn't enjoy getting his teeth cleaned, but he did like the bag of goodies his hygienist would give him afterwards, as well as the Macdonald's cheeseburger Momma would buy for each of them along with a small coke for the ride home. It was a stupid memory, not even one of the good ones, but it was enough to send Elliott back into his room weeping and frustrated.

The entire house was filled with those little ghosts. Worst part though, they were sneaky, always coming up on him when he didn't expect it. Elliott tried to keep them out of his head. He thought maybe there was a way he could build a wall around himself inside his mind. Maybe that would keep them out. He went through the motions of his day, did everything Ken told him to do with no complaints or even a comment, because the rest of him was actively trying to keep the ghosts of his past at a safe distance. They still seeped in, usually when his guard was down. He was heading down the stairs one morning and had to stop mid-way because another sweet memory of his mother caught him.

He just stood there on the step of the stairwell, looking down at the spot where they sat together a lifetime ago and let the memory play out in his head. What else could he do? It was a nice memory, but when it was over, Elliott felt a dark sort of emptiness inside him that he didn't like. He came to find that each little ghost left that feeling behind it when it went. After a single day, he felt drained and tired of fighting these ghosts in his house, so he told Ken he'd like to go to town. Elliott knew he would agree. Ken didn't enjoy staying in any one place for too long, however, the town wasn't much better. It had its own share of ghosts. The strongest ones were of his parents, of course, but there were plenty of others he found. They left behind their taint, their blackness. It seemed to fill up Elliott's insides.

Then the ugliness took hold of him.

Elliott remembered seeing the grey man in the dark clothes and when he tried to avert his gaze, his eyes landed on the bat that was just lying innocently on the side of the pavement. He remembered little after that. If he was being honest, he really didn't want to. It was a scary moment and best forgotten.

The fight he had with Ken afterwards was even worse. Elliott couldn't explain himself. He had threatened Ken with the bat. Well, he didn't actually say he would hit Kenshiro. At least, he was pretty sure he didn't. He had the bat raised over his shoulder, though, and he was ashamed to admit it, but he might have used it. On Ken. Elliott was deathly afraid of what he might do next. Luckily, Ken knew exactly what to do and what to say. In his mind, Elliott had stood in front of Ken's massive swell and felt the awe of its raw primal fury as it loomed over him, and yet he wasn't afraid. He felt comforted by its presence.

Ken's wave was like an unstoppable force of nature, but not against him. The massive swell loomed in front of Elliott like a wall, protecting him from the blackness of the outside world, and radiating a sweet sort of warmth that felt like an embrace. He had felt that warmth before. Elliott knew what it meant. He let it surround him like a suit of armor.

He felt better after that.

The ghosts didn't disappear, though. The suit of armor protected him, but they were still there, scratching at the seams, trying to get in. Some did. They weren't actual ghosts after all. They were his memories, and there was no escaping those. That's when he decided. It wasn't a straightforward decision by any means. He stayed up all night thinking about it, but he felt it was the best decision. He had to leave. This place wasn't his home anymore. He saw it more with each passing day. It was just a house

Elliott buried the thing that made this place special, and if momma was dead, he had to assume daddy would be dead too. Or worse. He loved her too much. Heck, his father once punched a man because he called Momma the c-word,. Just walked up and punched the man in the chops. He wouldn't let something happen to Momma unless something happened to him first. No, they were both gone forever.

"*You have to stop acting like a baby, Elliott,*" his father's words spoke to him in the night's darkness. "*You're not a baby anymore.*" Daddy was right, he was right when he first spoke the words, and he was right now.

He knew what the problem was. Even if he didn't know how it happened. His home wasn't his home anymore. So, if that was the problem, the answer to that problem was easy. Doing it, however... *You're not a baby, anymore.* Like removing a band-aid, he felt the best way to approach it was to decide and just do it, the quicker the better.

I should tell Ken about this, Elliott suddenly thought to himself. Elliott then threw back the covers and climbed out of his bed. After he rose, his stomach growled loudly. *Maybe Ken will make breakfast*, Elliott pondered as he made his way down the hallway.

-

"Ugh!" Elliott moaned loudly as he let himself fall to the ground after they had completed their workout for yet another morning.

This was how Elliott liked to spend the few moments immediately after the last squat, because squats were the last exercise in the routine. He would just let his muscles drop to the ground. There, he would lie on the grass and just let his body soak up the coolness of the ground while his body flushed out the burning sensation coming from his muscles. Seemingly all of them. At least that's what it felt like.

"You said this would get easier," Elliott complained breathlessly from the ground. That *is* what Ken had said. It didn't seem to be getting easier though.

"It will," Ken said with a bit of a chuckle, which confused Elliott.

He didn't understand what he had said that was humorous, but he just brushed it off. Either Ken didn't understand Elliott wasn't telling a joke, or Elliott didn't understand what was funny about the situation. In the end, he was too tired to worry about it.

"Just give it time," Ken said, in a tone Elliott recognized

When Elliott heard him say things in that gentle sort of tone, it meant Ken didn't want any follow-up questions t. Which was fine with Elliott because, he was content to look up at the puffy white clouds in the sky as they made their slow and steady trek overhead.

He was tired, but he was content. Calm even. All the jumbled thoughts that usually filled his head had quieted themselves. Maybe his brain was tired too. Elliott didn't know, but he was happy for the peace inside his head. He knew it wouldn't last after all. It never did.

"I think you finished faster today," Ken added, to make him feel better. Which it did.

"Really?" Elliott perked up and pushed himself up on his elbows to look at his friend. "You think so?" He asked, trying to think back to the exercises. It was hard for him to do because it was just a hazy recollection of repetitious movements and sore muscles. Time was a hard thing to conceptualize during the workout. Elliott didn't know how long it took for him to get through the whole routine. He knew Ken had finished well before him, but that was no surprise. Ken did the exercises like he was on auto-pilot.

"Well, it's not like I was timing you or anything," he said, walking the statement back a bit. "But I think so."

Ken came back from the truck with a pair of water bottles in his hand, as became their little post-exercise routine.

Ken handed him a bottle of water and sat down on the grass beside him. Elliott opened his bottle with one smooth twist of the cap and took a big drink. They drank their water and looked out over the emptiness in front of them. It was nice.

Elliott drank and let the cool fluid drain down his throat. It was glorious. As the bottle dropped from his mouth, he looked over at Ken and was pleased to find his friend had the slightest of grins. Ken didn't smile often, and it was nice to see a genuine smile on his face.

"You did good today," Ken said without looking at him as he took another drink from his bottle. He was telling the truth.

"Thanks."

Elliott enjoyed the compliment, but if he was being honest, he enjoyed the quiet little smile on Ken's face more. Elliott told himself that the look was pride. It wasn't the usual overjoyed display of pure enthusiasm that he was used to receiving from his mother, but, then again, Ken wasn't his mother. Ken wasn't a hugger. He didn't fawn over every little success Elliott had like his Momma had. With Ken, it was different. Ken reminded Elliott of a picture he had once seen. In the picture, which somehow showed the view from both above and below the water line, featured a massive iceberg. Elliott remembered how only a small portion of it poked above the water. Ken reminded him of that picture because most of what made up Ken was under the surface as well. On the outside, the slightest smile was the only outward sign of how he felt but, on the inside, his feelings radiated off him like a warm energy. To Elliott, that was better than the superficial gestures he got from gym teachers, coaches, or his own father. Those gestures, though nice and polite, were like getting an envelope in the mail just to open it and find nothing inside. Devoid of meaning. Whereas with Ken, he could just sit contently by his side, not exchange a single word, and Elliott could just bask in the warmth coming off of him.

"So, what now?" Elliott asked after he finished his bottle of water and a quiet few minutes had passed between them. "You want me to stab the hay bale some more?" Elliott liked the practise.

Unlike the other physical activities he had experienced, the ones where the principal goal was to have fun and try hard, the principal goal here wasn't to have fun, but to perform. Strangely, it was more fun than just playing, which was hard for him to wrap his head around if Elliott thought about it too much, so he didn't. He wanted few reasons or errant thoughts to complicate the time he spent with his friend.

"No," Ken said quietly as he lifted his head up to look over the empty landscape in front of them. Elliott would bet money he was looking for grey people. "I don't think so. We should head into town and do some work before it gets too hot out." He craned his neck to the sides as he spoke.

"Are we getting more supplies?" Elliott asked with a slight groan. He knew the answer before his friend even spoke. He wasn't even sure why he asked, but it seemed like the polite thing to say.

"Well, yeah," His friend said after he finished subtly checking the immediate area for any intruders. "We are going to have to stock up the house. I want to find another larger gas can to take, and we should find another food bag to take with us."

"Like the green one?" Elliott said and thought of the large green duffel bag that was stored in the living room at the end of the sofa. Although Ken had rarely opened it, except for the times he added cans and other foodstuffs, he made Elliott well aware of its contents and why it was important to have.

"I figure if there's going to be twice as many people in that truck, we probably should pack up twice as much food, just to be safe." That was one of Ken's favorite sayings, *just to be safe*. He said it all the time, though Elliott couldn't argue with his logic with the food, he was still somewhat disappointed. He had told Ken he wanted to leave. Yet, here they still were.

"When are we going to leave?" Elliott asked again. He had asked Ken that same question almost every day since that first early morning conversation they had. Each time, he received a different, vague answer. *Soon*, Ken would say. *Shortly*, was another answer he got. To Elliott, these were hollow answers. He expected more from his friend than that, which is why Elliott didn't feel bad about the slight amount of annoyance that seeped into his voice as he spoke.

"Getting kind of antsy, are ya?" Ken said, looking at him with a smile that didn't last long when he saw Elliott's expression. "Friday," he said finally. "We'll leave on Friday." Elliott just looked at him suspiciously.

"Tomorrow is Friday," he said plainly and watched the look of surprised burst across his friend's face.

"What?!" Ken said with genuine shock. "No, today's Tuesday, I thought."

"No, today is Thursday," Elliott said with absolute confidence. It wasn't the first time Ken got the days of the week confused.

"Oh, umm," he said, seemingly unaffected by the news. "In three days then. Just give me three more days to get the supplies I want and to organize the place a bit." Elliott smiled at the answer. It was definitive, unlike Ken's other answers.

"Okay," Elliott said contently with a certain grin on his face.

He had his answer.

Three days. In three short days, Elliott would embark on the adventure of his lifetime. He felt a certain twist in his gut that confirmed it. Elliott worried he might not be as ready as he had previously thought he was to leave the place that was once his home. None-the-less, He was happy to have an answer.

Elliott's grin fell away when his gaze happened upon the ragtag little garden in front of him. His mother was there, but not really because her body was buried by the tree. It was a little ghost of a memory playing out in front of him. He knew that.

She was younger than he remembered, crouched down in the garden, huddled over the medium-sized plants as she weeded in between the rows of vegetables. In the memory she wore her blue jean shorts and the Broncos t-shirt she liked, because she didn't mind if it got stained. On her hands, she wore the same white gardening gloves she always wore. The ones with the little blue flowers on it, the ones daddy got her for her birthday the previous year. She wasn't exactly happy with the gift when she first received it, but she used them often and grew rather fond of them. On her head was the large, floppy rimmed white hat she wore on hot days, her *sun hat*. Elliott watched as she rose from the plants and removed her tremendous hat to wipe the sweat from her brow with her free hand, unknowingly wiping a bit of dirt across her forehead.

Inside his mind, his brain was more than willing to provide many details about what he was seeing... or feeling? He supposed it would be *remembering.* *Would you like to know the date this happened? Do you know what store she bought that hat at? I do, I could tell you, if you'd like?* Elliott brushed the thoughts aside and watched as Momma looked up towards the house. He knew what would happen next. It was *his* memory, after all. Elliott's heart ached as he watched her soft face brighten and radiate with instant joy as she reached her arm into the sky to give a whole-hearted, joyous wave. Elliott couldn't help himself. The moment had him firmly in its grasp, and he just did what his heart told him.

"Who are you waving at?" He heard Ken's voice break in from the side. The sudden sound startled him abruptly, breaking him out of the fog of the memory. Elliott quickly lowered his hand and looked again to the garden, but this time he just saw plants.

"No one," he mumbled, suddenly feeling the ghost's icy touch on his heart.

-

That night, Elliott found himself awake at God only knows what time. It was dark. That's all he knew for certain. He turned on to his back and looked at the ceiling for a time. The light from the full moon cast a ghostly sort of light through the window. It was just enough to see, but not enough to make out any real detail in the space. He breathed deeply and shifted within the covers the of the bed to find a comfortable spot.

That's when he heard it.

He recognized the pained moans instantly. It wasn't

the first time he heard Ken's sleepy cries from down the hall. Elliott suspected it wouldn't be the last either. Ken was having a nightmare. It wasn't a common occurrence, but it also wasn't so uncommon that it was a cause for concern. It was just something Ken did sometimes when he slept. Elliott understood. He had bad dreams sometimes, too. Elliott's instinct was to go to his friend, and try to calm his troubled waters however he could, but he knew Ken liked to sleep armed, and he had occasionally warned Elliott not to disturb him when he slept. Heck, on the night he told Ken he was ready to leave this house, Ken awoke with a start and for a fleeting moment, it looked like Ken didn't recognize him.

Let sleeping dogs lie, he remembered his mother saying once. He didn't know exactly what that meant, but he took it as a warning that applied to his friend.

From this distance, Ken's wave was a mere shadow. Elliott had to concentrate on it in order for it to take shape inside his head. When he did, it seemed like Ken's wave was struggling against something. He couldn't tell, but now and then he heard his friend's low groans seep through the bedroom door. Elliott couldn't explain it, but he felt those sounds as if they were physical blows. Like some invisible hand was softly punching him in the stomach, and there was nothing he could do about it. He wondered if he should risk it and walk down the hallway. That alone would probably wake Ken up. He was a very light sleeper. Would he be mad, though? Ken rarely woke up in a good mood. He hid it well most days, but Elliott could tell his friend woke up like he was disappointed to find it was a new day. He didn't have to worry about it long, though.

Ken woke himself up.

There was a loud yelp. It almost sounded like Ken had called out a word, or maybe someone's name. Elliott didn't know for sure. It was impossible to discern what was said by the sudden, loud, and very brief noise. Maybe it was nothing it all. It had scared Elliott, though. In his bed, he jumped like a jolt of electricity suddenly went through his entire body. After, his brain worked furiously to figure out what the sound was, it came up with nothing he didn't already know. One thing he did know, however, is that Ken was now fully awake.

Elliott's eyes searched the ceiling as his ears strained to hear whatever sound might happen down the hall. So, he was prepared when he heard the first slight creak of the floorboards. It was a familiar sound to him. It meant Ken was out of bed and when Elliott heard the corresponding creaks, he knew Ken was moving around in his room. The noises from his room almost sounded like the floorboards were whispering to each other. Elliott quickly, but quietly, rolled away from the hallway door and pulled the covers up tight to his shoulders. He didn't want Ken to know he was awake. He didn't want to spoil what he was pretty certain was going to happen later. It didn't happen often and Elliott found it utterly fascinating. Besides, he always felt there was a secret line between adults and kids, one that he did not mean to cross in that moment.

He always knew when his mother was upset. No matter how hard she tried or how many smiles she threw out into the world, she could never hide what was happening on the inside from him. She always lied about it though. Always. Adults shielded themselves from kids, kept back certain parts of themselves they didn't want kids to see. It wasn't just Ken or his mother.

All adults did it.

Elliott didn't know why, but he'd come to accept this was how it was done, and he shouldn't question it. So, that meant Ken wouldn't even want him to know he was awake. Let alone why. So, he pretended to be asleep. Not that it was hard. Elliott had done it many times before in his old life. All you had to do was lie perfectly still with your eyes closed and not flinch. That was the important part, not flinching. He stared into the darkness behind his eyelids and tracked his friend's movements via the tiny creaks and squeaks of the floorboards he knew so well.

Elliott's heart quickened when he heard the floorboard outside his room sound off. Ken was checking in on him. He felt his friend's wave by the door, and for a moment Elliott struggled against the rising anxiety inside himself. Elliott fought to remain motionless and breathe normally, but then the floorboard sounded off again and he felt his friend's wave move away. Elliott waited until he heard the telltale sounds of Ken descending the staircase before he let out a deep sigh to relieve the pressure inside himself.

He turned over and silently threw the covers back and waited until he heard the front door open, and then close, before he swung his legs out and got out of bed. Elliott slowly approached the bedroom window and crept towards it as he peered out over the ledge until he saw his friend below. He didn't want to be too close to the window and risk being seen by Ken. Elliott didn't know why, but his friend seemed to go to great lengths to keep this part of himself a secret. He felt if Ken knew Elliott was watching him, he would be mad, like Elliott was intruding upon him. Elliott didn't understand it, so he proceeded with caution, just in case he was accidentally doing something bad.

Outside, the full moon glowed in the cloudless sky and cast the entire landscape in front of him in the same ghostly silver light that filled his room. It was a beautiful night. It saddened Elliott to think he and Ken might be the only ones who would enjoy it. He pushed aside all thoughts when

Ken's frame walked into view below. Elliott first saw him as he moved to the open tailgate of the truck.

Once there, he laid the wrapped bundle on the tailgate. Elliott smiled because he knew what was inside the wrapped bundle. He had only seen Ken remove it once before. Ken stepped away from the truck and when Elliott was fairly confident his friend had forgotten all about the possibility of being seen, he moved closer to the window to his usual spot where he had a full view of the area Ken liked to use to do his... *dances*? Elliott wasn't sure what they were called specifically, though he doubted they were called dances, but he couldn't think of a better word for it.

Ken approached the spot in the yard that he liked to use. From this vantage point, Elliott had a clear view of the section of grass that Ken had trampled down from repeated use. Once there, he stood facing away from Elliott. He stared at the dimly lit vista ahead of him for a moment while he stood perfectly still in place with his feet together. Elliott had noticed this was how Ken liked to start all his dances.

Even from this distance, he could see Ken's chest swell as he took in a deep breath of air and then slowly exhaled. Elliott watched expectantly as his friend first bent at the waist in a deep bow. Elliott had seen this in movies and knew it had something to do with respect, but usually the bow was to someone. Ken bowed to the vast, empty, silver-lit landscape in front of him and brought his hands out from his side in a wide arch until they were stretched high above his head. Then he brought them down the front of himself like Ken was pushing some imaginary piston down in front of his body.

Here we go.

His friend, suddenly and without any kind of external warning, sharply pivoted to the left. As soon as Kenshiro planted his feet, a strong-looking fist shot out in front of him. He rose slightly on his front foot before whipping his back foot and his other fist forward to attack at the same time. Ken settled back into the same stance. Next he pivoted again and punched in the same direction, but this time he punched from his side. Elliott watched transfixed as Ken moved with a sort of grace and bodily coordination Elliott didn't think was possible.

When he moved, Ken flowed through the air as if he weighed nothing at all, and at other times he looked solid like a statue made of carved stone. Elliott cooed as he watched his friend torque his upper body before jumping up, spinning around in a way Elliott couldn't even fathom, and kicking his outstretched hand with such force it sounded like a gunshot. Ken landed squarely on his feet and immediately kicked in front of him with his back foot before punching the air in front of him again. His hands did a sort of swirly motion in front of his chest that Elliott didn't quite understand, and then his whole body dropped down while pivoting somehow. Ken placed his hands on the grass and then his leg came forward suddenly, low to the ground, and swept the area in front of him. Without pause, his friend shifted his weight on his feet and then the other foot came out from under him and swept the same area. A blink of the eye later, Ken was back standing on his feet doing another whirlwind of attacks.

Watching him was like watching the tiny gears of a clock, all turning together to move the hands. When he was done, incredibly, he was in the same spot he had been when he had started, staring off in the same direction. Again, his hands came out in the same wide arch they had in the beginning, and Elliott knew Ken was finished with his dance when he bowed in the same fashion he had at the start. Only then did Ken's shoulders slump slightly. Only then did

Elliott see the effects of the dance's exertion on his friend. He saw Ken's chest rise and fall with each heavy breath.

Next, after a bit of a water break, Ken brought his metal pole out of the back of the truck, and with it in his off-hand, he approached his starting place in the yard. Again, he bowed, and then did the high arch with his free hand. Elliott had seen this dance before, Ken always did this one, and he even recognized some attacks from the dance.

He seemed to wield the heavy rod effortlessly as he went through the motions, his face blank and expressionless. Elliott concentrated hard and tried to push himself out towards the yard to feel Ken's wave. All he could feel was a shadow moving out in the world's ether, but he got a strange sense from it. It felt like Ken's wave was... *playing*? That didn't feel quite right, but it was the best way he could conceptualize what he felt in the distance, like playing... but with purpose. Or was it purposefully playing? Elliott didn't know. It was a complicated feeling he hadn't run across before with anyone else, but he liked it. Elliott quickly found the concentration it took to feel the wisp of Ken's wave took away from actually watching the dance, so he dropped it just in time to watch his favorite part. Shortly after that, Kenshiro had finished and the pole was replaced into the back of the truck.

This is it, Elliott thought excited as Ken downed the rest of his water bottle, he threw the empty bottle without a thought into the bed of the truck, and unwrapped the bundle on the tailgate.

From his vantage point, he couldn't see much of what his friend was doing down there, but his heart kicked a little when Ken freed the sword and it flashed silver as the moonlight reflected off the polished steel of the blade. He didn't know what kind of sword it was. Elliott had seen its kind before, in movies. He knew it was Japanese, like Ken, but that was about the extent of his knowledge on the secretive blade. The gently curved blade glistened and gleamed in the soft light of the moon as Ken walked to his starting point.

This dance differed from the rest. It didn't start with a bow, nor did it have the fancy arm motions at the start. He watched as Ken simply gripped the sword in both hands and began. Elliott watched the dance closely. Unlike the other dances Ken did, this one didn't have large, flowing motions or fancy kicks. This dance had short, quick motions with tiny shuffling steps that made it look like Ken was simply gliding over the top of the ground as he moved. He looked solid as he stood rigid with the sword in his hands in front of him. The sword, however, moved with surprising speed as it cut through the air in front of him and around him. Moonlight flashed off the mirrored finish of the blade at certain parts of the dance. This dance definitely differed vastly from the others, but it was no less beautiful.

Then he stopped.

Elliott's curiosity piqued as Ken lowered his hands without warnin. His eyes fixated on something off to the side and out of view, but Elliott could guess what it was Ken was looking at.

"Stupid grey people," Elliott muttered to the window in front of him. No one was around, so there was no need to hide his annoyance.

This would be the end of the dances for tonight. He knew his friend too well to think Ken would continue after the appearance of a grey person. No, Ken will deal with the grey person and then he'll check the yard, probably the whole property, to ensure he didn't attract anymore. Then he'll move the body over to the pile before he called it a night.

Ken turned backed to what he was looking at and simply waited with the sword in his hand by his side. Moments later a grey person walked in the frame. It was listing hazardously to the side and threatened to fall over with every step forward it took. Ken raised the sword up and held it again with both hands. Elliott bit his lower lip in anticipation.

This was new.

The grey person weakly stumbled forward with its hands out in front, clawing the air for Ken, and if Elliott had blinked at that moment, he may have missed what happened next. Ken moved forward. No, Ken exploded forward. His hands came up, and the sword flashed silver before it struck and then, inexplicably, Ken was behind the grey person with the sword still held high in the air.

Strangely, the grey person didn't turn to follow Ken's movement. Instead, it took another step forward and fell to the ground. Elliott watched with utter shock as the grey person's head just popped off its neck and rolled a short distance from where its body had fallen before it came to a rest. Elliott stared at the scene open-mouthed as his brain struggled to fill in the gaps of what he had seen. So much had happened in such a short amount of time it was impossible for him to track it. One moment Ken was standing there with the grey person moving towards him, and a heartbeat later Ken was behind the grey person's body as its head playfully rolled away from its owner.

After that, Ken cleaned the silvery blade and returned it to its sheath. He wrapped the sword up in the towel once again. Once he was finished for the night, Ken followed the script in Elliott's head, and if he had waited around to watch, he felt Ken would have followed it to a tee.

Instead, Elliott turned away from the window as Ken

turned away from the truck and started walking towards the entrance onto the property. The search had begun. There would be nothing else to see tonight. Elliott slid easily under the covers of the still warm bed, closed his eyes, and thought of the silvery blade before sleep took him away from it all.

-

Elliott's gaze meandered around to the passenger side mirror and locked on to the dark, hunched over figure that was slowly creeping up on the truck from behind. Elliott immediately recognized the gaunt posture of the grey person as it struggled up the road like it was dragging a thousand pounds behind it. It wore blue jeans and a dark hoodie that was missing one sleeve. He could see the lifeless sort of grey of its arm that was contrasted by the dark color of the exposed meat of the wound on its forearm. Elliott watched its reflection in the mirror for a moment longer, long enough to realize the grey person wasn't actually coming towards him.

It was just walking up the road in no particular direction. Its hands were down by its sides, its head was locked in place on its shoulders, and it only seemed to move when the body swayed as it made its way up the road towards the truck. If he were here, Ken would have said the zombie wasn't active. That's what he called it when the grey people got angry. *Active*. This one, however, was not active, so he wasn't in any real danger. His special power would make sure the grey person didn't notice him, and as long as he stayed quiet, the grey person would just carry on past the truck and continue down the road.

That's not what happened, though.

Elliott reached for the door handle and gingerly opened it. He knew that alone would make enough noise to alert the one grey person coming up on them, but Elliott didn't want to alert any more if he could avoid it. *'Always assume there's more than you see.'* Elliott stepped out of the truck and locked his eyes on the grey person with the dark hoodie as he closed the vehicle's door. It did not surprise him to see the grey person was noticeably moving with a purpose now. It was active. Its ugly blanched eyes were peering at him as if mesmerized as its body struggled up the pavement towards him.

Elliott moved briskly to the side of the truck bed, reached in to retrieve the gloves Ken advised him to wear, and quickly slid the oversized gloves onto his hands. They used to belong to his daddy. They used to be his favorite pair of gloves. The gloves were well worn, but they still had plenty of life left in them. *I guess these are mine now.* It was a bitter thought, but he didn't have time to deal with that stuff. He had a job to do. Ken was depending on him.

Elliott reached in and carefully lifted out his baby-spear from the truck's bed, like if he bumped it the wrong way the solid metal rod might shatter like porcelain. Which Elliott knew it wouldn't, but still, he marvelled at the lethal-looking point for a moment. Ken had him file the point down until it looked like the end of a finely sharpened pencil. Perfect for poking. Elliott moved away from the approaching grey person as he darted around the front of the truck and up onto the lawn of the house they were clearing. Ken exited the darkened interior of the home just as Elliott was stepping onto the lawn. Ken's eyes noticed Elliott even before he was out of the doorway, but Ken waited until he was closer before speaking.

"We got one?" Ken asked with mild curiosity. He had a semi-full trash bag in his one hand, which he set on the ground beside him as he came to a stop. Elliott just nodded and thumbed towards the grey person. His friend's eyes followed his gesture down the road until they locked onto the grey person in the dark sweater and blue jeans. "Okay," Ken said softly, as if he was saying it more to himself, as he scanned the area for any others. "You ready?" He asked and looked down at the weapon in Elliott's hands.

"Yup," Elliott said cheerfully, though he had butterflies in his stomach, as he usually did, but he didn't want Ken to know that. His friend might think he was still afraid of the grey people, which Elliott very much was, but he didn't want to risk his friend thinking less of him because of it. He knew what he had to do, what Ken expected of him, and he had done it before. Elliott wouldn't let a few butterflies stop him.

"Did you bring the rope?" At that, Elliott's shoulder slumped slightly.

"No," Elliott said, feeling suddenly stupid because he had forgotten the rope Ken used to hold the zombie still for him. "I'm sorry, I forgot." Elliott felt like he had already screwed this up and they hadn't even really started yet.

"Don't worry about it," Ken said to him and just waved it off. Ken was nice like that. They walked towards the truck together and Ken, once again, ran over the complete plan he had for the next few minutes. Elliott knew what he was going to say. He had heard the same speech a few times now, but listened earnestly anyway.

He walked with Ken up to the truck and monitored the grey person as his friend reached into the truck bed for the rope. With the long length of rope in hand Ken looked at him, and the down to the metal rod in his hands, Elliott grew nervous that maybe he was holding it wrong or maybe there was something wrong with his feet, but Ken just grinned.

"Let's do this." Inside his mind, he could feel Ken's swell rise and come alive with violent currents, they moved and shifted with a strange sort of purpose he didn't understand, but Elliott knew it was time to get serious. More so than Ken's tone ever could. Elliott merely nodded, and the pair moved into action.

Elliott felt like a wolf as they approached the grey person in unison. Their prey. Elliott liked to think of the grey people like that. It made them less scary somehow. Ken moved slowly towards the angry grey person and Elliott made sure he matched him step for step, like they had done in the past. The closer they got to their target, the more they separated from each other, forcing the grey person to choose which one of them it would pursue, because even the grey person knew he couldn't chase them both at the same time. Elliott kept a close eye on the bleached white eyes of the grey person, and tried not to pay any attention to the snapping jaws. The instant they left him and went to his friend, that was his cue.

"Hey, shitfuck!" Elliott blurted and felt a tinge of embarrassment at what came out. He wasn't very good at swearing. He wouldn't be deterred, though. "Look at me, you ugly son of a..." Elliott briefly panicked when he couldn't remember the right curse word that went with that expression and just said the first thing that came to his mind. "Cow!" He reddened slightly, but he could feel Ken was unaffected by anything he said. Ken was solely focused on the grey person. It didn't matter what Elliott said anyway, he just had to make noise, any noise. He could sing if he felt like it. Cursing at them, however, just felt right.

The grey person responded in kind to Elliott's insults. Its whole body turned back to him. It was decision time, and the grey person had stalked clumsily after Elliott. *Bad move, sucker*, Elliott thought to himself, while allowing Ken to quickly sneak in behind it. With practised ease, Ken hooked the grey zombie's neck with the rope. He then did this loopy thing with his one hand that caused the rope to kick up like it had suddenly come alive, and snake itself around the grey person's throat. He could see his friend pull back on the grey person's reins and all its forward momentum came to a grinding halt. Elliott watched the grey person teeter in place, and he feared it might just topple over, but it soon corrected itself as it pulled against the rope around its throat.

"I got it," Ken said holding the struggling dead man in the blue jeans in front of him.

Snow white eyes glared at Elliott emotionlessly as it peeled its lips back in a sort of snarl that was like how he had seen dogs do when they're really mad. It growled breathlessly at him, even as the rope around its neck bit deeper into the dry, scaly-looking flesh of its throat. Cold, arthritic hands, with swollen joints and overgrown fingernails were uselessly swiping at the air to reach him.

"You're up," Ken said. Elliott took a breath to steady himself and try to calm the butterflies in his stomach. It was at moments like this he wished he was more like his friend.

Ken was fearless.

Elliott took another breath and tried not to focus on the grey person's features as he lowered himself into the stance Ken had shown him. Elliott brought the sharpened tip of his metal rod to bear on the grey man in the dark hoodie in front of him.

As per Ken's teachings, Elliott was to rush forward in between those clawing limbs, to strike right under its chin and push the rod up with all his might. Seemed easy enough in theory. Standing in front of it, however, was a different matter. Elliott tracked the grey person's movements, looking for a way in through the pair of swiping claws, and got distracted by considering whether this grey person was taller than the others had been. His brain quietly informed him it wasn't. The grey person fought against the restraint around its neck as it snarled and snapped its jaws at him in a way that still made Elliott's skin crawl. Goose pimples broke out over his flesh. Elliott had to remind himself that he had done this before, a few times actually, and he shouldn't still be scared like this. Ken wouldn't be scared. Elliott couldn't help it, though.

"Elliott?" He heard Ken's voice quietly call his name from behind the grey man. Elliott snapped out of his funk. He had to move.

Now.

He followed Ken's instructions to a tee. Elliott pushed off the back leg of his stance and braced his arms as he propelled his body forward. Somewhere inside his brain, a distant voice cried out in protest at the insanity of what he was doing. Elliott only paid it enough attention to know the voice existed inside his head, but that was it. He didn't have time to listen to what it had to say. Something cold and scratchy touched his upper arms, but undeterred, Elliott pressed on. Elliott's brain screamed for his arms to move and his body responded by gripping the rod even tighter as his arms shot forward in unison.

His aim was perfect.

Elliott saw the tip penetrate the soft tissue under its jaw, just like Ken showed him. Elliott pushed the tip forward until his hands registered the light shock that traveled along the rod as the tip struck something solid. The baby-spear punched through the obstacle and continued on its path. The grey man made a strange growling sort of yelp as its body shook once violently. He felt the grey man's hands flop uncontrollably on his shoulders, and Elliott took that as his cue to yank the rod back. *To the hip*! He reminded himself as Elliott forcibly drew the rod out as he moved away from the falling grey person as fast as he had moved in towards it.

Success!

Elliott cheered silently as the grey person's body settled onto the road with Ken's rope still around its neck. Elliott let out the breath he had been holding and smiled proudly at his accomplishment on the ground. He let the rod hang, with its tip down by his offhand. Elliott found if he did this immediately after poking a grey person; he didn't have to worry about the black slime on the tip trickling down the shaft and onto his gloves. This way, the black goo could just drip onto the pavement until he could get a rag and clean it off properly.

"How was that?" Elliott asked excitedly and looked at his friend. "That was pretty good, wasn't it? I'm getting good at this." Elliott had a smile on his face. He couldn't help it. The butterflies he felt a moment ago in his stomach had disappeared and were replaced by a warm feeling of accomplishment. He could see it in Ken's wave. He was happy with it as well.

"Yeah, that was good." Ken nodded thoughtfully as he spoke. He bent down and unwound the length of rope that was around the grey man's neck. "You're still hesitating a bit, though." Ken looked at him when he rose.

"I was nervous," Elliott said defensively, knowing that *scared* would have been a more apt word, but he didn't want to say it. Not to Ken anyway. Elliott didn't know what else to say in his defence, so he pouted.

"It was good," Ken said again. "When you finally *did* attack. Nice clean angles. Mind you, I couldn't see a whole bunch from behind it, but." He held up his finger to emphasize the next bit. "What I saw looked pretty damned good." He smiled at the end. Which made Elliott feel better about the whole thing. "You're on the right track," Ken added, and held up his fist. "Pound it." Elliott didn't need to be told twice. He stepped forward and bumped the fist with gusto. "Good job."

They spent the remainder of the morning clearing out the rest of the houses on the block. '*For good measure*', Ken had said, but Elliott didn't know exactly what he meant. They had plenty of food. There were canned goods and dried goods in the cupboard. They had an entire section of one cupboard filled with vacuum sealed packets of different jerked meat. They collected ten water cooler jugs and lined up along the wall in the dining room. That was only their house.

"We need to go to the storage unit," Ken said after the last house had been cleared. He walked down the sidewalk from the house and tossed the garbage bag that was in his hand into the box of the truck. The streets were empty. Elliott had been sitting on the tailgate, waiting for him to return.

"Oh, okay, what for?" Elliott asked as he hopped down from the tailgate.

"I want to lock it all up and do some other stuff before we leave tomorrow." Elliott felt a pang of excitement when Ken spoke of their departure. It had been on his mind since he got up that morning.

They moved towards the truck. Elliott didn't bother lifting the tailgate. They didn't drive fast enough through town to worry about losing anything out of the back. Elliott cheerfully hopped into the driver's seat and waited for Ken to climb into the passenger side and give the signal before Elliott started the truck and put it into gear.

He drove east to Main Street and weaved his way through the collection of abandoned vehicles on the way towards the storage lot. He pulled up to the gate. Ken didn't say a word. He just hopped out and casually scanned the surroundings as he pulled the gate open for Elliott to drive through. After the truck crept passed the entrance, Ken just hopped onto the tailgate and Elliott drove the truck up to their storage unit.

Elliott climbed out of the truck just as Ken was pulling up the wide steel door of their unit. Everything was still in exactly the same place as they left it two days ago. Ken just stood at the entrance as he looked over the contents of the unit as if mesmerized.

"Whatcha looking for?" Elliott asked after a time of just watching his friend stare into the space.

"Nothing in particular, I don't know. Just making sure there isn't anything I'm forgetting or maybe there's something else we could put in here." Ken said as he stared thoughtfully at the contents packed against the wall. "I just wanted to have one last look before we go. You know, see if anything comes to me," he said and Elliott nodded even though he really didn't know what Ken was talking about. Elliott's eyes drifted to the large black muscle car parked in the unit. It was hard not to see. His eyes traced the graceful lines of the body along the sides. It was then that his brain reminded him of something.

Something important.

"You said we could take it for a drive," Elliott said, sounding a little more accusatory than he had planned, and motioned towards the imposing-looking vehicle. He probably didn't have to; Ken would have known instantly what he was talking about. How could he not?

"I said *maybe* we could," Ken mentioned absently, still mentally tallying up the contents of the packed wall. Elliott had kind of forgotten about the vehicle. A lot had happened over the last week after all.

"Could we? I've never ridden in a car like that." He looked at his friend when he spoke and again motioned to the black, mean looking car that was just sitting there. Elliott had only previously seen a car like that in the movies he would sometimes watch with his father. He never imagined himself actually riding in one, and it was right there. Practically waiting for them.

"There are a lot of other things we have to do…," Ken said without really finishing the sentence and just let the words hang in the air. Elliott could tell by Ken's wave he wanted to. Currents swirled within the deep calm with a sort of restrained excitement. There was a *yes* inside his friend that was just waiting to come out. Elliott just had to give it a path.

"We don't have to go far. Maybe just to the farm and back," Elliott gently prodded. Ken made a humming sound as he considered it. Elliott could feel he was close. "There's barely been a grey person all day." That seemed like a bit of an over exaggeration. If they didn't count the ones inside the houses, there were only three that stumbled onto the scene from elsewhere. If they counted the ones from the houses, the number was fifteen. Which in Elliott's mind wasn't insubstantial, and didn't believe Ken would be easily swayed. He had dealt with twelve of them after all. He had to think of something else.

That's when his brain chimed in.

"You said this was our getaway car," Elliott began and saw he had Ken's attention. "But we don't even know for sure if this car can get away from anything. We don't even know if it runs." Elliott said stone faced looking at his friend. Ken looked at him suspiciously.

"I see what you're doing," Ken said with a sly

grin. "So, what you're suggesting is we just take it for a short drive? Just to make sure everything works. We wouldn't want any surprises after all, right?" His friend said with a certain amount of mirth in his voice.

"Right," Elliott agreed innocently.

"We wouldn't have to go too far, and we'll be super careful, right? We probably won't even take it out of second gear," Ken said without the grin leaving his face. Elliott didn't quite get the joke, but he felt he was close to succeeding, so he pressed on.

"Safety is our middle name," Elliott said, hearing it before from a TV show he and his mother enjoyed, and he felt it was an appropriate thing to say. Ken laughed out loud at that, and Elliott could tell by the playful movement of the currents on the surface of Ken's wave that he had succeeded. It was Elliott's turn to smile.

"Japanese people don't have middle names." Ken chuckled. "That's a white boy thing." Elliott's shoulders sagged. Maybe he had been mistaken about the wave, but then his next words perked him up. "Go get the booster cables out of the back seat and pop the hood. I'll go grab the truck and bring it around."

Elliott worried the car wouldn't start at first, but then it came to life with a deep sounding roar that loudly resonated throughout the tiny space. The sound of it made Elliott jump. Ken had been right. If there were any grey people in the immediate area, they definitely would have heard the car coming to life.

"Will you listen to that engine?" Ken shouted so he could hear him over the steady rumble of the car's engine. "This thing is a beast," he said excitedly as he disconnected the cables. Ken stowed the cables back in the car's backseat and returned to the front of the two vehicles where he promptly closed each hood. "Hop in. Let's get going before we have visitors." Elliott quickly moved over to the passenger side and opened the door. He eased himself carefully into the fine leather seat that seemed to hug his bottom. It was a much nicer interior than the truck's.

Ken hopped into the truck first, so he could back the truck out of the way of the garage door. He then parked it off to the side and shut it down. Ken jogged back over to the driver's seat, and closed the door. With the door closed, the interior was somewhat shielded from the noise of the engine, but Elliott could still feel the rumble of it inside his gut.

"Ok, just a quick trip," Ken said to no one in particular as he let the park brake off, put the transmission in first, and eased the clutch out. Slowly, the black Mustang stalked out of the garage and rolled towards the front gate.

Elliott felt the swirling currents of Ken's wave dance and leap into the air. It was hard not to get swept up in the giddy feeling. It was a nice thing to feel from his friend as the car pulled onto Main Street where he stopped with the town shortly ahead of them. Ken looked to Elliott briefly and then back to the road ahead of them. He could see on Ken's face, as well as his wave, he was considering something.

"What?" Elliott asked. "Is something wrong?"

"You should put your seatbelt on." Ken never took his eyes off the road ahead of them as he gunned the throttle twice. Elliott didn't like his tone when he said it.

"Why?" Elliott asked not even trying to mask the concern in his voice as he reached over his shoulder for the seatbelt. Once in hand, he quickly clipped it into the buckle. When he finished, he looked over just in time to see Ken click his belt in as well. That concerned Elliott more than

Ken's tone.

Ken never wore his seatbelt.

"Because I changed my mind." Ken looked over and flashed an evil grin before he pushed in the gas. The engine roared to life around them, then Ken dropped the clutch.

There was a horrible squealing noise that erupted from the car. Elliott thought about bringing his hands up to cover his ears, but then the car exploded down the road. Gravity itself seemed to shift as it sucked Elliott back into the plush leather seat. He clenched his teeth together and reached out with his hands for something, anything, he could hold on to. One hand found the armrest, held onto it with a white-knuckled grip, while his other hand just flailed until it latched onto the muscle of his thigh. All the while, he watched helplessly as the car rocketed down the roa, straight towards the first intersection of the town and the roadblock of abandoned vehicles that was cluttering up the center.

"What are you doing? What are you doing!? WHAT ARE YOU-?" Elliott screamed in quick succession as the car roared headlong towards what he saw as their imminent doom.

His senses were alive. Information of all kinds flooded into Elliott's brain. It was all just white noise in the background that added to the moment's chaos. His voice caught in his throat when, a moment before Elliott was sure they would smash into the first truck at the intersection, he saw Ken in his peripheral vision pull madly on the wheel while he shifted gears, and the roar of the engine ebbed. Elliott was thrown towards the passenger door. He heard the tires scream again as the car banked sharply on the road right after the train tracks. They narrowly weaved past the power pole on the corner of the intersection as Ken turned the mustang onto Moore Avenue.

The screaming from the tires abruptly ceased as the car hit the gravel road and the engine roared again as Ken stepped on the gas. Elliott's brain informed him the car was moving sideways while also moving forward, and a moment later, he felt it. Elliott wanted to scream but his breath caught in his throat as the loud, menacing car drifted onto the center of the gravel road. The back end swerved around a bit before it settled onto the gravel. That's when Ken pushed the gas pedal down, and again Elliott felt an invisible hand push him back into the seat of the car. He held on as best he could as the car exploded down the road.

Ken had a wild grin on his face that Elliott didn't quite appreciate given the circumstances. Ken's wave was alive, the currents on the surface churned and swirled itself into a sort of white surf. It was hard to focus on his wave as the world moved past them in a dizzying blur.

Elliott heard tiny whooshes as the car exploded past street signs and power posts. They rocketed past Birch Street so fast Elliott hardly had enough time to register it. He managed a full breath as they left Locust Street in their dust trail, and for a second he thought maybe the worst was behind him. He realized just how wrong he was when Poplar Street suddenly appeared on the right-hand side. The engine's RPM's dipped just as Ken shifted gears again right before he cranked hard on the wheel. The gravity inside the car violently shifted as the monster under the car's hood growled loudly. He could hear the tires dig into the gravel of the road. The car sprayed tiny rocks past the rear bumper as it attacked the corner.

"Whoa." Elliott heard Ken say as the large car once again drifted into the turn as if the car was operating on a sheet of ice, but it overshot the road and swerved onto the lawn of the house on the corner.

Elliott's brain told him they had cleared out that house weeks ago, and provided an itemized list of what Ken had found. Elliott couldn't focus on that right now, even if he wanted to, as the angry car was drifting closer and closer to the white picket fence.

"Ken?" It was all he could get out. Elliott wanted to look at him, or anything else really, but his gaze was locked on the ivory white boards of the fence as it moved closer towards Ken's side.

Out of the corner of his eye, he could see Ken was struggling with the steering wheel in order to get control of the careening vehicle. Elliott's heart skipped a beat when the fence came impossibly close and then he heard it.

It sounded like someone was banging a rapid-fire drum beat on the rear bumper. Miraculously though, Elliott didn't think they actually broke through the fence. Ken let off the gas right before the heinous noise erupted throughout the interior of the car and it definitely felt like the car nudged into something. The engine barked up again and the wheels found some purchase on the soft ground, and propelled the car back towards the road. The car hopped up onto the road, and when he thought it was safe to do so, Elliott twisted in his seat to look back at the fence they left behind.

"I think you wrecked that fence," Elliott nervously warned his friend.

He could only make out the vague outline of the fence within the massive dust cloud they left behind them, but he thought he saw a piece that looked misshapen to him.

"Do you think I should go back and leave a note?" His friend chuckled from behind the wheel. It was a silly thing to say. Elliott angered after he came to realize the comment was sarcastic. He didn't like that. He felt maybe Ken was being mean to him. He didn't understand because, to his knowledge, he had been good today.

Ken's hand gripped the wheel as the next intersection rushed towards them at blinding speed. His brain told him it was Ryus Avenue ahead. Elliott didn't feel like he had full control of his eyes. His gaze was laser-focused on the road rushing towards him. Ken stepped on the gas as he cranked the wheel to the left. The monster of a car responded immediately as the engine revved up, and the back wheels started spitting gravel out behind them. The car slid onto Ryus like it was sliding across a sheet of ice.

"Car. CAR!" Elliott screamed as his eyes locked onto a small dusty-looking hatchback that was parked on the side of the road. He frantically tracked the hatchback as the Mustang slid side-on towards it.

"I see it," Ken replied calmly, which Elliott didn't understand given the gravity of the situation. He didn't look at his friend because Elliott couldn't turn away from the little blue car that was rapidly approaching the passenger window. *His* window.

Mercifully, he heard the dark rumble of the engine kick down and felt the vehicle's direction correct itself so it was moving forward again instead of sideways. The little blue car disappeared behind them. He turned back to follow it, but the only thing he could see out the tinted back window was a rapidly expanding cloud of dust. The car growled loudly again and Elliott turned back to the front just in time to feel the gravity inside the car shift again. Elliott braced himself just in time to stop himself from colliding with the passenger door; he found the seatbelt was doing little to keep him from flopping around.

Just like before, the maniac-car slid into the intersection to the sound of gravel being spit out the back, and again, Elliott's breath was caught in his throat until the strange motion of the car ceased and it continued accelerating madly down the gravel road. Something caught Ken's eye. Elliott saw Ken's head turned out of his peripheral. Elliott followed Ken's stare and saw a large, flat dirt lot that was completely empty except for the little tufts of grass that dotted the property. With a turn of the wheel and a bit of gas, Ken maneuvered the car nimbly onto the lot, and then the madness started. He cranked the wheel to the side and gunned the engine.

The Mustang roared all around them. Elliott could feel the sound of it deep within his stomach. Ken didn't just turn this time, the car just spun around in place. Elliott had a hard time with the feeling of the motion. The back end of the car was rapidly turning in a wide circle around the tight circle of the front. Dust kicked up all around them, choking off the visible light, casting the interior in subtle darkness and turning the outside world into an incomprehensible void. He didn't know how many complete rotations they did because all Elliott could focus on was how much he hated this car and how he wished they had never found it.

Then it ended.

The car engine died away to a low rumble and a second later, it came to an abrupt stop. Elliott rebounded in his seat as the car finally settled. The cloud of dust that surrounded them surrendered to the slight breeze and dissipated to mere wisps that floated gently by his window.

Elliott's fingers still tightly gripped the dashboard as his lungs finally released the breath he had been holding. He wanted to scream, but he jumped as Ken hooted loudly beside him without warning.

"Fuck, yes!" He said sharply into the steering wheel and then looked in Elliott's direction and promptly burst into laughter. "The look on your face…," Ken said and couldn't even finish the statement because he was laughing so hard. Elliott tightened his lip. He didn't like Ken's laughter, not this time. Elliott didn't like feeling like he was the joke.

He's making fun of me.

"Stop it!" Elliott shouted over to the driver's side, and using his left hand, he reached over and swatted Ken's shoulder angrily. "It's not funny!" He hit Ken's arm a few more times, but his friend just continued laughing at him. It just made Elliott madder, so he balled up his fist and hammered it down on his friend's arm to get him to stop.

That got his attention.

"Okay. Hey! Alright, FUCK!" Ken raised his voice, and it boomed through the interior as the last blow landed. Elliott recoiled back to his seat, still angry. "What the fuck has gotten into you?" Ken looked at him with those hard eyes.

"You did that on purpose," Elliott accused him.

"Well, yeah." Kenshiro just looked at him, obviously confused.

"You just wanted to scare me. It's not funny to scare people. I don't like being scared!" Elliott felt his eyes burn as the emotions swirled inside him.

"I'm not trying to scare you."

"You could have KILLED US!" Elliott raised his voice. He didn't mean to, it just happened. He crossed his arms because he didn't trust himself not to hit Ken again and stared forward.

"What? No. You're overreacting. We were having fun, I thought. I guess I was wrong." Ken finished saying and then sat back in his seat and puffed.

Elliott could feel his frustration. His wave suddenly

ceased all the joyous movements it was doing a mere moment ago and settled into a deep stillness. A silence grew between them. Elliott didn't know what to say. He was still angry, but at the same time; he didn't want Ken to be angry with him either. Ken sat reflectively in the driver's seat, moved his gaze forward and just sort of looked out the window. Elliott spied his head making tiny brief nods and quiet little shakes like he was having a discreet conversation with someone Elliott couldn't see.

"Uh-oh, Ken. Look." Elliott broke the awkward silence between them when he spotted the grey person down the road through the rapidly vanishing dust cloud that was around them.

Apparently, when the vehicle came to rest it had settled facing south. Elliott could see the grey person stumble onto the intersection they had just come from as the dust settled around them. From this distance, Elliott couldn't make out any real detail but he knew a grey person when he saw it. There was no mistaking that walk. Ken's expression came back to life as he adjusted his gaze until he saw the figure down the road as well.

"Hmm," Ken sat back in his seat and then turned to face him with an earnest expression. "Okay, there's something I'd like to show you because I think it's kinda awesome." Ken looked at him like he was proposing something, except he neglected to mention exactly what it was he was going to do. Elliott could guess, though, as the surface of Ken's wave shifted and turned eagerly.

"Is it more crazy driving?" Elliott said in an accusing tone. He just wanted to ask, but apparently, Elliott was still slightly cross with his friend.

"Yes," Ken responded unabashedly. "And no. It involves some crazy driving *skills*, but I've done it before, a few times actually, so it's not like it's *dangerous*," he said before quickly adding. "Not to us, anyway."

"I don't know if I want to." Elliott said while mulling it over in his head. He was curious, though.

"Listen, I'm sorry, okay? I didn't think you'd hate it so much. Most people find that fun," Ken said the last bit offhandedly, but that was the part that cut the most. *Most people*. Ken didn't mean it like an insult, like some people had in the past. The way he said it, maybe Elliott wasn't even supposed to hear it. Still, it stung to be reminded his friend was aware Elliott differed from other boys.

"I just didn't know you were going to do that," Elliott said defensively. "And it just sort of scared me. If I had known it was going to happen, I probably wouldn't have been so scared." Elliott then looked back to the grey person off in the distance. He didn't know how true that last statement was, and he didn't want Ken to see it on his face.

"Really?" Ken said, sounding somewhat amused. "Let's put that to the test, then." He put the car into gear and slowly let out the clutch. The large black car rolled forward out of the dirt lot, and Ken drove it slowly onto the road. Elliott assumed he was going to do something with the grey person. When Ken pulled onto the road, he was facing the wrong way, which only intrigued Elliott more. "Okay," he said and let the car idle in the middle of the road as he turned to Elliott with a bright expression on his face. "Now I'm going to back up really fast and then, at the right point, I'm going to turn the wheel, and the car is going to spin around really quick, and if I do it right," Elliott didn't like that Ken had said '*if*', but he continued to listen quietly, anyway. "That zombie back there should hit the quarter panel right. About. There, and send it flying," he said and pointed to the front corner of the car on Elliott's side, close by the wheel. Elliott looked to the spot he pointed out and then back to his friend.

"You can't do that," Elliott said after he thought about what Ken was suggesting. Ken only smiled at the challenge.

"You wanna bet?" Ken responded with a playful chuckle. Elliott was glad the playfulness in Ken's wave was back, even if it was to a lesser degree than it had been a moment ago.

"Not really," Elliott confessed. "But you can do it. If you want," Elliott said a bit sheepishly because he didn't really want to go through that craziness again, but Ken seemed to like it. If Elliott was being honest with himself, there was something thrilling about how the car swerved into the corners like a wild animal clumsily chasing after its prey.

"Okay, I will," Ken said and then gunned the engine a few times so the car growled around them. To Elliott, it seemed like the car was eager to get started, and maybe in some small way he was curious how this would play out. "Let me know when you're ready." Ken flexed his fingers on the steering wheel while he looked in the rear-view mirror, presumably checking on the grey person who was behind them. "You might want to brace yourself," Elliott looked at him wide-eyed with sudden concern, which Ken just shrugged off. "Just to be safe."

"I trust you," Elliott said, trying to sound confident, but at the same time he checked to make sure his seat belt was secure. He also felt he better grab onto the armrest on the door. When he was confident he was as secure in his seat as he was going to get, he turned to his friend and tried to speak bravely. "Do it."

The car's engine revved up, sounding like the war cry of some wild beast, before Ken shifted the car into reverse and let the clutch out. Elliott could hear the tiny plunking sounds that the wheels made as they dug in and sprayed the undercarriage with gravel. The vehicle shot backwards. Elliott reached out for the dash instinctively as he was thrown forward. Luckily, the seatbelt locked in place and prevented any further movement as the strap dug into his chest. Ken twisted his upper body around so he could look out the back window. The car accelerated backwards with such force it swerved to the sides. Ken struggled with the wheel to control the car as they sped towards the grey person. Elliott kept his gaze forward, specifically at the spot Ken pointed out on the side where the grey person would supposedly strike the car, but he couldn't help but see the ever-expanding cloud the car was creating on the road. He felt all the tiny changes Ken made on the wheel as he fought to keep the car moving in a straight line. It was like the car had a mind of its own as they sped along the road backwards towards the target only Ken could see. Elliott held on to the dashboard and fought against the butterflies in his stomach to simply breathe normally. He settled on long, frantic gasps.

"Get ready." Ken cautioned with a certain amount of tension in his voice. His wave was moving slowly and with a strange purpose, Ken was concentrating on something. Elliott hoped it was the road, as he squeezed the soft leather of the door handle tighter.

Elliott suddenly noticed a whirring noise that was coming from underneath the car. Part of him became worried maybe the manufacturers did not mean the vehicles to be driven backwards at such a velocity. *Is he hurting the car?* His brain wondered from the safety of his head. A moment later, the sound vanished, and the engine barked as Ken let in the clutch and cranked the wheel violently to the left. The surrounding universe spun around and Elliott braced himself as a strange force tried to throw him over to Ken's side of the car. A thousand miles away he felt the fabric of the seat belt dig into his hip, and his hand strained to hold its grip on the armrest. Just when Elliott was sure his hand would slip free from the leather handle, Ken won the bet.

Wham!

Elliott saw it. He was looking at the spot, after all. The dead man hit the side of the car in front of him, close to where Ken had pointed out, but the grey person struck slightly closer to the side mirror. Elliott only knew the grey person was a man because his brain was going off about how short his hair was, and how masculine the dried-out prune of a face it had. Because the grey person was only there for the time it took for the sound of the collision to reach Elliott's ears.

The next instant, it was gone.

Elliott saw the grey man cartwheel through the air with its arms and legs splayed outwards like someone attached him to an invisible pinwheel. It did one lazy circle in the air before the grey man's momentum died away and it collided with the ground.

"Whoa!" Elliott barked out in amazement. The grey man's leg touched first and it just flopped hard onto the ground. *That's about twenty-six feet.* His brain chimed in as the body came to a rest before the giant dust cloud they had made overtook the car. "Whoa," he said again, replaying the grey man flying through the air in his head. Elliott was smiling, he couldn't help it. "Ok, that was pretty cool," Elliott said, not minding that he had been wrong one bit. That *was* kind of fun.

"You see," Ken said, and slapped Elliott's arm in a playful '*I told you so*' gesture. "You can't call it '*crazy driving*'," Ken lapsed into a less than flattering impression of him. "If I know what I'm doing."

"Where did you learn to drive like that?" Elliott asked. He looked out the window to where the grey man landed, but all he could see was the cloud of dissipating dust that enveloped the car.

"That?" Ken thumbed in the general direction of the grey man. "I taught myself how to do that, wrecked more than a few cars in the process too," Ken said with a strange sense of pride. While Elliott's brain quietly wondered how many cars exactly. Ken continued before Elliott could ask. "I had a friend in high school whose uncle owned a body shop back in Los Angeles, in Brea, and we would drive out there on the weekends to help him with the shop for the day. After which, he would let us take his beat up old Chevelle for a drive on the dirt roads behind his shop. It was an old car and banged up to shit. I mean, there was nothing we could do to hurt this car that hadn't already been done. I'm not even sure that car was legal to drive, but man, could that car run." Ken remembered fondly. "We would drive up and down those roads for hours. I can't tell you how many times we hit the ditch or took out some guy's mailbox doing some stupid shit."

Ken stopped and just sort of looked off into the distance through the windshield. Elliott didn't know what he was looking at. He could tell from his wave that there was more Ken could say, but he probably wouldn't. Ken rarely talked about the time before the grey people showed up, and when he did, it was in tiny snippets. Like he was reading from the tiny scraps that had been torn from a book, except the story was his life.

"Look," Elliott said when he looked over at the grey man in the empty field on the left. The breeze had carried the bulk of the dust cloud away. The grey man wasn't trying to get up, or even trying to crawl towards them. It just moved. One of its legs flopped uselessly up into the air, and

Elliott could see its bulk shift on the ground like it was trying to move, but just lacked the basic structure to do so.

"I'll take care of it," Ken promptly said and reached for the door handle; he was out the door before Elliott could say another word.

Elliott watched him close the door and move around the front of the car, his narrow eyes searching the horizon like a jungle cat, as usual.

It was then his brain chimed in to point something out to him. *Ken only drives like that with his friends, and he drove like that with you. That means* you're *his friend.*

Ken pulled the tiny pistol free from its holster on the black vest as Elliott beamed inside the rumbling car. He had foolishly thought his friend was playing a mean trick on him by driving the car crazy like that. He thought Ken was enjoying putting Elliott through that, but he had been wrong. Again. He felt bad for how he had acted a moment ago, but the feeling was brief. Elliott thought about how Ken might tell other people about the time the two of them went driving together, and when he did, he thought about the pleasant look that would be on Ken's face.

Pop!

The tiny bullet kicked up a bit of dust as it tore through the grey man's head and buried itself into the ground. All motion ceased as the body settled to the ground. Ken walked away from it without another look as he holstered the pistol and made his way back to the car. Elliott shifted his gaze from him and back to the crumpled body in the dirt and thought about how it would lay there for the rest of its days. There would be no one to come by and bury it, or burn it, it would just stay in that exact spot until its remains turned to dust and blew away by the wind. *Is that what's going to happen to me?* Some frightened part of him spoke up. Elliott swept the thought aside. He didn't have time for sad thoughts right now.

"Okay, problem solved," Ken said a moment after he opened the door and sank into the leather seat of the car. "What do you want to do now? Should we head back, or do you want to drive around some more?" Elliott knew what he wanted to do instantly.

"We can drive around some more," Elliott said and turned to see Ken's sly grin.

"Crazy driving?" He asked with friendly caution. Elliott felt a tinge of shame, reminded of how he reacted before, but swallowed it down and tried to mimic his friend's subtle smile.

"Sure."

"Atta boy," Ken said and Elliott felt his wave kick up in excitement. He clicked his seatbelt back into place and throttled the engine up menacingly.

"But tell me when you're going to turn, so I can be ready."

"I can do that."

The sound of the engine filled the car once again and the black beast took off down the road like an apex predator after its prey.

-

"Elliott?" Ken called up the stairs from the main floor.

The sound of his voice echoed off the walls and with Ken's accent, it made the actual word hard to understand, but he had spent so much time with his friend already his brain barely registered the accent anymore. Elliott understood him perfectly. He even knew what he was going to say next.

"Five minutes, buddy. I hope you're getting ready up

there and not reading the comic books you can't take."

Elliott was not, though he had packed a choice selection for the road. Ken let him pack his backpack from school with anything he wanted to bring. Elliott, at first, felt a bloom of anxiety at the prospect of fitting his entire life into that one small bag. He reminded himself that Ken said they literally had all the time in the world, but at the same time Elliott was eager to leave. Elliott should have done this last night like Ken suggested. Elliott filled the bag with the pictures he liked, two albums and a few off the wall that he preferred. He was also sure to take the bracelet jenny had made for him during the Summer Crafts Fair when they first met. It was the first gift she had given him. The tiny beads spelled out his name along with *my friend* along its length. Elliott has had it safely tucked away in his sock drawer ever since. Now, he gingerly placed it into the front zippered pouch of the bag.

When he was finally ready, Elliott moved towards the front door and allowed his brain to take in every detail of his childhood home. Elliott reached for the doorknob, took one final breath of the air inside his home before he opened the door and left everything he had ever known behind.

"You ready?" Ken asked.

"Yeah," he said as he hung onto his backpack and made his way to the passenger side. Ken just nodded before he moved around the truck to the driver's side. Elliott wordlessly fastened his seatbelt before Ken started the truck and put it into gear. As the truck slowly rolled towards the front gate, Elliott couldn't help looking out the window towards the house.

"Don't worry," Ken said, trying to sound reassuring. "We have everything we need." The truck moved forward, and out from behind the house, the large tree under which they buried his mother came into view, just like Elliott knew it would.

Almost everything, Elliott thought to himself as they passed the large tree.

Chapter 7

Elle

Maggie lifted off from the tarmac of The Prescott like an enormous bird taking off into the sky, and Elle had the familiar feeling of as her heart falling into the depths of her gut. A part of her wondered if she would ever get used to the feeling of being in a vehicle that could move rather sharply in a vertical direction. One second, they were on solid ground and with a gentle pull of his left-hand, Martin brought them into the sky with little warning. She had never ridden in a helicopter before coming to The Prescott and meeting Martin, so she didn't have any experience to reference from, but she felt Martin sharply brought the craft into the air on purpose.

The first time she suspected he was trying to get a rise out of her. It was only natural. In her experience, there's nothing middle-aged men like more than to scare young girls with their immature bullshit. Her father did it, all of her uncles did it, even friends of the family, for Christ's sake. It wasn't malicious. She knew that, and sometimes it made for a good laugh, but more often than not, she remembered walking away from those exchanges feeling like a fool.

At least I don't have to worry about boys snapping my bra strap anymore.

Her step-dad and Kate's father, Joe, was one of the few people who regarded her more as a person and less like a target for some good-natured teasing. It was one thing she instantly liked about him. She didn't like many things about Joe at first, but it was the gentle form of respect he showed her that held the door open for him to enter her life. Bit by bit, he slowly wore her down. Elle never actively rejected any of the other men her mom dated, but Joe was the only one she liked.

She felt if Martin had ever dated her mom, he would have worn her down too with his quiet ways, so she gave him some slack about the takeoffs. She couldn't say for sure, but she had a strong feeling if there were paying customers in the back, instead of a bunch of empty gas containers, he might be more subtle with how he handled Maggie's take-off. She never mentioned it to him, though, probably for the same reason he actually did it. It was the only genuine thrill she got anymore that didn't involve a mortally dangerous encounter with the undead. Like a roller coaster, it was harmless. It was the illusion of danger that made it fun.

Martin slowly spun the craft until it was facing west as it ascended over the cityscape. Once they were facing the direction he wanted, Martin pushed the cyclic stick forward marginally and settled the craft into a nice cruising speed. The sudden momentum pushed her back into her seat as Maggie sped up through the sky and the city moved below them.

"So, where are we going?" Elle asked over the intercom. She looked at the displays on the center console until she spotted the digital compass. They headed north-west, which wasn't really a surprise.

"Jesus. Did you forget already?" Martin teased her over the intercom.

Martin gave her the full run-down of the plan well before they even thought about taking off. The two of them were heading to some small airport Martin was familiar with to refuel Maggie.

"No, I didn't," Elle snapped back playfully. "Some small-town airport you visited to help fix your buddy's airplane ages ago," she said with a slight drone in her voice. "I mean, specifically, where are we going?"

In reality, she didn't really care. Martin assured her this was safe and easy, and only required one other person as a lookout. Honestly, it was nice to just get out of The Prescott for a time. She didn't need more convincing after Martin said the words, *safe and easy*.

"Andover, New Jersey," He promptly answered.

"Never heard of it."

"No shit, that's probably why I didn't bother telling you in the first place." She didn't even have to look. She could almost feel the satisfied grin on Martin's face.

"How far away is it?" She asked, trying to keep the conversation going.

"Sixty miles, give or take. We should be there in about thirty minutes," he said with a certain amount of disinterest as he pivoted his gaze between the horizon and the displays in front of him. They fell into a comfortable silence until Elle thought of something that might get a rise out of him.

"How long did it take to *drive* to your friend's place?"

"Oh, fuck!" Martin blurted out suddenly and Elle smiled inwardly. "Don't even get me started on that nightmare," he said and then told the story.

Turns out Martin's friend, Cole, drove into the city to pick him up because Martin didn't have a valid driver's license. Which isn't entirely uncommon within the boundaries of New York City. Martin soon clarified he did indeed have a driver's license, but at the time, it had expired. Like he was worried Elle would have thought less of him if he didn't have one. Martin told a five-minute story of the events of the day before he circled around to answering her original question. Four hours. It had taken him four hours to exit the city and drive twenty-five miles Which again, wasn't entirely uncommon. That's why she asked. She didn't know anyone who left the city by car, with a few rare exceptions, and everyone who did, had a story about how terrible of an experience it was. Joe would often quip that New York City was a blackhole of humanity, easy to get sucked into, and almost impossible to leave.

They crossed into New Jersey the moment they past the Hudson River. Everyone knew that, but you'd never notice it from the landscape that passed beneath them. It was all just... city.

A flat grey landscape populated with an endless amount of differently colored boxes, all neatly arranged within larger box shapes with vehicle ladened streets running in-between. She had a teacher in High School, Mr. Handelson, who always liked to preach about how the New York metropolitan area was the greatest human engineering accomplishment of all time.

From this height, Elle had her doubts. At this vantage point, the city below looked more like a giant, endless maze for rats. In the end, it might have led to the downfall of the city, as the residents soon found out when the government called for the greater New York metropolitan area to be evacuated. A country's worth of people panicked at the same time. It was instant chaos followed by gratuitous slaughter. To her knowledge, only the residents of The Prescott survived.

"You ever see anybody else out here? You know, like other people?" She asked quietly, because she felt she already knew the answer.

"Not really. When we first started doing the runs, you would see pillars of smoke all over the city. That's about it. I've never seen people, though. You'd think if there were people down there somewhere, they would come running to the sound of a helicopter, but I've never seen one and before long, those pillars of smoke disappeared too."

"Do you think we're the only ones left?" As she looked down at the landscape below, she blurted out the question. She wasn't aware she was going to ask it, but now that it was out, she let it hang between them.

Elle knew full well it was a taboo of sorts to talk about the grim realities that might await them when they finally exited The Prescott. They all thought about it. How could they not? No one wanted to talk about it though, except maybe Kate, and in those conversations, Elle simply played her part. She would gently reassure her sister while keeping her own fears to herself. She felt she could talk to Martin though, like *really* talk to him. Maybe that's why the question slipped from her lips in the first place.

They had a strange relationship. She was mature enough to admit that. She could almost forgive Jacob's occasional teasing about it. Almost. She didn't know what category Martin fit into in her life. In one way or another, he fit into all of them, and none of them at the same time. He was more than a friend, but less than a lover. More than a teacher, but less than a father.

"Where's this coming from?" His voice sounded off through the headset in that tone only he could pull off. The one that left you with utterly no idea what was going on behind that kind, stone-like face.

"I dunno." She said out of habit. It was a childish response to a serious question. She could do better. "It's been a long time since..." She left it there not knowing what exactly she wanted to say, but took comfort in that fact she probably didn't have to say much else for him to understand. "Just wondering if there's anybody left out there. You know, maybe we're the last people on earth." She tried to sound lighthearted when she said it, like it was some kind of soft joke to lighten the mood. But she felt all she accomplished was revealing some of her hidden fears.

"Typical New Yorker mindset," Martin said with a good-natured chuckle, though she didn't think he was laughing at her attempted joke.

"What?" she said, sounding slightly hurt.

"Well, you spend your whole life in one of the biggest cities in the world, so you naturally assume this city is the center of the country, or the world, or whatever." Ahead of them was a large swath of green, watery land, like a swamp or something. Martin eased Maggie into a turn and, according to the digital compass display, the craft was slowly banking to the north. "It's not, and it never was. There are a lot of places out there with a shit ton of people in them. Trust me, we're not the only ones left," he said with a certain amount of confidence that Elle found reassuring. She glanced over at him just in time to see him look down at the picture of his daughter. "We can't be." He whispered before he returned his attention to the displays.

Of course, he thinks that way, he has to. For Martin, acknowledging the possibility they were the last people on earth, or even the United States, was the same as acknowledging his little girl was the one of the many who didn't make it out. Elle figured everyone held onto tiny little hopes like that.

"I hope you're right," She confessed.

"I am," he said with a certainty that she assumed only came with age. "Don't worry about it. You just got to take it day by day. Keep your mind on what's in front of you. For example, what's our current heading?" Martin asked and nodded towards the center display console.

"What?" she barked out nervously at the sudden pop quiz. She heard the term before. She was just stalling for time while she searched her memory. It had something to do with their direction.

"Don't bullshit me. I saw you looking at the compass. What's our heading?"

"North," she said, grasping at the first answer that came to her mind.

"Technically, yes, but that's not the answer I'm looking for. North is a general direction and in order to truly navigate, you need to know what your heading is." Martin spoke slowly and clearly through the headset. "We've been over this, you know."

"I know, gimme a second," she barked back with gentle irritation. "It's been a busy month. Shit, if I had known I was going to be tested, I would have taken notes." She quipped as she thought about the question. It had to do with their direction, and geometry, which she was never especially good at. She was a little ashamed of the silence that grew between them until she finally broke down. "Give me a hint," she said unabashedly, while Martin just laughed over the intercom.

"A hint? Jesus Christ, what would my old flight instructor say to that?" He said incredulously while still chuckling quietly, but then it passed. "Okay, fine. Think about how many degrees there are in a circle," he said, regaining his composure.

"Yes!" Elle yelped excitedly, cutting him off. It hit her like a lightning bolt, all the pieces came together inside her mind. She just had to visualize the circle and put the helicopter at the center, and put north at the top of that circle at zero degrees. Whichever way the helicopter was pointing in that circle was their heading. The digital display of the compass was what she looked at. She saw North was just a little top-dead-center to the left. Elle guessed the rest. "Twenty degrees, something like that." She instinctively shrugged when she gave her definitive answer. Martin just gave her a side eye glanced and then momentarily took his hand off the cyclic control to tap on the compass display, right above where he tapped on the side of the main graphic of the compass. It read:

HDG: 023

"Oh, twenty-three degrees. I was pretty close."

"Pretty close? Depending how far we're going, you could have been off your target by miles," he said again with a chuckle. "And we say it like: Zero-Two-Three degrees." Elle rolled her eyes discreetly at that.

"Ok, zero-two-three-degrees." She repeated the number back to him in an attempt to solidify the lesson in her mind. Then something hit her. "I thought you said this place was to the west. Why are we going north?" Martin grinned slyly, used his head to motioned out his window.

"I'm avoiding that fucking swamp down there. The last time I flew over it, I had a close call. I got about halfway across it then a flock of birds kicked up, like thousands of them, couldn't say what kind of birds. Ducks, maybe. Scared the living shit out of me. Chopped up a couple in the main rotor, but luckily that's as bad as it got. Something like that could have brought Maggie down for good." He spoke in the excited tones of a man telling a thrilling story, but there was no humor in his voice.

She swallowed hard at the realization that something as insignificant as a flock of birds could have been the doom for the last two dozen people left living in New York. Everybody was aware of the passenger jet that was forced to land in the East River shortly after it took off because it inadvertently flew through a large flock of birds. If birds were enough to bring down a large jumbo jet like that, she imagined it wouldn't be too hard to do enough damage to Maggie to bring her down too.

"I'm not going through that bullshit again. No sir, not to save five or ten minutes off the trip. Fuck that," Martin said with a hint of annoyance in his voice.

It once again occurred to her the immense strain that everyone at The Prescott had put on this man's shoulders. He was solely responsible for the only lifeline they had. He was the only one who could fly the helicopter. The only one who could fix it if it broke down. Martin also was the only one who knew where they could find fuel for it. At The Prescott, everyone looked to Mason and his group for protection and guidance, but it was quiet, humble Martin that bore the real responsibility of their futures in his hands. Elle couldn't imagine the strain such a heavy responsibility would have on a person after a while.

She has been on two missions, and on those missions, she accomplished goals that any able-bodied person could have done. There was nothing special about her that made her uniquely qualified. Hell, there were probably other people who were better qualified. She had just been the first to volunteer.

That first mission ruined her for a bit, more than a bit, if she was being honest. She still had trouble recalling the exact details of the mission. The insanity of the moment shredded the memory inside her mind. When she searched for memories of the event, she just recalled tattered sensory fragments. Some fragments stood out more than others. She'll never forget the sounds of thousands of low, pained groans and angry hissing that blended together to form a terrible wall of white-noise that almost had a tangible presence. The smell of rot and decay that permeated the air all around them. The high pitched staccato blasts from the soldier's rifles sounding off in the distance. Hundreds of clawed hands reaching for her.

These were the memories she guarded herself against. She built up little walls in herself to keep them secure and away from her conscious mind. Like a zoo of sorts. Elle kept these memories somewhere safe so she could revisit them on her own terms without them affecting her. Other memories struck like a thief in the night, quiet and unsuspecting. Like the smell of cordite that seemed to follow her around everywhere she went and struck like a knife between the ribs.

Yep, she was a wreck. Not like Martin. Who was the only person who could fly the helicopter, and who went on every mission, and somehow managed not to be unstable like herself or a complete asshole, like three out of the four members of Mason's crew. The man was a goddamn rock.

Martin kept the craft on the same heading and they cruised along the New Jersey coastline to the north. Out of Martin's window, was the expanse of green and dull blues of the swamp water. Out of her own window, were the dull greys of the cityscape and the black ribbon of the Hudson River. The occasional tree dotted the otherwise bland landscape below. She briefly looked over at Martin before returning her gaze to the window.

She wanted to talk, but for the life of her, she couldn't think of what she wanted to talk about. Sure, there were things she needed to say, but where to start, and what to say? When she has that figured out, when the formless anxieties inside her gut finally take an actual shape inside her head, then she'd talk about it. Right now, she just wanted something to distract her from the constant sound of that fucking engine.

"Have you talked to Jackie lately?" She asked the moment the question popped into her head. She tried to make it sound casual, maybe even friendly. But to her own ears, it still sounded uneasy. "How's she doing?"

"Not bad. At least the infection has finally cleared up. She was worried she was going to lose more of her arm. Thankfully, it didn't come to that," he said in a calm, level tone of someone making straightforward conversation. Damn him.

"I haven't seen her around much." Truth be told, Elle hadn't seen her at all since they carried her off the helipad after La Guardia. Elle felt she should have gone to visit her. *Like she would want to see me*, a familiar voice inside her head reminded her.

"Yeah, well," Martin started cautiously. "She's still adjusting to things. She doesn't want people staring at it." He didn't have to say more. Elle knew what *it* was. Hell, if she was being honest with herself, Jackie's missing hand would probably be the first thing Elle's eyes would lock on to. She doubted she could control it. Her gaze would just gravitate to it. "Right now, she seems comfortable to just hang out in her room, and everyone is more than happy to let her."

"Does she still blame me?"

"Dunno. You haven't come up the few times I have actually talked to her. She mostly hangs out with Derek these days, but all those fuckers live on the same level, so I'm sure she has plenty of other people she can complain to," he said, maintaining the same slightly disinterested tone.

"Derek seems to think it's my fault," she said venomously as she thought back to the assault in the stairwell.

"Fuck that guy," Martin said with gusto. "I swear to

god that guy has the most punchable face I've ever seen," he said and Elle let out a bit of a laugh. "Every time I see that face, I just want to punch it." Martin smiled.

"And what would we do when you break your hand?" She asked in jest.

"You obviously don't know me very well if you think I can't fly with a broken hand," Martin said with the sort of fatherly machismo she expected from him. She made sure he was looking at her this time when she rolled her eyes. He just smiled. "Speaking of which, I think you're due for another flying lesson. You ready?"

"What?" she barked out suddenly on reflex even though she heard exactly what he said. "What the fuck are you talking about?"

"What do you mean?" Martin asked, managing to look slightly hurt. "I thought you wanted to learn to fly."

"Well, I... I," Elle stammered, suddenly struck by her own words. It seemed like a lifetime has passed by since she uttered them.

"Listen, we're not going to get a much better opportunity, so it's kind of shit or get off the pot time," he said in a playful tone, but still meaning every word.

"Ah." The weak sound escaped her mouth that was still hanging open. Elle didn't want to look him in the eyes . Instead, she looked at the vast array of digital displays in front of her. She couldn't begin to-.

"Don't look at those. Look at me." She did. Martin looked at her dead in the eyes and held his gaze there for a moment. There was a connection there. She felt it. "You can do this," Martin said in a slow, deliberate voice. He let it sink in, and then said it again for good measure. "You can do this." After that, he turned back forward. "Considering the things you have done lately, this shit should be a walk in the park."

That caused her to consider the things she had actually accomplished instead of how it broke her along the way to accomplishing them. Elle *did* fix the helicopter. She *helped* Emilio set up a greenhouse within the building. Elle retrieved the seeds on the food run *by herself*. She managed to shoot her weapon and even downed a few zombies for good measure. *You can do this*, Martin's words resonated in her head.

Asshole!

"Okay. Okay," Elle said nodding slowly. "What do I do?" She asked, sitting up straighter in her seat and shaking her hands out in front of her to prepare herself for whatever was going to happen next.

"Take the cyclic control with your right and reach down and grab the collective with your left. Just like you did the first time. The rest is easy," Martin said with a smile. She didn't think about it. Elle didn't want this moment ruined by whatever was rattling around inside her head. She just did it.

Elle took the controls in her hands. She gripped them firmly and already felt her palms getting slick on them. Martin still had control, though. She could feel his subtle movements through the stick in her hands. Once she was ready, though, he released his grip on the controls. The helicopter bobbed a little in the air as control of Maggie transferred to her. Instinctively; she tightened her grip on the controls and both her arms seemed to solidify with the tension she held. Like stones at her side.

"Relax," Martin soothed. "It's like driving a car. Hold on to the stick, but don't strangle it." He gently advised as Elle took a few deep breaths so she could relax her grip… slightly.

Her heart was pounding inside her chest. She didn't dare move the stick between her legs in any way, lest she actually affect how they were currently travelling. It seemed to take everything she had just to keep the craft flying in the same manner as Martin had a moment ago.

"Good." Elle jumped slightly as his voice came through the headset, but luckily, the jolt didn't translate through to the controls. "Okay, let's have some fun," he said and instantly she wanted to object, but before she could, he spoke again. "See this?" He asked and out of the corner of her eye she saw that he was pointing to something on the center console.

"Huh-uh." Elle answered even though she didn't look at the thing he was pointing at. She couldn't. Elle locked her eyes on the airspace in front of them. She wanted to look at what he was pointing at, but somehow that was a leap her body wasn't ready for. Beside her, she heard Martin's sigh.

"Yeah, okay, but I need you to actually look at it. Take a fucking breath already and relax. We're in the wide-open sky. You're not going to hit anything." He didn't do his little chuckle at the end that time. She did as she was told, starting with the deep breath, or two. Then she forced her head to turn and look at the console. If only for a moment.

It resembled a digital clockface, but it wasn't a clock. It was obviously a gauge of some sort. However, Unlike the fuel gauge, this one encompassed the complete circle, numbered increments that increased by ten, with smaller increments in between. She didn't count the smaller ticks between the numbers, but she assumed there would be ten of them. Then, as if on a timed spring, her gaze whipped back to the space outside the front of the craft.

"That's our speed, it's measured in miles," he said and she just nodded while keeping a close eye out the windshield. "How fast are we going right now?" He asked innocently. She should have guessed he was going to ask that.

Fucker.

Elle primed herself for another quick look. She found the gauge easy enough, and this time, with the benefit of knowing what she was looking at, she somehow became more familiar with it. She didn't bother trying to decipher the digital needle position on the gauge, because on the bottom of the incremental circle was a numeric readout.

"One hundred and nineteen miles per hour," Elle said with a little tension in her voice.

One hundred and nineteen goddamn miles! Jesus! She wondered if Martin would tease her over her nervous tone. If he did, she wouldn't have a problem telling him he could go fuck himself. She had a lot on her plate at the moment.

"Okay, let's slow down to 80 miles per hour. Just ease back on the stick to slow us down." Elle did as she was told.

Easing the stick back while maintaining a tenuous eye on the speedometer. *Was it even called a speedometer?* She didn't know, and it didn't seem overly important. Elle added it to the list of questions she was sure she would have for Martin later, after she had time to think.

"Perfect." Martin cheered as the gauge finally finished its slow countdown to eighty. "You see? It's not so hard. Now just keep on this heading until we reach the interstate." Martin pointed in front of them.

Elle could see it off in the distance. On their left, they were running parallel to another massive road, probably a different interstate, though she didn't know which one. She followed the road ahead of them to a massive turnpike. The rest of the buildings looked like the massive roads merely pushed them aside as the two multi-lane interstates collided with each other at the turnpike and continued to snake its way through the cityscape in opposing directions. They cruised towards it at such a speed Elle didn't think she had much time before the next direction.

"Okay, just move yourself over a bit until you're centered over the road. Ease the stick over to the left a bit."

"Okay," she said and with sweaty hands she moved the stick to the left ever so slightly. Elle felt her weight shift in her chair as the craft's nose started drifting to the left. She lined the nose up with the massive road beneath them as it followed a bend in the dark river beside it. Then she remembered something that caused a spike of dread within her as she saw a thin ribbon of green below. Just beyond the road she was supposed to line the craft up with. "What about the birds?" She squeaked slightly.

"I'm keeping an eye on it. Stop worrying so much. That's supposed to be my job," he said, probably expecting a laugh. "Just do what I say and let me worry about everything else. If something comes up, I'll take over, quick and easy. So, stop pissing your pants over there. Shit, you're making me nervous, for Christ's sakes."

"Fuck you," she said with a bitterness only a friend would see through. "Don't tell me not to worry. That's all I do. It's what I'm good at." A brief chuckle rewarded her sourness over the intercom. Then it was back to business.

"That's good," he said as they approached the turnpike. "When the helicopter is moving forward like this, it operates a lot like an airplane regarding the turns."

"When do I use the pedals?"

"Don't worry about those," he said absently. "Okay, now bring us back the other way until the nose is lined up with the road and then follow it past the turnpike up here. Just go straight through. Up ahead, past it, was a T-section where three giant six-lane interstates come together. Once we get up to that point, I want you to follow the road going off to the left," Martin said and then motioned out his window with his thumb, as if she might have forgotten which way left was.

Maggie crossed over a vast concrete parking lot. It must have been the size of three football fields and was completely empty before they finally reached the interstate. Elle listened closely as Martin directed her over the road and had her bring the helicopter up to twenty-five hundred feet by pulling up on the collective lever ever-so-slightly. Up ahead on the right-hand side of the interstate, beyond a cluster of indistinguishable buildings, was another swampy green patch. Elle suspected Martin was concerned about the birds here as well.

"Wait. If we can just fly over the birds, why are we going this way? Why not just fly straight there?" She looked over to him just in time to catch him nodding appreciatively.

"Clever girl," he said as if impressed by her and held up two fingers. "Two reasons. One," he ticked off a finger, the middle one. "The higher we go, the more fuel we spend." *Makes sense*, she thought, if they weren't going to refuel, anyway. Regardless, she let him continue. "And two, it's more fun." She looked back to the front, feeling slightly annoyed at his answer.

Who has time for fun? She thought sourly.

The road ahead bent slightly to the right and then, after a few miles, shifted back to the left. Without permission or instruction, she shifted the cyclic stick in front of her and Maggie's nose lined up with the roads through the slight bend.

I'm in control, she told herself as she nervously steered

Maggie down the interstate. Elloise Russo, a twenty-three-year-old native of Queens, was flying a helicopter over New Jersey.

During her stay at The Prescott, especially over the last few months, there had been many occasions when she wished her mother were there with her. What she wouldn't give to just fall into her lap and have her mother stroke her head like she used to when she was a child and was upset about something. A few times, she wished she was there so she could advise her on what to do or how to handle some people. However, this, *this* was the first time she wished her mother was here so be proud her. *Look at me, Mommy! I'm doing it*! It was an entirely selfish thought, but she was flying. *She* was flying! This wasn't like their joyride over the park and the east river. That was like comparing learning to drive in a parking lot to the first time out on the highway.

"You're right," she said, feeling slightly ashamed at her previous annoyance. "This is better." Martin said nothing, and they just continued on over the road.

They sailed over the New Jersey turnpike and Elle risked a brief look down at the road. From this height, she could see the stagnant river of vehicles that were left on all the lanes of the turnpike, even the ones leading into the city. She didn't imagine anybody was too keen to head into the city during the evacuation. Knowing her fellow New Yorkers, somebody probably bust through the lane barriers and started using the east bound lanes to go west. She looked to her left, following the line of cars towards the city. She didn't get far, though.

They followed the highway into the city to the west, and before the wide bridge that crossed the black-watered river that fed the swampland they had passed, was a military roadblock. *Was that a tank*? Elle thought to herself as she spied an impossibly wide blocky-looking vehicle in front of the concrete barrier that was placed across the entire highway. She didn't know, and it really didn't matter now, it was just part of the landscape. Elle turned away, wondering if the blockade kept people out of the city, or in it. In the end, it didn't matter because by the time the first warning went out to the public; it was already too late. They just didn't know it yet.

After the turnpike, it was a straight shot to the interstate convergence up ahead. Elle kept her hand steady on the stick and maintained her bearing towards it.

"Okay, let's drop down to, let's say, three hundred feet for the turn and then after, just follow the interstate," Martin said, pretending to sound bored, but she knew better. "Why don't we make it interesting and increase our speed up to one twenty while we're at it, but not until after the turn, mind you?"

Elle looked over and saw his hands resting on his lap. Casual enough to look relaxed, but also within close reach of both control sticks. *Good*, she thought. It was easier to focus on the tasks ahead of her, and enjoy the experience a bit with a comforting knowledge she had a safety net ready to catch her if she made a mistake.

As her turn approached, she ran through the controls in her head and what she would have to do to make Maggie turn to the left. *This is crazy*, she reminded herself. She could have laughed out loud. Elle had seen crazy. She survived it. This wasn't crazy. It was a simple mistake to make because the line between fear and enjoyment could sometimes be a fine one. Especially after a person crosses over into adulthood. She didn't blame the voice in her head for making the mistake. She simply corrected it. *No, this isn't crazy*, she gently reminded herself. *This is* fun.

She looked at the display for their speed. Elle held the craft at eighty miles per hour as she began her turn over the highways. She had never driven a car eighty miles per hour, nor has she been a passenger in a car that went that fast. Luckily, the height of the craft made their speed less daunting. She couldn't even think about after the turn, when she was supposed to speed up to well over a hundred miles an hour. A hundred-goddamn-miles per hour! It was unthinkable, and yet…

"More." Martin calmly instructed from beside her. She answered by shifting the cyclic further to the left, and Maggie responded instantly. Elle eyed up the bend in the road and compared that to the rate they were turning, and she thought it was wrong. She was taking it too wide. "More." Martin confirmed her thought before she adjusted it. She had been right. She grinned and nudged the stick further to the left.

It was too little, too late. She ended up taking the turn a little wider. Maggie strayed outside the lines of the massive ten-lane interstate highway. Martin teased her quietly, as she knew he would, as she adjusted Maggie's course and brought them back over the interstate.

On Martin's word, she brought the craft's speed up to one hundred and twenty miles an hour. She watched the little digital needle on the speed gauge climb over the tiny ticks with ever-increasing anxiety until she reached their cruising speed. That's what Martin called it, anyway. To her, it felt like they were doing much more than simply *cruising*. She was flying, goddamnit!

From this height, their speed didn't translate well, and ahead of her the interstate slithered gently through the cityscape. There was nothing she could hit, and her path was clearly laid out in front of her. She breathed easier. Her heart rate fell back to the point it was completely unnoticeable. Okay, she thought, maybe *this* was cruising.

"Okay, doing good, just maintain this altitude and speed," Martin said while keeping a close eye on the very things he was telling her to watch. "Just relax into it."

She felt like she was taking a test and Martin was the teacher, watching over her shoulder to make sure she didn't cheat. She knew better, though. *Safety net*, she reminded herself. Martin's last words were the ones that stuck with her the most. *Just relax into it.*

"So how fast can this thing go, anyway?" She asked playfully after a spell. She had just navigated a very lazy, backward S-curve in the road. Elle stayed within the boundaries of the interstate, which wasn't hard, really. She felt relaxed and confident enough about what she was doing, as well as the road ahead, to risk conversation. So, of course, she started by teasing him.

"Don't even think about it," he said, taking the bait perfectly.

"A girl can dream, can't she?" She said in her flowery voice.

"Uh-huh," he said, giving her a side-eye. "Just keep up this same airspeed and altitude, hotshot."

"For how long?" She asked more for the conversation than the information. She didn't care how long it took to get to their destination. As long as she was flying, the farther the better.

"A while yet. You'll know when you're getting close when there's more green around us than grey." Martin motioned outside the helicopter. Around them, the cityscape spread out still in all directions. After a moment of silence, Elle realized she had never been in a place where there was more green than grey. That was the curse, as well as the allure of the big city. You think you know everything there is about the world without the benefit of actually seeing it.

"Then what? Where do we turn off?"

"Highway two-oh-six," he said promptly. "Going north."

"So how am I supposed to know which highway it is?" She asked quickly before steering through a series of slight bends in the road below them. She didn't think she would be capable of doing both at the same time.

"Well, for one, I'll tell you," Martin said and chuckled at his own wit. "We could have plotted our course beforehand to get us there. Then it's just a matter of heading, airspeed, and time. However," he said, bracing her for the next part. "That requires a shitload of math. Which I'm not really thrilled about," Martin said with a blasé tone while waving it off.

"You're going to show me that part, though, right?" It was her turn to give him the side-eye stare.

"I can. Next time we take a run out this way, I'll have you plot us a course we can follow that will take us straight there. If need be, we can always read the signs on the overpasses."

"You're shitting me, right?" She blurted out. She had to call him on that one because there is no way that's true.

"Not me, personally, but I've heard of people doing that. Truth be told, if I didn't have a map, and I had to get somewhere I was unfamiliar with. Sure, I could see myself doing that," Martin said thoughtfully, but with a hint of cautious humor, like he was admitting to something that was a last-ditch effort. She hoped he was kidding.

The conversation died away naturally between them and they fell into a comfortable sort of silence only close friends could tolerate. Which was fine with her. Elle kept a close eye on the road up ahead and subtly steered the craft through the bends. She felt she was getting the hang of it. She didn't have the control of the stick that Martin had, though.

When Martin turned the craft, it felt like they were riding an air current to their new bearing. When she shifted the stick, Maggie would jerk to the side like the helicopter itself was jumping out of the way of something. It wasn't subtle. She didn't blame herself for it. She would learn. Elle could only get better. After all, she had kept Maggie's nose in the center of the large interstate since Martin had her turn onto it. Some of the sharper turns made keeping the craft on track difficult. She knew what the problem was. Elle was being too timid with the control between her legs and starting her turns too late. She made a note of it.

The dull grey desert of the cityscape passed by them in predictable ways. Industrial zones gave way to commercial zones, which slowly blended in with residential zones. Then there was usually a green space of some sort before the cycle started over. *Are those separate cities we're passing by?* She thought to herself as she looked out the side window and saw the cycle renew itself, with another industrial zone starting up. Further ahead she could see a large mall in the distance. If she was passing through individual cities, it was impossible to tell, as their borders seem to blend into one giant sprawl.

"Wow," Elle said with a defeated exasperation in her voice as she looked out at what she assumed was the biggest traffic jam in human history. Since she took control and kept Maggie over the highway, she has kept an especially close eye on the road below them. In reality, she was observing the vehicles, because the road itself wasn't visible except for the odd gap between the abandoned cars.

"We were never going to get out, were we?" Elle inquired and risked a look at Martin.

She didn't need him to say anything. The proof was below her. She and her sister had to abandon their car they were driving shortly after the Queensboro bridge when they heard screaming erupt from all around them. There was no way they would have made it out of the city. By the looks of it, not many people did.

"No," Martin breathed. "Not your fault, though. It was a clusterfuck from the beginning. First, they quarantined the metropolitan area to try and keep the infection out. Which was impossible. Then, after it was obviously too late, they reversed course and told everyone to evacuate the city. You were smart to get off the streets when you did."

"I guess."

It was hard to celebrate the decisions of the past when she knew they led her to the place she was now, but deep down she knew Martin was right. It just didn't feel like it. She was happy they were alive, but she couldn't comment on their future prospects. That was something she tried not to think about.

Again, they felt into a comfortable silence and let the roar of the turbine engines fill the void between them. She busied herself with the smooth operation of Maggie. At least, she hoped it was getting smoother. Martin commented a little on it. He was content to watch the landscape past them by through the side windows. When he wasn't looking out the windows, he was checking the displays on the console to make sure she was still flying within his parameters. Elle paid him no mind as she weaved Maggie clumsily along a series of gentle bends in the massive freeway below her before she came along a fairly sharp turn in the road. She readjusted her grip on the cyclic stick in front of her, took a deep breath.

"What is that?" Elle asked on the other side of turn.

In front of them she saw the great grey cityscape give way to a thick forest that spread out to the north-west. To the south, the city persisted even though she saw more green permeate through the dull greys. There was one more massive overpass where the city ended and beyond that, the forest took over the landscape ahead of them. Her eyes traced the river of vehicles on the road to a point, which was right before a large bridge where the highway separated into two pieces that stretched across an actual river. There, the constant stream of abandoned vehicles on the road below came to an abrupt end.

"That's a roadblock the army set up to check people for signs of infection before they entered the city. Then, when the shit hit the fan within the city, they used it to check for infected people on their way out. All they did with slow the evacuation, though." Martin said in a rather sad voice.

As they approached the disturbance on the highway, Elle made out the large green vehicles that were parked across the interstate. She saw two large white tents erected on both sides of the road, as if the circus was in town or something. She quickly checked her speed and altitude before returning her gaze to the approaching scene. One thing caught her eyes that furrowed her brow further. Close behind the tent was a giant hole in the ground. There was no other way to describe it. Both sides of the road had a large, almost perfectly square, excavation was dug deep into the ground. All the surrounding trees had been removed to make room for the tent and the ominously fenced-off pits.

"What's with the pits?" She asked timidly, because part of her was afraid of what the answer might be. They were still too far away to see what may be inside them.

"Those aren't pits," Martin said. His tone alone confirmed what he was about to say next. "Those are graves."

It didn't hit her as hard as she thought it would. Maybe because she saw the blow coming, or maybe she was just getting used to the gut punches the world handed out these days. She didn't know. She thought she would be more upset, and in a way, the realization did disturb her, but not nearly as much as she thought it should. Those were Americans down there in those pits. *Mass graves*, a voice inside her head, corrected her. *We don't do that sort of thing*. It was a sign of how fragile the American moral superiority was.

"Fuck," she cursed, quietly and bitterly. It was all she felt she could say on the issue.

She felt the outrage in herself, but she didn't know where to direct it. She couldn't blame the soldiers for removing the infected. It was a shit job, but nobody would argue with its necessity, except for maybe family members at the time of the removal. She couldn't blame people for trying to sneak out infected loved ones. For hanging on to the vain hope that maybe, just maybe, they would find a cure in time. That's what Americans did. They hoped for the best.

"How'd they know?" She asked solemnly.

"I think they did a temperature check first, and then if they found someone with a fever, they would separate them. Probably haul them into those tents down there to inspect the person for bites. I imagine for someone who was bitten, that would be a one-way trip," Martin said, trying to be impartial and doing a good job of it.

"Do you think they let them say goodbye first?" She asked as they came upon the roadblock.

It was a chaotic scene. At some point, it looked

like motorist got tired of waiting and tried to run the roadblock. Vehicles had turned off the highway and ran along the side of the road in the ditch, hoping to find a way through. Many didn't. She saw burnt out wrecks on the grass in front of the dense shrubs that ran along the road. She only had to look at the large caliber guns that were mounted on the military vehicles to imagine what happened to those who tried to flee past the checkpoint. *They had to know*, she said to herself while thinking of the infected people who might have been sitting in their car with their families and seeing that roadblock in front of them.

"I don't know. The army was pretty upfront about their zero-tolerance policy there at the end, and I personally would have hoped that anybody who was infected would have seen the writing on the wall." She risked a look out the side window to see if she could see down into the depths of the graves.

Over the intercom, she heard Martin about to say something, but he cut himself off before the words found a way out. Knowing him, he was probably going to advise against looking into the grave. It was too late, though; she was already peering over the edge of the large open grave that was roughly half the size of a football field. She didn't know why exactly. Part of her felt it was her responsibility to see it. Like survivor's guilt or something. She *had* to see it.

Time seemed to slow down over the seconds it took her to look into the sad abyss. With a heavy, uncertain heart, she gazed into the pit. Even though, Elle was not entirely sure what she would see, or how she would react to what was down there. At first, Elle was relieved. From this height, she didn't see too much, just a uniform indiscernible blackness. As her gaze lingered, though, Elle saw bits of color peek through. Her eyes focused in on the color, and she recognized the bottom of the pit wasn't as uniform as she originally thought. There was an entire landscape down there, and she took a long breath as her brain recognized some of those shapes.

Thankfully, Maggie cruised over the spot just as her mind picked out the individual, mud-covered bodies at the bottom of the mass grave. One moment she was seeing the evidence of humanity at its breaking point, and the next it was behind them. *Maybe that's for the best*, Elle said to herself as she looked forward over the newly green landscape ahead of them.

She silently flew forward over the interstate while actively trying not to replay the image of what she had seen. Below her, the west-bound lanes still had a vast collection of vehicles. It was near the impassable traffic jam Elle had seen on the road before the checkpoint. Here, the cars on the roads looked like the people must have abandoned them because they just parked haphazardly along the edges of the interstate every fifty meters.

"Where do you think they were going?" She asked and glanced over at Martin, who just shrugged.

"Dunno. Maybe Wilkes-Barre, there's an Air Force base there. Fort Dickinson, I think. Maybe the army set up a green zone there or something. Maybe they were just running, who knows," Martin said with a certain amount of disinterest. Elle couldn't blame him. In the long run, it didn't matter where they were going because they didn't make it there.

Elle needed to change the topic. Desperately.

"So, are you going to tell me what makes this trip so '*safe and easy*'?" She said his words back to him in a poor imitation. Martin looked at her and smiled like he was a child with a secret. Which he was. She expected Martin's little rundowns on their missions well before the actual trips. This time, he simply said, *'You'll see'*. Martin wasn't a mysterious man. This was a change for him. If it was Jacob or Blaine, she would have wanted to know what was going on immediately before continuing. There was something in Martin's eyes when he told her last night, though. A sort of roguish playfulness that hinted towards something... different.

"You may not know this, but private airports were the first ones to shut down. Back when they thought it was a flu or something. The one we're going to has been locked up tight since before the quarantine."

"Okay," she said, prompting him to continue because she still wasn't seeing it.

"It's practically a zombie-free zone," he said and she could only look at him with a puzzled look. "It's private. So, it's out in the middle of nowhere, and it's completely fenced off and locked down. First time I was there to scout it out, there were like only three zombies down there. One of them was the grounds manager. He was a good guy." Martin gave the man a moment of thought before continuing. "We can land there and maybe have hours before we have to worry about the fucking undead showing up." Martin was getting more excited about it as he spoke. It was kind of infectious. "It's fucking glorious. There's still a mostly full bottle of Jack Daniel's in the office, and my buddy kept a carton of cigarettes in his desk." He was talking like someone planning a vacation. It was kind of cute. "You're welcome to do what you want, but I'm planning on getting a little drunk, smoking a few cigarettes, and playing some pool."

"Your buddy had a pool table at his shop?" Elle asked, genuinely curious.

"He was divorced," he said it like that explained

everything, and maybe it did. "It was a shop slash man-cave. Now, it's my little getaway."

"And Mason is fine with all this?" Elle asked cautiously. She knew what Martin probably thought of Mason's opinion, but she had a hard time believing their stern-faced leader would be okay with a day trip, especially if it was only for the two of them. She had trouble believing Derek would also pass on this if he knew about the pool table.

"Mason thinks it's farther away than it is, and I might have exaggerated on how long the refueling process takes," Martin said with a certain coyness.

"How long does it take?" Elle asked with a certain mirth in her voice. She didn't mind pulling the wool over their protectors. Especially if it gave them time away from them.

"Literally, maybe ten minutes. As far as Mason and his lot know, this is a long, boring milk run with a lot of tedious labor, and nothing to shoot," Martin said with a chuckle.

"How much time does that give us?" Elle asked cautiously. Considering the strange possibility of being outside without worrying about being attacked by hideous monsters. Or seeing tall looming buildings all around her. Or hearing constant gunfire. *This is going to be weird,* she told herself as she kept her course down the road, *but a good weird.*

"Two hours," he said promptly before adding: "Give or take."

"What kind of cigarettes?" She asked, knowing full well she wasn't a smoker anymore, unless she drank a bit first.

"Pall Mall." He answered in a curious tone.

"Fuck sakes," she said disappointed. "You even smoke like an old man." She couldn't help the grin on her face as she stared forward. In her peripheral vision, she could see him peering at her. It was easier than saying thank you.

"Did you just ask that just to hurt my feelings?" He replied, sounding shocked at the concept.

"Maybe a little," she teased. Elle thought about the time she had ahead of her. It didn't seem real. Time in the outside world, free from the threat of the undead. For a short time anyway, but still. It was hard to imagine. "I could play some pool, but I don't know how much I'll drink."

"Good, because you have to get us home," he said casually. Elle knew him well enough to know he was joking. At least, he better be. To be sure, she shot him a look filled with daggers.

"Don't even fucking joke," she said with an honest smile. Down below on the interstate, she realized something that she maybe didn't see before and if she did, her brain didn't register it. "I don't think it would look too good if we came back with you all liquored up. That's *if* we made it back at all." She said while watching the road below her.

On the interstate, the west-bound lane was cluttered with the long-abandoned wrecks of the people who tried to escape the horrors of the city and failed. As she went along the road, she kept the helicopter's nose on the green strip of grass between the west and east-bound lanes. Across the grass and on the other side of the barrier, the east- bound lanes were completely empty as far as her eye could see. Not a single car was on that road. Not one. She found this odd and maybe even slightly discomforting. She couldn't put her finger on it why it bothered her, though. Maybe it was the simple fact she had never seen a road without a car on it before.

There was something ominous and sad about the look of it, like the entire country had already written the New York city area off and all that was left was to wait for it to succumb while the masses fought tooth and nail to escape the carnage. She looked at the empty lanes for a couple moments longer before she realized, at least in part, why the sight bothered her. It was symbolic. Maybe that's why it was lost on her initially. She didn't have time for symbols. This one seemed to hit home, though. Elle moved her gaze back to the center console to make sure she was on track. Just in case Martin surprised her with another quiz. She tried to forget about the empty road and what it represented, but the stain of the thought lingered.

Nobody is coming to help you, those empty lanes said to her. It wasn't a new revelation to her, quite the opposite. The empty lanes of the interstate just reinforced some of her own private fears.

Nobody is coming.

Nobody is left.

Nobody.

Chapter 8

Jeremy

He awoke with a terrible, sucking gasp, like he had been thrown, kicking and screaming, into consciousness. Suddenly he was looking upon the world with a set of wild eyes that searched for the predators he had been running from in the blackness he had just escaped.

It wasn't a dream. It was something *more*.

Other people, he knew, talked about dreaming like it was some magical fucking pony ride into some fantastic land where your subconscious came alive while your body rested. That wasn't his experience. Sleeping was like a death to him. A void. A formless space where he shed his body and just existed in an unknowing stupor until he opened his eyes again and emerged out of the darkness. Sometimes, though, like tonight, it felt like he was escaping something. Something with teeth.

Rows and rows of them.

He sprang in conciousness with a jolt that coursed through his body like a bolt of lightning. He found himself seated in his chair without the benefit of a real good recollection of how he got there. A moment passed and his breathing slowed as he came to recognize his office by the dim light and shadows cast by the candle's flame. He was safe.

His pack inhabited the entire forty-second floor, his allies surrounded him. People who, may not die for him, but they would definitely kill for him, which, in his mind, was better because it was more reliable. You can't trust a man to die for something, not truly. Men don't have it in them. People are animals at their core, he knew that, animals don't believe in sacrifice because they knew there was no greater good. There's only survival. When the wolves come, all the sheep scatter, and the weak get singled out and slaughtered. That's how it works, that's how it's *supposed* to work. That is the only true law, the law of nature. This group understood that. He was fortunate in that regard. They knew how to fall in line when the chips were down. His little pack of killers.

For a moment, he swore one shadow in the corner... shifted, as if guided by some kind of malicious intellect. He gazed at the spot in the darkened room, as if daring the shadows to move. After a time, he shook the thought from his mind, forcing himself to believe he was mistaken. That there was nothing there, and there never was.

He rubbed his short salt-and-pepper hair with both hands before rubbing the sleep from his eyes. *It's late*, he told himself as his mind swam precariously within his head. He held his skull in his hands and looked out through his fingers to the line of cocaine that remained on the ornate wooden desk in front of him. Just a little past that thin line of white powder was a large crystal glass that was still half full of that expensive bourbon. Details of last night slowly permeated out of the fog of his mind. There was a card game Dennis had thrown together. They had been doing shots. He took part until he felt the drunkenness set in and then he excused himself. Loose lips sink ships, and he had an image to maintain.

Sometimes he wondered if his little band of killers followed the rank or the man, he didn't know, so he figured it was best to keep the facade up when he could. He sat there during the game and put up with the drunken high school antics of these lost and lonely adults as best he could, but when he ground his teeth just to keep his mouth shut, he knew it was time to go. He remembered politely saying his goodbyes to everyone and nodding to Dennis on his way out. The two of them had been through a lot before this shit-box of a place. They came here together, and if he had anything to say about it, they would leave here together as well. Just like they had planned in the beginning. Besides, Dennis Martinez was a handy person to have around.

Fuck it. The thought radiated so strongly in his head he almost said it out aloud as he eyed the single line of coke on the desk, it was practically singing to him. As if pulled by strings no one else could see, he leaned forward. Using a familiar motion, he pinched off one nostril with his finger and dive-bombed that line, sucking up the drug with practised ease.

"Fuck, yes!" He growled loudly as he felt the sweet burn boring its way into his skull.

He bolted up from his chair like it was on fire, the edges of his vision pulsed with his heartbeat. He smacked his palm down onto the solid surface of the desk once, twice, three times as the fire spread throughout his mind. When it finally ebbed, he reached for the bourbon and swallowed it down in one pull. Again, he felt the liquid trace a line of fire down his throat.

"Breakfast of champions," he said, chuckling a little while putting the empty glass down before turning around to face the giant floor-to-ceiling windows of this ridiculously large office.

Nobody had ever called him a champion. They did not groom him for greatness like some of these white-collar pricks. He felt like he was standing in the office of some asshole who had never had to *really* work for anything, a real silver spoon type. The kind of guy that was blessed with status, wealth, and opportunity from the moment his mother spit him out of her greasy slit. More than once he looked around the office with its large ornate desk which was probably supposed to symbolize power, or some shit like that. The tasteful shelves with a life's collection of expensive looking knick-knacks and books that have probably never been read, and probably never will be now. Not to be overlooked, was the posh black leather furniture set. Two chairs placed opposite to the desk, and a long couch with two more large chairs that were placed around a glass coffee table at the other end of the office by the door.

They said when the founders of this nation first started building Washington D.C.; they built it to be so architecturally grandiose that it would intimidate any foreign dignitaries who came to do business. It was the capital city of the new empire, after all. They conceived this room for the same purpose, to influence and intimidate the people who entered it. People like him. The commoners. The architects meant this room to suggest, *Look at all that I have. I have everything you have ever desired. You could have it too. I could let you have some of it, if I like you.*

He knew the type. After a while, with these rich pricks, it stopped being about the money. It became about control. It wasn't enough they were on top of the heap; they had to control who rose out of the muck. That's what brought a smile to his face. All their little tricks, schemes, and machinations, that were all designed to keep people like him out of places like this.

"And yet here I am," he said, looking into his shadowed reflection in the window.

Beyond his image was mostly blackness out there in the zombie world. The giant windows faced out towards the Park. He was on the one of the highest floors of The Prescott building, a space normally reserved for titans of the business world, and now it was his. He looked out into the darkness of the city. He could still make out the moonlit rooftops of the other buildings nearest them. He then peered deeper into the blackness of the night. He smiled broadly, satisfied with what he had accomplished for himself thus far. He knew that in a year's time, give or take, everything that blackness touched would be his.

He leaned in close and pressed his cheek up to the cool surface of the glass to try and see all the way down to street level. It was, of course, impossible. He was too high up and there wasn't enough available light. No matter where he looked, everything just descended into blackness. *No matter*. He knew what was down there. He could almost feel *them*. Rotting away... Slowly.

Much slower than they should. He knew this for a fact. The rats didn't eat them. Hell, the one plus side of the undead horde infesting New York is they seemed to drive all the rats away. He didn't think bugs cared for them, either. He had been up close and personal with a lot of those ugly, undead marvels enough to notice none of them had maggots or any other little critters crawling on them, or in them. Decomposition should have made them dried up husks by now. No, something was preserving them. He didn't know what, but he felt in his heart the undead didn't have another year left in them.

"Just a little more time, that's all I need," he said to his reflection. He didn't have an exact timeline because it wasn't an exact science, but if he could just keep the sheep in line a little longer, then he could have it all. "Oh, but I shall miss you," he cooed almost musically down into the depths of the blackness of the streets below. "My sweet children." He wasn't lying. There was a strange pull on his heart when he thought of the world without zombies.

Two to five zombies were a problem for an average person, but not because people didn't have the faculties to handle the problem. They didn't have the will. They lacked the drive to look something in the eye and do lethal damage to it. It's difficult for the sheep to smash someone's skull, or drive something sharp into its brainpan, especially when the thing you're trying to attack wants to eat you. Violence like that was beyond them. Generations of living under someone's boot had bred the will to survive right out of them.

That's why he hated New York so much. A goddamn massive sheep farm was all it was. The end result of a centuries-long effort to turn real people into *consumers*. Sheep. He looked out over what he could see of the darkened city and marveled at the complexity of it, the sheer goddamn magnitude of it all. All these buildings were just neat little containers for humans, one for when they are at work. Doing jobs they don't like, jobs that suck the very thing that made them special right out of them. Stealing away everyone's uniqueness until they all dressed the same, looked the same with the same haircuts, and had the same stupid expressions on their dull faces.

The other container was where they slept, raised the next generation of consumers, and housed all their useless stuff. Their masters led them to believe it's a castle, a sanctuary, a place they can go where they will be safe. All bitter lies to keep them in line, to keep them consuming. The sheep tell themselves if they just made a little more money, then things would get easier. Just a better job to afford to go to school, so they can get an even better job and make more money. It doesn't stop there. No, the more they make, the more they consume. And if the time comes when the sheep can't afford to consume anymore. *Well, no need to worry your pretty little head over a small thing like that, friend. We have credit. You can't pay me back right away? Don't you worry about that, just pay us when you can and we'll let the interest take care of the rest.*

Consume. Consume. CONSUME!

So yeah, he had had to admit when he first saw a zombie bite into someone; he had a good laugh over it. One of the great lies of the modern era was that they let the sheep believe they were lions. It led them to believe the sheep were superior. It was funny watching the sheep finally see beyond the veil of lies.

He knew the look.

He tried to show a few people the truth in the past, so, it was easy to recognize the disheartened look of someone seeing the light for the first time. Of course, the zombie spread the truth better than he could have even imagined. A whole toothless nation fell before them in a matter of weeks. The entire system just fell apart like he always knew it would. He remembered laughing uncontrollably in his bed for days while the city burned and screamed outside his window.

He couldn't help it.

His whole life, the system labeled him as unworthy of its attention. There was a glorious period in his life when he could be who he was meant to be. A period where he didn't follow their rules. The same rules meant to keep him in the station they saw fit for him. He discovered their rules didn't apply to him because he found the will to follow his own path. At that time, he was a bird who had found his wings. He found his purpose, his *true* purpose, and he followed it wherever it took him. He followed *the Itch*.

It didn't last long, though.

Soon, the sheep assimilated him back into the grand machine and they forgot about him. His time had passed. So, when the zombies exposed the truth to the sheep all over the nation, he laughed, and laughed. His time would soon come again, and this time, there would be no going back to the system, because the system was gone. Forever.

And here he was.

He was number one.

Top of the list.

Head of the heap.

"King of the mother-fucking hill," he said to his shadowed reflection. It smiled back at him like a devil that had a secret to tell.

It was the drugs; he knew that. He knew the shadowy figure in the window wasn't real, even though he felt real, or felt like he should be real. Like the dark figure, who looked less like a real person than an approximation of what an actual human might look like, represented who he was better than his genuine face. The grin on the reflection slightly widened at the thought of people seeing that darkened, distorted face before kissing this world goodnight. It was enough to make him giggle. Yeah, it was definitely the drugs.

"I need a smoke," he said aloud and then turned to the desk.

In the partial darkness, he couldn't see much. He had a flashlight and knew very well where it was on the desktop, but did not want to break the gentle solitude of the candle-lit room. He had always felt safest in the darkness. Besides which, he had better-than-average night vision, which came in handy. With the level of light available to him, he could easily see the pack of cigarettes on the desk's surface.

Using the tactile information from his fingers more than his sight, he fished a cigarette out and then tossed the pack back onto the desk. He retrieved the book of matches out of his pocket and lit one, held the fiery bulb up to the end of the smoke with a sort of grace that came with years of experience. As he tossed the match away from him, and watched its arch as it travelled across the room like a tiny comet. The flame was eventually extinguished and disappeared into the darkness. Leaving only a thin trail of smoke before the blackness consumed it, like it consumed everything else.

He looked back to the window and took another heavy pull of the cigarette. He watched with keen interest as the burning end flared up and briefly illuminated his reflection in the window. Exposing more of himself.

If the sheep only knew what walked amongst them…

He let the thought linger for a moment in his brain. He felt good. He couldn't deny it. He liked this place, he could tolerate the people, and he even had an outlet for *The Itch*. What more could he ask for? Sure, he was playing a dangerous game with these people, but that's what made it interesting. He held no illusions when it came to them. If they knew who he was, and more importantly, *what* he was, they would kill him.

Oh sure, they would hem and haw over it. The decision wouldn't come easy, by any means. *Motherfuckers would probably take a vote, by secret ballot most likely.* Sheep didn't like to make the hard choices. In the end, though, he would still catch a bullet from them. Or, maybe not, but they would insist it be painless. That's how these people worked. So, he played dress-up and put on a show for the masses. He did it before, he could do it again.

The funny thing was, and this always put a smile on his face, was how goddamn easy it was. In a city of millions, he seemed to stick out like a sore thumb, and he always felt like every damned move he made they recorded, scanned, analyzed, and finally logged away in some database for later use. Here, he was like smoke. He could go anywhere, whenever he wanted. He could carry a knife in plain sight, or a gun, and nobody cared. There was no way to vet anything he said, and even if they could, this lot wouldn't, because they're too occupied with their own sorrowful bullshit to notice who was right in front of their eyes. As long as they were safe, had a bite to eat, and a place they could cry about all the shit they had lost, these people could care less about who was sharing their space with them.

And who exactly provided this safety? He did. How exactly did he provide this safety? Well, simple, by doing the exact thing that put him away. It was a cosmic joke that only he truly understood, and he loved it. It just proved the hypocrisy he knew existed, but nobody ever wanted to admit to. The only difference between a killer and a savior is the clothes he wears and the situation he is in. If he had killed all those goddamn people way back when to protect some national interest, he'd be a goddamn hero. They would have had parades for him. He had talent; he was special, but he didn't play by their rules. The sheep punished him for seeing through their thin veil.

He took another heavy drag and watched his reflection flare up with the cigarette. He, too, looked like he was burning. Something about that thought intrigued him. He didn't have time to think on it too long though because in the window he spied another light source being reflected. Somewhere behind him, a light flashed briefly as someone moved through the common hallway these executive offices shared.

Who could be up at this hour? He wondered playfully.

The sky had been overcast all day, so outside the window was only darkness. No stars, no moon, barely enough light outside to see across to the adjacent building. It had to be after midnight. Maybe as late as two o'clock in the morning. Far too late for there to be anyone casually roaming around the darkened hallways of The Prescott. He didn't have to think long about what to do next. His body reacted to the idea of a hunt. Even if he was only going to find out who might be lurking around his space at night. Still, he got a little hard thinking about the prospects.

"What's the harm?" He asked the darkness as he turned towards the door.

He paused for a moment as he briefly considered taking something. There were many guns and knives in his possession. He had two pairs of brass knuckles, which was just a term, because he suspected they actually made them out of steel. Which, in his mind, was better. He had a baseball bat that he knew was leaning up against the far corner. He had many toys he could bring. In the end, he breathed out a long sigh, and simply walked out of the room. He didn't need protection, and he didn't need the temptation. He had to be smart about this after all.

He left his flashlight on the desk as he walked into the darkness of the room, and crept across the large office with confidence. He didn't need to see everything; he knew this office like the back of his hand, as well as most of the floor. He could navigate well enough using only the meager amount of light there was and his knowledge of the layout. He sneaked into the large foyer and counted twenty paces as he crept forward towards the receptionist's desk. Using his hands, he moved around the right side of the desk and counted ten more paces towards the glass door of the entrance into the law firm he claimed as his own. He didn't remember what the name was because, in the end, it didn't matter. Though, he did like to refer to the firm as Cheatum & Howe. He let the door whisper shut behind him and just stood in the blackness of the shared hallway and listened. He craned his head up and turned it slowly first to the left, and then to the right, trying to get a sense of the space. Instinct told him when to move forward, and he didn't hesitate when it did. He kept low and took seven quick, careful steps forward towards the elevator bank. From there, he used his hand to follow the wall to the hallway that led to the stairwell. On the wall, as usual, he found a selection of small flashlights hanging beside the door. He carefully slipped one free from the hooks. It was only big enough to fit into the palm of his hand. Sightlessly, he turned the cylinder in his hand until he felt the tiny rubber button on the side that activated it.

The stairwell door presented him with a slight problem. It was a big metal door with a metal handle and thumb-latch that operates the catch on the door. He knew it wasn't locked. That wasn't the problem. The problem was, it was loud. They did not design commercial doors like this to be quiet. He brought his ear up to the door's somewhat cool exterior and listened. His hand slipped around the door's handle with his palm sliding onto the thumb latch. When he couldn't hear any sounds coming from the stairwell, he slowly and with steady pressure, squeezed the latch and the handle together. It was a similar motion to how someone might strangle someone with their bare hands.

Snick!

The small metallic noise seemed to resonate in the darkened hallway. It was a sharp sound, and an instant later it was gone. Before he opened the stairwell door, he waited for sharp click to die away. He knew this door. When it opened or closed, he knew it didn't make a sound. He had made sure of it. Again, he waited until instinct told him to open the door. He tried to make it look casual as he braced himself for what was on the other side.

More darkness.

He slipped into the blackness of the stairwell like he was entering a friend's house. He let the door close behind him and then assisted in easing it to a relatively quiet close. The catch slamming home still sounded like a gunshot as it pierced the absolute stillness of the stairwell.

Like before, the noise echoed sharply and then it quickly died away. He stood in the absolute darkness waiting, feeling his erection throb in his pants, as he waited for a familiar sound to come. He slowly felt his way towards the stairwell's inner railing, feeling slightly impatient. It was a fifty-fifty guess which way the figure had gone. Up or down.

He smiled wickedly as he figured the odds might be a bit more stacked in his favor as his brain replayed the brief scene he witnessed in his head again. It was a small frame that moved towards the stairwell. He only saw it for what seemed like the briefest of moments, but the more he thought about it, the more he felt that frame was familiar. If he was correct in his assumptions, he would find out soon enough, as the sound of the rooftop door closing would be the telltale sign he was right. If he wasn't, maybe it would be best if he returned to Cheatum & Howe and poured himself another glass of that expensive whiskey and drink it leisurely while he smoked cigarettes behind his desk and waited for the sunrise. Like a real executive. Maybe he would even jerk off.

Slam!

The sound of the rooftop door colliding to a close was unmistakable. It echoed loudly down the stairwell from above him and when he heard it; it flipped a switch inside his head. All other thoughts were pushed aside instantly. *I got you now*, he thought as he climbed the steps towards the roof. It was an odd thing to have pop into his head because he didn't remember having any malicious intent when he began this journey. He was just going to have a look, after all. Like a well-fed cat that still hunted a mouse even though it had no need to kill it. He still wanted to go through the motions. He still wanted to play with it a bit before he retired for the evening.

The push bar on the inside of the rooftop door made opening it silently all too easy. It was like a gift as it opened with hardly a sound. He eased it shut and moved into the nearby shadow to listen for a spell. New York had certainly changed. It used to be that no matter where you were in the city, no matter how quiet you believed it to be, you could always pick out the background noise of the maelstrom. The sounds of traffic, sirens in the distance, airplanes overhead, boats in the harbor, et cetera. It was the goddamn symphony of cacophonous sounds that were the earmarks of man's existence on this planet. The white noise that followed the sheep around no matter where they went.

Now it was gone, replaced with only the sound of the void. The deep hollowness that echoed throughout the dead space. The hunter's calm. It made the sound of sobbing coming from somewhere up ahead of him much easier to hear. That sound stirred something dark inside of him, like how a wolf feels when it hears the pained mewing of an injured calf. It tickled him in a way he wasn't expecting.

None-the-less, he moved forward around the metal staircase that led up to the helipad, and into the deeper darkness of the space under the overhang. He crept up to the small storage room, hugged the walls as he peered around the corner and up to the railing along the helipad. He didn't see anyone, not yet, but he still heard their sobs somewhere above him and maybe a little further on. With three quick, elongated strides, he moved out from the overhang, around the front face of the storage shack, and slipped back into the relative security of the overhang in the blink of an eye.

He approached the corner of the roof and he knew he was getting close when he could smell the cigarette smoke on the breeze that always seemed to blow up here. He risked a look out from the overhang just in time to see the burning heart of Jackie's cigarette flare up in the night. The red hues that shone on her face against the black backdrop of the night sky was…, magical.

Lava tears flowed down an ember face that stared vacantly at the ugly stub at the end of her forearm where her hand used to be. There was a longing in her face that he witnessed in that moment, a sort of anguish that stirred something inside of him. It wasn't sexual, nothing so easily explained as simple chemical desire. He couldn't explain it. Maybe it was curiosity or maybe his intent was crueller and more intrusive, but he suddenly knew he had to get closer to her. To what she was feeling. After all, he had a right. He had been the one who was joyously tasked with removing her hand.

He moved into the seclusion of the overhang, tucked himself right up against the building and put his hand against it and counted his steps as he went. After fifteen steps, he felt he was close and moved away from the building. It was dark on the roof, but there was still enough ambient light to see the cigarette butt next to the dark spot on the concrete ahead of him. *This is the spot.* He lowered himself into a seated position on the roof, still completely hidden from Jackie's view if she looked down.

He sat there cross-legged in the darkness, pleased with himself as he listened to Jackie renewed her sobs with a fresh vigor. He just took it all in, as they say, and thought about how he would spend the rest of his morning.

That's when the sound came.

A tiny sound of something colliding with the concrete somewhere in front of him. His heart skipped a beat when he concluded it was a wet sound. He looked again to the dark spot on the concrete and the realization came in a flash. *Tears*. After that, his hand just sort of moved on its own as it reached slowly forward to cover the dark spot with his palm up. He wondered, if she were to look down to where her tears were falling, would Jackie see his palm below her just waiting to catch the next one? Would she scream? Part of him wanted her to, even though he knew that was a dangerous thought to have. *I should leave*, he thought to himself and began to withdraw his hand.

Then something small struck his palm. Something insignificant kissed his flesh, close to his middle finger. It was a small, warm something and when it struck, it exploded into smaller pieces of wetness that blossomed in his hand. His body shook when it happened, which was weird, because he was expecting it to happen. Hoping even, but he didn't think it would feel so... liberating.

His breath caught in his throat as his whole body shuddered, as if in ecstasy. A warmth bloomed inside of him that radiated out from his palm. He pulled his hand back into the darkness and held it in front of himself. He couldn't see it. The tiny spot of wetness, the tiny piece of Jackie that he had stolen away for himself. He felt it, though. Using the fingers of his other hand, he gently massaged the slippery piece of Jackie into the flesh of his palm. Part of him imagined his skin soaking up her essence and making it a part of himself.

He let out a long sigh after he could no longer feel the wetness in his palm because the hard realization of his mistake seeped into his consciousness. He shouldn't have come here. He shouldn't have left Cheatum & Howe, or walked through that stairwell door, or made his way to the roof, and he definitely shouldn't have tempted *the Itch* the way he did up to this point, because now *the Itch* was awake. The beast had set its thousand-eyed gaze firmly upon Jackie and it would not settle on just a piece.

He moved as if his body was on autopilot as he retraced his steps carefully and silently back to the stairwell door. He eased the latch down on the door, pulled it wide open and let the hydraulics close it with its usual noisy bravado. He counted to five in his head as he internally put on his human disguise and walked towards the metal staircase.

"Is anybody up here?" He called out into the darkness in the deep commanding voice everyone recognized as he stepped on to the first rung of the staircase and waited for the reply.

In his head, he weighed his options on moving forward. After all, maybe Jackie didn't want company, maybe she was hiding and didn't want to be found. There were a dozen reasons for her to remain silent. Self-preservation was at the top of the list, but she didn't know that. If she didn't reply, tried to be sneaky about it, he would simply walk up to the helipad under the guise of simply checking on the group's most valuable resource. The helicopter. He could say he heard someone in the stairwell and was just checking on it, you know, just to be safe. It was believable. That was his job, after all. Keeping everyone safe.

"Yeah. I'm here." Jackie's weak voice called back from atop the helipad.

He took that as an invitation and climbed the stairs. She was still where he had left her a moment ago, on the opposite side of the helipad, standing by the railing. She was looking over at him with her big doe eyes, like the weight of the world was on her shoulders and she was looking to him to relieve her of her burdens. Luckily for her, he was thinking the same thing.

"Hey," he said without waving as he approached her in the darkness. He tried to sound concerned, but not like a motherly concern, more like you're-not-supposed-to-be-here kind of concern. He laced his tone with a hint of authority. "What are you doing up here?"

He didn't have the flashlight in his hand, he wondered if she would question that. As he stepped closer to her, he could see on her face she was occupied with something else. He didn't care what it was at the moment as long as it kept her distracted.

"I couldn't sleep." Jackie admitted shyly, and she turned her body in such a way that allowed her injured arm to hide from sight behind her. "I needed a little peace and quiet."

"You couldn't have picked a better spot," he said, motioning around the general area as he came to a stop before her. "Nobody will bother you up here."

What he meant was, nobody will *hear* you up here. It was a warning of sorts. *The Itch* liked it when he played with them in such a way. Before she could ponder his words too much, he diverted to something else. Something more…, sensitive.

"How's the arm?"

"Oh, hmm," she uttered shyly as he looked down at the bandaged remnants that she was coyly keeping out of sight. "Not bad, I guess," she said, settling on those words out of politeness.

"Can I see it?" He asked, gesturing to her hidden arm. On instinct, her body flinched away from him, like the very idea of showing it to someone was repulsive. He knew he had no right to ask, and if he was anybody else, Jackie would probably have told him to go fuck himself. Mason wasn't anybody else, though. He was in charge. So, Jackie instead presented her wounded arm to him without saying a word.

Mason didn't really want to look at it. If he did, probably would need a flashlight. He didn't though, and maybe Jackie thought that was a bit strange of him, but he didn't care. He didn't want to see it. Mason wanted to feel it. To get a real tactile sense of it. He reached for her arm and gently wrapped his hand around the meat of her triceps to hold the arm in place. He could feel her body tighten up at the unexpected touch, but she didn't pull away. Why would she? He was the great white protector, after all.

Her body heat felt electric through the skin of his hand. Under his fingers, he could feel her pulse. He went through the motion of inspecting it, but in the night's darkness there was little to see, though that didn't seem to cross Jackie's mind at all as he was gawking at it. Mason reached out with his free hand and traced the line where the bandage met the skin, and it eased it down and around to the actual nub of where the rest of her arm should be. He might as well have been a teenage boy touching a breast for the first time, judging by how his body reacted to the feeling of the injury.

"Hey!" Jackie yelped slightly as she weakly pulled her arm away from his touch.

"Oh, sorry," he said because that is what normal people said in those moments. "Did that hurt?" He asked with genuine, sinister curiosity.

"No, it just felt weird." Jackie sounded ashamed.

"Does it still hurt?"

"No, not really. Not anymore," she said and then stood silent for a moment before adding: "It itches real bad, though. I can feel it. Right there." She held her half-arm out in front of her and used the cigarette in her hand to point to the space where her hand would have been. "Right in the center of my fucking palm. It comes and goes. Bill said it will go away, eventually. I hope he's right, because it itches like a bitch," she said sourly.

He could tell she wanted to say more. He could see it in the dejected way she looked out into the blackness of their surroundings. Like she was looking for something that she secretly knew wasn't there. A tear drained away from her right eye, which she quickly wiped away.

"I'm sorry, John," she said for reasons he wasn't able to fathom. "I guess I'm still a bit of a wreck." She took a drag off of her cigarette.

He became transfixed on Jackie's neck. Even in the darkness, he swore he could see the slight rise and fall of her pulse on the skin of her neck, right by the carotid. It was like it was calling to him, well, not him specifically, but *The Itch*. It was calling out to *the Itch*.

"Hey," he said in an upbeat manner as he looked her coldly in the eyes. "You want to know a little secret that helps me get through the dark times?" He smiled a friendly smile as she looked up at him with a tiny glimmer of hope.

"Sure," she said, taking another hit of her cigarette. "I'll take all the advice I can get at this point," Jackie said with a snort and a bit of a cynical smile. He leaned in close to her and whispered it right into her ear in soft tones like he was legitimately telling her a secret. Which he was.

"My name isn't John." It would be the last secret Jackie would ever learn. He said it and moved away from her and shrugged innocently as if to say, *what are you going to do*? Her one eyebrow cocked up slightly as she looked at him, confused for a moment.

That was when he struck her.

It was such a quick motion and all the elements of the attack were working against Jackie. His hands were already up when he shrugged. All he had to do was ball up his left hand good and tight, pivot slightly to shift his body weight to the right. He didn't hold back; *the Itch* wouldn't allow it. He drove his balled fist into the right side of her head with as much force as he could muster. He felt his knuckles in his hand pop from the force of the impact. A glorious warmth spread over him as he witnessed her body pitch to the side and fall to the ground.

The Itch had taken over.

Jackie fell hard to the ground, but she was still conscious. She was badly stunned. He looked down at her with a certain measure of enjoyment as her eyes rolled around in her head as she desperately tried to focus on something, anything. Her arms blindly reached out and flailed around her as her tiny little sheep's brain tried to come to terms with what had just happened.

It was then that *The Itch* spoke to him.

As it sometimes did. It didn't use words; it hadn't for a long time. The sheep's so-called medications wore their relationship down to simple thoughts. The itch gave him an idea and showed him a goal. Much like a gardener would hand somebody a seed and show them the fruit it would produce, the rest was up to him. He looked down smugly at Jackie struggling to gain some sense of the danger she was in. The vision filled him with a brilliant sort of warmth.

The Itch had gifted him with the one thing he had been missing. Purpose, real purpose. It was all so delicious to him. There was no other word for it. He could think of nothing else that would be as satisfying to him as the course *The Itch* had shown him. That's what he needed right now.

Real satisfaction, not the pretend nonsense he has been doing with the undead. Something with some substance behind it that placated to his more… visceral nature.

It was so perfect. All he could do was smile.

Then he felt himself growl gleefully as he lunged for her. He grabbed a fistful of the dark-colored shirt she was wearing, and he roughly lifted her off the ground. Jackie struggled to lift her neck and look at him.

"Whud?" It was more of a sound than an actual word. It didn't matter, he wasn't listening to her anymore.

He balled up his other hand in a tight fist and threw it at her in a sharp blow. He struck her cleanly on the bridge of the nose. A muffled yelp erupted from the woman as his fist crushed her nose and whipped her head back to strike the concrete of the helipad with a hollow sort of *thunk* sound. He was careful not to hit her in the mouth. He would need those teeth intact later. Mason thought about hitting her again. He wanted to. It was a legitimate struggle not to. He forced himself to let go of her shirt and let her chest fall back to the ground. He looked down at his handiwork.

If she was stunned before, now she was hanging onto consciousness by a thread. Her eyelids fluttered weakly, and she wheezed on the ground, blood leaking down her face and onto the helipad. She coughed once and a glob of dark fluid shot out of her mouth and landed on her cheek. He watched with interest as the dark glob rolled down her face, leaving a dark trail behind it.

It was beautiful, in a way.

As he settled down onto Jackie's chest and pinned her good arm to her side. He smiled to himself. Although he had fucked this woman a few times before, this was the first time the woman legitimately aroused him. *Life's strange that way. Why are all the best moments in life so damned fleeting?*

He reached down and wrapped his hands around Jackie's throat and squeezed.

Instincts must have kicked in because the woman's eyes opened wide and focused in on his face. Just like he preferred them to. This was an experience that the two of them were partaking in together. He wouldn't want to rob her of the realizations that death brought. Hell, that was the whole point. Sure, he enjoyed it immensely, but it wasn't just about him. *The Itch* taught him it was rude to deprive people of a good, meaningful death. When possible, he always tried to make the end something he and the sheep can experience together. If he had more time, he might have been able to draw this out a little for her, but there was still much he had to do before his night was over. He was sad about that, but he would make the most of it.

His heart hammered away in his chest like a locomotive burning down the tracks. He breathed in deeply, and every time he exhaled, he felt a little giggle escape his lips. He purposefully left the woman with the use of her ruined arm. It immediately shot to her throat, where he was currently squeezing the life out of her. He imagined in her head she was telling the hand that was no longer there to grab a hold of his wrist to try and break his grip. Then the little nub of an arm reached for him, and he imagined her missing hand was clawing at his face as her body weakly bucked underneath him. There was no way out for her. The physics of the situation were not in her favor. It was just a matter of time.

"Shhhh." He looked down at her with what he approximated as sympathy as she fought for her life beneath him. He tried to be soothing in these moments for them.

He ruined it a moment later when the impulse took over and he darted forward to lick the blood from the side of her face. He could feel the wetness on his lips and cheek when he came back up. The woman looked at him with blood-shot eyes he could barely see in the darkness, but he could still see their pleading nature, and he could see they weren't really looking at him anymore. Jackie was beginning her journey. It wouldn't be long now. The woman's stump of an arm knocked against his forearm rather hard. Then a second time, with a weaker and less focused blow. Then once more it bumped against the meat of his forearm before it fell to the ground. The bucking ended as her body settled peacefully beneath him. Her blood-shot eyes looked out at the dark world with a soft sort of love and admiration. That was death's last gift to the sheep. He could feel her pulse come to a slow end beneath his fingers. He knew she was gone, but he couldn't bring himself to let go of her.

Mason felt his eyes slightly watered, and he was suddenly overcome with emotion. He leaned forward and gave the woman a single delicate kiss on her forehead, right above where he had struck her the second time, before he released his grip.

He slumped his body back and craned his neck towards the dark heavens. Mason breathed heavily and felt the cooling sensation of the thin sheen of sweat that was on his skin. He felt spent as a familiar calm washed over him. He was alone again. The itch was nowhere to be found inside his head. It was like lust in that way. Immediately after the need was sated, the itch went quiet inside him. It crawled back into its dark place with a full belly and slept. He breathed in as he found a clarity he had not had for some time. He let out a final deep sigh and looked down at the tool he had created for himself.

Four minutes.

In his newfound clarity, he saw a way forward. It went against his more basic desires. He had strong notions of just letting Jackie's zombie loose on an unsuspecting floor and just letting nature take its course. *Maybe the queer's level*, that thought crossed his mind. He didn't have a problem with queers like some people did, but there was something about that particular queer that rubbed him the wrong way. Mason didn't know what it was because he didn't waste time trying to figure out why he didn't like some people. He just accepted it.

Mason also entertained the idea of walking Jackie's zombie down to that Russo girl's floor and letting it snack on some young meat. Though, he would want to make sure that Bill also was made into a meal for it. He was a concern. He didn't like the way Bill looked at him sometimes. Like that old black bastard knew something about him he didn't want known. It would be so easy to use the growing menace underneath him tonight, but no, he wouldn't do that. Using his tool now would raise too many suspicions, and they would ask too many questions. Questions he may not have a suitable answer for. No. He would wait for the right time because that was the plan *The Itch* had gifted him.

Three minutes.

He moved swiftly as he first rose from the body. On another day, under different circumstances, he would take great interest in the fascinating change going on inside the woman's body. He would watch with keen interest at all the different physiological changes that would turn the woman's body into Jackie's zombie. In his mind, he would try to identify the exact moment the woman's body was no longer just an inanimate thing and blossomed into being Jackie's zombie. Yes, on any other day...but this wasn't such a night. Mason had a plan, a timeline he had to meet, obstacles to overcome, and attentions he needed to avoid. He had to move. He grabbed the woman's shirt and pulled it over her head as the body laid motionless on the ground. Then he went to her feet and removed her running shoes, which he untied the laces from each shoe before he tossed the shoes over the railing and down to the zombies on the street level. He took off one sock before he used one of the laces to tie the feet together rather tightly.

Two minutes.

He pulled the upper body forward off the ground so he could use the last shoestring to tie the woman's hand behind her back. He then took the woman's sock and jammed it roughly into her mouth before taking the shirt and tying it around its head to keep the balled-up sock in place. Those teeth didn't discriminate after all. It's one thing he respected about the undead. Everybody was on the menu.

One minute.

He pulled the body forward off the ground and hoisted the woman's relatively small frame onto his shoulder and then used his legs to lift the bound lifeless body off the ground. He held onto the body in such a way that its head was out in front of him, so he could track it. And if the need arose, he could just smash its skull into the wall. He didn't honestly think that would happen, though. This was a good plan. He felt it would succeed as long as he did his part. He maneuvered the limp body into a more comfortable position before he made his way to the stairs.

He reached for the handle of the stairwell door when he first felt the body on his shoulder twitch slightly. He froze in his tracks. Inwardly a wicked smile stretched across his black soul. Another twitch came from the body, and this time, he witnessed the head of Jackie's new body roll slowly to the left, and then slowly back to the right, as if being reborn left it unfamiliar with how its body worked.

"Good morning, sunshine," he said lovingly. "I have big plans for you, darling, real big plans," he said with a certain amount of pride as he reached for the stairwell handle again. "You're going to help me thin the herd a little," he said gleefully before he entered the darkness of the stairwell.

Chapter 9

Kenshiro

You take any creature out of its natural environment and there will be problems, Kenshiro told himself on several occasions over the last two months. *It's only natural.* He knew there would be adjustments that needed to be made. He never expected Elliott to just seamlessly slip into the new life Kenshiro provided for him. If anything, Kenshiro tried to steel himself against the coming storms.

Elliott didn't disappoint.

In those times, when the teen was red-faced and shouting in Kenshiro's face about how wrong everything was around him, Kenshiro breathed deep and rubbed Emily's letter through the material of his pants. The first couple weeks were the worst, until he learned to take Elliott's fury and just direct it somewhere else.

"Is there anything we can do to make the bedroom less horrible for you?" Kenshiro learned to challenge the boy with trying to find the solutions, instead of focusing on the problem.

Elliott complained a lot about things just not *feeling* right. Sometimes it was a problem they could fix, usually by moving some furniture around and taking down the pictures in the room. Other times, the only solution was for them to sleep in the same room, some times in the same bed. Kenshiro found that solution less than ideal, because Elliott was a restless sleeper and usually kicked or slapped him at least once during the night.

There were a lot of fights in the beginning. Sometimes

Elliott was unreasonably stubborn, and other times it was Kenshiro who refused to bend. Harsh words were said on some occasions. Other times things were thrown, though, never at each other. Sometimes the silence between them lasted into the next day. They weren't perfect. They weren't even perfect for each other. However, they made it work. They both put in the effort when the time came to do so, and they never faulted the other for their failings.

They made their way east across the United States using the secondary roads that ran like veins across the individual states. They stayed away from major centers as they hopped from one safe house to another. Kenshiro didn't trust Elliott to tackle new towns, not yet. Not until they functioned better as a team, so they moved from one safe house to another and stayed in relative comfort as they planned their next moves.

They trained in the morning, and Elliott practised with his weapon in the afternoons. It had become their routine, and Elliott didn't seem to mind it one bit. He was growing stronger, by the day it seemed. Kenshiro taught him all manner of attacks and defences Elliott could use against the undead with his little weapon. The teen just seemed to soak up the lessons like a greedy sponge, though he was still a bit squeamish when the time came to actually apply the lessons. Kenshiro was fine with that. He wasn't in a rush to put Elliott in front of the undead.

They crossed the Mississippi River north of St. Louis. Luckily, the bridge crossing he had used last year was still upright and intact. They continued east from there, the safe houses on this side of the river were fewer and farther in between. It made Kenshiro nervous as he kept a close eye on their food supply.

-

"I'm getting hungry," Elliott said, breaking the silence

within the cab of the truck.

He was bored, that much was obvious. They started the day listening to their favorite Kenny Rogers CD on repeat. At this point, it had become less than Kenshiro's favorite. However, they knew all the words and Elliott enjoyed it when they sang along together. After that became tiresome, they just sat in silence as the CD played on until Elliott eventually turned that off. Then they just sat and listened to the constant hum of the tires on the road.

"Can we find some place to pull over and eat?" Elliott asked in a fairly bland tone.

He had been quiet for some time, content to just watch the seemingly endless green landscape go by. Elliott admitted he had never been this far east, and the lush green landscape was a stark contrast to the arid one he had come from.

They were in Pennsylvania on the I-80 interstate that ran through the state's northern half. Kenshiro liked it because, after Ohio, it was mostly a scenic drive that avoided most of the major cities all the way to the east coast. He remembered this highway being fairly quiet, desolate even, where the biggest concerns were avoiding the numerous abandoned cars on the road. There were the occasional undead who walked along the side of the pavement here-and-there along the interstate, but that was only on the sections that didn't have a barrier. Ultimately, it wasn't much of a concern to him. Just another thing to be mindful of.

They had come from a fair-sized farmhouse that Kenshiro had marked down in the Atlas as being a house that was cleared, but had little in the way of supplies. It was southwest of Mercer, Pennsylvania. A city he has never dared visit because it was entirely too large. In the Atlas he wrote, *seen from the road. Can only get to it on east bound lane.*

They stayed there four days, two days longer than he wanted, but they found the house had a good DVD collection and almost all the most recent superhero movies. Many of which Elliott had not seen yet.

They trained in the mornings. Elliott rarely complained anymore. In the afternoons, they retreated away from the heat to watch movies inside the house while the generator they traveled with ran inside the large storage shed across the yard from the house. They used four long extension cords that they found to run a line from the shed to the house, which plugged into a power bar that ran the television and the DVD player. In the evenings, after they finished dinner and yet another movie, they went out into the cool evening air and dispatched the undead that had collected around the noisy storage shed. Most nights they had a little over a dozen bodies slowly circling the small isolated shed. After they cleared the bodies away and shut down the generator, they walked the large yard together. They talked about stupid things as the sun descended into the western sky as they searched for any stragglers.

It was a good routine. A pleasant break from the usual. Honestly, if Kenshiro could have, he probably would have stayed there longer.

After four days, however, Kenshiro looked at their remaining food supply and did the hard calculation in his head. *It was time to go*. They hadn't depleted all their food, but enough of it was gone for it to be a concern. During the quiet times at night, Kenshiro studied the Atlas in the dark, and he planned their route to the next house.

There was a safe house, a *fully-stocked* one, about a hundred and twenty miles further east on the interstate. They drove down I-80 at about thirty miles an hour, with the number of cars that they had to swerve around, going any faster than that would be foolish.

"Sure," Kenshiro said while slowly swerving to avoid a compact car that was abandoned in the left-hand lane of the road.

As the truck rolled past, he dared a look inside the car only to see a dark shape within clawing weakly at the dusty passenger window, and then it was gone.

"What do you want to eat?" Kenshiro asked with genuine interest.

Elliott didn't want to leave the house. Last night, they had an argument about it. He only relented when Kenshiro agreed to take the DVDs Elliott still wanted to see. It was the easiest decision Kenshiro ever made. He still felt a bit of a cloud between them, though, so he saw this as a way to score a few points with the quiet teen.

"Pancakes," Elliott said coldly while gazing at the road ahead of them. Kenshiro looked over and eyed him suspiciously. They had run out of pancake mix weeks ago.

"We don't have any mix. You know that."

"Beans and bacon, then." Elliott shot back immediately. All Kenshiro could do was sigh loudly as it became apparent this wasn't going as smoothly as he had hoped.

"We don't have any of that either. I know you know that," he said, feeling annoyed but still trying to rein in his frustration. Elliott had a mind for lists of all sorts. Kenshiro had no doubt that Elliott knew exactly what they still had for food, and was just being difficult.

"You asked what I wanted. That's what I want," Elliott said curtly, like an impudent child.

"You know goddamn well what I meant." Kenshiro snapped back and immediately regretted it.

"That's what you said!"

"Fine," he growled. "Great, in fact, very helpful, thank you." Kenshiro bit his tongue. He wanted to say more. Hell, he wanted to yell, but Kenshiro settled on simply breathing heavily for a moment or two.

This was not unfamiliar territory for him.

Ahead of them loomed a large sign that stated the I-79 turnoff was up ahead, with meant there would be an overpass. It would be a nice place to escape the midday sun while they pulled over and had lunch. He relayed the information to Elliott, who seemed utterly disinterested in the knowledge, but he would change his tune when he saw the lunch Kenshiro had in store for him.

The two of them would take the time to set up the small propane burner and they would have baked beans that were actually baked. They didn't have plates, so one would have to eat his portion out of the can while the other would have to enjoy the beans straight out of the pan, which wasn't a problem. They would wash down the beans with a nice bottle of lukewarm Iced Tea from the large container of drink crystals they found a couple days ago. Then they would end the meal with a portion of sliced pears. Sliced pears weren't Elliott's favorite, but they ran out of mandarin oranges days ago and he was pretty sure sliced pears were, at least, one of Elliott's top five.

It would have to do.

He hoped it would be enough to lighten the mood inside the cab for the rest of the journey to the next house. They had at least a couple more hours of weaving through the obstacle course of abandoned vehicles that was the interstate before they reached St. Petersburg. It seemed like a big ask at the moment, but it was all Kenshiro had.

He brought the truck to a slow stop in the center lane about a half hour later in the overpass's shadow. He didn't pull over to the side of the road, there was no need to, he simply stopped the truck in the lane it was in and placed the transmission in park.

"Wait here," Kenshiro said as he reached for the door's lever.

"Okay." Elliott looked out the windows, taking in their surroundings.

Past grievances were forgotten and now the teen was all business. Just like Kenshiro had taught him. *Good boy*, he thought to himself, but remained silent because Elliott sometimes didn't like it when you made a fuss over him. Instead, Kenshiro simply nodded and exited the truck.

The afternoon air was relatively cool and completely still. Not even the tall grass on the sides of the highway showed any signs of movement. He breathed in air that was heavy with humidity. It had been like that for the past couple of days. The sky beyond the overpass was clear, but it felt like rain could be a possibility if the temperature dipped low enough. Thankfully, they would be at the safe house well before any storms threatened them.

As he moved back to the bed of the truck to retrieve his spear, Kenshiro casually slipped the tan leather work gloves he gained from the small, neat little farmhouse in La Veta. The gloves were well-worn and had several spots where the spear had worn through the leather completely. By the time Kenshiro lifted his rebar spear out of the back of the truck, he had spotted two undead that would need to be taken care of. He was sure there was more out there, somewhere.

One was an undead man they had seen on the approach to the overpass. It was on the other side of the traffic barrier that ran along the side of the highway. They passed it only a few moments before they had stopped underneath the overpass, and now the short-looking zombie in a horribly ragged business suit was walking with a renewed vigor up the road towards them. The other one he could see had been a woman at one point, judging by its hair and the shirt it was wearing, and was making its way through the waist high grass to the south of the interstate a few yards ahead of where they stopped on the road.

Kenshiro walked the long way around the back of the truck while keeping a keen eye out for any other movement until he reached Elliott's window. He looked in towards his friend and held up a still gloved finger. Elliott followed the procedure they had worked out beforehand perfectly. He almost looked bored as he leaned over and pressed the horn button on the steering wheel. The truck's horn chirped loudly and the sound of it pierced the quiet air like a sharpened knife, and then it was gone. Kenshiro didn't exactly hear anything as a result, but he felt the air stir immediately after the noise ended, like they had awoken something. He waited for a moment with his one hand on the spear at his side. He didn't have to wait long before the first body fell.

It happened in front of them, maybe because they were parked more to that side of the overpass, he didn't know, but when the first body tumbled down from the overpass above them, Elliott hopped slightly in his seat. It happened too quickly to pick out any of the body's defining features. Before it came to a violent end on the asphalt, it looked like it was about the size of an adult male. Kenshiro saw the body fall, and make one awkward rotation in the air before it belly-flopped onto the road with a noise that sounded like a wet sponge hitting the ground. The zombie's head landed solidly on the hard road, promptly split open, and emptied its contents out onto the surface of the interstate in a truly gruesome fashion.

When the second one fell, it wasn't much of a surprise to either of them at that point, and they watched with morbid excitement as the second one fell painfully onto the hood of a pickup truck. The impact must have broken every bone in its lower body, before it bounced off and settled onto the pavement. Another one fell to the road behind them. Kenshiro heard the wet sound of the zombie's impact and when he turned, he saw a new body in the center lane of the eastbound side of the interstate, the same lane they were currently in. Kenshiro eyed the new corpse on the road skeptically. It confirmed his suspicions when the heap of decayed flesh wheezed angrily as the first signs of movement came. The zombie's head rose to stare at Kenshiro with those milky, soulless eyes and then moved its body as if it was trying to figure out what still worked, in an effort to drag itself towards its prey.

Kenshiro waited a moment to see if any others would fall from the overpass above. He looked back to the one that had bounced off the hood of the abandoned truck to the left-most lane of the interstate. It was moving and hissing as well, though it was clear the fall had severely damaged its lower half. Its shattered legs were being dragged behind its body as the undead woman clawed its way along the pavement towards him. He watched the undead woman struggle along the ground, mindlessly dragging its ruined legs behind it while its unblinking eyes focused solely on him. Any other creature on earth would have had the good sense to just die. That's what made the undead so unnatural, so incredibly fucking evil, because they didn't follow the natural rules. Not for the first time, Kenshiro became transfixed with the sheer single-mindedness of them.

What could do that to a person? What could turn a living, thinking human being into THAT? In the last days of humanity, the world clawed at itself to figure out what was causing the transformation and how they could stop it. The lights went out all over the world before they found the answer. It remains humanity's last great unsolved mystery. He didn't know, that was for sure. Kenshiro knew the undead quite well. He felt in any situation he could accurately predict what a zombie would do. In a way, they were like old friends. But he couldn't even guess what brought the plague upon humanity, or how, on a biological level, it worked. There was nothing on this earth, that he knew of anyway, that could cause those kinds of changes to a human body and mind. He wasn't a doctor, though, or a scientist. There were entire scientific schools Kenshiro was utterly unaware of. In life, he was bestowed with a few natural gifts, and a scientific mind wasn't on the list. He knew how to survive them. For now, that would have to be enough. He wasn't out to save humanity after all. That job was beyond him. Maybe it was beyond any single person, he didn't know. He was only responsible for himself and one other. Some days, even that felt overwhelming.

He was stirred from his thoughts when he heard the passenger side window roll down. Kenshiro looked over to see Elliott's face. He looked as bored as only a child could look.

"Can I get out now?" He whined harmlessly. "There's only four of them." The corner of Kenshiro's mouth curled upward at that. He could easily remember a time back in La Veta when Elliott refused to leave the truck if there were *any* zombies present.

"Just hold on," he answered back absently, returning his gaze back to the undead.

The female in the tall grass was almost at the edge of the road. He turned back and saw the zombie in the ragged business suit making his way along the guard rail still. Every so often, it would bump into the wooden post on the ground and threatened to fall over before its legs would awkwardly adjust and kept it upright. Soon though, the barrier would force it to turn and without the necessary coordination to maneuver itself over the guardrail, it would instead simply tumble face-first over the obstacle. Kenshiro doubted he was lucky enough to have it fall directly onto its skull with enough force to do the job for him, but it was nice to dream.

"I just want to be sure." With that said, Kenshiro's instincts told him it was time to move.

He left Elliott sitting in the truck without further explanation and stalked towards the back. Kenshiro first strode up to the crumpled zombie on the pavement. He looked down at its ruined form that had somehow propped itself up on its one remaining good arm. The broken zombie snapped at the air between them and somehow even produced a weak snarl. Kenshiro drove the spear point into its eye socket and let the propped-up body fall to the ground before he pulled the spear free from its skull. At almost the exact moment, the undead man in the tattered suit flopped over the guardrail and onto the asphalt of the interstate.

With a flourish, Kenshiro brought the spear up over his head as he spun the end around himself one time, to gather momentum, before he brought the end of the spear down to crash into the side of the undead businessman's head. The end of the spear made contact just as it was rising with a sickening crunching sound that erupted in the afternoon air. The zombie was violently propelled into the guardrail, its ruined skull bouncing off the metal with a sound of a weak bell being struck. Leaving a black mark on the guardrail to mark where its skull had struck the metal, staining it possibly forever.

He held the spear tip out in front of him as he walked towards the undead woman who had emerged from the grass and was now approaching the guardrail at the other end of the overpass. Their eyes met; he could see the ferocious hunger that had twisted its features. As he got within range, he hoped, at least on some level, the zombie could recognize the seething hatred he had for them as well, before he destroyed them forever. He swung the spear like he would if it were a baseball bat. What the swing lacked in technique and grace, it more than made up for in raw destructive force. Kenshiro could feel the steel of the rebar bend slightly on impact like a hardened spring as the point sunk into the undead woman's skull. The force of the impact knocked it off its feet and sent its body into the dirt, where it laid still.

He looked over at the last one.

The zombie woman with the ruined lower body had changed its trajectory on the pavement to track with Kenshiro's movement. Undeterred by its shattered legs, it clawed its way towards him. Maybe gaining an inch with each weak pull. At this rate it would take hours for it to reach him. Kenshiro didn't have that long. He walked behind it and placed his boot on its back, forcing its upper body down onto the pavement. From there, Kenshiro reared the spear up and plunged the tip solidly into the base of its skull. He felt the body jerk once under his boot, and then nothing.

He pulled the spear free from the body and looked around himself as he stood in the overpass's shadow. Kenshiro could hear nothing more around him but the still air. It was deathly quiet. He took in a deep breath and let it out slowly as he listened intently. He remembered a time when the absence of sound was disorientating to him. He had spent his whole life with noise, so much so his psyche depended on it, so when it was finally gone, it instinctively gave him a sense of dread.

Now, silence was a tool he used to not only hide from the undead, but he also used it to find them. The undead had no use for stealth. They didn't hide. They spent their entire existence simply bumping and crashing into things until they found their food. If there was a zombie in their immediate vicinity, he felt he would hear them, but he heard nothing. He had hoped for birds, as he always did, because the sounds of birds meant the area was free of the undead. He rarely heard birds in his travels, and right now was no exception. *They are out there somewhere.* He felt that truth in his heart, but there was nothing he could do about that. Beyond the road, as far as he could see, was just waist high grasses and dense patches of trees. There were literally a million places a zombie could hide out there and remain unseen.

How long to you really think you can keep doing this? A familiar voice spoke up in his head. *Honestly?*

This, coming up in a few short months, will be his second winter in the zombie world. That was the only measurement of time he had for his tenure anymore. God only knows how many months it has actually been. Kenshiro started out on the road in the spring. Maybe it was early June or late May. He didn't remember anymore. He remembered little from before the zombies. He knew a lot of factual things, the things you can never really forget. Like going to the movie theatre, buying popcorn, and sitting down to watch a movie with your friends. He, of course, remembered all of that, but he didn't remember what popcorn tasted like. Or chocolate. He knew his father liked a particular brand of Old Spice, original scent, but he didn't remember what it smelled like. He remembered every facet of Amy, every detail of her face, every little wrinkle it would make when she smiled, but he didn't remember the important stuff. Like how she felt when she snuggled up beside him on a warm morning when they both were just waking up. Or how she sounded when she was happy, or sad, or upset. All those things felt so long ago, so far away from where he was right now. *This* life feels like all he has ever really known and all that other stuff wasn't real. Like it was from a dream he had once.

How long? The voice asked again, taunting him. Kenshiro's hand dropped to his thigh where he could feel the letter through the material of his pants.

"As long as it fucking takes," he answered back bitterly to the empty landscape before turning and heading back to the truck.

In the truck, Elliott watched him intently as he moved around to the passenger window.

"Okay, we should be good for a while now. I want you to set up the burner while I keep an eye out." He learned shortly after meeting Elliott that you never phrase a request like: would you like to, or, can you? Elliott's unique mind would simply answer the question in front of him instead of inferring the request. Although, despite that, Elliott still insisted upon proper manners. "Please," Kenshiro added, and he couldn't help the slight grin when Elliott understood today's lunch would be warm.

"Really?" Elliott asked excitedly. It was truly a sign of the times when a heated meal was something to get excited about, but he was thankful for it none-the-less.

"Why not?" Kenshiro stepped back from the door as Elliott reached for the handle or risk being struck by the door as Elliott threw it open.

"Okay. I can do that, lickity-split," Elliott blurted out as he hurried past Kenshiro.

"What did you say?" Kenshiro inquired with a bemused

chuckle while looking at the teen incredulously.

"What? Lickity-split? It means fast," Elliott said looking a little disappointed Kenshiro was unfamiliar with the term. He could only smile as the teen went to work setting up the burner on the tailgate.

Lickity-split? Kenshiro wondered with some amusement if it was a nonsensical term Elliott had just made up because it sounded funny to him. In the twelve years he spent in the United States before the zombie uprising, he had never heard that term used before. Like, what was a *lickity* and why would you split it?

He stood by for a moment and watched Elliott set up the tiny propane burner. Elliott dropped the tailgate, being careful not to make any excessive noise, and then fished the small metal burner, the fuel hose, and the propane tank out of the back of the truck. Elliott placed the burner on the tailgate and the propane tank on the surface of the interstate and then connected the burner to the tank with the hose.

Kenshiro left Elliott to his work and checked the few abandoned vehicles idly that were in the overpass's shadow with them. There were only three. Two on their side of the interstate, and one on the westbound lane. It was on the other side of the small strip of overgrown grass that separated the two halves of the interstate.

Elliott's unique and utterly confounding ability of being invisible to the undead came with a few caveats. If one zombie became aware of Elliott's presence, it ruined the effect and they all were aware of him as if the teen were like any other person.

Right now, if some undead were to stumble onto them, like it was investigating some of the noises they had made a moment ago, it would be stricken with that strange sniffing-seizure until Elliott moved a certain distance away, or the undead suddenly realized Elliott's presence. In Kenshiro's experience, the only thing that can penetrate the seizure-like funk the zombie fall into is if some noise alerts it. However, that only works if it is just Elliott. Zombies in that situation would forgo the seizure and lock instantly on Kenshiro instead, as if Elliott wasn't even there. He had actually seen the undead walk past Elliott to get to him. The only way Elliott's ability could protect both of them is when Kenshiro couldn't be seen.

In that circumstance, an invisible bubble, the exact radius of which is still a bit of a mystery, springs up around the teen that zombies passively avoid. The undead may walk into that bubble, but when they do, he had seen them inexplicably change course to one that would take them away from Elliott instead of towards him. It was never anything as drastic as a zombie turning a hundred and eighty degrees around, but it would slowly veer off in another direction away from them. In all the nights he had spent in Elliott's company, Kenshiro had never awoken to the undead being outside... yet.

He walked up to the pickup the one zombie had crashed into when it fell from the overpass above. Kenshiro looked with morbid curiosity at the damage the zombie's body had done to the hood. It was minor. Kenshiro looked into the passenger window, prepared for just about anything, and was happy to see the cab was empty. There was nothing to interest him inside. Kenshiro moved up to the midsize sedan that was parked quietly on the north-side shoulder of the road.

He saw a figure in the driver's seat as he approached the vehicle from behind, but when he walked up to the driver's window, all he saw was a body in the advance stages of decomposition slumped over the steering wheel with a fairly sizable hole in the back of its head. *Somebody got tired of running*, he thought with a certain amount of empathy. Kenshiro looked at the gun resting on the corpse's lap, an old-looking revolver which wasn't much use to him, it had the withered, dried out fingers of the body still wrapped around it.

He paused at the steel traffic barrier separating the interstate for a moment and peered into the thin strip of waist high grass beyond, looking for signs of movement and listening intently for anything that might be waiting for him in that grass. Zombie-landmines were a genuine concern in tall grass. He didn't see any depressions in it. As far as the eye could see, that thin strip in the middle looked almost completely uniform. Still, he used his free hand to knock slowly on the steel rail. The steel rang softly three times, and he waited a couple of breaths while watching the grass closely. When nothing came of it, he hopped over the rail, gingerly waded through the grass and scaled the railing on the other side.

The car was empty. The inside looked like the car had been on a long road trip before it rested under this overpass. Empty plastic water bottles and food containers littered the back seat. Judging by the moderate film of dust that covered the car, he figured it had been there a while and barring some miracle, which Kenshiro couldn't even fathom. It would be there for the foreseeable future. Like centuries, until it rots away to plastic paneling surrounded by a pile of rust.

When he finished with the car and was, at least for the time being, satisfied they were alone, Kenshiro looked back to the truck where Elliott was quietly stirring the small pot of beans. The smell of it had yet to hit him, but his mouth was already watering in anticipation.

He walked back over to Elliott and stood guard with

the spear in his hand until Elliott gingerly served him the beans. Kenshiro took the pot and sat on the tailgate while Elliott scooped his portion back into the can and sat cross-legged on the surface of the interstate across from him. They ate their meal in silence for the first bit, each spooning their meal into their mouth with purpose, as was their way. Soon, however, Kenshiro felt the teen's eyes on him, and he waited for the inevitable.

"Do you think we'll ever have a home again?" Elliott posed the question to him. It wasn't what Kenshiro was expecting to be on Elliott's mind.

"What do you mean?"

"Well," Elliott started, putting in an obvious effort to translate his thoughts into actual words. "We've stayed at a lot of places, like a lot," he said with emphasis. But none of them felt like home, you know?" Kenshiro didn't, he sorely wanted to, and he couldn't even blame it on the undead.

He thought back briefly to when some place felt like home, tried to ascertain what that feeling might even be. All his mind could conjure was a picture of his mother in his mind's eye. It wasn't even her, not really. He had lost the exact image of her some time ago. All that remained for him was an impression of her. Not so much who she was as much as who she was to him. Kenshiro gave his friend no sign he knew what he was talking about, so instead, he simply sat by and let the teen finish his thought.

"So, I was just wondering if it was always going to be like this or are we going to find someplace where we can stay for a long time? Like we did in La Veta. We stayed there for over a month."

"You don't like the road, huh?" He asked gently.

"No," Elliott replied quickly and defensively. "I like

it. It's just…," he said, but then abruptly stopped and stuck his finger into his mouth and started sucking on it thoughtfully.

Kenshiro just looked at him patiently and scooped another spoonful of the warm beans into his mouth. They really did taste better when they were heated. Elliott was momentarily lost in his thoughts as he searched for his words inside his head. Kenshiro didn't need him to say anything. He had known the teen long enough to know he liked things a certain way and took comfort in a routine. A consistent routine was a hard thing to accomplish on the road.

"It's not home." Elliott broke the pause in the conversation and looked at him in mild distress, as if to say that what he said wasn't *all* that was bouncing around his head, but it was all he got out.

"Hmm." He made the quiet hum and nodded his head like Elliott didn't need to say anymore. "Okay. Fair enough," Kenshiro said and then gathered the last remaining beans into one spot in the bottom of the small pot before he scooped them up and popped the spoonful into his mouth. "I may have a solution," he said, and Elliott's face lit up. "Finish your food before it gets cold." He warned and gestured to Elliott's half-full can. "I've been looking in The Atlas the last couple of nights, looking for a place on the Atlantic coast, and I have a few towns that could work for a possible safe house." Elliott stared at him keenly as he spoke, so much so he almost missed his mouth with the spoonful of beans. "A few of them are right on the water, too. I was thinking if we find one that suits our purposes, maybe we can stay there for a week or two. Maybe even a month." Kenshiro could see the excitement building within the boy. "If," he said again, this time holding up his finger to caution his friend. "If we find one, that works. If not, we have to get back on the road," he said with a hint of sympathy.

"Do you think we could find a boat?" Elliott said, wiping some of the bean juice that was on the corner of his mouth off with his forearm. "Maybe we could learn to sail?"

"No," Kenshiro said playfully, yet firmly, while shaking his head. "We have enough to worry about. We don't need to add getting lost at sea to the list." He couldn't help himself but chuckle a bit at the end. *The things this kid comes up with.*

"Yeah," Elliott said with a snicker as well, "I guess you're right." He rattled his spoon around the bottom of the can, hunting for the last few beans before popping the spoon into his mouth. With the can empty, he rose, picked a spot in the tall grass between the east and westbound lanes and purposefully tossed the can away.

"You ready for dessert?" Kenshiro said, rising off the tailgate.

"You betcha."

"Can or pot?"

"I'll open the can," Elliott said, smiling as if he had won some contest. Kenshiro held his spoon out in front of him for Elliott to take and add to the dishes to be cleaned. He was secretly happy Elliott chose to open the can because he felt he needed more practise at it. Elliott always fumbled with the can opener, trying to get it properly attached to the can before he could turn the crank on the side of the device. It was a small thing, but for some reason, it irked him slightly to see Elliott struggle with it because, in his mind, Kenshiro felt it should be easy. Almost natural.

Kenshiro fished a water bottle and a small rag out of one of the food bags. He poured a small amount of water and used his finger to clean the inside of the pot. Kenshiro sloshed the water around in the pot before lifting it to his mouth and drinking the watery bean juice down. He used a little more water to rinse the pot out one more time and clean off the spoons. Kenshiro swallowed that down as well before he used the rags to dry out the dishes. He stored the pot back in its rightful spot and walked back to the tailgate where Elliott sat, swinging his legs beneath him. Kenshiro handed his friend his freshly cleaned spoon back to him and took up his spot on the tailgate. As was their routine, the opened can of pear slices sat on the tailgate between them.

"To another day." Elliott toasted with such a cheery voice he might as well have been singing the words as he held up his spoon between them. The sourness from earlier apparently was forgotten completely.

"To another day," Kenshiro responded somberly, but still somehow sounding resolute, and gingerly touched his spoon to Elliott's.

The toast had been something they had done weeks ago, and slowly it was becoming another routine of theirs. To surprise Elliott, he had put a six-pack of grape soda in a stream overnight and the next day when they cracked open the first of the cold cans; Kenshiro had made the toast. It had been a good morning leading up to that moment. It felt right. Elliott latched onto the toast and now and then, he worked it into their meals. Kenshiro didn't mind. Elliott would do it even when they fought, and it became a way for them to break the ice between them when things became tense.

"Do you think when we make it to this new safe house, the one on the water, we could put in a TV like the last house had?" Elliott asked sheepishly after finishing his first peach slice and wiping the errand juice on his chin off with his forearm again.

"You really like that house, huh?" Kenshiro couldn't

help but tease the boy.

"It was sooo big," Elliott said suddenly excited. "I've never seen a TV that big before."

"It *was* pretty big. Must have been seventy inches, or something like that.," Kenshiro said, indulging the boy. "Would a big TV make the new safe house feel like home?" Kenshiro asked slyly. Though part of him became slightly concerned that Elliott might come to expect such luxuries in the future. They wouldn't always be able to watch movies. He hoped his friend understood that, but at that same time, it was hard not to become infected with Elliott's joy over the prospect.

"I don't know," Elliott said, looking at him earnestly, like he had taken the time to consider the question thoughtfully first before he answered. Hell, maybe he did. "It would be pretty freaking awesome, though." Elliott dipped his spoon into the can for another peach slice.

Kenshiro's unexpected, muted laugh did not even bother him.

-

Forty-five minutes later, he could hear Elliott hum along with Kenny Rogers, that was quietly playing once again on the stereo. After lunch, Kenshiro had driven for maybe a half hour and had every intention of driving the pickup all the way to St. Petersburg. By his approximation, would take about another hour and a half. Though, shortly into the drive, his lower back ached again and his eyelids became heavy.

It took little to convince Elliott to drive.

He basically just had to suggest it. Elliott wasn't the best driver, but he was careful. Maybe too careful. When Elliott drove, the truck never broke twenty miles an hour, and he braked for obstacles well before the truck ever got close to them. Hell, he even insisted on using the signal lights and wearing a seatbelt. He knew in his heart, Elliott would get them to the turnoff safely. *Just not quickly*, he mused from the passenger seat with his eyes closed. He couldn't help but listen to the music silently playing, but he tried to push the noise of the country music aside and concentrate on the constant hum of the tires on the road.

Before sleep took him, Kenshiro thought about their destination. St. Petersburg. He remembered he had cleared the small town of every trace of the undead when he had stayed there last. If it was the same place he was thinking of, it was a pleasant town that was very spread out with nice paved streets. The safe house would be the first house on the left as they entered the town from the interstate. If his memory was correct, there should be enough supplies in the house to last them at least a week. It should have a nice waist-high fence around it and a large detached garage on the south side at the end of a wide gravel driveway. *If* it was the place he was thinking about. He drifted off, trying to imagine where the undead were most likely to seep back into the town, where the highest concentration of them might be…

"Wh-whoa!" Elliott's frantic voice pierced Kenshiro's slumber like a bullet. His sleep-addled mind, for some reason, conjured up an image of a cliff in front of them that Elliott was inexplicably about to drive off of.

Before his eyes even opened, he could feel the signs of the adrenalin dropping into his system. His heart started hammering away in his chest, each beat felt like a tiny explosion that threatened to rip his heart into pieces. Time slowed down and, in an instant, Kenshiro was hyper-aware of the danger that had sprung up seemingly all around him.

Kenshiro's eyes opened just in time to feel something collide with the truck somewhere behind him on his side. Something large. The sound of crumpling metal erupted in the truck's cab as the gravity inside the truck itself shifted. They were still moving forward, but for a moment, the momentum in the truck changed and suddenly shifted them to the side. Kenshiro flinched away from the unknown assailant attacking the truck and reached out blindly for something to steady himself in his seat.

That's when the passenger window exploded inward.

He was still trying to recover from the first strike when another followed quickly behind it, but this time, it struck the passenger door. Glass sprayed the side of his body as he brought his arms up to protect his face and head in the next few moments.

Something burst through the window. Kenshiro saw it out of the corner of his eye. It had a brown snout and black, panicked eyes. That was all his mind could register before something jabbed him in the arm painfully. Noise filled his ears, too much for him to distinguish in the frantic moment he was in. He knew he yelped loudly as the pain bloomed unexpectantly in his arm, but he didn't hear it as he recoiled away from the howling beast ravaging his door.

Beside him, his mind registered Elliott's high-pitched scream and in the next moment, the acceleration of the truck pushed Kenshiro back into his seat. The creature at his side violently thrashed about before it was sucked back out the window. He, thankfully, had the presence of mind at least to look out the windshield, only to have a feeling of doom that cascaded down inside him as he saw the small faded blue sedan in front of them and he felt the speed in which they were approaching it. He didn't have to think about what would happen next. It was painfully inevitable to Kenshiro what would happen.

All he could do was try to brace for the impact.

There was a terrible crunching noise that filled the cab when the two vehicles collided with each other. There was no preparing for it. All he could do was let it happen and try to deal with the consequences on the other side. The gravity inside the truck shifted violently again, and without warning, Kenshiro's body was propelled forward into the chaos. Something struck his leg first. There was an undeniably sharp pain that echoed throughout his body, but before he could cry out, something hit him in the chest and stole his air. There was a sickening feeling of weightlessness before something jumped up and hit him directly on the right-hand side of his forehead. A dull pain erupted in his head before something roughly deposited his ass back on the seat and his body pressed against the cushion of the seat. Kenshiro rebounded forward again dumbly before settling into place on his side of the truck.

There was a familiar loss of self. It was dark, but his eyes were open. Quiet, though he heard his friend calling to him in the background. Kenshiro knew this space. The void between consciousness and the darkness. He'd been here before. *Just breathe*, Kenshiro told himself and searched for the feeling of his chest rising and falling in the ether of his mind. When he found it, he told himself to take a deep breath, fill his lungs as much as possible. His body obeyed, and a sharp sting in his ribs brought him partially out of the void.

"Ken?" Elliott was crying horribly beside him and roughly shaking his shoulder. "KEN!?" His friend's shrill sounding voice made him drunkenly flinch away from the offensive noise. Kenshiro suddenly was overcome with the urge to shush the boy. *Quiet*, he thought weirdly, *you'll wake the neighbors. You don't want to wake the neighbors.*

"I'm fine," he said automatically. Kenshiro didn't know what he was saying. Well, he did, but he didn't know why he chose those words in particular. Slowly, he was coming back to the moment. He was groggy, suddenly exhausted, but Kenshiro knew one thing for sure. He was not fine. "I'm fine," he said again with a little more conviction for Elliott's sake.

"I'msorryIdidn'tmeanto," Elliott said, but his words were strangely mumbled. Pain radiated from his forehead and made it hard to concentrate on what his friend was saying. His dull mind desperately reached for the meaning in Elliott's words, like it was hanging just out of Kenshiro's reach.

"Thosedeercameoutof-nowhere." He looked over at his friend, tried to focus on his face. Something was wrong, something about what had just happened left him with a prickly feeling of urgency.

"I'msorryIbrokethetruck." Elliott's face was wet and twisted up with an emotion he couldn't quite put his finger on, but Kenshiro was positive it wasn't a good one. "I'msostupidstupidSTUPID!" Elliott shouted, and Kenshiro flinched away from the outburst.

"Elliott, it's okay," he said weakly, trying to soothe the boy. "Let's just… let's just have a look," Kenshiro said with weary words and as he fumbled for the door handle. It surprised him to find tiny pieces of glass covering him like someone had dropped a bucket of diamonds into his lap.

That's strange.

He looked at the tiny sparkling fragments strewn about his person with an idle confusion. *I know what did this.* He concluded after a moment. In his mind, a discordant series of memories flashed in the background. Something broke through the window. *Wait, what did Elliott say a moment ago?* He didn't remember, but he got the impression something had surprised them. He wiped all thought of the incident from his mind, like it no longer bore any importance, as his hand latched onto the handle of the door and gave it a weak push.

Opening the door took a lot more effort than it should have, and Kenshiro took a moment and looked out it into the disturbing vast world that laid beyond. His mind swam helplessly as he looked out into the expanse without really focusing on any one thing. He was supposed to do something, he couldn't remember what it was exactly. Kenshiro felt the diluted sense of urgency like whatever it was, it was important, but he...

"Baka!" He growled as it came to him like something that formed in the smoke of his mind.

He was supposed to be checking on the damage to the truck. *Jesus, how hard did I hit my head?* Kenshiro wondered, bringing his palm to the spot on his forehead that had a pulsing ache that seemed to seep into his head and interrupt his thoughts. He probed it softly, feeling the large bump that was probably still swelling. He pulled his palm away, blinked heavy a couple times to clear his vision, and looked down at his palm. There was no blood present on his hand. *That's good*, he thought absently as he stepped out of the truck.

There was a sharp stab in his right leg when he lifted it out of the truck, but when he felt the pain, it was distant, like it was far away somehow and could be ignored. He *had* to check the truck and they *had* to get back on the road. He didn't know why, but he felt a dire need to keep moving and the truck was the key. He had to. It was easier to ignore the stabbing pain the second time when he placed his boot down on the solid surface of the road. It wasn't too bad after all.

Then Kenshiro howled.

When he put actual weight down onto his leg, there was a white-hot explosion that enveloped his lower half. He cried out as his leg sacrificed him to save itself, and Kenshiro fell the rest of the way out of the truck and crumpled to the ground. Instincts took over as his body contorted on the way down to lessen the fall as much as possible. He landed hard on his right shoulder and more pain erupted from his arm and cut off his cry as the agony stole his voice from him. His body jerked and rolled him over onto his other side as so much pain coursed through him, Kenshiro felt like his spine might explode out his back.

Breathe, dammit! A voice screamed inside his head and he tried to follow the command as best he could. Kenshiro came out of his former stupor and fully into consciousness like it was the painful conclusion of a long fall. He clamped his jaw shut, so he breathed forcefully through his teeth and errant strands of spittle escaped his mouth and flew onto the pavement in front of him. His mind was on fire with agony like every brain cell he had was trying to process the pain he felt, but couldn't keep up. There was a sound he heard through it, a noise he recognized. Kenshiro turned and looked underneath the truck to the other side just in time to see two skinny legs hop into view and dash towards the back of the truck.

"Ken?!" He heard Elliott's voice call out to him, but there was something else.

A tiny pitter-patter rang out in his head like the sound of a rattlesnake. It sounded all too familiar to him, like someone gently slapping a pool of water.

"Ken?!" He heard Elliott cry out again, but he ignored

it as he adjusted himself so he could look towards the source of the slapping noise at the front of the vehicle.

Fuck!

There he saw the tiny stream of green fluid slowly dripping into the puddle the leak had formed on the surface of the road. *Coolant.*

"Ken." Elliott almost skidded to a halt beside him. "Oh my god, are you alright?" Elliott's voice pleaded with him, almost begging Kenshiro to say everything was fine. He was awake now, fully awake, and nothing was fine.

"Elliott, quick, help me up," he growled and rolled over onto his back. He looked up at the boy's red face, and held up his uninjured arm. "I think my leg is broken." Elliott gasped at that but then reached down and awkwardly wrestled Kenshiro up onto his good leg, where he tittered precariously.

"You're bleeding too, real bad." Elliott whimpered beside him and pointed to his wounded arm that throbbed painfully. He just waved it off and motioned again for Elliott to help him up, which the boy promptly complied. Despite his best efforts, Kenshiro growled loudly as the two of them struggled to get him on his feet. When he finally was up and balancing on his remaining good leg, he felt a gloss of sweat on his face and Kenshiro felt like he was going to throw up.

"We're in trouble, Elliott," Kenshiro confessed weakly once he was confident he could speak without spewing his lunch all over the road. Elliott didn't need to be told they were in trouble. Kenshiro could see the extreme confusion and apprehension on the teen's face. "Help me to the back, and then I'm going to need you to get me the first-aid kit."

Kenshiro was tired, more tired than he could ever remember being in his whole life. *Keep going*, he pleaded to himself, *just a little longer*. His body, once a trusted ally, now threatened to quit on him in his time of dire need.

"I'm sorry," Elliott said weakly as Kenshiro put his arm around him and hung his weight on the teen's shoulders.

"It's not your fault, buddy." He replied without thinking. Maybe it was Elliott's fault, maybe it wasn't. He didn't know, but right now, it wasn't important. "I would have done the same thing," Kenshiro lied.

The last thing he needed right now was for his friend's judgement to be skewed by feelings of guilt. Elliott seemed to accept what he said as the truth, because he didn't say another word. Instead, he dropped the tailgate and stood back as Kenshiro eased himself onto the edge. Again, he grunted and hissed loudly as he pulled his injured leg up onto the tailgate. Pain caused the edges of his vision to flare red. Elliott squeaked up a tiny sob watching the effort.

"The first-aid kit, Elliott?" He gently reminded the red-faced teen, who shook his head back into focus. He rushed to the side of the truck and reached over to grab the green bag with the reflective strip. Kenshiro relied on the three large bags, so he often instructed Elliott to pack them according to his specifications. Elliott knew where everything was. He quickly unzipped the bag and stuffed his arm into it, frantically feeling around the insides for what he was looking for. A moment later, the teen triumphantly pulled the white metal box out of the bag. He hurried and handed the steel box to Kenshiro.

"Good boy, now grab me the big black rifle from the gun bag," he said, but then quickly added, "and bring the hatchet." Elliott looked surprised and concerned at the addition of the hatchet, but he said nothing. He nodded dutifully and went about his tasks.

Kenshiro sat with his injured leg resting length-wise

across the tailgate while his good leg dangled off the back of it. It throbbed horribly. Each heartbeat set off a tiny explosion in his leg, just below the knee. *First things first*, he said inside the chaos of his head. Pain signals were coming in from all over his body. It was like a white noise inside his head, making it hard to concentrate. He, almost drunkenly, looked to his wounded shoulder for the first time. Whatever attacked him... *It was a deer, a fucking deer!* He reminded himself. The sleeve of his t-shirt was ripped to shreds. On the exposed skin, he saw a gnarly gash that carved out a channel in his flesh that started at his shoulder and ran down his arm, before it ended just above his elbow. It painted his entire arm below the gash red with the blood that seeped from the wound.

Fuck.

Kenshiro unzipped his combat vest and groaned sickeningly as he eased the heavy vest off his body just as Elliott appeared into view with the big rifle in one hand and a hatchet in the other.

"Gimme that," he said, and took the rifle from Elliott. It was heavy, and he struggled with it more than he wanted to admit when Kenshiro set it on his lap. "Put this on," he said with little fanfare as he held the vest out to Elliott. Elliott just stared at it for a moment.

"I'm not leaving you behind," he said with whatever conviction he could muster with tears in his eyes.

"Just take it," he commanded sternly. "You're going to need it."

"But-," Elliott resisted.

"Damnit, Elliott! Just listen," he snapped at the teen and looked at him harshly. Kenshiro maintained eye contact through a full breath before he continued. Elliott remained silent as he reached out and took the vest from him. "I need you to take that hatchet and go into the trees over there," he said and pointed out past the traffic barrier and into a clutch of trees a way off to the side of the road, "and cut me off two sticks about this big." Kenshiro used his hands to approximate how long he needed the sticks to be, "and about as thick as your thumb. Then bring them back to me." Elliott nodded solemnly as he slipped the vest on and zipped it up. It was obviously too big for the teen's frame, but it was functional. "And Elliott?" Kenshiro said suddenly, right as his friend turned to accomplish the task set out in front of him. "Take the pistol out. Be careful, and watch out for the undead," Kenshiro said slowly and deliberately before gravely looking at the boy. "Aim for the head, like we talked about." Elliott didn't like guns, nor was he overly effective with them, but he knew how to use them. Kenshiro made sure of that. He just hoped it was enough.

"I'm scared, Ken." Elliott sobbed. He tucked the hatchet into his belt and pulled the tiny twenty-two automatic pistol from its holster on the vest and held awkwardly it in his hands, like it was dirty, but he was holding it. That was the main thing right now.

"I know," Kenshiro said like it was an apology, and maybe in a way it was. "I know, but we'll get through this. You just have to listen to me and do exactly what I say for, like, twenty minutes. Can you do that?" He asked. Everything he felt, the pain, the fear, the guilt, he forced all of that into a box in his head and stored it in the back of his mind until he could deal with it later. He did this for Elliott. Twenty minutes.

"I can do that," Elliott said in a cracked voice that was utterly unconvincing.

"Okay. Get to it then. Remember, be safe, and hurry

back." Elliott didn't respond. He simply nodded once and deliberately clicked the safety on the pistol to the 'off' position so Kenshiro could see it. At that, Kenshiro returned his nod solemnly and Elliott turned and headed off over the traffic barrier and into the trees.

He waited until he was sure Elliott was gone before Kenshiro let the first tear fall.

"Baka!" He cursed himself when the bitter disappointment boiled up from within him and manifested itself with a sob.

Kenshiro sat there with his broken leg out in front of him on the tailgate, his right arm painfully throbbing as it hung limply at his side, with blood seeping from it. He had so utterly failed, and it left him broken and bleeding, and now was a walking beacon for every zombie within a mile of their position. He hissed out curses to himself in his native tongue. It felt right. He had doomed them both because his back was a little sore and he was drowsy. He had become soft, complacent in his perceived ability to survive, and he allowed this to happen.

A sound caught his attention. A weak, animalistic cry from down the road. Kenshiro looked up, wiped the tears from his eyes so he could see, and saw the source of the noise.

On the asphalt, maybe twenty feet back down the road from where they had come, was a large buck struggling to stand. Kenshiro looked just in time to see it lift itself up onto its front legs. The fur on its head and neck was matted and stained crimson and its back legs were completely lifeless. *Its back must be broken.* The buck got itself part ways up on its front legs before it cried out in pain and its front legs buckled underneath it. The buck's mass lurched forward in a desperate attempt to flee its own death, only to crash clumsily back onto the pavement of the highway. There it laid still for a moment before it craned its neck towards Kenshiro. Its large antlers digging into the road as it did. For a moment, their eyes met. His heart sunk and fresh tears welled up in his eyes as Kenshiro saw his own fate in the sad eyes of the dying animal.

You're not beat yet, a familiar voice rang out in his head. It didn't surprise him to hear it, because she had always been there when he needed her the most. *So, stop fucking acting like you are. If you count the one currently connected to the truck, you have two good batteries. You have jumper cables, tools, and enough fuel to get you to the safe house. You have everything you need, so stop feeling sorry for yourself and get to work. You owe it to Elliott.*

Kenshiro growled weakly in frustration. He *did* owe it to Elliott. He dragged that teen out of his home and did the worst possible thing he could do for him. Kenshiro gave Elliott hope. He, by no means, meant to do such a thing. In his eyes, he was merely trying to keep the boy safe. It was the boy's nature. Anybody else would have grasped the prospect of the endless struggle ahead of them and felt the weight of it. Not Elliott. He lived each day, with little thought for tomorrow, but he also carried a lot of his past with him. That was one thing they had in common, because Kenshiro was very aware of the past he allowed to haunt him. Now, because of his failure, if he died, Elliott would be alone in a strange place he didn't recognize or be able to navigate, with few supplies, and only with a basic understanding of how to survive. If Kenshiro allowed himself to die now, he would be killing two people.

Frustration brought his fist down on his good thigh. Spikes of pain reverberated from various spots throughout his body, but he didn't care. He deserved to feel that pain. The buck on the road behind them moved, and it caught his attention. Again, he met those black eyes. *Don't let them win*, Kenshiro imagined those eyes were saying to him. *Don't let them beat you.*

He pursed his lips together, and angrily wiped the tears from his entire face like the fluid suddenly sickened him. He wiped the wetness that remained on his palm onto his pant leg. He would like to say he simply flipped a switch in his head and he was back on track, but unfortunately his broken psyche didn't work like that. It was a process. Like starting a giant steam-operated machination, it took time to light the fire, build the temperature to a boiling point, and let the pressure inside raise to a workable level.

DON'T LET THEM WIN!

For the first time since coming to rest on the tailgate, Kenshiro looked around himself. With fresh eyes, he searched his surroundings for a way out, just in time to see the first undead emerge from the foliage on the other side of the interstate.

He groaned painfully as he reached further into the bed of the truck to grab one of the food bags. His fingers just barely hooked around the shoulder straps of the camouflaged bag and he tried to brace himself for the pain that was involved in pulling the weight of it towards him. His pained groans twisted into an animalistic growl as he leveraged himself back up to a seated position and pulled the bag along with him.

He stowed the rifle to the side, but made sure it was in easy reach. He then opened the bag up and fished around for a water bottle. Kenshiro placed the water bottle and the first-aid kit beside him on the bed of the truck. He grit his teeth as he struggled out of his shirt. He used the material to wipe away the fresh blood from his arm and then upended the water bottle over his shoulder and let it cascade down his stained arm. The water stung slightly, but not nearly as bad as when he took the soiled shirt and cleaned the blood from his arm. He had to rinse and wipe three more times before it satisfied him that he had cleaned all that he was going to with the stained shirt.

Behind him, he heard sounds of something moving frantically through the tall grass, it momentarily made his heart skip before he heard his friend's voice.

"I got the sticks, Ken." He heard Elliott say from somewhere behind him.

The teen appeared at his side with a triumphant look on his face and two sticks in his hand that were exactly as Kenshiro had described them.

"Good work." He took the sticks from Elliott and placed them beside his injured leg. Kenshiro looked at Elliott, intent on saying something but the words faded into the smoke and haze of his head when he went to speak. He was profusely sweating from exertion. Kenshiro felt like he had run a marathon already and had one more ahead of him. "I need you to hop into the back with me and pull out the large compression bandage from the first-aid kit." He spoke the name of the bandage slowly for Elliott, even though he knew all the packets of bandages were labeled with easy-to-read lettering. "I need you to help me with my arm."

Elliott didn't need to be told twice. He nodded once and moved into action. It reassured Kenshiro when he saw his friend's eyes. He wasn't crying anymore. Apparently, that phase had passed, and now Elliott had a resolute look on his face of a man deeply set in accomplishing a task. Which was good, because the task ahead of them seemed monumental. The teen swiftly moved to the passenger wheel well, he planted his foot on the wheel and leapt into the back of the truck with ease.

"Easy," Kenshiro growled loudly as the body of the truck sank and rebounded, causing his leg to blossom with a fresh red-hot pain.

"Sorry," Elliott said absently as he hunkered down beside Kenshiro and flicked open the latch on the first-aid kit. Elliott hunted around the contents before coming up with the correct packet. He tore into the plastic with his teeth. Inside was a large sterile piece of gauze and the wrapping.

"Pour some peroxide on it first," Kenshiro said, using his good hand to point to the small brown bottle nestled into the side of the kit. Elliott grabbed it and then gave him a sheepish look that kind of looked like an apology. Which Kenshiro didn't like. "What?" He asked suspiciously.

"It's empty. I used it up and forgot to tell you." Kenshiro wanted to scream, but just forced himself to breathe deeply.

"Okay. Fine. Just use the antiseptic cream, then." He pointed to the bottom corner that had a variety of small packets lined up neatly along the sides. Elliott flipped through them until he found the right one.

"It's expired," Elliott said after reading the label, sounding defeated.

"I don't fucking care. Just put it on," Kenshiro hissed angrily. It didn't need to be perfect; they were beyond any hope of that. In his head, precious seconds were counting away.

Kenshiro's thoughts vaporized as he felt Elliott apply the cream to his wound with what felt like a rusty rake. He clamped his eyes shut as he felt the cream scold his flesh. Kenshiro clenched his jaw to suppress the animalistic cry that wanted to escape his lungs as the boy thoroughly spread the cream around the inside of the wound. He looked over with a sort of mind-wrenching horror and saw the tip of the boy's finger disappear into the interior valley of the wound.

When that passed, he instructed Elliott to fold the gauze pad over in half, then fold it again, until it looked like a small, white sausage and then apply it to the wound before he began wrapping it up. After that was done, He pointed to another gauze packet, and he told Elliott to do it again, this time only folding the gauze pad in half once before he fastened it into place. He had the teen put a third bandage on, just applied the full pad to his arm, and wrapping it up. When he was done, the completed bandage formed a large hump on his arm that sort of looked like a large diaper. He didn't care, Kenshiro just prayed it would soak up the blood long enough so they can get them out of the area.

With that done, he had Elliott wash whatever blood remained off his arm and torso, and then throw the soiled shirt with the rags into the tall grass, well away from their smashed-up truck. When Elliott returned, Ken was eyeing the pair of sticks nestled in beside his broken leg ominously.

This next part will not be fun.

"I'm going to need two fresh shirts," Kenshiro said while easing the long straight blade from the sheath on his injured leg. "Cut one of them into three or four strips we can use to make a splint on my leg-,"

"Shouldn't we use one of the towels for that?" Elliott interrupted him, and by the look in his eyes, immediately regretted it.

"I don't fucking really care what you use, Elliott. Just get it done," Kenshiro said in a strangely conversational tone.

Internally he was bracing himself for what lie ahead. Elliott went to work frantically, going through the bag Kenshiro kept the clothes they travelled with. He felt the truck lull slowly back and forth with the boy's urgent movements.

In the end, Elliott ended up cutting one of the big plush towels into the required strips for the splint. Kenshiro noted each strip was about two inches thick as he took them from his friend, who looked at him with great concern on his face.

Kenshiro put a strip at the bottom of the leg, just above the ankle, and another about midway up his shin. The last one was directly inline with the point of impact. He had Elliott cut the lower half of his pant leg away. They both grimaced at the sight of his swollen and discolored leg.

"Don't worry about that," Kenshiro said at the sight of it for Elliott's benefit, but it might have been for his as well.

Doubts coursed through his mind like lightning bolts. *Just leave it. You don't know what you're doing. You're just going to make it worse than it already is.* It was just noise in the background he didn't pay any attention to. There was only one voice he was listening to, and it was the one that said if he didn't do this, they would both die.

"Okay," he said, reaching down and placing the sticks at the sides of his leg to show Elliott where he wanted them. "So, hold these and then tie the straps around the leg to hold it in place."

"What are you going to do?" To that, Kenshiro smiled weakly while looking at his friend earnestly.

"I'm going to try to not pass out. That's my job."

With that said, he put on the fresh shirt and leaned back against the truck bed. He took a few quick, deep breaths before reaching down and grabbing the fourth strip of the towel Elliott had cut off for the splint. He balled it up, but before he stuffed it into his mouth to muffle whatever sound he was going to make, Kenshiro looked at his friend gravely.

"And Elliott?" He waited until his friend was looking at him before Kenshiro continued. "It has to be tight," he said with a certain amount of sympathy in his voice.

"Okay," Elliott said nervously while he finished lining up the sticks and gently tying the strips just tight enough to hold them in place. Even at that small pressure, Kenshiro groaned through the material of his gag. Elliott looked to him for confirmation, and in his pleading eyes, Kenshiro saw a look that begged for forgiveness. "You ready?" Kenshiro replied by taking two sharp breaths through his nose before nodding.

Elliott grabbed the two ends of the knot on the bottom strip and mercilessly pulled them tight. The pain was immediate and overwhelming. Kenshiro clamped down on the cloth in his mouth and groaned loudly through the material. Then Elliott moved onto the second one mid-way up his shin bone. Again, Elliott pulled the two ends of the knot tight and the pain inside him became a living, breathing thing. It bit and clawed a path up his spine and straight into his core. Kenshiro arched his back and stared at the overcast sky with bulging eyes as he found there was no escaping what he felt, nor was there any way to dull the pain. It was something he had to experience. His cries broke into sobs as he looked back to Elliott. He looked back at Kenshiro, gravely concerned with fresh tears rolling down his red cheeks. Kenshiro breathed in quick gasps, He looked at him apologetically as Elliott took the ends of the last knot, the one right over the wound, into his hands. Elliott didn't need to say anything. Kenshiro could see the apprehension on his face.

"Do it! Do it!" Kenshiro shouted as best he could through the gag in his mouth.

Elliott broke out into a fresh sob as he held his breath and pulled the two ends of the last knot. The two of them screamed together. Kenshiro slammed his back against the truck bed and pounded his fists down and howled into the gag in his mouth. There was no hope of placing this pain in a nice tidy box and storing it in the back of his head for later. This was a whole new level of agony. His whole body spasmed and squirmed, trying to contain the immensity of what he felt into his relatively compact frame.

A million miles away, back in the real world, he heard Elliott cry out his apologies and then throw his arms around Kenshiro's shoulders. It was impossible to tell whether Elliott was trying to comfort him or hold him in place while the pain had him in its grasp. At first, he dared not return Elliott's embrace because the pain might cause him to squeeze the very life out of the teen. After a few long, torturous seconds, the pain ebbed… slightly. He collapsed into Elliott's arms and they held each other for a moment. He was present enough to feel the warm drops of the boy's tears soak into his new shirt.

Inexplicably, Kenshiro looked up and turned his head towards the dying buck on the interstate. A morbid curiosity maybe. He had to squint his eyes and try to see through the red haze of the agony that clouded his mind. It took a genuine effort not to let the pain consume him entirely. Sweat was rolling down his face from exertion and he felt hot, like there was a furnace boiling away on the inside.

Kenshiro idly watched the road while Elliott continued to hold on to him. The buck still lived, though Kenshiro suspected its time was near. It weakly moved its head to the ground, arching its neck as if it was trying to see something. Kenshiro followed its gaze as the buck made a weak yelping sound and saw four undead at the guardrail on the far side of the interstate. He struggled to discern anything about them other than they were moving with purpose. Their dull, milky eyes firmly locked on the still bleeding buck on the road.

They're coming.

His eyes darted to more undead emerging from the treeline that ran along their side of the road. Two popped into view and, before Kenshiro could look away, another one stumbled onto the scene closely behind the first two. He waited for the familiar adrenalin kick to jump start the engine of his body, but it never came. Kenshiro just felt tired. He wasn't even all that afraid. He knew he should be, but it was hard to feel anything other than the pulsing pressure in his leg and the constant ache of his shoulder.

"Okay, Elliott." He was trying to sound calm and reassuring, but hearing the tension in his own voice, he just hoped he would not make Elliott more anxious about their already dire situation. "It's time to get to work," he said in an effort to make it seem routine. Elliott made him proud when he forcibly wiped the tears from his face and settled into a stern expression before replying.

"I'm ready."

It didn't take Kenshiro long to spot a new vehicle. He would have preferred another truck, but there was none to be found. There were cars and SUVs, and his troubled gaze locked onto one car in particular. *That one!* Something inside him knew that was the vehicle he needed to pick, and he went with it. Kenshiro didn't have time to think, or he didn't think he had time to waste. It was hard to concentrate and time seemed to move in strange waves where one moment everything seemed to move incredibly slowly, and at other times he seemed to lose whole minutes. A muddled plan formed in his head. He used slow deliberate words, and with some effort, he relayed the plan to his nervous-looking friend. It broke Kenshiro's heart to see how strong Elliott was pretending to be. They were both nearing their breaking point. Kenshiro was so proud of Elliott; he promised himself that when this was over, he would shower the teen with praise. He just had to get them there.

"Do you understand what we have to do?" As best he could, he tried to look into his friend's eyes, but found his vision was swimming all over the place. It took effort to focus on one thing.

"I think so," Elliott said but then added, "yes." It would have to do. They were out of time.

The buck's pained cry caught both their attentions, and they turned in unison just in time to see the first zombie fall upon the dying animal on the highway. Kenshiro saw the undead man in indiscernible dark clothes fall into the matted fur on the buck's hindquarters. He watched with dark fascination. Its head reared up and a pained cry escaped its bloodied snout as the zombie bit into the animal's back. The undead man pulled its head back to reveal a full mouth with bloody clumps of hair protruding out the front of its mouth. They did not watch long enough to see the undead man begin to chew while the other two zombies descend upon the helpless creature.

Time to go. The words didn't have to be spoken between them.

Kenshiro did a quick assessment of the encroaching undead into their area. From what he could see from his vantage point, three were feasting on the helpless buck that could do little else than call out with a low, hollow-sounding wail. Two more were making their way through the tall grass. Kenshiro didn't remember seeing those ones before, and guessed they appeared out of the treeline to the south. He looked to the treeline with his hazy, swimming vision, and he saw something moving in there. A lot of somethings. He looked to the opposite side of the interstate, across the barriers and the thin strip of tall grass to the eastbound lane, and his heart sunk deeper in his chest. A group of undead were making its way across the interstate. A pair were in the process of awkwardly tumbling over the steel barrier that separated the eastbound lanes from the center strip of tall grass. All of them moving much too fast for his liking. The only thing going in their favor was the living, bleeding buck on the road. Like a goddamn blinking sign that read: free food. That would change soon enough.

As if on cue, Elliott started the truck. It took a few seconds of the engine cranking over. In the back of his mind, Kenshiro was frantically contemplating the possibility of the truck not starting, but reluctantly, it caught and came to life. The engine didn't sound right, but that was okay. It just had to last a little longer.

Kenshiro had chosen the police cruiser that was parked on the side of the interstate maybe twenty feet further up the road. He carefully slid his weight deeper into the bed of the truck. Each tiny movement caused his leg to explode with a fiery bloom of pain that spread like a tsunami throughout his body. All he could do was grind his teeth together and hiss out forced breaths.

When Kenshiro felt he was secure, he collapsed onto his back, reached over and weakly pounded on the side of the truck. Elliott put the truck into gear and first backed it away from the sedan they hit, before turning the wheel and creeping the broken vehicle down the road. It didn't take Elliott long to park the truck alongside the cruiser with the nose slightly angled into the front of the police car. It was too soon. Kenshiro felt he could have laid in the back of the truck for days.

Back to work, a voice inside him scornfully spurned him on.

He reached out with his good arm to help leverage his upper body into an upright position just as Elliott exited the truck. Painfully, like there was any other way, Kenshiro inched himself back towards the tailgate, grunting and groaning with each fractional motion his injured leg made.

"It has keys." Elliott knew better than to yell. It was barely audible from the back of the truck but he could still hear the teen's excitement in his words. He probably should have felt, at least, a small sense of relief, but Kenshiro made the mistake of looking at the wailing buck on the road.

He was looking for the undead, of course. Kenshiro didn't expect to notice anything else of interest. The buck already had a large amount of undead on its body. Chewing away at its flesh. He heard the buck's pained wails as they crossed the distance between them, and penetrated the red haze of his mind in a way Kenshiro didn't expect.

Then, for the third time, their eyes met, and the large, pleading eyes transfixed him. Even at this distance, Kenshiro could read the anguish in its eyes, and it struck him. Kenshiro's mind inexplicably flashed a memory by his mind's eye that he didn't want to see. For the briefest of moments, his addled mind forced that image into his vision and it replaced the buck's dark eyes with *hers*. Kenshiro's eyes stung as he saw those soft green/blue eyes say their last goodbye one second and in the next moment...

He knew what he had to do.

He didn't know how the large M4 rifle came to be in his hands, nor did he care. He struggled with his good arm to raise the rifle up and pressed the butt into his right shoulder. His left arm was supporting most of the weight of the rifle. All his right hand had to do was pull the trigger,.

Even then he breathed out through clenched teeth to raise his hand up to the pistol grip of the rifle.

"Ken, what are you doing?" Elliott asked, sounding worried as he came around the passenger side to the back and saw him looking down the iron sights of the large rifle. "That's gonna make too much-,"

"Shut up, Elliott." Kenshiro angrily barked in a gravelly voice he didn't quite recognize. "I know what I'm doing." He lied.

Instinct and experience told him to leave the undead to their feast, and the buck was more use to them alive right now than dead. Animals didn't change, at least Kenshiro didn't think they did. In all his time out in the zombie world, he had never seen an undead animal. Even if they changed, though, that mass of hungry, undead mouths will render that carcass useless before it does. Still, he looked through watery eyes and struggled to line up the sights. Frustration forced the next words from his mouth in a hiss.

"I will not let them take her." In Kenshiro's head, the words explained everything, but when he heard them with his own ears, he recognized the slip he had made and just prayed that Elliott missed it.

When he pulled the trigger, he didn't see a deer at the other end of the iron sights of the rifle. He saw Amy. The only woman, other than his mother, that felt like home to him. He saw her sweet face, twisted up in pain and fear, looking at him with an expression that begged him to do the unthinkable. Just like then, the finality of the decision gave the trigger an impossible weight, but just like then, he still managed.

BLAM! BLAM-BLAM-BLAM!

It took four shots before Kenshiro hit his mark. Each

shot, the butt of the gun punched him painfully in the shoulder. The resulting agony made him whimper slightly with each shot. He couldn't help it. When it was finally over, he saw the buck's weight settle in the highway's asphalt. The feasting undead were mostly unphased by the sudden explosion of sound., though, the two who were on the approach shifted their paths mid-step and started towards the truck. When he was done, he used the thumb of his right hand to flick the rifle's safety on and then used his good arm to toss the rifle behind him like it suddenly disgusted him.

"Help me," Kenshiro said, reaching out with his good arm while avoiding his friend's eyes. Elliott said nothing, simply obliged and help wrestle him out of the truck and back onto the road. It felt like all the blood in his body drained into his wounded leg until it threatened to pop like a balloon. Kenshiro just concentrated on his breathing as Elliott help him to the side of the truck. From there, Elliott stared at him. *You good?* Kenshiro nodded and growled out an affirmation.

He left Elliott to carry out his duties. Kenshiro put most of his focus on keeping the tsunami of agony in his head at bay and remaining upright. His head hurt and he felt like he might throw up at any moment. He tried not to pay attention to any of that as he reached for the long black bag of guns. He retrieved the black leather carrying case for the scoped .22 rifle, the zombie killer, and fumbled with the zippers to open it. He wiped the sweat out of his eyes before reaching for the rifle with his good arm. It was blessedly light compared to the lethal bulk of the carbine, but even so, he leaned heavily against the side of the truck as he brought the rifle up to his shoulder. His mangled shoulder screamed in protest. All he could do was clamp his jaw shut, breathe forcibly out through his teeth and try not to pay attention to the little moans that escaped his throat.

Trevor taught him to control his breathing when shooting, to pick his targets with care and consideration, and above all, to control his emotions. All that went out the window when he looked back down the road and saw that there were now more zombies towards them than there were still feasting on the carcass on the asphalt. He looked through the scope and suddenly could see them so close up that he could see which ones were missing teeth. He focused his aim on the right most zombie, paused for a moment to place the crosshairs firmly in the center of the snarling face and squeezed the trigger.

BAFF-BAFF-BAFF-BAFF

He fired and a slight arc of agony reverberated throughout his body, but it was nothing compared to the bone-jarring recoil of the M4. He kept the rifle steady and looked out at his targets with both eyes open.

In his right eye, he saw the magnified crosshairs of the rifle, in his left eye he saw the scene in front of him. When the first bullet hit its mark, he moved his aim to the next target directly to the left and fired. In quick succession, the closest zombies fell to the pavement. He barely even registered it as he aimed at the next undead face, a woman with long dirty, light-colored hair and a nasty gash on her forehead, and fired. He worked his way back to the right and methodically picked them off one by one while keeping a count of the rounds he fired in his head. It took effort, far more than he was expecting, but he was managing.

"There are four coming in from the front," Elliott quickly said as he rushed by.

"Shooting front!" Kenshiro said in a raised voice before hopping painfully on his good leg to turn himself to face the front of the truck.

He saw them but before he raised the rifle up to his

shoulder, Kenshiro took in their surroundings. More were approaching. Kenshiro could see numerous bodies stumbling towards the steel barriers of the interstate on both sides. He didn't bother to count them. It didn't matter how many there were, their survival came down to only two real factors. Ammunition, and time. He had three tiny magazines for the rifle, all fully loaded with ten rounds each. He had shot twelve already. Thirty zombies, assuming his aim held out, after that he would have to fish through the box of shells and frantically reload the magazines by hand. He tried not to think about what would happen after that point.

While he was keeping the undead at bay, Elliott was madly going about his tasks. Out of the corner of Kenshiro's eye he saw the teen wildly throwing the contents of the cruiser's trunk off to the side of the road until that space was clear. Then Elliott went to the truck and began moving the bags over, starting with the heavy weapons bag, then the clothes and personal shit, and then topped off the space in the trunk with the camouflaged food bag. Elliott stuffed the rest of their supplies in the back seat.

Kenshiro's brain made note of the long, towel-wrapped bundle that was also transferred into the back. *Good boy*. With everything going on, he was briefly but profoundly ashamed he hadn't thought of that bundle even a little as he gave the teen his instructions. Given their current state of affairs, Kenshiro might have forgotten about it all together.

Kenshiro reloaded the rifle with the last loaded magazine he had when he spied Elliott struggle to lift the large car battery over the side of the truck. Elliott was red-faced with exertion. He finally managed the heave the battery over the side of the truck's bed and slowly lower it to his side before he awkwardly walked the part to the front of the police cruiser. Elliott quickly hustled back empty-handed and then pulled out the small metal tool-kit they had. It had everything in it Kenshiro would need to replace the battery. He grunted in pain as he raised the rifle up and shot two more zombies who had approached the metal guard rail on their side of the interstate.

When he lowered the rifle, Elliott was at his side with a look of intense focus. His friend didn't even really look at him as he allowed Kenshiro to lean on him so Elliott could help him make the ten-foot journey to the front of the vehicles. Even with Elliott's help, Kenshiro couldn't help but whimper with each shuffled step as they slowly made their way to the front of the cruiser. Elliott said nothing. He solely focused on the job in front of him, completing the tasks Kenshiro had given him. That was the boy's true power, to be completely unaffected by the gravity of the situation he was in as long as he had something to do while it was happening.

Kenshiro blinked hard a few times to keep his vision from swimming long enough for him to locate the battery, determine how it was held in the cruiser, and pull out the tools. It was a straightforward job. When he was younger and working at his friend's family shop, this was a mindless routine.

Now, it was his life's work.

Like everything he had done in his life led up to this point was to prepare him for this exact ordeal. The battery terminal bolts were standard, but he cursed loudly as he fumbled with the tiny sockets in the tool-kit to find the right fit for the hold-down bolt. Sweat fell from his face as he worked. Kenshiro risked a quick look to the back and, sure enough, Elliott was emptying one of the jerry cans of fuel into the car's tank. They had two cans full of gasoline, but Kenshiro instructed Elliott to hold off on the second can until the car started. When he gave his friend the instructions, he thought maybe they could try another car if this one didn't start, but Kenshiro didn't think that was possible anymore. This was it, their one chance. It had to work.

Once the hold-down was off, Kenshiro used his good arm to lift the battery out and squealed in agony as he attempted to toss the heavy weight to the side. He managed to weakly leverage it enough for it to fall pass the body of the vehicle. At least they didn't have to worry about driving over it, but the motion made him lose his balance and his body automatically tried to compensate by putting his broken leg down.

Kenshiro almost crumpled to the ground right there, but he reached out his injured arm and caught the front of the car enough to keep him upright. All it cost him was pain. A lot of it. He saw stars as he struggled to put the new battery into place. Immediately, he saw the dimensions weren't right for the hold-down, so he threw the hold-down apparatus into the tall grass and hooked up the terminals. As he did, he tried to think back to when he last charged this battery. A week? More?

It's charged, he repeated inside his head like a crazy, hope filled mantra. *It's charged. It's charged. It's charged.*

"I have the cables." Elliott appeared beside him moments after he had finished with the last terminal bolt. Kenshiro instructed Elliott to attach the jumper cables to the truck. He had Elliott open the passenger door of the truck and start it. Again, the truck cranked for a moment or two longer than Kenshiro liked before the engine noisily finally caught and came to life. Then, as Kenshiro watched on from behind, he had Elliott get into the dusty driver's seat of the police cruiser and instructed him to turn the key to the ON position.

Something resembling hope bloomed inside of him as

the lights of the dash flared to life, and the vehicle's door alarm bonged loudly. He instructed Elliott to cycle the key to the OFF position and then back to the ON position three times, to prime the fuel system. The cruiser had been here in this very spot for almost two years. He imagined the old battery was completely useless and the fuel lines had nothing more than air in them.

"Okay, Elliott," he said weakly, taking a long breath before continuing. "Try to start it." Elliott looked at him, seemingly undisturbed by the stakes in front of them. Elliott nodded his reply and turned the key to the START position.

Please, please, PLEASE!!!

To be continued...

To my new readers

Thank you! Thank you so much for continuing to take a chance in me, and this series. I am well aware of the stigma around 'zombie' books. For the most part, I agree with them. However, if you watch some of the earlier George A. Romero movies, especially Day of the Dead, I believe you'll find his portrayal of zombies is more like an environmental disaster. Like being trapped at sea. In that sense, the undead are just a medium in which to tell great stories that involves really interesting characters. Plus, as a martial artist, there is no greater glory than to fight someone who doesn't block, and moves slowly. I *really* enjoy that part too. lol. Again, I really hope you're enjoying what you've read so far, because shit is about to get crazy. I'm really excited to get the next book out. Book Three is going to be amazing! Now, we know all the characters and the rules of the world they live in. We've had some ups and downs, and explored the character relationships. In short, we've set up the chess board.

Now, it's time to play!

To be continued:

Check out the continuing story of the exciting four-part undead saga in.

Ronin of the Dead: Book Three

Excerpt from
Ronin of the Dead: Book Three

Chapter one

Elliott

Elliott lifted his foot off the ground and placed it on the first step and, slowly, he put his weight down on that foot. He finely tuned his ears for any noise that might occur while his body was preparing his flight response. Adrenalin made his hands shake as he reached for the railing to pull himself up onto the step. Elliott held his breath as he lifted himself onto the first step and didn't exhale until his full weight was on the step and still no sound came from the wooden board.

That wasn't so bad.

Elliott repeated the same process for the next step. Although as he was applying his weight onto the next board, he heard it. A subtle groan of the wood that resonated through his ears and stole his breath away.

He froze.

He didn't dare move a muscle until he looked over at the grey soldier who, thankfully, was still trying to shake the helmet from his head. To be sure, Elliott checked the other greys in the vicinity before he let out the breath he was holding. They, too, were still caught in the sniffing effect of his superpower.

Just a little longer. Just a little further.

The door at the top of the platform was unlocked.

Elliott tried to imagine he was climbing a giant mountain, his ascent was fraught with danger, and ahead of him was the summit. Elliott couldn't turn back now. He was so close. He gripped the handrail, ready to abort if needed, and slowly continued to press his weight onto his foot. The board protested, still with the same low groan as before. He pressed more of himself down onto his foot while observing the grey soldier in his periphery as Elliott locked his focus on the entrance to the store. The groan ceased the moment his bottom foot lifted off the first step and he slowly rose himself up onto the second step. He stood there a moment and exhaled in one long, jagged breath.

You're doing it! Elliott cheered to himself internally.

With his free hand, he carefully wiped the sweat from his brow. It wasn't especially warm outside, but still he felt perspiration soaking into his shirt. He was going to have to change when he got back to the house. He made a quick note of it. Elliott took a deep breath before he tackled the third step, again using the same tried, tested, and true process he had developed. As he lifted his foot, Elliott wondered just how amazed and/or proud Ken would be when Elliott tells him the story of how he saved him. Ken would take the medicine Elliott would find for him, the Chesty Cough syrup, and he would recover in a few days and then, after Ken felt better, they could go find another safe house and…

STOP!!

Elliott's body sort of shuttered to an awkward stop that threaten his balance. Thankfully, his hand on the railing could stabilize him enough for him to set his foot back down quickly on the second step.

The nails! Look at the nails! His brain screamed at him.

Elliott adjusted his gaze and looked down at the nails

at the ends of the third step. He didn't like what he saw one bit. The two by six had four nails that secured the board to the frame of the staircase. Elliott could clearly see each rusty head of the nails on his side of the board were poking up from the surface of the wood. *Don't step on that.* He couldn't tell just by looking at it when the noise would happen, whether it was when he put his weight onto it or off, but Elliott just knew that board would make too much noise at some point. He could practically hear the noise that the board would make, like an old rusty hinge or maybe some high pitch animal cry. Whatever it was, it would be too much. The grey soldier to the left would spring into action first and then Elliott assumed it would spread to the others like an invisible wave.

Then, as Ken would say, he would be *fucked*. Ken also said, in tough situations like this, Elliott should always weigh his options carefully. He knew he had to hurry, that Ken badly needed the medicine, but Momma said once that *haste makes waste*. Well, Ken had said something similar as well once, but Ken's version didn't rhyme.

Focus!

Elliott thoughtfully placed the tip of his finger into the corner of his mouth and sucked on it. When he thought about difficult things, he liked to do that. He didn't really have any options, per se. He knew what he was going to do. Elliott just wanted to think about how best to overcome the problem of the noisy step in front of him. He took a moment to think about all the ways his brain could imagine avoiding the unsecured board. However, after about a second or two of some serious thinking, he came back to the first solution that came to his mind. He'll just step over it.

Elliott, to be doubly sure, surveyed the surface on the wooden platform he was about to step up onto. He made a special note to look at how well everything was fastened together. Elliott's brain suspected the boards that made up the floor of the landing were newer than the boards on the steps. The platform boards seem to have screws in them rather than the nails that were used on the steps.

If Elliott's father had seen that, he would have said that the builders were half-assing the job. Elliott smiled inwardly at that. His father had a lot of weird sayings like that he really didn't understand. Elliott missed him.

Convinced the platform was safe, well, safer than the step at least, he reached up further on the railing for support before lifting his foot up and over the murderous step and placed his sneaker down on the platform. He was happy with himself with how easy it was to actually slowly hoist himself up onto the platform. *I'm getting pretty strong,* Elliott thought to himself with pride as he looked down on the staircase he had successfully, and silently climbed.

Elliott turned to the door and crept right up to it so he could look through the glass and see if there were any grey people inside waiting for him. Inside was mostly darkness and shadows except for the few patches of light that came through what few windows the store had along the side of the building. It was enough to see and navigate the aisles of the store, so it was enough. That's all the mattered. He had brought a flashlight, just in case, but Elliott was thankful he didn't have to use it.

He closely surveyed the store as best he could through the glass of the door that was littered with little signs that had little or no meaning to him. Inside the store, Elliott slowly looked over at the disarray that was beyond the door. The store looked like a real strong wind had just blown through and sort of tossed a few things around a bit. Not everything. He could see a few shelves in the back looked relatively untouched.

There! On the Floor!

Elliott's eye immediately gravitated to the spot, and he instantly recognized the medicine bottle that was amongst a few other items on the floor. It wasn't the cough syrup he was looking for, but he could just tell by the shape of the bottle and what he could see of the label. It was cough syrup. *I can fix this!* The thought burst through him like a joyous energy. He wanted to burst into the store, snatch up what he needed, and just run back to the house as fast as he could. Instead, he took a breath to calm his nerves and continued to survey the scene through the door. The shelves closest to the door were mostly empty, and straight on from it, Elliott could see the cashier's counter. The register was on the floor in front of the counter, with the money drawer open and empty. A multitude of coins were strewn about on the floor. The dull, lackluster shine they gave off hinted at how much dust had collected on their surface. There was lots to see, but no grey people.

The inside was safe.

Elliott reached out for the push bar and slowly applied pressure on the cold steel until the door moved silently inward, to his utter delight. He thought of what else he should look for inside the store. He had brought a backpack that was mostly empty. *Food.* As the door moved, he considered how much actual, usable food he might find inside the store. The knot in his stomach still gave him a sense of urgency, but Ken always said to never waste an opportunity. Besides, how long could it possibly take to-

TING-A-LING!

With his hand still on the steel push bar, Elliott recoiled away from the high-pitched sound like it was an explosion, which it might as well have been. No, he thought instinctively as he first looked at the source of the noise, a golf ball-sized bell that was attached to a weird-looking spring that was connected above the door, and then he looked to the grey soldier to confirm what he already knew in his heart.

Manufactured by Amazon.ca
Acheson, AB

11122657R00216